"Would you ever do something like that? If you loved someone enough, would you follow him into the dark?" He looks at me with those jade green eyes and, for the slightest of moments, I think I see dark amber fire rings dancing around his pupils.

My impulse is to look away, but I don't. "No," I say. "I'm not a follower."

INTO THE DARK

THE
SHADOW
PRINCE

BREE DESPAIN

EGMONT
Publishing
NEW YORK

EGMONT
We bring stories to life

First published by Egmont USA, 2014
This paperback edition published by Egmont Publishing, 2015
443 Park Avenue South, Suite 806
New York, NY 10016

1 3 5 7 9 8 6 4 2

www.egmontusa.com
www.breedespain.com

THE LIBRARY OF CONGRESS HAS CATALOGED THE
HARDCOVER EDITION AS FOLLOWS:

Library of Congress Cataloging-in-Publication Data

Despain, Bree, 1979-
The shadow prince / Bree Despain.
pages cm. -- (Into the dark ; book 1)
Summary: In this modern retelling of the Persephone myth, Haden Lord,
the disgraced prince of the Underrealm, has been sent to the mortal world to
entice a girl into returning with him to the land of the dead.
ISBN 978-1-60684-247-8 (hardback) -- ISBN 978-1-60684-406-9 (ebook)
[1. Gods--Fiction. 2. Princes--Fiction. 3. Fate and fatalism--Fiction. 4. Love-
-Fiction. 5. Mythology, Greek--Fiction.] I. Title.

PZ7.D4518Sh 2014 2013
[Fic]--dc23
2013033192

Paperback ISBN 978-1-60684-567-7

Printed in the United States of America
Typography by Torborg Davern

In loving memory of Audrey Biesinger.
A woman for whom there was no quest too daunting,
no task too hard, and no journey too far to undertake
for faith, family, friends—or even just the sake of a really
good story.

I miss you, Grandma!
Bree

THE SHADOW PRINCE

chapter one

HADEN

I did the unforgivable the day my mother died, and for that I've been punished every moment of my life.

He's too weak-minded.

Impulsive.

He's too much like her.

He's too human.

It has been ten years, and regardless of everything I've done to try to change their minds, the Court still speaks of me as if I am unworthy of my birthright.

I try to lock away my doubtful thoughts as I watch the Oracle make her way up and down the ranks of Underlords. She is here to help Choose the Champions, and despite the fact that Rowan and the other Elites make it a point to tell me that I will *never* be Chosen, I intend to be one of them. This moment is what I've been preparing for. It's what I've lived for.

The Oracle has passed two entire rows of Underlords without stopping to inspect a single one. Her presence is accompanied by a buzz of energy and excitement that flows through the crowd of spectators. Most of us have never seen an Oracle before, and to hear one speak is a rarity usually reserved for kings and priests. To be Chosen by the Oracle would be an honor unparalleled by any other in this realm. One collective question occupies everyone's mind: *Why would the Oracle deign to participate in the annual Choosing of the Champions?*

Perhaps the rumors are true.

Something more important is going on—this year's Champions will be required to do more than procure new Boons for the Court's harem.

The Oracle passes two more Elites without even glancing their way, and then stops abruptly beside Rowan, King Ren's prized son, and the favored of the Court. Surely he would be their first choice for one of the Champions if the decision were left solely to them. The Oracle reaches out her pale blue fingers and touches Rowan's forehead. He looks stunned for a moment, blinking his eyes. As the Oracle pulls her hand away, she pinches her fingertips together as if she were pulling a thread out of Rowan's skull. She cups the invisible thread in her hand. Her face is shrouded in layers of gauzy veils to protect her holy visage from our unclean eyes, but I can tell that she's studying what she holds with great interest. Master Crue told us that an Oracle can draw memories and thoughts from a man's brain—take a sample of his soul, so to speak—with only her touch.

Rowan's surprised expression slips away and a smug smile plays on his lips. Whatever thought or memory of his the Oracle tasted is one that makes him feel even more confident in his position. No doubt one of his many victories—like the time he slaughtered the gladiator, an untrained sap, before the man had even had a chance to draw his sword.

I ache to knock that smug look off Rowan's face, but then the Oracle brushes her hands as if wiping his memory from her fingers.

She leaves his side and proceeds on with her task. I catch his eye and smirk. What did he think, she was going to stop the Choosing Ceremony right then and declare him the sole Champion? Rowan glares back at me and starts to make a crude gesture in my direction. Master Crue must have caught our exchange, because I hear him clear his throat. He makes a stern, "eyes forward" gesture. I snap to attention, with my shoulders back and my arms straight at my sides, one of them resting against the ceremonial sword in my scabbard. As much as I want to keep watching the Oracle as she makes her rounds, I keep my focus trained on the back of the Underlord standing directly in front of me.

I notice that one of the leather straps holding up his bronze breastplate is twisted, as if clumsy hands had put it on. He's shaking, too. I wonder if it is nerves. Is he anxious about being Chosen? Or anxious about being passed over? I don't recognize him from behind, but from his size, I guess he is only fourteen. He has two more chances to be selected after this year—unlike myself. I am almost seventeen. I've been passed over twice before, and this is the last year I am even eligible for Champion. Anger creeps up inside of me. How dare this boy be nervous?

I almost want to bring the flaw in his armor to the attention of one of the Heirs. The boy would receive a beating for sure for his ineptitude. But then I realize that the way his muscles tremble isn't from nerves, but from strain. It seems he is unaccustomed to wearing the heavy bronze armor of the Underlords. That's when I know that boy must be a Lesser—a second- or third-born son of an Heir, bred purely to serve the Court. The only time they wear the armor of the Underlords is during the annual Choosing—when they get to pretend they're like the rest of us for the night. I don't know why the Heirs allow it; it's not like a Lesser has ever been chosen as Champion.

Then again, it is not as if anyone expects me to be Chosen, either.

The Lesser boy must've noticed my gaze on his twisted strap, because he turns slightly and tries to adjust it. Something about the side of his face makes me feel as though I should know him, but I do not make it a habit to associate with many Lessers. His green-stained fingers fumble with the twisted strap. I know he won't be able to fix it on his own. He looks at me for a second, seemingly asking for my help. I snap my gaze above his head, pretending I didn't see him. *Helping a Lesser.* Like I need that on my record.

A nagging pain twists in my gut and I am suddenly reminded that I would have had the same life as a Lesser if it hadn't been for the oath my mother had made my father swear when I was born. That oath was the only reason I had not been cast out of the ranks of the Underlords completely when my father disowned me. *The day I lost my honor . . .*

The Lesser boy gives up on fixing his strap just as the Oracle glides into view again. She starts up our row, and I see now that she doesn't walk but floats slightly above the ground. I try to forget about my bad memories and focus my thoughts on something that would impress the Oracle if she chooses to look inside my head. I run through my accomplishments and land on the memory of my hunting down and killing the hydra for the Feast of Return last spring. It had eluded even Master Crue and my other teachers, but I had tracked it into the cliffs above the river Styx. I was the one who had carried it into the Great Hall on my shoulders . . . only to have it taken from me by Rowan and his cronies before the Court witnessed my victory.

I was so angry. Almost as angry as the day my mother collapsed and I sent a Lesser to fetch my father. He was so slow in coming, I . . .

I shake my head and try to find an untainted memory as I watch the Oracle pass Underlord after Underlord, drawing nearer. I cannot let her see my shame. I silently curse the boy in front of me for dredging up memories of my darkest moment, when the Oracle comes to a sudden halt beside him. Her face is still veiled but I can tell that she is staring at him. He twitches under her inspection. I watch the way he tries to make himself appear bigger in his oversized armor. She tilts her shrouded head as if listening for something, and stands there for so long, I feel the crowd straining with anticipation.

The Oracle is so close to me now that I can feel the icy chill that emanates off her body. Gooseflesh prickles up on the parts of my arms that are not bound by the leather and bronze of my armor. She is only two steps away from deciding my fate. I can't bare to watch her. I glance at King Ren while he sits waiting at the edge of his ebony throne. He looks annoyed and expectant. Then I notice Moira, Ren's latest queen, sitting beside him. She is draped in a gown made from shimmering fabric and jewels, but it does not hide how pale and withered she has become—like a bony shadow of her former self. She holds a silver scepter—the weight of it looks like it might rip her thin arms from her body. *She will die soon, just like every other Boon who has been brought to the Underrealm. Just like my mother . . .*

No, no, no, I scream silently at my mind's betrayal. *I cannot think of this now. I will not.*

I suck in a deep breath and rack my brain, searching for my proudest moment. The Oracle steps abruptly away from the Lesser boy's side and closes in on me. I shake as her glittering blue hand reaches toward my face. I close my eyes and concentrate on the image of myself slaying a chimera in the arena in just thirty-one seconds, besting the other Underlords in my age group by half a minute. Surely that was my proudest moment. My greatest victory. The crowd had even cheered for me. . . .

All except for my father and the Court . . . They did not see my accomplishments because they did not care to look. No matter how hard I tried, they will not forget what I did to earn my disgrace. . . .

I feel the Oracle's icy touch land lightly on my skin, just between my eyes. My vision flickers black for a moment and then I see myself at the age of seven—as if gazing into a mirror from the past—sitting in my bedchamber. *I hear my mother's hollow voice as she cries out. . . .*

I feel a sharp, stinging sensation in my forehead, like someone is pulling a string through my skull, and I am snapped back into reality. My vision focuses and I see the Oracle drawing her pinched fingers away from my forehead. And I know what memory of mine she holds.

"No! You can't see that!" I try to grasp the Oracle's blue hands, but as I reach for her, she disappears, and all I clutch at is the air. The ranks of Underlords gape at me for trying to touch the Oracle. Master Crue begins to stand. The Oracle reappears next to the altar in front of the throne, cupping my most shameful memory in her hands. I am too far away to stop her from watching the scene that she has stolen from my mind.

She holds her pinched fingers out in front of her veiled face. My heart feels as though it might break through my rib cage. Will she demand that I be cast from the ceremony after what she sees? I want nothing more than to stop her from seeing, but before I can even think of what to do, she drops her hand, and her body goes as rigid as the marble statues that line the perimeter of the throne room. Her priest, a short, balding man in a red tunic, steps forward.

"One Champion only can complete this task," the priest says, but his voice echoes like wind whipping through a long chamber, and I realize the Oracle is speaking through him, using his voice as her own. *"The son of King Ren is he."*

Rowan stands tall and begins to take a step forward to the altar, but then the Oracle raises her blue hand and points one of her long, glittering fingers, not in the direction of Rowan, my twin brother, but toward me.

"Your Champion is Lord Haden," the priest says—my name echoing in the chamber, which has fallen as still as death.

Elation rises in my hammering chest.

That is, until a cry of outrage rushes through the Court of Heirs with a force akin to the wake of Charon's mighty boat.

"This is absurd," Lord Lex, the king's chief advisor, says, rising from his seat among the Court. "The boy lacks proper training. He is not one of the Elite. He's too emotional. We all know that."

My hands tingle with heat. I ball them into fists but keep them tight against my sides. An outburst would only prove him right.

"It should be Rowan," Lord Killian, my father's second advisor, demands. "The Court agreed on Rowan. He should be . . ."

"The decision has been taken out of the Court's hands," the Oracle's priest says, using his own raspy voice. "The Oracle was brought here to make it for you. She has made her decree; it is now your pleasure to listen and obey."

"It is you who must obey!" another one of the Heirs demands, but his blasphemous comment is almost drowned out by the other members of the Court who add their protestations to the din.

I have heard rumors of strain between the members of the Court—I have even heard of whisperings against my father's rule among the Heirs—but there seems to be one thing that still unites them: their disdain for me.

I don't know why I didn't realize that this is exactly how it would play out.

The elation I couldn't help feeling when the Oracle said my name twists inside me until it becomes something darker. Perhaps this is more than the usual scorn of the Court against me? Perhaps this is all some kind of sick joke? Something orchestrated to humiliate me for hoping that I could rise above the lot I have been cast? Hope is a shameful emotion after all—another useless thing my mother must have taught me.

I keep my eyes trained on the Oracle. She is unmoving, swathed in her many veils. I wish I could see her face. I ache to know what she was thinking when she made her decision.

I need to know *why*.

"Silence!"

All voices cut off at once, and all eyes turn toward the towering throne.

King Ren Hades rises from his ebony seat. His long black hair is plaited in a ceremonial braid like mine and the other Underlords'. The firelight from the torches surrounding the altar reflects in the polished gold of his breastplate. He holds his open hand out in front of him. Threads of blue lightning hiss up from his palm and encircle his hand. It is meant to be a warning.

"Oracle," he begins, "I brought you here to predict the best possible outcome, but you have obviously chosen wrong. The boy is unfit. . . ."

"You dare question an Oracle?" the priest asks.

"I am king here," Ren says.

"*And I am the infallible voice of the universe*," the priest says, his voice that of the Oracle. "*I have chosen my Champion. The boy is the one who can save you.*" The Oracle's bluish skin pulses purple and then deep red when she turns toward King Ren, her veils rustling about her as if blown by an invisible gale. The ground beneath my feet trembles, and I know I am not the only one who feels it. "*Only ruin lies in wait for those who disobey the words of fate.*"

The ranks of Underlords behind me jostle for a better view. Even the Lessers have dared to fall out of position.

The lightning in Ren's hand pulses brighter and coils its way up his arm. "Is that a threat?"

"*I speak only the truth*," responds the Oracle. "*You are the one who summoned me here. You and I both know why.*"

King Ren's face grows dark. He advances upon the Oracle, with the lightning crackling in his raised hand. The ground shifts again, and I almost lose my footing when I leave my place in the ranks. The Oracle's words have emboldened me, and I don't think about what I am doing before I throw myself down on my knees between her and King Ren.

"Stop!" I say. "I can do this. I have lived and breathed preparing for this. I am more than ready for wherever this quest shall take me. Let me prove myself to you." I look up at King Ren and see his shock that I have dared to address him directly. His jaw is hard set and orange rings of fire pulsate around his pupils. "Allow me to do this. Please, *Father* . . ."

King Ren looks down at me, meeting my eyes for the first time since the day he told me I was no longer his son.

Gasps of surprise ripple through the crowd of Underlords

behind us. My father breaks his gaze with me as someone else comes to stand before him. My brother Rowan lowers to only one knee beside me.

"Send me, Father. I am loyal, and I am no *nursling*." He casts a pointed glare in my direction. "I will not fail you." Rowan has left behind our ancient dialect and spoken each sentence in a different language used in the Overrealm—French, Arabic, Cantonese—probably thinking that because I am not an Elite, I will be unable to follow his words.

"I am not a nursling," I say to Rowan in perfectly accented American English. "You have stolen honor from me before, but I will not allow you to take this from me as well."

The Oracle moves to my father's side. She has turned icy blue once again, and the cold wind that swirls her veils about her body makes me feel chilled to my soul. My father snuffs out the bolt of lightning that had been building in his hand. He squares his shoulders and stares at the Oracle like he's trying to see past her shroud, into her mind.

"You are absolutely certain this boy is the right choice for Champion? We've been preparing for this particular quest for almost eighteen years. Surely Rowan, or one of the Elite, would be better suited. . . ."

"Sending him is the only way. He is the one."

The one? The only way? His quest has been eighteen years in the making? What exactly is going on here?

Lord Lex steps forward. "What if we did away with him?" he asks. "Would the Fates choose another in his place? Rowan is ready and willing."

My mouth goes dry.

The Oracle's skin turns bright red. *"Your words are insulting to* the Fates. They will punish this Court for your hubris."

"Be still," Ren says. "Lord Lex does not speak for me."

"Forgive me, Your Excellence." Lex bows his head, but a cross look plays on his face. "I only speak in your best interest. Need I remind you what the consequences are for *you* personally, if the boy fails?"

"No, you do not," King Ren says with a quiet forcefulness.

He turns and says something to his guards that I cannot hear, but I guess their meaning when two of them advance toward me. One guard grabs me by the arm, yanking me to my feet, while the other one pulls my ceremonial sword from my scabbard. He jabs the blunted point into my back, between my shoulder blades. I don't try to resist, but as they propel me toward the torch-lit altar, I feel as though I am a prisoner headed toward execution.

I search the faces in the crowd of servants who flank the Court and find the one person who might care about what happens to me. My cousin Dax tries to give me a reassuring look, but his face has grown as pale as the marble floor beneath my feet. I look away from him and concentrate on the carvings that adorn the alabaster altar I'm being propelled toward. The stony personages of the first Hades and the original Boon, Persephone, stare forlornly back at me. When we reach the altar, one of the soldiers sends a swift kick to the back of my legs, forcing me to fall to my knees.

"I would have knelt on my own, harpy mouth," I snarl at him.

He responds by slamming my head against the altar. My jaws smash together when my temple hits the hard stone. Strange bursts of light cloud my vision, and the black, oily smoke from the torches chokes my lungs, but I make it a point not to show any signs of pain. I stay perfectly still, with the side of my face pressed to the cold altar, and watch my father advance on me.

I hear the ring of metal against metal as King Ren draws his sword from the scabbard at his hip. His is not a ceremonial blade—its sharp edges gleam in the torchlight. I try to look up and meet his eyes once more, but he does not return my gaze.

The fear that my father has chosen to listen to Lex's suggestion strikes into my heart. *I am to be done away with so they can choose another.*

I grip the edge of the altar to stop my hands from shaking and wish desperately I had something more to offer to prove my worthiness of this assignment. My father glares down at me. And I see it. Behind the fresh anger that flashes in his eyes, it's still there: that look he used to give my mother before she died—the look that transferred to me after what I did all those years ago— like what he saw before him was the embodiment of every failure, disappointment, and shame he had ever experienced.

As swiftly as fear had struck me a moment ago, a sudden calm replaces it. Resignation. I will not beg as he expects. I will not plead my case again. Instead, I look at him undaunted and ask a final question. "Is your hatred for me so great, Father, that you would risk bringing down the wrath of the Fates on the entire Underrealm in order to deny me my destiny?"

Ren's jaw tightens. He lifts his sword, grabs me by the hair at the back of my neck, and yanks my head up from the altar's cold surface. I say nothing more. If this is what he wants, then so be it. Let it come.

Ren swings his blade at my neck.

I will it to be quick and clean.

The sharp edge of the sword slices into my thick braid until it cuts all the way through. The blade nicks the back of my neck just above my shoulders. My skin stings from the shallow cut but I do not flinch.

"Do not call me that again," he says calmly and lets go of my head. My temple bashes into the altar once more. A cut breaks open above my eyebrow. My blood drips onto the alabaster, staining the cream-colored stone with beads of red.

I am slow to follow what happens next, but I try to focus as King Ren drops the braid he has cut from my head into a large silver bowl. He snaps his fingers and a young servant scurries forward from somewhere in the throne room and lifts the bowl. The boy follows Ren while he approaches the Oracle, the heavy vessel straining his small arms.

My mind is muddled and I almost miss the moment when the Oracle pours some type of shimmering liquid into the bowl with my hair, and then dips a dagger into the mixture. The priest whispers what sounds like an incantation, and then the Oracle hands the knife to King Ren, her blue skin darkening to a turquoise green as he takes the blade from her.

He hesitates. Or perhaps my brain is working too slowly.

"Make the vow," the Oracle's priest says.

King Ren holds the dagger out in front of him. I can barely hear anything over the sound of my pulse pounding in my head and my heavy breaths huffing against the stone altar. I make out something he says about the water from the river Styx, the river of unbreakable vows. . . .

I blink. When my eyes flutter open, the Oracle is standing in front of me.

"Show him," King Ren says.

The Oracle's glittering blue hand reaches for me, her icy touch lands once again between my eyes. Her fingers are so cold. I wonder what memory she will steal from me this time, but instead, my thoughts coil inside my brain and my vision flickers black for a moment. A string of images enters my thoughts, layering upon each other until they form one fluid, moving picture.

At first, the images tell a story I already know. It's the old myth we Underlords are raised on. It's stitched into every tapestry and carved into every door I have passed in my lifetime, even on the altar I lean upon now, but then the pictures shift and I see the silhouette of a girl standing in a bright light.

We've found her—the Cypher. I hear the Oracle's words inside my head and not with my ears. *We have found the one who can restore what has been taken from the Underlords. You are the Champion whom fate has chosen to bring her to us.* The outline of the girl grows more defined but I still can't make out her face. *You will have six months to convince her to return to the Underrealm with you. But she must come willingly. No human can pass through Persephone's Gate without the mortal's consent. This quest is your destiny. The fate of the Underrealm lies on your shoulders, young Haden.*

I nod and the Oracle's icy touch lifts off my skin. The images in my head flicker to black. I open my eyes and look up at her covered face.

"Do you understand what you have been shown?" the priest asks.

I don't know if I do—I have never heard anything about a *Cypher* in any of my lessons—but the entire *living* population of the Underrealm is watching me, and I dare not say that I don't understand.

"Yes."

"Very good."

"What is her name?" I ask the Oracle. *I need to know her name.*

The Oracle takes three steps away from me and then turns to

King Ren. She indicates the knife in his hand.

"Finish it. Seal the will of fate," the priest says for her.

Blue wisps of lightning crackle forth from Ren's hand and wind their way up the dagger he holds.

I have been struck by lightning several times in my nearly seventeen years—in training and in fights—but I am unprepared for the jolt of pain that sears through my body as my father stabs the electrified dagger into my tricep. I go limp against the altar.

Ren pulls the knife from my arm and then makes several small, burning incisions into my skin—cutting and cauterizing my flesh at the same time. I cannot see what he is doing but it feels as though he is carving letters into my skin.

"You want to call me Father?" he says. "To be my heir? To have your honor restored?"

"Yes," I hiss through gritted teeth.

"Then you bring this girl to me," he says, squeezing the wound he's carved into my arm. It takes every last bit of strength I have not to scream. "You return victorious, and I will crown you as my heir and allow you to call me *Father* once again. But if you do not bring her to me when the gate between the Underrealm and the mortal world reopens in six months' time, then mark my words, your hair is not the only thing you will lose."

He slides his knife up to my throat to illustrate his point, then stalks away to his throne, gesturing to the ranks of Underlords who stand behind me and the crowds of onlookers beyond them. "Out!" he demands. "Everybody, out!"

The crowd quickly snaps back into its lines and begins to leave the throne room, following his order. I start to rise, but my head swims and I steady myself against the altar. I am stuck in a position that looks as though I am half bowing, half standing as the bystanders file out around me. I do not understand what is happening. After all the protestations, I have finally been Chosen. Which means the ceremony is supposed to go on. I am supposed to be endowed with the blessing of the Court. A wreath of laurel leaves is supposed to be placed upon my head, crowning me with glory. There is supposed to be a feast of celebration in honor of the Champions. The servants have been preparing it for weeks.

Instead, everyone is being sent away.

Ren looks in my direction. "I said for *everybody* to get out." He speaks with a quiet composure that makes me shiver more than if he had shouted with rage.

I stumble through the now-empty throne room. My head aches, my arm throbs, and my neck feels naked and exposed without my hair. All I want to do is return to my bedchambers and collapse, but I know the challenges of this day aren't over yet, and I'm not quite ready to face them.

The aftereffects of the lightning that ravaged through my body make it hard to concentrate on staying upright, let alone anything else. Knowing I can't be seen by anyone at this point, I lean against one of the golden doors at the end of the torch-lit corridor. The strangest mixture of grief, relief, and pride grips me, and I let out the smallest of sobs.

When I regain my composure, I inspect the cauterized scars on my arm and discover the words that Ren has carved there.

It's the name of the girl I have six months to convince to return with me to the Underrealm. The girl who can give me the status to be elevated over Rowan and the other Elite. The girl who holds the key to restoring everything that has been taken from me:

Daphne Raines.

chapter two

DAPHNE

"It's do or die, Daphne," CeCe says, with a sassy, almost devious tone as she wades through the sea of red balloons that separate her workstation from mine. Despite her flame red hair and freckled skin, she always reminds me of Billie Holiday with her warm, old-school, jazzy vibe. "Ask him while you have the chance."

I know she's right. Mom could be back any minute, and I am more likely to get a positive answer from Jonathan than her. Especially after the look Mom had made when she answered the phone call that came about ten minutes ago. I figured it must be the bank again, considering she took the handset outside and then all the way into the bungalow she and I live in behind the flower shop. It is calls like this that make me so determined to do what I have in mind.

"Go for it, Daph," CeCe says, and pushes me through the bouquets of red and orange balloons we've been inflating for Ellis High's September Social. Jonathan and his magenta apron come into view.

I clear my throat. It's not that I'm reluctant to do what I need to do—it's that I know I'm a terrible liar. But is it lying if you're just omitting a small portion—okay, about 56.2 miles' worth—of the truth? "Hey, Uncle Jonathan . . . ," I start to say, but the loud clank of the bell over the front door of the shop interrupts me.

Jonathan looks up from the ribbons he's been cutting into balloon strings. "Can you get that?" he asks, referring to the customer who must have just entered the shop.

"Indie's up there," I say. "She can handle it."

Jonathan balks. "You know she doesn't have cash register privileges yet."

I give CeCe a stricken look. I don't want to lose my chance.

"I'm on it," she says, and then mouths to me, "Do it!" as she disappears into the balloons on her way out of the back-room workshop to the storefront.

"Welcome to Paradise Plants!" I hear Indie say so enthusiastically, I can imagine the unsuspecting customer jumping at the sound of her voice.

"So . . . Uncle Jonathan," I try to say so nonchalantly that it ends up sounding pained instead. I turn away slightly so he can't see the blush that hits my cheeks. I grab a stray balloon by its string and twist it into the nearest bouquet of red and orange. *No big deal. Just doing my work and striking up a conversation with my favorite uncle, who isn't actually related to me.* "Um . . . so . . . when I'm done with this, do you think I could get off early? I mean, the decorations are being picked up in a few minutes, and I know we still have some cleanup, but CeCe said she'd stay later so I could beg off a little early. If that's okay with you?"

Jonathan cuts one more ribbon and then squints his eyes in a way that makes me worried that my not-quite-lying omission of the truth came tripping off my tongue so fast that he didn't comprehend my words and I'm going to have to start over again. Then he gives me a jolly grin. "Need extra time to get ready for your dance date, eh?"

"Yeah," I say, concentrating a little too hard on tying the strings of my balloon bouquet into a big knot. "You know me. Gotta look my best for that big date!"

"Daphne," Jonathan says, his tone shifting ever so slightly lower.

I glance at him and see that his grin has disappeared.

He shakes the spool of ribbon in my direction. "Cut the crap, honey. I do know you. Enough to know you rejected *both* the boys who asked you. Even after that sweet Richards kid sent you a chocolate-dipped-fruit arrangement from that store in Hurricane. You threw it in the trash."

"Because I'm allergic to strawberries. You know that."

"Yes, but you could have let me eat them," Jonathan says with a pout and drops the spool on his worktable. He reaches into the front pocket of his bright magenta apron. "And I also know where you *plan* on going this evening instead of the dance." He pulls out a folded-up flyer and splays it out on the worktable. He stabs one of his large fingers at the words: ALL-AMERICAN TEEN TALENT COMPETITION HOSTED BY SOUTHERN UTAH UNIVERSITY. ONE NIGHT ONLY!

Oh.

Crap.

The flyer must have dropped out of my apron when I hung it up during my break. I'd been keeping it in my pocket for good luck. Load of good that had done me.

"Jonathan, I can—"

He holds up his hand in a *stop* gesture. "Just be glad I found this and not your mother. You know the conniption she would have if she found out you were planning on sneaking off to Cedar City for the evening. You made a deal with your mother not to leave Ellis Fields again without her permission."

Yes. I know all too well. In my almost seventeen years, I had been on one, and only one, trip outside of my hometown.

Ellis Fields is a tiny speck that you can only see on a Google map of southern Utah if you zoom in real close, tucked into Apollo Canyon and surrounded by miles and miles of nothing but desert and red-rock formations in every direction. My mom is so rooted here that the town legend goes that her ancestors were here even before Ellis was founded. And leaving it isn't exactly easy, especially when your mom forbids it and you don't have a driver's license yet. A lesson I'd learned the hard way when I was almost thirteen years old. After fighting with my mom for, like, the ten thousandth time about how she never let me go on class field trips or even to the Zion outlet malls, which are a forty-five-minute drive outside town, I'd tried to run away to Saint George on my bike. But I crashed while careening down Canyon Road. I ended up sitting on the side of the remote highway, dehydrated, with a flat tire, a broken arm, and a concussion until Mom and Jonathan found me an hour later, merely one hundred yards from the NOW LEAVING ELLIS FIELDS—COME BACK SOON! sign. I did eventually make it to Saint George that day, but it was to spend the weekend at Dixie Regional Medical Center.

That's when the infamous deal had been struck. While hopped up on painkillers and still freaked out about my near-death experience in the desert, I'd agreed to stop pressing my mom about leaving Ellis—and not run off again—and she'd agreed to give me a longer leash once I got my driver's license. I'd been dreaming of ultimate freedom, but at just over two months shy of my seventeenth birthday, with *still* no license in hand (no thanks to my mom), I was beginning to think I'd been duped into a really bogus deal.

"But look"—I point at the flyer—"second prize is *twenty-five hundred dollars*. That's exactly what Mom needs to replace the flower cooler in the front of the shop—and you know the bank isn't going to give her another loan. It's *one night*, Jonathan. Please?"

"But what about first prize?"

"What about it?"

"It says here"—he practically stabs the flyer with his ribbon scissors—"that if you win first prize, they'll haul you off to Las Vegas for the next round of competition, and then possibly New York City after that. It won't just be one night *then*. Your mother would never stand for it, and I'd be a dead man for letting you get into this mess."

"Who says I'm going to win first prize?"

Jonathan rolls his eyes. "One thing you don't need to be is modest, Daphne. You and I both know you've got first place in the bag."

"Well, I'll never know if you don't let me go." I give him a teasing smile. "I might stink at singing and nobody in this tiny town knows the difference." Ellis High School is so small, we don't even have a real music department.

"Please, Daph. I'm from Manhattan. Don't tell me I don't know amazing singing when I hear it."

"Then let me go and prove it to myself. If I win first, then I'll bow out and take second place and the prize money."

Jonathan takes a swig of Diet Mountain Dew from his ginormous *Jersey Boys* mug. I can tell he's swishing the soda in his cheeks like he does when he's contemplating a difficult floral design. He swallows hard. "Sorry, honey. No way, no how. Your mother would kill me if I let you leave Ellis and something bad happened to you out there."

I wrap my fingers through the strings of the balloon bouquet I'd forgotten I was even holding until now, and bite back the urge to make a frustrated *urrrrrrg*.

"How were you even planning on getting to SUU in the first place? Don't tell me you were planning on driving without a license?" Jonathan asks with an accusatory tone.

"No." I've had a driver's permit for over a year, but state law requires forty hours of driving time behind the wheel with a parent or guardian before I can apply for a license. Since Ellis is only 4.6 square miles and my mom won't let me take the car out on the highway, it was taking an eternity to rack up the hours needed to get my license. *There's nowhere in Ellis you can't get to on your bike,* she always says, but I know she's dragging her feet on the issue so she won't have to fulfill her end of our bargain. And the more I point this out to her, the more excuses she comes up with for not being able to take me driving. At this rate, I won't have a license until I'm eighteen and can get it without her consent. "There's this new senior at school who has a boyfriend at SUU. She says I can hitch a ride with her to Cedar City and back. That's why I need to get off early."

A very cross-sounding tone comes off Jonathan. Telling him I am hitching a ride with someone I barely know isn't helping the situation, but I don't have many options. Most of my school friends haven't had licenses long enough to be legal to drive with another teen in the car, and CeCe, who claims to be night-blind, wasn't too keen on the idea of navigating the canyon roads after dark. Not that she'd be excited to drive me out of town in the daytime, either. I swear, it's like half of the adults I know are just as reluctant to leave Ellis as my mother. Despite being from *the* big city, even Jonathan rarely leaves town other than his yearly pilgrimage to the designer outlets in Primm, Nevada. It's, like, once people come here, they never want to go anywhere else. Mom calls Ellis an oasis in the desert and our own private paradise—hence the name of our shop—but at an average temperature of 105 degrees in the summer and the looming walls of red-rock mountains on every side, this town feels more like a stifling prison to me sometimes.

"But what if *you* took me instead? That way, you know I'd be safe. Maybe I could even get an hour of driving time on the way? We'll tell Mom we're going to movie night. She'll never even know we were gone." I smile. "I'll let you give her the prize money. We'll tell her you won it from a design contest or something."

Jonathan shakes his head while making a *nuh-uh-uh* kind of noise, which reminds me of the way Frankie Valli sings. But behind the scolding tone, I catch something else. Just a hint of sympathy. Just a little bit of give, maybe?

That was something I could work with. I say in a singsong voice, "You'd be both of our heroes, Uncle Jonathan."

A smile starts to edge at Jonathan's lips as though he likes the idea of being a hero. Then he quickly shakes his head as if trying to get water out of his ear, and the happy look is gone. Along with the tone of sympathy. "Sorry, sister. Not happening." He picks up his scissors and cuts a ribbon with a snip so abrupt that I know I've pushed it too far with that one.

I didn't want it to come to this, but I know what tactic I need to try now. The truth.

"Fine, Jonathan. You want to know the real reason I need to go to this competition—besides winning the money for Mom, that is?"

Jonathan makes another sharp snip. "If it will explain why you'd break your deal with your mother over some silly teen idol contest."

"Mrs. Arlington, the cashier at the music shop on Main, who gave me this flyer, said that there would be talent scouts from SUU, the University of Utah, and other colleges at the competition," I tell him, knowing this tactic may very well backfire. College is another one of those topics my mother and I don't see eye to eye on.

"Daphne, you and your mother will discuss this when you're older. . . ."

"Yeah, right. Mom's big plan for my postgraduation future probably involves me getting some online associate's degree in business management, and then inheriting the flower shop from her. But I've got bigger dreams than making corsages for other girls to wear to dances and wrapping up 'I'm sorry' flowers for every doghouse-ditching guy who comes into this place. I graduate in less than two years and I want to go to college. A real college."

Assuming Jonathan is right about my voice and I can manage to land a scholarship somewhere—*anywhere*—that is.

Getting a scholarship was step number two on my "prove to the world I can become a music star all on my own" master plan. (Step one being two hours of self-imposed music practice a day, no matter my homework load.)

"Opportunities like this competition don't exactly come this close to Ellis very often. But if I can't even get fifty miles away from here for *one evening*, how am I ever going to convince Mom to let me go away for school?"

Jonathan puts down his scissors. "Your mother has her reasons for wanting to protect you."

"Which are what? Her own paranoia that the outside world is some big, bad place? What does she think is going to happen to me 'out there' anyway? Is she afraid I'm going to sneak off with some guy and get pregnant, just like she did? Or is she more afraid that once I step foot outside town, I'm never coming back? Does she think I'll abandon her, just like my father?"

Jonathan's lips pull into a tight, thin frown and I know I've struck on something. A remorseful tone wafts off him as he sighs.

Truth is, I don't know how to make it work. How do I go after my dreams and not end up leaving her in the red dust of southern Utah because she refuses to budge from this spot? "I love my mom, but someday I am going to have to leave. I need to know what else is out there in the world. I need to know if I can make it on my own."

"Daphne. I know you can make it on your own—but this is a conversation you should have with your mother. Later when . . ."

"Later will be *too late*." I place my hand over his large fingers before he can distract himself with cutting ribbons again. "Please, Jonathan. Let me go tonight—"

The shop's bell interrupts me once more, only this time it's much louder, like someone has opened the front door in a hurry. I wonder if Indie has sent another customer running.

But instead, a few seconds later, Indie comes bounding into the back room. Or at least she tries to before hitting the barricade of balloons.

"Hol-y amaze balls, Daph-ne," she says, jumping up to see me over the balloons. "You will never guess who is in the shop—like, never, ever in a mil-lion freak-ing years!"

When Indie gets excited, she talks in short, staccato notes and acts like she's had five espressos in the last half hour, even though

25

Mom says she's supposed to be on a strictly stimulant-free diet. I'm not sure where Mom got this information, nor where she found Indie. Despite being on a limited budget—because she flat-out refuses to accept any child support from "that man"—my mother has a tendency to bring home strays. Of both the animal and human variety. Most of her person rescues stay only long enough to collect their first paycheck, but others become part of the family and never leave. Like *Uncle* Jonathan, who's been with us for so long, I can't remember when my day wasn't greeted by one of his Technicolor aprons, and CeCe, who'd practically become my sister since my mom brought her to the shop five and a half years ago, looking like a drowned rat—CeCe, that is, not my mom. I still am not sure where Indie is going to fit into the mix.

"Come on. You have to see him!" she says when I don't follow her.

Jonathan and I glance at each other, and he chuckles. He always says that a flower shop is the worst place in town for meeting cute guys. You'd have better luck at the library. Because the guys who come in here already have someone to buy flowers for.

"She'll learn." Jonathan laughs again with a merry tune, the tension between us melting away. The skin around his eyes wrinkles with his smile all the way up to the graying hair at his temples. I can't help thinking that I won't allow myself to grow old while waiting for my Prince Charming in a place like Ellis. My mom thought she'd found her prince once, but he'd hopped off like the frog he really was before I'd even been born.

As far as I'm concerned, no guy is worth waiting anywhere for, nor following, for that matter—prince or not.

"I'm ser-i-ous, you guys." Indie grabs my arm through the balloons. "You have to see this or you will nev-er be-lieve me. Crap,

26

where did I put my phone?" She drags me, with that red and orange balloon bouquet still in my hands, to the front with her. Jonathan follows, making a bemused humming sound. I hope he doesn't think our discussion is over.

The first thing I notice is a long Hummer limousine idling in the no-parking zone in front of the shop entrance. But before I even have the chance to be irked by the illegal parking job, or wonder why or *how* someone had gotten a limo for the dance around here anyway, Indie jerks my attention to the flower cooler, whose motor is chugging and buzzing like it's about to die any second. Or rather, Indie turns my attention to the back of the man who is standing in front of the cooler.

"See," she whispers.

The shop's fluorescent bulbs reflect off the back of the man's leather jacket, and his boots are just as shiny. He wears dark wash skinny jeans that look far too tight for comfort. In fact, everything he wears looks stiff and perfect, like someone else picks out a new outfit for him every time he steps out of his house. Considering it's ninety-eight degrees outside, that person hadn't done a very good job. The woman next to him looks just as crisp in a black suit and a patent leather briefcase that coordinates with her glossy red heels. She clutches the briefcase to her chest as if she's afraid one of the potted azaleas is about to fling itself at her.

I glance at CeCe, who is ringing up a bundle of red roses and baby's breath for a very nonoriginal customer at the register. She shrugs to show she has no idea what Indie is going on about.

The leather-jacket man seems intent on a bunch of ranunculus blooms, which are wilting in the half-dead cooler. The glossy woman clears her throat. The man brushes his long, wavy hair over his shoulder and turns toward us.

Indie squeals.

CeCe swears.

"It's really him!" Indie says. "It's *the*—"

"Joe Vince," Jonathan says. He makes a move like he wants to block the man from my view with all three hundred pounds of himself.

I hold my hand up to stop him.

The man's lips part into a cheeky grin. He winks at Indie and then looks at me. "'Ello, Daphne," he says. "It's been a long time."

I let go of the balloon strings.

"Dad," I say.

"What are you doing here?" Jonathan demands.

"Didn't your mother tell you?" Joe says to me in his British accent, which must have once charmed my mom off her feet. "A judge granted me custody. I'm taking you to live with me in California."

A loud bang echoes above my head as one of the red balloons bobbing against the rough popcorn ceiling bursts.

chapter three

HADEN

Rowan lies in wait for me in the antechamber beyond the throne room. I would not expect any less from him.

I slow to a halt and try to place my hand on the hilt of my sword to show him I am ready for any attack he has planned, but then I remember the weapon was taken from me by one of Ren's guards.

Never mind. Hand-to-hand combat suits me just fine.

Several Underlords step around me, most gawking as they go, trying to get a good look at the king's disgraced son, who is now the lone Champion for our year.

The Lessers, who are not allowed to wear armor outside of the ceremony, stop to remove their bronze breastplates and leather wrist cuffs before returning to their labors. I am not surprised to see Lord Lex standing near Rowan and a couple of other Elites who've congregated near the exit. My hands grow hot, prickling with energy, as I think of the things Lex suggested in the throne room.

Lex whispers something to the Elites that I cannot hear. Rowan nods and laughs, glancing in my direction. Fire rings gleam in his eyes.

I hope to the gods that Rowan issues a challenge now. It would be my duty to riposte.

Lex clasps his hands in the sleeves of his robe and takes his leave, presumably to join the other Heirs. Only a handful of Underlords remain in the antechamber now, and I wonder if Rowan wants our fight to be a private affair, rather than the spectacle I predicted. I decide to push the issue by advancing toward Rowan—when someone collides with me.

At first, I think I am being attacked from the side, and I raise my hand to strike, but then I see that the clumsy fool who has gotten in my way is nothing but a scrawny boy. With a twist in the strap of the heavy, ill-fitting breastplate that drapes over his sagging shoulders. He's the Lesser who stood in front of me during the ceremony.

"Watch it!" I shout instead of striking him.

The boy glances at me and gives the smallest nod. Again, I feel as though I should know him. "My apologies, my lord," he says, and scurries away as fast as he can toward the exit.

It is now that Rowan chooses to make his move. But it's not toward me. He signals two of his chimera-faced lackeys to follow his lead. They step in front of the doorway, and the Lesser boy, not paying attention, runs right into Rowan's chest.

"Where do you think you are going?" Rowan asks him.

The boy trembles. Rowan's menacing glower makes him take a step back. "Returning to my barracks, Lord Rowan," he says. "As I was instructed."

"And you were going to take your borrowed armor with you?" Rowan points at the stack of breastplates where the other Lessers have left theirs behind. "You *know* what we do to thieves."

"Yes," the boy says. "I mean, no. I wasn't stealing. I just forgot.

I was distracted." He glances slightly back toward me.

My impulse is to look away, but I can't.

"Then let us help you get out of it." Rowan wraps his hand around the boy's left wrist cuff, and one of Rowan's friends clutches on to the twisted leather strap that lies across the boy's back.

Before the Lesser can even try to fight back, Rowan and his crony both yank viciously on the boy's armor, pulling him in opposite directions. The boy screams. The noise echoes off the walls and fills my ears, but I can still hear the sickening sound of his shoulder being dislocated from its socket.

I react before I even have a chance to think. I push my way through the bystanders who still remain in the antechamber. My hands clutch into fists. I can feel a current of electricity surging up my body.

Rowan lets go of the boy and pushes him away. The Lesser whimpers and sinks to the stone floor, his arm hanging at an unnatural angle. Rowan opens his mouth to laugh, but I smash my fist into his jaw before he can make a sound. He slams into the doorjamb, and I hit him with a bolt of lightning to the chest.

Rowan's two friends try to grab me from behind, but he waves them away. Rowan charges at me. We grapple, knocking into the stacks of discarded armor, sending them scattering. I smash my forehead against his and slam him to the ground. I pin him there with one of my knees on his chest.

A second bolt of electricity shudders through my body. The energy bursts into my arms and explodes from my fingertips.

Rowan writhes in agony as I direct the crackling streaks of blue lightning into his rib cage a second time. I imagine the electricity clenching his heart in a taloned grip, squeezing the life from it.

The energy dissipates so quickly, it nearly knocks me back.

Rowan tries to roll away. I grab him by the throat with one hand and lift my other over his heart, preparing to blast him again.

Rowan and I both know a third jolt of lightning will stop his heart completely.

"Say it." I keep my voice cold like King Ren's, not giving away the anger that boils behind my words.

"Never," Rowan says.

A gasp ripples through the small crowd of Underlords who've circled around us. I can feel Rowan's pulse hammering against my hand. Energy that has been building up inside of me courses through my free arm, and I flex my fingers as wisps of blue light lace between them like webbing.

Rowan doesn't flinch. Neither do I.

"Say it," I demand. "Say it, or you're done."

Another sound of shock escapes the crowd of Underlords. They know the rules of a proper challenge. The loser must invoke *elios*—a cry for mercy—or face death at the hands of the victor. The others wonder if I mean what I threaten. Their doubt gives me more strength to accomplish the deed.

"Lord Haden, don't," Dax says. I know it must be him without taking my eyes off Rowan's face. Dax is the only one whose standing is low enough among this group to feel free to show concern. "Rowan has had enough. Let him go." By the sound of his voice, he's moving closer. "What would your father think?"

I know exactly what Ren would think. *Only a coward wouldn't finish off an opponent who doesn't properly relent.*

I've never lost a fight. I've never backed down. But I've also never been in a brawl that has escalated quite this far. I've never had to kill another Underlord before.

Rowan smiles mockingly. His teeth are stained with blood, but

I can read the scorn in his expression. I'm stronger than Rowan. He knows that. I clearly have the upper hand, so why would he choose this moment of all times to taunt me?

The energy I hold in my hand swirls itself into an angry ball of white-hot lightning. It's almost too hot to bear. I must throw it soon, or it will incinerate my fingers. "He has to say it." I shake Rowan by the throat. "Say. It." I keep my voice cold and steady even though I want to scream at him. I want to force the word out of his mouth. I'd reach my hand down his throat and claw it out of him if I could.

But of course he will not make it that easy.

"Then what would your mother have said?" Dax asks.

His words cut as deep as a dagger to the back.

"Don't bring her into this," I say.

"Yes, little prince, what would Mother have said?" Rowan says with a sadistic gleam in his eyes.

We must show mercy and kindness to all, my young prince. No matter their lot in this world . . .

I take my sight off Rowan's sickening smile and look up at the huddled throng that has grown larger. The Lesser boy stands a little apart from the others, holding his arm in a way that makes it look like he's trying to push it back into its socket.

The boy looks away from my stare. As he turns his head, I register the thin scar across his cheek. I *do* know him: Garrick.

The boy is not just any Lesser. He is my and Rowan's younger half brother. The bastard Lesser son of one of the many concubines our father had taken up with before my mother was even on her deathbed. Garrick used to follow Rowan and me everywhere when we were children, trying to make friends with us even though he was no better than a servant. He was the Lesser who was there when my mother died. He was the one who witnessed what I did to earn the disdain of the Court. . . .

I haven't seen him since he was reassigned to work in the Pits eight years ago.

Rowan groans and the crowd shifts closer, cutting Garrick off from my view as it closes in on us. All wanting to see what I'll do next. The ball of lightning surges, blinding everyone else out of my vision. All I can see are the slits of Rowan's fiery eyes as he glares up at me.

Was Rowan really ready to die to prove some point?

No. His point is that I'd let him live. . . .

He wants to prove that I'm a coward so he can try to get the Court to override the Oracle's decree.

I flex my fingers, and the ball of lightning morphs into a bladelike shape in my hand that I can slam into his heart like an electrified stake. "I *will* kill you," I tell him. "Unless you say it."

And I mean it.

Something changes in Rowan's eyes as I hitch my arm back to spike the lightning blade into his heart. A sickly, sweet scent, like rotting pomegranates, wafts up from his body.

It's the smell of fear.

At the last second, I shift my aim. The lightning spike explodes against the stone floor, leaving a blackened crater next to Rowan's head, and nearly takes off his ear. Chinks of marble go flying, sending the crowd scattering.

I let go of Rowan and climb to my feet. The hand I held the lightning in throbs, but I refuse to look at it. Rowan clutches his chest while his friends help him to his feet. As soon as he is standing, he pushes their hands away. Like he hadn't needed them in the first place.

Rowan squares his shoulders and walks toward the great golden doors leading out of the antechamber. The remaining crowd follows him—ever on his side. He lets the others pass by him into the corridor, and just before leaving, he turns back. His eyes land on me as I tuck my burned hand behind my back. I'd held the lightning for a moment too long, and it hurts like Tartarus, but I won't show any sign of pain with Rowan—or anyone else—watching me.

The crowd follows his glare.

Rowan is the one who lost the fight. He's the one who was at my mercy—but he looks at me like *I'm* the one who should feel ashamed. They *all* look at me like that. His mocking smile returns. His lower lip cracks and bleeds, but he only licks the blood away.

"Defending a Lesser? Sparing an opponent?" Rowan says. "How adorably predictable, nursling. Did *Mother* teach you such useless manners?"

"Shut up," I say, and raise my uninjured hand.

Rowan makes a scoffing noise. "Your impulsiveness is so predictable. Ironic, I know. That's why I know you'll fail. Even if by some miracle Father goes through with his decision and actually allows you to pass through the gate tomorrow, you're still going to lose. Because you're weak."

"I'm stronger than you. I just proved that."

"Brute strength and good aim aren't going to get you anywhere on this quest of yours, Haden. You lack the proper training. You're a simple foot soldier, not a Champion. That takes brains, not brawn. Do you have any idea how to convince this Boon to return to the Underrealm with you? Do you know how to manipulate someone into doing and saying exactly what it is you want from them? Because all this little fight proved is that *I* do. You played your part so well, little nursling."

I open my mouth, ready with a comeback, but all I can think is that no matter what I say, it'll be exactly what Rowan expects.

"And when you *do* fail in this quest, I'll be the one the Court turns to, to clean up your mess." His smile widens. "No matter what you do, I'm still going to be the one who wins." He sweeps through the doorway.

I can't help it. A great, raging burst of lightning escapes my hand. I fling it at Rowan. The electricity explodes against the heavy golden doors just as they bang shut between us. The force of the lightning ricochets off the gold and takes out the two alabaster statues that stand guard at the exit. I throw my hands over my head to shield myself from the flying stone bits.

Only Dax and Garrick remain in the corridor with me—the only witnesses to my losing control. But I can *feel* Rowan's smugness seeping under the doorway as he walks away with his adorers.

I think I even hear laughter.

The blood from my head wound drips off my chin and pools in the hollow of my collarbone. My hand is black and singed. Sweat prickles up from my pores as my body tries to cool the hot electrical currents that swirl inside my chest.

Garrick steps close to me. Too close. I smell the stench of Keres on him. I think he is about to bow down in front of me and thank me like I'm some sort of Hercules for saving him. Instead, he uses his uninjured arm to push against my chest as hard as he can. His weak shove has no effect on me, but the rage on his face does. "You stupid brute," he practically spits.

I blink at him in surprise. "That's no way to show gratitude, Lesser," I say, pushing him away from me.

"Gratitude? Do you know what you've done?" He tries to take a swing at me with his good arm, but I block it, forgetting about my burned hand until pain reminds me. "You tried to make Rowan invoke *elios* on my behalf." Garrick gingerly clasps his dislocated shoulder. "This is *nothing* compared to what he'll do to me now. And then he'll take his accusations of theft to the Court. I'll be dead by the end of the week."

I take a step back. Garrick had been sentenced to work in the Pits—a life of hard labor: caring for the monstrous Keres, which were banished to the depths of Tartarus centuries ago—after he was accused of stealing from the palace. A second strike against him—if the Court believed Rowan's accusations of trying to steal the armor of an Underlord—and the punishment could possibly be even worse than death.

Garrick charges at me, swinging his good arm. I grab him by his fist. His fingers are stained green from working in the Pits, and he's so underfed, from years of fighting for scraps with the other Lessers, I could crush his hand if only I squeezed.

A buried memory flits through my brain, and I remember how Garrick had tried to help me when my mother collapsed. . . .

No, I tell myself. *What Garrick did wasn't help. Lessers serve. It's what they're born to do.*

"Get away from me, Lesser!" I thrust his hand away. "Don't you dare touch me with your dung-stained fingers. Your kind has already left. Follow them."

I raise my fist as though I'm going to attack him if he doesn't listen. Garrick rushes toward the golden doors.

"You might want to consider leaving that armor here," Dax says.

Garrick skids to a stop. He hurriedly and clumsily pulls at

the straps of his breastplate, but he can't free them with only one hand. His face reddens as he glances back at us. I look away. Dax sighs heavily and then goes to help him. Once the boy is free, Dax tells him to visit the healing chambers.

"Lessers are not allowed . . . ," Garrick starts to protest.

"Tell them that Champion Haden sent you," Dax says.

Garrick nods and exits without another word. I hear his feet slapping against the marble floor as he runs away. The sound of it sends another flash of unpleasant memories through my mind. Garrick's sandals had made that same noise when I sent him running to fetch my father when my mother needed help. I remember how long I waited for my father to return with him. I remember how I . . .

The shame of those memories overwhelms me. Suddenly, all I can think about is the blood that stains my face. I try wiping it away with my leather wrist cuff but I can tell it only smears the blood more. The wound won't stop bleeding.

"I have to go." I step quickly away from Dax and head toward the exit, bits of alabaster statue crunching under my feet. "The Court can't see me like this. *He* can't see me. If they call me back in there"—I gesture toward the throne room where my father remains—"I have to go. . . ."

"Lord Haden, wait," Dax says. "You should remain here, in case—"

"I can't." I pull away from him and flee from the antechamber as fast as possible. If the Court is going to punish me for what happened with Rowan, they'll have to come and find me on their own.

chapter four

DAPHNE

I don't know why I called him that. *Dad.* The man who stood in front of me now may have been my biological father, but he had never been my *dad.* That title is supposed to be reserved for the man who teaches you how to ride a bike, or who picks the splinters out of your skin, helps you with your homework, and argues with you about your curfew. Not for the person who married your mom in a Vegas drive-thru chapel after one date, only to leave her three days later to become a rock star. I wouldn't have even recognized Joe if I hadn't seen his face splashed all over the covers of tabloids in the grocery store checkout stand.

I'm so stuck on this *dad* detail, I don't follow what Joe is saying. I can see his lips moving and I can tell he's using the same practiced tone of voice that he employs during TV interviews, or while accepting awards at the Grammys, like he's giving a rehearsed speech. But I don't actually hear the words he's saying until he places one of his hands on my shoulder and says, "That's why we have to leave tonight."

"What?" I step back abruptly, and my heel makes a squeaky noise against the linoleum floor. Upon Joe's request, we and the glossy woman moved our conversation to my mother's small office in the back of the shop for privacy, but I know Jonathan, CeCe, and probably Indie, are listening at the grate on the other side of the wall. I wish one of them could fill me in. "I'm sorry. What did you just say?" I ask Joe.

The grin my father has plastered on his face falters at the edges. "We need to go tonight," he says. He waits for a moment, probably for some sign of understanding from me. When I don't respond, he goes on. "To your new school. In California. The one we've been talking about for the last few minutes."

"What?" I take another step back. "I don't understand what you're saying."

He loops his fingers behind his giant—and, no doubt, real platinum—skull-shaped belt buckle, and rocks back on his heels. "Bugger. I thought you were taking this too well." He runs his fingers through his long hair and clears his throat. "I know I haven't been there for you, Daphne," he says, starting his little speech over again. "I want to make things up to you. This school—Olympus Hills High—can open up opportunities for you that I never had and that you can't possibly get here. The training you could get for your voice alone, and the education is top notch. It's what you deserve. Your voice is amazing. . . ."

He would think so. He claimed that I had *his* voice.

"You can only attend the school if you're a resident of Olympus Hills, and I just happened to have finalized the purchase of a home there last week. You would live with me. We could get to know each other."

I probably look like some kind of dead fish with the way my mouth is hanging open. I don't even know what to say to this . . . this proposition.

My father checks his watch. His smile vanishes altogether.

"This is a big deal, Daphne. You have no idea how many strings I had to pull to get you in." His voice is edged with a pleading tone that surprises me, and I notice for the first time how much older he seems in person than in the images I've seen of him in the Star Tracks section of *People* magazine. "If we don't go tonight, you will lose your place."

"Tonight?!" This isn't happening. "But there's this talent competition tonight. I'm supposed to audition for scholarships for college." And school is starting, and CeCe's birthday is next week, and Mom needs her flower cooler fixed, and I'm supposed to start teaching guitar lessons for the kids in my neighborhood to help bring in extra cash. All I've ever wanted is to graduate and get out of Ellis, but suddenly I can think of a million reasons why I need to stay. Why I'm not ready to leave. Not yet.

Joe clasps his hands. "Daphne, darling. If you're Joe Vince's daughter and you graduate from a place like Olympus Hills, you won't have to audition for scholarships anywhere. Schools will throw money at you to attend. Not that you'll even need it now. But only if you come with me—"

"She's not going anywhere with you."

My mother sweeps into her office, and Joe stops speaking midsentence. He looks at her wide eyed, almost as if he's a little afraid of her, and I can't help but notice that even the glossy woman with the briefcase and the slick chignon is taken aback by my mother. The two are polar opposites. While the woman is petite, and gives off a very even, uncluttered tone, my mom stands over six feet tall and is wearing her signature green maxi dress and the pollen-stained apron I've rarely seen her without. Instead of heels, Mom's feet are bare. My mother never wears shoes, as if all those NO SHIRT, NO SHOES, NO SERVICE signs don't apply to her. It's like she believes the grass won't grow and the flowers won't bloom if she doesn't glide over the earth with her naked feet each day. Her hair tumbles about her shoulders like waves of golden wheat, and her eyes, bright blue like the color of delphinium blossoms, pierce right into Joe. The tone that comes off her is like the crescendo of a symphony. I'm tall like my mother, and people say I look just like her, but I don't know how I can even compare when it comes to presence. She's like a force of nature.

"Don't even try me," she says to Joe.

He clears his throat. "As I told you on the phone, Demi, I have a court order."

The woman in the suit dress snaps open her briefcase and pulls out a document that supposedly proves that Joe is my new legal guardian. How he got a judge to grant him custody of the teenage daughter he's seen only four times since I was born is beyond me. I mean, Joe doesn't make the tabloids because of his more *sober* exploits. Then again, he probably has enough money to keep half the lawyers in California on retainer.

Mom doesn't even look at the paper. "I don't care what that document says. You can't just waltz in here and take my daughter away."

"*Our* daugh . . . ter," Joe says, but Mom gives him a look that makes him stammer.

"I don't care what I have to do to block your so-called court order. I don't care if I have to sell my shop to pay for it. I will not let you take Daphne out of Ellis Fields."

It's at this moment that I make up my mind. The shock and numbness of the situation have started to wear off, and I know what I have to do. Because there's no way I'm going to let Joe destroy my mother's dreams all over again. There's no way I'm going to let her sell her shop—her paradise—because of me.

"I'll go," I say, stepping between my feuding parents.

Through the grate, I can hear Jonathan and CeCe gasp. Indie makes some sort of high-pitched, hiccuping noise.

My mother turns toward me. "Daphne, no."

I square my shoulders and look right at her. "I'm going," I say as definitively as I can. "I *want* to go. This school is everything I've ever wanted. I'm going."

My mother looks as though I've smashed one of her prized oleanders onto the floor and then kicked the dirt at her feet, and a low, disappointed tone comes off her.

Joe blinks at me in relieved surprise.

"We need to leave," the glossy woman says. She taps the screen of her phone. "We'll lose our spot for takeoff if we don't get to the airport ASAP. Daphne, you have seventeen minutes to pack your essentials. We'll send for the rest later—assuming there's anything worth sending for." She puts her phone into her briefcase and then takes me by the elbow to escort me out of the office. I look back at my mother, but she's turned away from me.

"Wait," I say, breaking away from the woman's grasp. "Mom, look at me, please."

"We don't have time for this," Little Miss Glossy says.

"Yes, we do." I stand next to my mother. I place my hand on her shoulder. I've always been able to read people by the tones and sounds that come off them—but at the moment, I wish I couldn't. There's a raging ensemble of emotions behind my mother's stiff expression, a chorus of anger, feelings of betrayal, remorse, and fear.

"I'm sorry, Mom. But I have to do this. As much as this store is your life, music is mine. And just as much as it would be impossible for me to stop singing, it would be even more impossible for me to watch you lose this place. Not when the solution is so easy."

"Leaving your home is that easy for you?"

"No, that's not what I mean." I squeeze her shoulder. "It's going to be okay, Mom. I'll be back for Christmas break." I glance at Joe and he nods, confirming that this would be part of the plan. "You don't have to worry about me."

"Bad things happen out there. Believe me, Daphne, I know." More remorse wafts off my mother, and I know she's thinking of her one excursion outside of Ellis Fields as a teenager—spring break, her senior year, with some high school friends. That trip was how my mom ended up with an ex she barely knew, and a baby she'd never planned on. Not to mention one of her best friends had run off to New York City with some guy, never to be heard from again.

"Some good things happen out there, too," I say, and give her a look that says, "How else would you have gotten me?"

All the stiffness in my mother's face melts away. Water fills her eyes and she grabs me in a close hug. "I know," she says. "You are my everything. That's why I don't want to ever lose you." Her grip on me tightens. "Please, my little sprout, stay here."

I bite back the urge to tell her that I've changed my mind, that I am never going to leave, but I can't fight the tears that roll from my eyes as I let my mother hold me like I was a little kid who's fallen and skinned her knee.

"We now have thirteen minutes until we need to leave," the glossy woman says.

I break away from my mother's hug. Anguished notes fall off her like teardrops as she realizes that her pleading won't keep me here.

"You know, you could always come with me," I say. "Open up a new shop in California?"

She shakes her head, with a sad little smile. "Who would take care of all of Ellis's strays?"

I'd known she'd never go for it, but I had to at least ask. "Okay, then, cross my heart and hope to die, I swear I will never run off with some random guy." I make an X over my chest, and my mother laughs tearfully at my corny rhyme.

"Twelve minutes," the woman says and takes me by the elbow again. I have no choice but to let her drag me out of the office.

We pass Jonathan, who gives me a sad frown, and CeCe, who acts as though she wants to try to stop me, but rethinks it when Glossy Woman throws her a look that could melt ice. Indie, ever oblivious, gives me an enthusiastic double thumbs-up.

The wall of heat outside the oasis of the shop's AC hits me and I suddenly feel overwhelmed—not just by the prospect of packing up my life in such a hurry, but also by knowing that, in twelve short minutes, I have to figure out how to say good-bye to the only life I have ever known.

chapter five

HADEN

Morning has arrived by the time someone comes to fetch me. I'm not surprised that it is Brimstone who finds me in the screech owl roost in the tallest tower of the palace. I know she's coming, because the owls become agitated, screeching and puffing out their feathers as she slinks into the room. She's a tiny little thing, but a good deal bigger than the puff of fur she'd been when I rescued her from one of the owls' clutches when she was only a few days old. As a runty newborn, she'd been tossed out of the nest by her mother, left to die in the Wastelands. That's why I'd saved her—and that's why she rarely left my side and could always find me no matter where I was—we'd both been rejected by the only family we'd ever really known. That made us kin.

Brim meows like she's scolding me and hops onto my lap as I sit on the window ledge.

"I know," I say, stroking my hand over her gray fur so she won't get angry. "I should have told you where I was going."

I slide one of my fingers over the silver bracelet she wears as a collar—trying not to think of the person it used to belong to. Brim huffs and then looks over at the door, as if waiting for someone. I know that if Brim has found me, Dax is only a few seconds behind. Not that either of them had to look that hard. Dax is the one who showed me this place, back when he was still an Underlord and everyone in my age group aspired to be just like him. It's the one place in the Underrealm where one can see not only the royal stables and the pomegranate groves, but also the asphodel meadows, which stretch for miles beyond the palace. When I was younger, I used to sit up here, watching the owls fly in and out of the roost. I used to stand in the stone-framed window opening, stretching my arms out, and dreaming about taking flight. About being free.

But where would I have even gone?

There's nothing beyond the meadows but the Wastelands. The place where the shades—the souls of the dead—wander, wailing their tormented cries, as they search for a way out of that final resting place of grief and shadow.

I may not come to the roost to fantasize about flying anymore, but it is still my favorite place to sit and think. I'd packed what few belongings I might need from my bedchamber for my quest, and then came here, where I've spent the entire night running through every lesson I've ever been taught about the Overrealm. History. Politics. Mythos. Fighting styles. Anything the Court might choose to test me on before sending me through the gate. All in an attempt to drown out the things Rowan said to me.

And I know it's not enough.

"It's time," Dax says solemnly as he comes to stand in the doorway.

"I'm not ready," I say.

"Everyone is waiting for you."

"I can't go through the gate. Not yet. I need more time. I need more training."

"There's no more time to be had. You know the gate only opens twice a year. Today's the day, my friend."

"What if I wait six more months? I can go when the gate opens then. I can get the training I need and go later. . . ."

Dax folds his arms in front of his large chest. "Don't be absurd."

"Why is that absurd? The Elites receive years of specialized training in case they are Chosen. Why send someone like me without it?"

"Because you're the one the Oracle chose. For this time and this purpose."

"But what if I'm not the right choice? Rowan is right. I'm predictable in my impulsiveness. I'm weak."

Brim sinks her claws into my knee.

"Rowan is wrong," Dax says.

I glance at him.

"Don't listen to a word that *koprophage* says. I know you better than anyone. Yes, you're impulsive, but that doesn't make you weak. It means you listen to your emotions."

I suck a breath in between my teeth. That's an insult if I've ever heard one. Emotions are something to be stamped out, controlled, not *listened* to.

"What I mean to say is that you are equipped with unique traits that make you well suited for the mortal world. They're the reason why the Oracle chose you—I'm sure of it."

I shake my head. He might as well have called me a human— and meant it as a compliment. Dax has never been the same since his time in the Overrealm. It's as though being declared a failure permanently altered his psyche. I want to laugh at him but something stops me. "They should declare the Oracle addled, just

48

like you," I mumble instead, "if she thinks the entire future of the Underrealm lies on my shoulders."

"Did she tell you that?"

I nod. "Obviously, she's gone insane." I pick up a rock from the ledge—probably something one of the owls brought up here—and chuck it toward the moat below. Brim tenses and follows the rock with her eyes, but she knows better than to jump from the window to chase it. Her getting wet wouldn't be good for anyone involved. "Perhaps I should tell the Court that I resign as Champion. Tell them to send Rowan in my place."

"You will do nothing of the sort," Dax says. "This is your chance, Haden. Your chance to show them who you really are. They think Rowan is the best in your age group, but that's only because they ruled you out long ago. *Make* them pay attention now."

"They're never going to look at me as anything other than the embodiment of disgrace."

"You don't know that. . . ."

"Stop." I glare at him. "We both know the truth. There's no point in coating it in siren songs. What would you know about success anyway? You were kicked out of the Court altogether. You're barely better than a filthy Lesser."

Brim yowls. She never likes it when I harden my voice at anyone.

My harsh comments are meant to hurt Dax, but he barely lifts an eyebrow. Six years ago, Dax had been considered the best of the Elite. As Lord Killian's son—the Underlord credited with bringing back an entire sorority of Boons from his quest—great things were expected of him. He'd been Chosen by my father to bring back a Boon who had been hand selected for Dax by the Court. But six months later, when the gate opened for the return, he had been the only Champion to come back alone. He'd failed, and suffered the wrath of the Court as a consequence. He'd been stripped of his rank, cast out of the Underlords, and had lived as a servant ever since.

"It's time to go," Dax says, like he won't take no for an answer.

I pick up another rock, toss it up in my hand, and catch it. Dax's words about this being my one chance to prove myself start to edge into my despair. Isn't that the reason I've always dreamed of being Chosen in the first place? Ren had even said that if I succeeded, he'd grant me back my rightful place at his side.

But he'd also made it very clear what would happen if I don't succeed. His oath to my mother prevents him from casting me out of the ranks of the Underlords as he did with Dax. Which means if I fail, he can do something much worse. My jaw clenches as I remember the feel of Ren's knife on my throat.

I fling the rock out the window. It flies so far that it misses the moat and disappears into the treetops of the orchard. I turn back to Dax.

"What if I fail?"

"You *won't*," he says so definitively that I don't want to argue. Dax has always had that power over me. "Besides, you'll have me to help you."

I really look at him for the first time since he entered the roost and see that instead of his servant's robes, he's dressed in strange dark blue pants made from a thick cloth, and a short-sleeved tunic, which has a picture of something that looks vaguely like a horseless chariot on it. It reminds me of the odd garments many of the Champions and Boons are dressed in when they return from the

Overrealm. Over his shoulder, Dax carries a satchel that looks like it's packed to capacity.

"You're coming with me?"

He shrugs. "I convinced Lord Killian that since you are the sole Champion this year, you should be allowed a small entourage for your quest. I assumed you'd like a guide who's been to the mortal world before."

I try to stifle a grateful smile. "But you botched your quest."

"Then who better to make sure you don't do the same?" Dax puts his hand on my shoulder. "Haden," he says, lowering his voice, "the fact that Killian agreed to letting you take a guide and my knowing what the Oracle said to you about the fate of the Underrealm resting on your shoulders only serve to confirm my suspicions. There is more going on here than anyone is telling you."

I nod. "The Oracle said that the Boon I am after can restore something that was taken from the Underlords. She said something about a Cypher."

Dax startles when I mention that word. "So the rumors are true. . . ."

"What rumors?"

A shadow blocks the light in the doorway, and I look up to see one of King Ren's guards leering at us. "Is he coming with you or do I need to drag him there?" he asks Dax, with a self-satisfied grin that makes me recognize him as the harpy who kicked me in the knees at the altar yesterday.

"He's coming on his own," Dax says.

The guard grunts and moves back out into the hallway.

"What rumors?" I ask again.

"We'll discuss this later—when there are fewer ears to overhear. Now it's time to go."

Panic swells inside of me. "It's too soon." I take a step backward, but Dax grabs my arm. "Leave me," I seethe at him. I know I am being irrational, but I can't help myself. I'm not ready for this.

Dax lowers his voice. "Haden, you *must* go now. It will be worse if they have to force you. The dishonor alone . . ."

I want to strike him and make my escape, but his words about dishonor make me hesitate. Brim paces in the windowsill, growling in a way that makes both Dax and me bristle. The owls flutter and hop in their nests, screeching frantically.

"What is it, girl?" I say, anxious to soothe her. Getting a hellcat mad—especially in such a confined space—is never a good idea.

Then I see three shades come into view over the horizon. Shades usually stay far away from the palace, their moaning the only evidence of their existence, but sometimes hunger drives them into the outskirts of the asphodel fields. Hunger—insatiable hunger—is all they know in this world. One of the shades throws himself down on top of an asphodel plant, shoving the ghostly gray blossoms into his sagging mouth. The other two clamor to get ahold of some of the flowers, but he pushes them away. I wince as their moans morph into shrieking screams. They've turned on each other, clawing and gnawing at each other's faces and limbs. They'd kill each other if they weren't already dead.

This is the plight of those who die without honor.

Heroes, Champions, those who know glory in this life go to Elysium when they die. I hear it is paradise. But those who are never given honor or who have had it stripped away from them, like myself, are doomed to wander the Wastelands for all eternity—trying to fill their cold, empty souls, which cannot be satisfied, no matter what. It's the worst-possible existence, save the fate of those who have openly wronged the gods.

Yesterday, when my life was in Father's hands, I'd thought I was ready to die if that was what he chose. I'd been resigned to the idea. But this ghastly reminder that dying without honor is a fate worse than death itself makes me realize that I am not resigned at all. I will not accept such a terrible destiny without a fight.

Dax is right; the Oracle has handed me the chance to show everyone what I am truly made of—to have my honor restored.

And I *will not* allow myself to fail.

I grab my bag, which holds what few belongings I am allowed to take. It is heavier than I remember and I wonder if I am feeling the weight of my quest on my shoulders. I hitch it up, ready at last, and let Dax propel me through the doorway. A loud clank echoes in my ears as he pulls the door to the roost shut behind us. Four guards, who've been waiting in the hallway, flank us immediately. The only path for us now is forward. Toward whatever destiny the Fates have measured for me.

chapter six

DAPHNE

The next few hours after I agreed to go with Joe are filled with so many firsts that I am not sure my brain knows how or where to process and store it all: My first time hearing the wind whip through the sunroof while riding in a limo down Apollo Canyon. My first time experiencing the cacophony of excited, dreading, and anticipating tones of people arriving and departing on new adventures in an airport. My first time on a plane—and a private jet, at that. My first time outside of Utah. My first time stepping foot in California, with its soupy humidity clinging to my skin, and realizing sound resonates differently in wet air than it does in dry. My first time seeing LA—granted, it was mostly a bunch of blobs of lights, and traffic noises, as it was pretty late on our way to Olympus Hills.

But of all the firsts, the one I'm having the hardest time processing is the first time seeing the sparse dots of houses and shops in the red dirt as we flew over Ellis Fields from the airport in Saint George.

Because that image meant I had done it—I had said good-bye to everyone I loved.

"Call me at least once a week," Jonathan had said with a hug and a big kiss on my cheek. "I want every juicy detail, you hear me." I could hear low notes of disappointment in him, but he'd managed to keep a smile on his face.

"Of course."

"I'll pack up the rest of your things tonight and make sure they get FedExed tomorrow. I just expect Mr. Tight Pants here to pick up the bill," he said with a smirk.

Joe nodded, and Marta—the glossy woman turned out to be Joe's "personal assistant slash handler slash babysitter" (her words, not mine)—handed Jonathan a card with Joe's address and account information for sending my things.

Indie gave me a melty Twix and half a bag of minipretzels for the plane. A gift I ended up being grateful for later, as the only service on Joe's jet was of the bar variety.

"Do you have everything you need in the meantime?" Mom had asked. It was the first thing she'd said to me since I'd left her office in the shop. I'd expected another plea from her to stay, and almost felt disappointed by her question instead.

"Yes." I was bringing with me my toiletries; three changes of clothes; my favorite sandals; Gibby, my acoustic-electric guitar; and much to the limo driver's—who had to bungee it to the roof— dismay, my white and lemon yellow cruiser bike. Everything else I could live without for a few days.

"I am still not okay with this," my mother said when Marta insisted we were two minutes off schedule and "must go now." But she still gave me one last hug before Marta pushed me inside the limo with Joe.

As the limo started to pull out, CeCe, who had been called away by the people from the school who had come for the balloon bouquets, came running out of the shop just in time.

She waved both hands frantically, as if afraid I wouldn't see her otherwise. I rolled down the window and shouted, "I'll call you soon. I promise!"

And then that was that. I'd watched through the back window as we drove away, leaving my old life behind in billowing clouds of burnt sienna dust.

I still can't get the image of my tiny town, with its tiny houses in the middle of nowhere, out of my head as we pull up to the security gates of Olympus Hills. The driver rolls down his window to show his pass to the guard, and I hear a cacophony of voices outside, shouting strange questions. At least half a dozen flashes pop on the other side of my window.

"What is that?"

"Paparazzi," Marta says, stopping me from rolling down my window. "They can't see you through the tinted glass. And don't worry; they can't get past the security gates, unless explicitly invited by a resident. That's the beauty of Olympus Hills: it's a private community, so no rats allowed."

"Be nice, Marta. Those rats butter our bread," Joe says. Or at least I think that's what he said; all the words were kind of slurred together.

Marta had given me some brochures on Olympus Hills on the plane, and since she'd spent most of the journey sending emails on her iPad, and Joe had passed the time taking full advantage of the rolling bar cabinet that a buxom flight attendant would bring by every time he snapped his fingers, I'd had plenty of time to brush up on Olympus Hills trivia.

The brochure had described the place not as a town, but as a "luxe, master-planned community." A description that seems very apt as we cross through the gates and into the neighborhood streets. Marta allows me to roll down my window once the gates are behind us. I want to see as much of everything as I can, even if it's dark out. The streetlights illuminate houses that are twice the size of any home in Ellis Fields. "Holy crap."

"These are the smaller homes," Marta says. "There's a lake at the center of the community. The houses get progressively more impressive, the closer their proximity to the lake. Joe's new house is right across the street from the shore, of course."

"Of course," I say, and watch as the houses grow larger and larger until we turn onto the road that circles the lake. I lean out my window, trying to get a better view of the water. We didn't have a lake in Ellis, so this is another first for me. One I'd been excited for since perusing the Olympus Hills brochure. It had said that the lake is shaped like a figure eight, with two islands in the middle. Everything is supposed to be connected by walking paths and footbridges. I can't see much in the dark except the lights from the building on one of the islands reflecting on the water. That must be the school. The brochure had said Olympus Hills High is on the larger island.

I may not be able to see much of the lake, but there is plenty to hear. The calming flow of the water; the happy, pulsing beats of insects skittering across the surface; the rhythmic swell of the wind through the reeds. As we pass the smaller island of the figure eight–shaped lake, all the subtle sounds are drowned out by a song that reminds me of a mother's lullaby. Well, a lullaby sung by *a mother*, not my mother—who might possibly be tone-deaf. I point at the tree-covered island and ask, "What's there?"

"The grove," Marta says. She shivers and indicates that she wants me to roll up the window. "Nobody goes there."

"Why?" I ask.

She picks up her glossy briefcase. "We're here," she says as we pull into the crescent-shaped driveway of a building that resembles more a gargantuan Grecian temple than a home.

During the drive, I'd noticed that most of the homes resemble an interesting mixture of modern architecture meets ancient Greece. "I guess they take the *Olympus* part of Olympus Hills seriously around here?" I say when we get out of the limo.

"You could say that," Joe slurs. They're the first words he's said directly to me since leaving Utah.

Marta unlocks the front door and then ushers us inside a grand entryway, the likes of which I have seen only in the movies at Ellis's single-screen cinema on Main Street. White marble floors lead to a pair of twisting staircases that fill the foyer, which is big enough alone to hold my mother's two-bedroom bungalow. A crystal chandelier drips from the center of the high vaulted ceiling. Little rainbows from the prisms reflect onto the tall white walls.

"Wow," I say.

"This place is smaller than Joe's homes in Malibu and Paris, but it'll do for now," Marta says. "Real estate in the area is hard to come by. I had to twist a few arms, didn't I, Joe?"

Joe grunts. He drops his leather jacket on the white marble floor and then disappears into one of the rooms off the west wing.

"Never mind him. Joe always needs a little alone time after we travel," Marta says. She checks her watch. "I have a few minutes to spare, if you would like a tour?"

I nod.

Marta explains, as we tour the house, that the first floor of the west wing is the main living quarters, with the kitchen, family room, a movie theatre—which includes what she claims will be a "fully operational concessions stand" once the house is completely unpacked and stocked—a "playroom," filled with Joe's collection of retro arcade games, and a ballroom for throwing parties.

She also informs me that the east wing of the first floor is her private living area, with its own smaller kitchen and a few guest bedrooms...but I don't get a tour of that. The second floor of the west wing holds Joe's master bedroom—a master bathroom that could put any spa to shame—a private rehearsal studio that seems especially *lived in*, considering Joe has been here for only a week, and a private office that looks like it's never been touched.

It strikes me how white everything is here. White walls, white marble columns and floors, white furniture, white carpet in the bedrooms, and even a painting taller than I am that is a canvas filled with globs of white paint. With the amount of dust that gets tracked into our bungalow back in Ellis, we'd never owned anything remotely white. Because it wouldn't have stayed white for very long.

"Does Joe have, like, a staff of thirty people to keep this place clean and running?"

"Your father employs a full live-in staff at his two other homes, but besides myself, Joe has insisted that he doesn't want any other live-ins here. A cleaning staff will come in once a week, but I am hoping he will reconsider bringing in his personal chef from the Malibu house, as cooking is not in my job description. I don't suppose you know how?"

"I make a mean bowl of Cinnamon Toast Crunch," I say, even though my repertoire is a little more advanced than that. No way am I going to spend my time cooking for Joe.

It's after midnight, and my legs are feeling fatigued by the time Marta leads me to the second floor of the east wing.

"This is your private area of the house," Marta says. "You'll have your own family room with a television, and there are three bedrooms, each with its own bathroom, but we thought you might like this one best, as it looks out on the pool." She opens a door and flips on the light of my new bedroom. It's also decorated in mostly white furniture, with pops of teal in the plethora of throw pillows on the plush, tufted duvet of the canopy bed. More teal pillows crowd the white, tufted sofa. I even have my own crystal chandelier. A gilded mirror hangs over a glossy vanity table, and a floating white shelf, which spans the length of one of the walls, is jam-packed with stuffed animals with various shades of white fur.

"Joe had his designer do this room up just for you."

"It's . . . um . . . nice." I frown at the white teddy bears staring down at me. "Joe realizes I'm not a six-year-old, right?"

Marta makes a noise that almost sounds like a laugh. "Joe does have a tendency to go a little overboard."

A MacBook computer sits on a white desk in front of a large window. I pull back the gauzy drapes and look into the backyard. Where this house has an advantage over my mother's bungalow in hugeness, it pales in comparison when it comes to yard. We have almost an acre of land in Ellis behind the shop, where my mom can fit her greenhouse and a barn for taking care of the various animals she brings home. Here, the yard comprises a stone patio, a long, skinny lap pool, and a narrow strip of grass. The almost equally ginormous house behind Joe's feels like it's only a few yards away.

I yawn. The fatigue of what must be the longest day of my life pulls me toward the very girly—yet admittedly comfy-looking—bed. I sink into the mountain of pillows.

"I'll let you rest now," Marta says curtly. "I would give you a tour of the community tomorrow, but I have another pressing matter that will take me away for the day. I will leave a map and a detailed itinerary outside your door by six a.m. Your audition is at three thirty p.m. tomorrow. Don't be late."

I sit up fast. "My audition?"

"For the music program at Olympus Hills High. Joe was able to pull a few strings to get you into the school, but if you want to be on the music track, you must audition for the program. You are scheduled for tomorrow afternoon."

"So soon?" The tiredness I'd felt only seconds ago is gone. I should have realized that there would be an audition right away, but I am wholly unprepared. I didn't pack any of my sheet music, leaving it behind for Jonathan to send later. I haven't done any research on what kind of music the director of the program prefers. I don't know if any of my three outfits are fit for auditioning at a private school.

I take two deep breaths and tell myself not to freak out. I'd already prepared a song for the Teen Talent Competition that I had planned on attending this evening. *I am ready for this. . . .*

"The other students in the program auditioned at the end of last year, and school has been in session for almost three weeks. If it hadn't been for a sudden opening in the program, you wouldn't be getting the chance at all. Mr. Morgan is holding preliminary auditions for this year's musical tomorrow. He said he would allow you to audition for the program and the play at the same time. You are supposed to prepare three songs."

Three? I'd spent all month perfecting my one song for the competition! "What play are they doing?" Hopefully, it was something I already knew a couple of songs from. *Les Misérables. Carousel.*

Seeing this town's apparent love for all things Greek, I wouldn't be surprised if it was *Mamma Mia!*

"He wouldn't say. It's supposed to be three songs of your own choosing."

"But I have no idea what else to sing."

"I don't see what the big deal is. Sing a few of your father's songs," Marta says, like it's a definitive solution to all my problems.

"Not in a million years," I mumble as she leaves and closes the door behind her. I can hear the click of her heels on the marble floor echoing as she goes. Now that I am alone, my new room feels too cavernous for comfort. I want to call home, but it's far too late at night. My mother would have a heart attack, thinking there had been some emergency.

I push the throw pillows off the bed. *Not a big deal?* This audition is *the* big deal. This music program is the entire reason I'd left home. It is my entire purpose for being here. All my future plans rest on it, and now the audition is being sprung on me before I am ready.

What if this has all been for nothing?

For the first time since I agreed to let Joe take me away from my home, I start to wonder if I've made a really big mistake.

CHAPTER SEVEN

HADEN

It's a long journey to the outskirts of the Underrealm, where Persephone's Gate stands at the end of a long ravine. The Underlords, and even the Lessers, flank both sides of the walk to the gate. Normally, their swords would be raised in honor to the Champion as he passes. I know better now than to expect such pomp on my behalf. All except the Lessers and the other servants are dressed in armor. Mine has been removed and I've been forced to don strange clothes like what Dax is wearing. My pants are made from a similar heavy cloth, but they're an inky black instead of blue, and my collared black tunic has many fasteners down the front. Both items of clothing are too tight, as though they'd originally been selected for someone slighter than myself.

This idea makes me look for Rowan in the flanking crowd, but instead of him, my sight lands on Garrick, the scrawny Lesser I tried to defend from Rowan's assault. His arm looks better now, thanks to a visit to the healing chambers, but for some reason, seeing him once more causes a twisting feeling inside my chest.

When Garrick had been reassigned to the Pits after he was

accused of stealing, I'd been glad to see him go. Relieved to be rid of the walking reminder of my shame. But I can't help wondering what his life has been like in that terrible place. *And if he knows what part I played in what happened to him . . .*

At least he hadn't been attacked by Rowan again, like he feared. Not yet anyway.

"Just keep walking," Dax says. I didn't realize that I'd stopped moving.

The ground trembles, and a faint green light begins to pulsate in the archway at the end of the ravine. The gate is beginning to activate. The old myths say that the gate was built for Persephone, the first Boon to be brought to the Underrealm by the original Hades. Persephone's mother, the harvest goddess, created the gate to ensure that her daughter could return to the Overrealm for six months out of every year—as was decreed by Hades's brother, the Sky God, in order to appease the keepers of both realms. But that was back when the Sky God cared about making peace. Back before the war between the gods. Before the dark day when Hades was slain by the Sky God and the Key to the Underrealm was lost. This made it so Persephone's Gate is now the only entrance or exit that exists between our world and the Overrealm that a living soul can pass through.

Unfortunately, the gate is active only for two twenty-four-hour periods a year. Once in the fall and once in the spring. Those times have been reserved for the entering and exiting of the Champions, sent on their quests to the Overrealm.

The gate's green light grows richer until it reaches a shade similar to emeralds. The ground shakes again, the tremor knocking an elderly Lesser off balance as I pass by with Dax. I step around the man and hear a familiar, derisive laugh. I look up toward the

Court, which surrounds the gateway, and find Rowan standing with Lex and Killian.

I stop in front of the pulsing gate. Dax stands behind me. I look away from Lex, Killian, and Rowan, waiting for one of them to make an accusation against me pertaining to the fight after the ceremony. But no one speaks.

Sweat beads on my brow as I realize there is one person who is missing from this scene. My father is not present.

Dax leans close. "I'm sure he's just attending to some pressing matter," he says, as if he can read my mind.

Master Crue, one of my teachers, steps to the front. I wonder what I will be tested on now, and try to remember everything I ran through during the night. But Master Crue merely gestures at the light that has filled the archway and says, "Godspeed, Champion Haden. May you be crowned with victory upon your return in six months' time."

Dax nudges me and I take a step forward—then come to a halt. Dax almost slams into my back.

"Wait," I say loudly enough that the Court can hear me.

"Gods, no," Dax whispers.

I look at Master Crue and then to Lord Killian. "I'm allowed an entourage, yes?"

Master Crue nods, indicating Dax behind me.

"But I can take more than one other with me?"

"Yes," Killian says hesitantly.

"Then I want to choose one more." I look at Rowan. "I choose my brother. . . ." I pause just long enough to watch my words dawn on Rowan. He starts to step forward, just like he had when he thought he was being Chosen by the Oracle. "My half brother, that is." I turn back and look at the frail boy in the crowd. "Garrick."

65

A collective gasp ripples through the ravine. Garrick stumbles forward, looking as though someone pushed him. He seems bewildered and a little panicked as he falls in line with me and Dax. I don't give Lord Killian or anyone else time to protest and I step up to the gate with my entourage.

"Take these," Dax says, pressing something into my hand as the three of us enter the pulsing green light. I look down to see that he's given me a pair of dark-lensed spectacles, and almost drop them as I suddenly lurch forward. It feels as though I'm being yanked by an invisible cable attached to my shoulders, but when I look at my feet, I realize I am still standing in one spot. Wind lashes at my face. I close my eyes, feeling as though I might lose the contents of my stomach. The yanking sensation stops abruptly and I fall to my knees. The dim green glow behind my eyelids has shifted to yellow. I open my eyes only to be blinded by an engulfing yellow light, so intense I feel as though my eyes might melt.

"Put them on," I hear Dax say.

I realize he means the spectacles and I shove them onto my face. The dark lenses mute the yellow glow, but only barely. After a few aching moments, my vision clears enough that I can discern the shapes of trees and rocks, and a great yellow orb on the horizon, peeking between what looks like two mountaintops. Garrick is huddled on the ground next to me, his hands clasped over his face.

"What the Tartarus is that?" I say, pointing at the orb without actually looking at it.

"Sunrise." Dax pushes up to his feet. He's wearing his own pair of dark lenses.

I hear a foreign noise from somewhere in the near distance. I blink several times and make out what seems to be the outline of a person emerging from the trees in front of us. The silhouette steps forward. "Welcome to Olympus Hills, my lords. I'm certain you will love it here," a voice says in a tone so . . . perky . . . it hurts my ears.

I close my eyes but the light still burns behind my lids.

And humans call the place where I'm from hell?

chapter eight

DAPHNE

This place is heaven, I admit to myself as I pull open the drapes in the main family room, revealing the incredible view of the lake. Seeing it in the daylight, I know why the real estate around here is so coveted. Jogging trails, trees, bushes, and flowers of almost every kind surround the lake, and I just can't get over how *lush* everything is. I knew that Ellis was in the middle of the desert, but I never realized exactly what that meant before. Or exactly what I'd been missing.

Mom would love it here, I think with a pang of guilt. Although she probably wouldn't be able to get over the fact that the long lake is man-made—according to Marta's brochure. I can't really tell, except for the odd figure-eight shape, that it isn't naturally occurring. I snap a picture of the lake through the window with my new phone—one of the things Marta left, along with a map and a daily itinerary, outside my door this morning.

I text the picture to Jonathan and CeCe with the note:

Arrived just fine. This place is gorgeous! (Please show my mom.)

Mom doesn't have a cell phone. She says she doesn't see the point since everyone she knows lives within walking distance. But maybe if I can get Jonathan and CeCe to show her enough pics, she might change her mind about coming to visit when she sees how beautiful this place is.

"Daphne, is that you, love?" I hear Joe's groggy voice from behind me.

I step away from the view. The light from the window hits Joe's face where he's splayed out on the family room couch. He cracks open one eye, then the other. He blinks a couple of times and then squeezes his eyes shut. "Be a good girl and go away."

I sigh and shake his booted foot, which dangles over the side of the couch. "Get up, Joe. Marta's itinerary says that you have an interview today. And I'm headed out. So if you don't wake up now, nobody will be here to act as your walking snooze button."

Joe lifts his arm and squints at his wrist, but his watch isn't there.

I check Marta's notes: "If Joe can't find his watch, it's probably in the fish tank. Again. He likes to test the water-resistance warranty." I'd thought that was a joke when I'd first read it, but sure enough, I see a couple of clown fish pecking at the platinum watchband at the bottom of the aquarium, which takes up most of the north wall in the family room.

"Bloody hell, is it morning already?" Joe asks, his British accent almost as heavy as his hangover.

"No, Joe. It's one in the *afternoon* already. And we've already had this conversation. Back when I woke you up at noon."

"Well, then, why did you wake me up again?"

"I told you, some reporter is coming over. Marta had to go somewhere for the day, so she charged me with making sure you wake up." Along with a laundry list of other tasks. I'd been here for fewer than sixteen hours, and it was already feeling like Marta was trying to shove most of her "babysitting" duties on to me:

1. Wake up Joe at noon. **Check.**
2. Wake Joe up again at one. **Check.**
3. Remind Joe that he booked an interview, even though I explicitly told him I'll be gone for the day. **Check.**
4. Either I or Joe's manager will be there in time for the interview to field questions. However, since Joe refuses to let me hire a decent staff for the house, remind him that he is therefore in charge of making sure things are tidy before the reporter arrives. . .

Oh boy. "I think you might want to clean up a bit." I hitch my thumb at the row of framed platinum records, hanging at precarious angles above the couch. A pizza box had been made into a tepee on the end table, and there are so many half-empty glasses and bowls residing on various chairs and tables in the family room and bits of ground chips living in the white carpet, you'd think he'd thrown a party after we got back last night. Yet from what I could tell from my room in the east wing, it had just been Joe and his greatest hits on Guitar Hero in here.

"A reporter? Why does a reporter want to come here?" Joe sits up. His rings clack against the glass-top coffee table as he searches for his glasses.

"I don't know. Why *doesn't* a reporter want to come here?" According to Marta, Olympus Hills is where the rich and famous come to live when they get sick of LA. If a reporter is being allowed inside Joe "the God of Rock" Vince's mansion, it is probably quite the scoop. "All I know is that Marta said to make sure you're up before the reporter arrives." I check my list. "Also, to make sure you're wearing pants." Thankfully, he is. Very tight leather ones, but pants they are. "Marta said you want to make some sort of announcement to the press."

I can only hope that announcement doesn't involve outing the secret of his long-lost backwater daughter to the world. Mom always said it was a miracle that the paparazzi had never found us in Ellis. It's almost like we were invisible to the rest of the world there.

"Oh, right, that." Joe finds his glasses: thick-framed, nerdy, hipster specs that clash with his leather pants, skull rings, and long, rocker hair.

Three things I know for sure about Joe so far. The longer portions of his hair are extensions, he never wears his glasses in public, and even though he tries to pull off an übercool, leather-clad, Top Forty rocker persona for the press, when I listen real closely, I can hear that he has more of this geeky, Indie singer-songwriter vibe. It's always baffled me, the few times we've met.

He presses the thick frames onto his face and makes a strangled noise as he surveys the mess around him. He turns a wide, toothy grin on me. "Fancy helping a poor bloke clean up a bit?"

"Not on your life."

"Come on, Daph, no love for your poor old dad?" He wiggles his eyebrows above the rims of his glasses, that cheeky smile on his face. "Quality daddy-daughter time," he croons.

"You are not my dad." He isn't going to let me forget that I called him that back at Paradise Plants, is he? "And cleaning up after your drunken binge doesn't make for quality lushy-louse–daughter time."

My anger shows in my voice too much, but at the moment I don't care. Joe didn't say a word to me on the entire trip from Ellis to here, and he'd disappeared the second I arrived at my new house, and the only reason that he's even paying attention to me now is because he doesn't want to clean up his own mess. I have no idea why he wanted custody of me if he's just going to ignore me as much here as he did when I lived a thousand miles away.

Joe places his hand against his chest and gives me an expression that almost looks genuinely crestfallen. But from the smell of stale whiskey and pizza that wafts off him, he is probably just trying to stifle a burp.

"I'm leaving to go find someplace to rehearse. My audition for the music program is today. That's the whole reason you wanted to bring me here, isn't it?" I pick up my guitar off the postmodern lounge chair, which clashes with the ancient Greece–inspired architecture of Joe's mansion. I use my fingernail to press down the peeling edges of a sticker of the Parthenon on my guitar case. The whole thing is covered in stickers of places I plan to visit someday. The Colosseum, Taj Mahal, Eiffel Tower, the pyramids of Giza.

Joe's eyes look huge and bloodshot as he blinks at me from behind his thick lenses. He doesn't answer my question, just looks at his wrist again as if trying to read his missing watch. "What day is it?" he asks. "The twentieth?"

"It's the twenty-first."

"Already?" Joe jumps up from the couch, and then catches himself against the armrest, like he's dizzy from standing up too fast. He's probably trying not to puke.

I grab my tote bag and hitch my soft guitar case over my shoulder. "Marta gave me a map. I'm going to find my way to that grove we passed last night. I need a good place to rehearse," I say, and head for the grand foyer.

I'd allowed myself exactly three minutes last night to freak out about the audition—a trick I learned from CeCe, who had trained to be an actress before she ended up in Ellis—and then set to work. I'd used my new Mac to peruse my iTunes account until I'd made a list of possible songs to add to my audition piece. I'd spent most of the morning running through the lyrics, but now that Joe is up, I feel the need to get out of the house. I could hear the grove's soothing song through my open window most of the night, and since Marta claimed that nobody ever went there, it seemed like a place worth scouting out as a practice spot. I've always preferred rehearsing in nature. When I was little, my mom used to claim that the flowers in the greenhouse grew twice as big because I sang to them.

"You can rehearse in my studio," Joe calls after me.

"Your studio smells like Cheez Whiz."

"Right. That it does." Joe stumbles into the foyer behind me. "I know, how about I buy you a new guitar? That's quality daddy-daughter time, right?" He reaches behind him and pulls out his wallet—where he fit a wallet in *those* pants, I don't want to know—and opens the billfold. "A few thousand ought to do it. . . . Huh. I seem to have misplaced all my cash. . . ."

"I think you donated it to the local liquor store." I open the front door. I don't have time for his attempts at pretending to be a good parent.

"Wait. My AmEx is upstairs. . . . Wait here."

"You've got an interview, and I need to rehearse." I pat my guitar. "I like Gibby anyway."

Doesn't he remember how I got her?

"But I don't want you rehearsing outside. Not today. What if it gets dark before you get back? How will I know where you'll be?"

"It's one in the afternoon, remember? And you've never known

73

where I was at any given point in time for the last seventeen years. Today shouldn't be any different."

"Just wait," he says. "If you don't want a new guitar, let's get you a new amp. A nice Fender? I'll tell that reporter to come back tomorrow, and I'll make sure I get you to the school with enough time to run through your audition piece a few times in one of their practice rooms."

I pause. *I could really use a new amp. . . .*

I sigh, wondering how much I'll regret the decision I'm about to make. "Okay, but only if we're quick. And I get to drive."

There is one benefit to Joe's constant need for a designated driver—I am going to rack up the remaining hours behind the wheel I need to get my license in no time.

"Brilliant!" Joe waves his hand at me in a wait-here motion. "I'll be right back with my card. I'll help you rehearse when we get to the school." He tries to bound up the stairs two at a time, but either his pants or his hangover slows him down. He whistles the melody from one of his songs as he disappears out of my sight.

I wait for a few minutes. The large clock in the foyer sounds like a countdown timer, the time I have left to rehearse ticking away. I realize I can't hear his whistle anymore.

"Joe?" I call up the stairs. "Did you get lost?"

This house is so big, I might not put it past him.

Joe doesn't answer. I wonder if I should wait here longer or go looking for him. My guitar grows heavy against my back. My shoulders ache. I suddenly feel like I'm ten years old again, waiting at the window—with a hefty telescope in my arms—for Joe to come pick me up so we can go stargazing. I'd waited until almost midnight that night, until my mother had insisted I go to bed. *I'm sorry, honey. I just don't think he's coming. . . .*

74

Standing here in his cavernous foyer, I hate that one small promise of a shopping trip can make me feel like that little girl all over again. Why am I putting myself in this position? Why am I letting Joe back in again just so I can be disappointed?

But shouldn't I be happy that he wants to spend time with me? Shouldn't I be forgiving? I mean, he brought me here, he's giving me everything I've ever wanted, he's giving me the opportunity to follow my dreams. Shouldn't I be grateful? If the man wants to spend the afternoon with me, shouldn't I let him?

But I already know how this is going to turn out. Whether it's here or at the store or later today at the auditions, he's going to forget or he's going to get distracted, or something, and I'm going to be left waiting once more like that disappointed little girl.

No, I'm not going to let that happen. I'm not here for daddy-daughter bonding time. I'm not here to reconnect with my long-lost father. Joe is a means to an end. A ticket out of Ellis and an opportunity for a top-flight education. I'm here for myself. To achieve my goals, and right now, that's getting into the music program at OHH. After that, it's making a name for myself in the music world—all on my own.

And I don't have time for distractions.

I don't bother calling Joe's name again. I don't go looking for him upstairs. *Ten bucks, he's probably already forgotten why he even went up there, or is puking in a bathroom,* I tell myself as I slip out the front door.

With my guitar case hitched over my back and my tote bag secured in the basket of my white and lemon yellow cruiser bike, I set off to find that grove to rehearse.

Alone.

chapter nine

HADEN

I have been told to wait. So that is what I have been doing, but I don't know how they expect me to do so for much longer.

After making introductions, the overly enthusiastic man—who told us his name was Simon Fitzgerald but that we should call him Simon—brought us to a house. It was a short walk from the grove, but between the aching behind my eyes and Simon's insisting on pointing out and naming everything in English that we passed, the journey was as tedious as Sisyphus's toils up the mountainside.

Simon's cheery commentary of "This is a road. This is a bridge. This is a mailbox. This is a doorbell" doesn't let up like I hope it will when we enter the house. "This is a refrigerator. This is a microwave. This is a coffeemaker. Have you ever had coffee? No, you other two wouldn't have, would you? You simply must try it! This is a fabulous roast. Here, take a cup. . . ." He hands me a cup full of hot, brown liquid. It smells acrid and acidic to me. I pass it to Garrick. He sniffs it and his face goes from pale to green. "This, over there, is a plasma TV. It's simply wonderful, isn't it?" He looks at Garrick. "Oh no. Oh boy. And this, over here, is a toilet . . . ," he says, grabbing Garrick and ushering him down the hall and through a door. I wince at the sound of vomiting.

"Can we dismiss this Simon guy yet?" I ask Dax. The pain behind my eyes has swelled into the rest of my head, and I am starting to worry about getting sick, like Garrick. "I haven't forgotten that you've promised to fill me in on what you know. I need to get started on my quest. I don't have time for this fool to name every object in this house."

Dax holds up his hand to quiet me. "Do not let his disposition deceive you," he whispers. "Mr. Fitzgerald is not your servant, he is not your friend, and he certainly isn't a fool. It is best not to cross him, understand?"

I nod, thankful all over again that Dax is here to guide me.

"Ah, now. No worries," Simon says, coming back into what he'd labeled the "breakfast nook," wiping his hands on a towel. "Our young friend is going to spend some time getting acquainted with the bathroom facilities. I am afraid some folks don't pass through the gate as easily as others. How are you feeling, my lord?"

The smell of the coffee Garrick left on the table makes my stomach swim, but I don't want to give away any signs of weakness. "Fine," I say.

"I'll give you boys the rest of the tour later. We have many arrangements to make. You don't fit the description of the Champion I was told to prepare for. . . ."

"There was a change of plans," Dax says.

"Very well. That happens." Simon pulls a flat, rectangular device from his pocket. "Remove your sunglasses," he says to me.

I realize he means my spectacles and I pull them off. Simon sticks the device right in front of my face. It flashes a bright light in my eyes with an artificial-sounding click.

"Harpies!" I clasp my hands over my face, my eyes burning even more.

"Sorry about that," Simon says. "But I'll be needing a photograph of each one of you. I didn't expect to see you again, Dax. What a pleasant surprise." I hear the weird clicking sound again and assume Simon used the device on Dax. "I was afraid they might chop off your hands or something equally unpleasant when you returned the way you did—"

"It's nice to see you again, Mr. Fitzgerald," Dax says, politely cutting him off. Dax never talks about his time in the Overrealm. I wonder what I might be able to learn about it from Simon—if I ever dare to ask.

"Yes, yes, reunions are always wonderful," Simon says. I am still seeing a bright white spot in my vision as he looks me over from head to toe and scratches his chin. "We will need to make some . . . er . . . adjustments. Dax, you will help me. In the meantime, Lord Haden, my house is your house, so make yourself at home."

"What exactly do you do for a living?" I remember from my lessons that people in the mortal world have different jobs that they perform and are then compensated for—not compulsory assignments required by the king. Whatever it is that Simon does for a living, he is compensated well—in mortal terms—for it.

"A little bit of everything." Simon's grin stretches far across his face. "I guess you could say my specialty is procuring *things* for people." He opens the thing he called a refrigerator and pulls out a glass of green liquid and takes a swig. "Gotta keep the ole immune system up. Especially with so many teenagers living in the house again. Want some? I'll make you all some smoothies if you want. I just got a new Blendtec."

He holds the glass up. It smells like fermented weeds. My stomach churns. I shake my head. "Is there a place I can put my things?"

"Oh yes, yes. I forgot to show you to your rooms."

After that, Simon escorts Dax and me up the stairs to our bedchambers. To my surprise, my room is much larger than the one I had been reassigned to in the palace after my father expelled me from the royal living quarters.

Simon names a few of the things in the room, and then with his most enthusiastic expression yet, he says, "This room is fantastic. The best room in the whole house. I trust you will be comfortable waiting here while Dax and I finish our arrangements?" His smile is so wide and his teeth gleam so white, I almost don't catch the true meaning of his words. I am being ordered to stay here and wait, something I am not comfortable agreeing to.

"But when can I get started? How do I find this Daphne girl?"

"Be patient," Dax says from behind Simon in the doorway. "Lord Haden, I know you feel anxious. I know you're eager to begin your quest, but it's imperative that you don't do anything until the arrangements have been finalized. Take this opportunity to rest from your journey. Wait here."

Simon's eyes narrow slightly as he looks at me. "Say yes," he says in a way that makes me feel compelled to agree whether I want to or not.

"Yes," I say.

"Fantastic!" he says. "You and I are going to get along just peachy."

He closes the door behind him and Dax. I hear the distinct sound of a key turning in the lock, and panic wells up inside of me. The feeling increases with every moment that passes. I listen by the door for some time. At one point, I hear Simon escort Garrick to his own room across the hall. A few minutes later, I hear another voice in the house that sounds distinctively female. This sets me to pacing the floor, from door to window and back again. At another point, I think I hear Dax and Simon leave the house.

But when will they be back? How long will these arrangements take?

I find myself pacing again, biting my fingernails—another trait of my mother's that I unfortunately inherited. It feels as though several hours have passed since Dax and Simon left me. I have done as I was told. Heeded Dax's warning not to be impulsive. But every moment that passes and I am stuck in this room is a moment that I am not working toward accomplishing my quest. Waiting is not acting. And not acting is akin to failing. How can I wait anymore?

I clutch at my hair and sit on a chair in the room. There's a bed here, too. Dax told me that I should take this opportunity to rest. He knows I didn't sleep last night. *Rest* is a luxury. Being alone is, too. Especially in the middle of the day. I guess I could collapse on the bed. Let myself stop thinking, for once. Take pleasure in a few moments of solitude—of not being watched or judged by anyone. No one expecting me to do anything for the moment. Rest is what I need. I should give into the fatigue that pulls at my body. I should let it all go for now. . . .

But I don't know how anyone can sleep when it's so cursed bright.

The sun has shifted much higher in the sky, causing the light that pours in through the window to grow even brighter. I have to wear the dark glasses even inside the house, which should be a deterrent to wanting to venture outside, but the muscles in my body ache from inactivity. The queasiness that plagued my stomach before has shifted into a weight that sits in my gut like a heavy stone. It *feels* as though I have been waiting for hours, but I have no idea how long it has really been.

It strikes me that I do not know how time moves here in the mortal world, compared to the Underrealm. What feels like hours to me could be mere minutes. Or perhaps *days*? Could the rising of this *sun* signify the passing of whole days before my very eyes? Why didn't Master Crue cover this in my lessons? What other gaps are there in my education? Perhaps I am even less prepared than I thought I was.

I have been told that I have six months to complete my quest, but what if, *here*, six months are a matter of weeks in comparison?

I know that if I am patient, I can ask Dax or Simon to explain how time works here, but I can't bear not knowing how much time I have left, nor how much time has been wasted—by *waiting*.

I can think of one way of checking the time. The gate is supposed to be active for twenty-four hours. If I can trace my way back to it and it is still active, then I will at least know that it has only been hours. Not a whole day or possibly even a week—or maybe more—that has been wasted.

I go to the window and find that it opens. It's a two-story drop, but that doesn't hinder me. Neither does the idea of being seen.

Stealth is one of the things I *have* been trained in. I excel in it, actually. Out of necessity to avoid Rowan and his cronies, not to mention the prying eyes of the Court. I know I can find my way to the gate and back without being detected. Just stick to the shadows cast by the sun. I can be there and back before the others return.

No one will even know that I was gone.

chapter ten

DAPHNE

I don't need Marta's map to find the grove. I follow the path on my bike, finding my way by sound. Like the grove's song is calling to me.

Most people would say that sounds weird. Or obsessive.

That's how most people would describe my relationship with music. Many of my teachers did. A group of doctors had. I am always following some sound or song, trying to find the source. That time I crashed my bike on Canyon Road and ended up in the hospital in Saint George, the doctor had looked at me like I was crazy when I told him I was chasing a song and didn't realize how fast I was going down the hill.

"Chasing a song?" he'd asked. "Like you heard someone's car radio?"

"No, it was a Joshua tree. It was singing at the bottom of the hill. Its song was so pretty, I wanted to find it."

"The tree was singing?" His eyebrows drew together. "Do other things sing? Do you hear them all the time? Do you hear music now?"

I nodded, thinking he was the crazy one. I never understood why other people didn't hear the things I did. The different tones, sounds, melodies that came from living things. The doctor himself had a harsh, high-pitched tone, like the repetitive *ting* of a triangle. I didn't care for it. He sent another couple of doctors to talk to my mom and me. I didn't like their tones, either. And before we left the hospital, they'd diagnosed me with something called musical OCD. They said my connection with music went beyond interest or talent. They called it an obsession. They said I *shouldn't* hear the things I heard. They said I was so obsessed that I didn't know how to relate to the world around me in any other way than through sound and music. So, therefore, in order to cope, I attached musical notes and tones to everything around me.

They said the music wasn't real, that it was all created by my dysfunctional brain.

They recommended therapy and medication. To this day, I still don't know if my mom curtly refused their diagnosis because she hated the idea of taking me out of Ellis twice a week for therapy, or because she believed my insistence that the music was real. Either way, I am glad she didn't let those doctors try to medicate the music out of me.

I use the sounds I hear to navigate my life. I use it to pick my friends. I am always drawn to people with warm, inviting melodies. I love grouping together the things and people whose tunes best complement each other. Like composing my own little symphony of friends. And it helps me read people's emotions based on the shifts in the tones they put off. I use music to discover favorite things and find my favorite places. Even the earth itself has a song that I can hear when I am being very, very still.

That's the real reason I want to rehearse in the grove. I want to be wrapped inside the grove's song, and add my own music to it.

I cross the footbridge that leads to the grove on the smaller island of the lake. I get off my bike and walk it through the ring of tall poplar trees, which border the grove. They remind me of spires, stretching up as if in homage to the heavens. Smaller aspens and laurel trees fill in the center of the grove, creating a thick canopy of darkness—even in daytime—that must have been what kept others away. Normally, I am not keen on dark places, but the grove's melody draws me in.

I leave my bike propped against a poplar tree and then settle onto the ground with my guitar. I lean my back against a strangely shaped laurel tree that reminds me of a tuning fork: the way its trunk is split in the middle so it grows upward in two separate curves. I pull my guitar from its case and run through a few bars without singing. I need three songs for the audition this afternoon. Two of them, I am sure about, but I am still wavering on what to do for the third. Should I choose one of my own songs so the music director would see that I'm interested in songwriting, in addition to singing? Or should I stick with popular songs that everyone will know and feel connected to?

I guess I could sing Joe's star song, since it would cover both options. That bitter thought trickles through my mind before I can stop it. I shake away a flood of additional thoughts that try to break through the floodgates. I've already lost too much time to Joe today, and I need to focus on rehearsing.

I run through several voice warm-up exercises, and then after some thought, I pick a song I wrote for my mother. I play it a couple of times on my guitar, and then start it again. This time, I join in with my voice after the intro.

The laurel tree I lean against seems to tremble at the sound of my voice. Its vibrating hum joins my song. It feels as though the grove comes to even greater life as I sing, sending the echo bouncing against the branches and leaves of the trees. The aspens create a quaking, clattering rhythm that keeps up with the melody of the song. Birds chirp, dragonflies buzz, and even the wind feels as though it is keeping harmony with me as it swirls my long hair around my face while I sing. I'd known there was something extra-special about this place before I'd entered. I could tell by the way it had called out to me. I've always loved singing with nature as my audience, but I'd never before had nature *join in* with me like this.

Perhaps this experience really is a symptom of a dysfunction in my brain—but there's no way I would classify it as a *disorder*.

I stop playing the guitar abruptly. The grove quiets in a way that reminds me of the intake of a breath, anticipating the next note. I sing the last line of the song without the guitar accompaniment, while the trees reverberate around me. The vibration of the tuning fork–shaped tree tingles up my spine and into my arms. When I finish the song, the grove falls silent again. Followed by the sound of a very real gasp . . .

I jump up, almost dropping Gibby. Somebody else is here. I can *feel* someone's presence, even though I can't see anyone, and I know I hadn't imagined that human-sounding gasp. The grove is still quiet—too quiet. Shouldn't it have taken up its own song again by now? What is it waiting for?

"Who's there?" I ask.

Only silence answers, but I know I'm not alone.

Perhaps there is some paparazzo lurking in the bushes. Marta said that they couldn't get past the security gates, but I'm sure someone unscrupulous and crafty enough can figure out how to sneak past the guards. Maybe this one had gotten wind of Joe Vince's prodigal daughter and was looking for a photo op?

"I know you're there," I say. "So you might as well show

yourself, get your picture, and get lost."

The air grows warmer around me, and I can feel someone coming closer. I shiver despite the budding heat.

"How did you do that?" a strangely accented voice asks from somewhere in the dark of the grove.

"What?" I look in the direction of the voice, but I can't see anyone. "Who's there?"

"What was that you did with your voice?" It sounds as though the questioner has moved even closer. "Just now. I heard you."

I put a hand to my throat. "You mean my singing?" I reply to the darkness.

"Singing. Is that what you call that?"

"Excuse me?" My cheeks flush with heat. I step closer to the location of the voice. "Listen, jerk, I don't know who you are. But if you came here to make fun of my singing, you can go . . ."

The leaves of one of the aspen trees silently quiver, and someone appears out of the shadows—almost as if he materialized from the darkness.

I step back, uncomfortable with the seclusion of the grove for the first time. The person is cloaked in shadows, but I can tell he's a man. Or perhaps a boy. But definitely male. He steps closer and his features come into view. I take him in from head to toe. It would be impossible not to. He's tall, even taller than me, and I tower over most of the guys I've ever met. His black jeans look brand-new, and his black shirt still carries the creases from sitting on a department store shelf. Both hug his fit body in a way that makes me take in a quick breath. While his clothes seem expensive and refined, the rest of him looks untamed in a way that reminds me of a wildcat. . . . Or more like a pirate? His cheeks and jaw are hard and muscular, and his thick hair, the color of ebony, falls in chunky, uneven strands, like somebody took a raw blade to it, just above his shoulders. Long black bangs hide his eyes.

"I'm not here to create amusement," he says and steps even closer, closing the gap of safety between us. My heartbeat kicks up a notch.

"Um . . . what?"

"I just wanted to know what that was you did with your voice. And with that." He gestures at my guitar. "I've never heard anything like it before."

I'm confused. Does he mean that he's never heard the grove's acoustics before, or that he's never heard *music* before? I am about to ask when he brushes his dark hair out of his face, revealing eyes the color of jade, except for the bright swirls of amber radiating like flames around his pupils.

My throat feels tight as I try to speak. I can't recall what I was about to ask. This boy, with fire dancing in his eyes, intrigues me, but at the same time, he reminds me of why I used to be afraid of the dark. Back when I was younger, I thought monsters lived in shadows and could only be seen out of the corner of my eye.

I should be wary of this stranger. But I'm not. I stand motionless, returning his gaze, as transfixed as if I were in the spotlight on a grand stage. Finally, he blinks, and I glance down at his mouth.

"Are you real?" he asks.

I try to laugh, but no sound comes out. Am *I* for real? I am the one who should be asking that question.

He slowly stretches his hand toward my face but then pulls it slightly back. I notice a pallor under his olive skin, but a strange heat seems to radiate from his fingertips. I look into his eyes again and move my hand toward his. The curious, pulsing heat of his skin draws me to him. We are about to touch, his fingers breathing warmth against mine. He looks away from my eyes and notices the name pendant—a sixteenth-birthday present from CeCe—that I wear around my neck.

"Daphne?" He reads my name. His hand drops, and that strange heat falls away with it. "*You're* Daphne Raines?"

"Yes," I say before thinking better of giving this stranger my name. The trance he held me in is broken. "How do you know my name? What—are you some kind of reporter?"

I notice now that this boy has no sound. No tone, no melody, no song coming off him. Just silence, like the too-still grove that engulfs us from the view of any witnesses.

I also realize that he doesn't have a camera. He's not a reporter looking for a picture.

He takes a quick step back, like he's about to run away, but then stops. He looks me square in the eyes, but this time, the intensity of his gaze only frightens me. "Will you come with me?" he says, reaching for my arm.

chapter eleven

HADEN

I make it to the gate unnoticed. In the mortal world, the gate is cloaked to resemble two curving trees that create an archway at the north end of the grove. The green light has grown fainter. I wonder if it is even visible to human eyes, but as I hold my hand out, I can still feel it pulsing with energy. The gate is still active, which means it is still the same day in which I arrived.

I have overreacted for no reason.

I am about to return to Simon's home, feeling reassured and slightly chagrined, when a sound catches my ear. It's a high sound, but not like the screeching of an owl or the wailing of a nursling. It's a flowing sound that evokes the image of a river or the wind streaming through the treetops—and yet still like no other sound I have ever heard.

I cannot stop myself from following the echoing noise. I track it through the thicket of trees until I come to the center of the grove.

There I see a young female, sitting against a strangely shaped tree. She cradles a large object on her knees, and strums the strings that stretch from its wide base up a long wooden neck. The object reminds me of the pictographs I often pass in the murals that cover the walls of the palace. It vaguely resembles a lyre—the great weapon the Traitor had used to deceive Hades all those centuries ago. But the object the girl holds does not seem like a weapon. Her picking and strumming the strings are what create the reverberating sound. I remove my sunglasses to be able to see her better in the shady grove, and I watch, curious, as she opens her mouth and starts to speak.

No, not quite speaking. Her voice sounds different from that. Her words are drawn out, ebbing and flowing at times and flitting at others, blending with the sounds that come from her strumming. It grows in intensity, swirling around the grove and washing over me. It pulls at me, evoking something I have not felt since I was in the presence of the Oracle: the feeling of wonder.

When the girl stops speaking and the sound dies away, a gasp slips out of my lips.

She stands, her abruptness making it clear that I have given myself away.

"Who's there?" she asks. Her voice sounds different from before. Lower, but still appealing.

I know I should leave, but I can't. I need to know what it was that she did with her voice. I want to know how.

She steps closer. The way she moves is almost as appealing as her voice. I feel energy swirling in my chest, growing stronger the closer she gets. I move in nearer to her. She does not see me yet, but she shivers.

I ask her what she'd done with her voice. I speak English, but I realize too late that I haven't concealed my Underrealm accent.

I step closer to her, still cloaked in shadow.

She places her hand on her throat. "You mean my singing?"

"Singing." I know that word; I have just never heard the sound that it applies to. It has always been an abstract concept to me until now. "Is that what you call that?"

She's angry at me. She thinks I am toying with her for my own enjoyment. She will leave if I don't do something. I step out from my hiding spot in the dark.

She takes a step back, as if nervous. I don't want her to go.

I try to reassure her as I come closer.

"I just wanted to know what that was you did with your voice. And with that." I point at the object she holds. "I've never heard anything like it before."

She gives me a confused look, and I wonder if she does not understand my question. I want to explain further, but I am distracted by her nearness. Energy pulses through my body, stronger than my heartbeat. The sunlight streaming through the canopy of the grove glints off her golden hair, and the curves of her body make my hands prickle with heat that is unlike what I normally experience before a surge of lightning. Her blue eyes, brighter than the mortal world's sky, meet mine.

I stand still, letting her look at me. I can feel the fire swirling in my eyes. Finally, I blink, unable to bear the intensity.

"Are you real?" I ask her. I have heard stories of mystical creatures that can enchant men with their voices. It is one of the reasons this singing—music—is forbidden in my world. And she is unlike any mortal female who has ever been brought to my realm.

I have also heard stories of sprites that can create mirages.

I raise my hand toward her face, wanting to touch her to see if she *is* real, but I hesitate, not quite wanting to know the answer. She lifts her hand toward mine, and I can feel electricity pulsing into my fingers. I look from her eyes to her mouth and then lower. A golden pendant sits in the hollow of her neck.

It spells something in English. It takes me a second to translate it. "Daphne?" I ask, dropping my hand. Can I really be reading that correctly? Can it really be her? "*You're* Daphne Raines?"

"Yes," she says.

The energy coursing through my body intensifies with her positive response.

I cannot believe my good fortune. For once in my life, the Fates have smiled on me. I have followed my impulses—no, my instincts—to this place, and here *she* is.

I've found her. My Boon. My prize. My destiny. Just waiting here to be plucked, like an asphodel blossom. With the gate, pulsing with life, only a few yards away, at that. This couldn't be more perfect.

An idea strikes me like an arrow hitting a bull's-eye. Why wait six months to do what I can accomplish right now?

I could be the fastest-returning Champion in the history of the Underrealm. Surely that would warrant glory and honor like no one has received before me. Rowan could not call me a failure again. My father would not look at me as though I am a disgrace.

But at the back of my mind, a worry pulls at me, making me wonder if the situation is too good to be believed. Why would Dax implore me to be patient if my quest were this easy to accomplish? I hesitate for a moment. . . .

No, I must act.

I reach for the girl's hand. "Will you come with me?"

She pulls away. "Um, no."

"I need you to come with me," I implore.

"I need to leave," she says quickly, hitching up the long object she'd been strumming on a few moments before. It did not seem dangerous then, but now she holds it as if it can be used as a weapon.

It doesn't frighten me.

"Say you'll come with me." She has to say it. I know that from the Oracle's instructions. She has to go willingly. I need to convince her. I advance toward her. I can be persuasive like Rowan. "You have to say you'll come."

"Get away from me, perv!" She backs away. "Creep!"

I reach out again, trying to clasp her wrist. Electricity surges into my arm, and before I can stop it, a spark of lightning escapes my fingers. She yelps with pain and twists out of my grasp. I reach for her again, and her fist—thankfully not the one holding the wooden object—goes flying at my face. I am so surprised by the action that I don't have time to block the blow before she punches me. Hard. In the jaw. I stop, completely stunned, and clasp my hand to my face. I'm not injured. It would take more than her small hands to hurt me. But I am still shocked. I did not know Boons are capable of violence.

I don't regain my composure quickly enough to stop the girl from getting away. She grabs an object, which I recall from Simon's monologue is called a bicycle. She glances back at me as she flees, fear dancing in her blue eyes.

chapter twelve

DAPHNE

My hand hurts from punching him, but it's caused enough of a diversion for me to get away. I run for my bicycle, realizing that I don't have time to stop for my tote bag or guitar case, but I won't leave Gibby behind. I sling her over my back, with her strap resting against my chest, and jump onto my bike. I glance back at the stranger, and then pedal as fast as I can from the grove.

Gravel spits out from under my tires as I hit the narrow trail that leads from the grove to the bridge. I don't know if he follows, and I don't stop to check. I cross the bridge that connects the grove's island to the paved jogging paths that surround the lake, and keep on going.

I careen down the trail, gaining speed, putting as much distance between me and the stranger as possible. I don't see the girl until it's too late. I try to stop, but the brakes on my vintage bike are old and I don't normally ride this fast. I try to skid around her just as she looks up and counters in the wrong direction. I clip her elbow with one of my handlebars.

"Ouch!" she shouts and tries to push me.

"Sorry!" I swerve away from her, and it takes all my balance to stay upright as my bike keeps skidding along the path. I glance back at her once I've regained control.

"You're such a freak!" she yells when she sees me looking. She clasps at her scraped elbow and starts jogging up the trail despite the fact that she's wearing a miniskirt with pink and silver wedge platform sandals. Hardly the right outfit for a run.

That strange boy is nowhere to be seen, but I still don't stop for anything until I get to the school.

chapter thirteen

HADEN

I could have caught her easily. But it is the fear that I saw in her eyes that stops me. Makes me realize my grave mistake.

I have done it again.

I've acted without thinking.

I have been here for fewer than twenty-four hours, and I have already erred in the most terrible of ways. If Rowan were here, he would delight in telling me that I have no idea of what I am doing. That I am failing before I even get started.

She fears me now, instead of trusting me.

Another pulse of energy swells in my chest. I grab the branch of the nearest tree. I squeeze the energy into it until the branch disintegrates. The ash slips through my fingers.

I am fighting the urge to fall to my knees and send up a prayer to plead for forgiveness from the Fates, when I hear the crackle of footfalls on the forest floor. A low hiss echoes through the grove. Someone else is coming. I can't afford to be seen. I can't afford to make another mistake. I pick up one of the items that the girl left behind, then slip behind the partially burned tree.

I disappear into the shadows.

chapter fourteen

DAPHNE

My legs shake from riding so hard as I roll my cruiser into one of the slots of the bike rack. My voice warbles when I try to whisper to myself to calm down.

"I'm okay. Nothing bad happened. Not really."

But the question I can't get out of my mind: where did he want me to go with him?

As if.

I might have been dumb for talking to him in the first place. But I'm not a complete idiot. I'd never follow some creep into the woods.

I try to tell myself to calm down, but my voice warbles and I can't help thinking about all those "stranger danger" lectures my mom used to drill into me as a kid—like how if I ever encountered something weird or dangerous, or if someone I didn't know tried to get me to go somewhere with him, I should run away and find someone trustworthy to tell.

But who would I even tell in this particular situation? Joe? He's the last person I'd confide in. I'd feel stupid going to the police— nothing had *exactly* happened. Maybe this is a job for the security guards at the main entrance into Olympus Hills? They should be responsible for whatever weirdos they let through the gates.

But I imagine trying to explain what happened and it coming out all wrong: an attractive guy, wearing tight black clothes, with long rough-cut hair, looking like he'd wandered off the set of a pirate movie, talked to me about my singing and then asked me to go somewhere with him? Yeah, the guards would probably say that he was just trying to hit on me.

Maybe I had completely misread the situation?

CeCe always teased me about how I have no idea when guys are flirting with me. She said it's because I've got a wall around me that's a mile high, so I'm either completely oblivious when guys try to flirt or I think they're trying to make fun of me.

I'm not here to create amusement. . . .

That's what the guy in the grove had said when I accused him of making fun of my singing. It was such a weird thing to say. Maybe he's even more socially inept when it comes to the opposite sex than I am?

But any idiot should know that you don't go around trying to grab a girl's arm like that.

And social awkwardness doesn't explain his eerie, fiery eyes, or the strange heat that seemed to be radiating off his skin. It had actually hurt when he had tried to touch my arm.

I look down at my wrist. My skin stings, and there are four red marks on my arm. They're long and thin, like the shape of fingers. Right where the guy had touched my skin.

That definitely isn't normal.

I notice the time on my watch. It's almost three o'clock. I'd been in the grove much longer than I'd realized. That's not nearly enough time for me to bike down to the security station and back before my audition.

My audition!

Why am I letting myself get carried away when I have much more important things to worry about? Forget about weird guys in the woods; I have only thirty-six and a half minutes to finish preparing for my audition.

Leaving my bike in the rack, I make my way between the granite columns at the entrance of the school and into the main hall. It's large and echoey, and I can hear singing drifting through the halls. Auditions for the musical must have been going on all day. I follow the sound through the school until I find the auditorium. I peek through the heavy double doors. Someone is onstage, singing a song from *Evita*, while a few clusters of students sit in the auditorium seats. Back at Ellis High, which comprised five whole rooms, we had to do all of our performing on a platform in the cafeteria. I've never sung in a room this big.

The girl on the stage stands perfectly still, her hands clasped in front of her chest and her chin out. Her voice is strong and even, and I can tell she's had years of professional training, but if Jonathan were around, he'd probably tell her to be more expressive with her body, not just her voice. The only adult in the room is a thin man with graying hair, who sits at a table, making notes in a binder. I assume he's Mr. Morgan, the music director. When the singer draws out her final note—a bit too long, in my opinion—I push the auditorium door open and slip inside.

Mr. Morgan calls out a name I don't quite catch. A guy comes out from behind the curtains on the stage. He wears skinny jeans, a white button-up shirt, a small open vest, and a tweed, narrow-brimmed fedora. He lifts his hat and gives a curt bow to Mr. Morgan, revealing his floppy black hair. He announces the songs he's going to sing to Mr. Morgan and then puts his hat back on. I take a seat near the back of the auditorium. The accompanist on the piano starts the intro, and with a snap of his wrist, Fedora Boy grabs the microphone stand and croons into the mic with all the flare of Frank Sinatra.

I'm still shaking a bit from my close encounter of the weird kind, so I try to run through a few relaxation exercises that CeCe taught me, but Fedora Boy's voice is so warm yet powerful that I find myself distracted. I like the sound of this guy's voice, and it relaxes me more than the breathing exercises. There's something familiar about him—something I hear in him and the way he moves his body while he sings. He reminds me of someone, but I can't place it. I find myself smiling when he starts his third song. I must have caught his eye, because as he finishes his last line, he plucks his fedora from his head, dips it down when he bows, and then winks . . . at me.

"Well done," Mr. Morgan says to the boy. "But the winking was a bit much."

Fedora Boy smiles wide and hops off the stage with a goofy swagger that makes me giggle inside. Mr. Morgan picks up his coffee mug and announces that he's going to "take five."

I realize just how dry my throat is from my bike ride, so I pick up my guitar and head out a side door to find a drinking fountain. Only twenty minutes remain until my audition, and a raspy voice isn't going to impress anyone.

The hall is dark and empty. I find the drinking fountain, but as I'm leaning over to take a sip, I think I see something move in my peripheral vision. A low hiss buzzes in my ears. I pop upright, water dribbling on my chin. I look left and right, but all I see are shadows.

My mouth feels even drier. I take a second sip. This time, I hear a sound from behind, like the *ratta-tat-tat* of a snare drum, and I know I am not alone. I whirl around and find the boy in the fedora standing there. He smiles wide, and the drumming sound grows stronger. I realize the syncopated beat is coming from him. It's his song. His inner melody, which only I can hear. It's a warm and inviting sound, not like the cold hiss I'd heard just a moment ago, and it clicks with his Sinatra vibe. He's a crooner at heart.

"Hey," he says. "Glad I caught you. You must be New Girl."

"Yeah," I say, looking over his shoulder to make sure he's the only other person in the hall. Maybe I'm still just shaken from what happened in the grove, but I have the weirdest feeling at the moment—like we're not alone. Like someone is watching me.

Maybe I *should* tell someone about what happened. . . .

"Hey, do you know where Mr. Morgan might have headed off to?" I ask. "I need to talk to him about something."

"Nope. I'm sure he'll be back in a few minutes. Pleased to meet you, by the way." He presses his hat to his chest and offers his hand for me to shake. A real handshake. Not a stupid "fist bump and blow it up" like most guys. "I'm Tobin Oshiro-Winters."

I shift my guitar to my other hand, and I take his outstretched one. He smiles wider in return, and I realize who he reminds me of—in both the friendly tone that wafts off him and also his toothy grin. He's the male, part Japanese version of CeCe back in Ellis Fields.

"Nervous?" he asks.

"No. Um." I realize my hand is shaking a tiny bit in his grasp. "I guess so. I'm on deck," I say, meaning that I'm up after the next person.

"Oh," he says. "Well, don't worry too much. I'm pretty sure Mr. Morgan has never eaten a student."

His friendly beat grows so strong, I know right then that Tobin and I are going to be good friends. Just like CeCe and me. Some people just click that way. Two melodies that complement each other.

"Hey, is your arm okay?" he asks, noticing the marks on my wrist.

"Oh, that. I must have brushed up against something in the grove."

"You went to the grove?" There's a strange note of disconcertment in his voice.

"Yeah," I say, pulling my hand behind my back. "I think I've got a rash or something."

"It looks more like a burn. Do you need . . . ?"

"It's fine," I say, but for a split second, I wonder if I should tell Tobin about what really happened. Maybe that would shake the weird feeling that has been following me ever since. I can tell from how much I like his tone that he's someone I might trust.

I open my mouth to say something about the grove, but I don't get the chance.

"Besides, you have to be pretty talented to get a scholarship here," a high-pitched voice says as three girls enter the hallway from the auditorium, using the same door I had. "I bet she's really good."

"Hey, ladies!" Tobin says, catching their attention. "Have you met New Girl?"

The three look at me, and I can tell from the expression that crosses one of the girls' faces that *I* was the subject of their conversation. The other two seem mostly uninterested.

"I'm pretty sure New Girl has a name, but she hasn't shared it with me yet." Tobin raises his eyebrows at me expectantly, and

I realize my lack of social grace has struck again.

"Raines. Daphne, Raines," I say, doing a silly James Bond impression. Because impersonations always make things less awkward. . . .

One of the girls laughs along with Tobin. The short blond one rolls her eyes, and the brunette yawns.

The girl who laughed gives me an amused smile. "I'm Iris Thompkins," she says. "It's nice to have another schollie around here."

"Schollie?"

"A scholarship kid," Tobin answers. "Iris thinks there are too many spoiled kids of famous people at this school. Don't you, Iris?"

She blushes and gives him a shut-up sort of look.

Tobin doesn't seem to notice. "Iris is always saying that the last thing we need is another brat kid of a celebrity mucking up the works around here."

She gives him a pointed glare and rocks her head toward the brunette.

"You mean someone who deserves to be here by talent?" the blond one asks, nudging her friend. "Not because her daddy pulled some strings?"

"Whatever," the brunette says and yawns again. I recognize those vacant eyes of hers and realize she's the spitting image—in a younger version—of the actress in Jonathan's favorite rom com.

"Anyway," Iris says, trying to get the conversation back on track, "*all* I was saying is that it's nice to have another schollie like me around."

"Oh. Yeah." I feel heat rushing into my cheeks. "How can you tell I'm a schollie?" I don't want to admit that Joe Vince is my father. Not yet anyway. I'd let these kids pass judgment on me after I had a chance to sing. If they don't think I deserve to be here afterward, then that would be a whole different issue.

"Your outfit," the tiny blond girl says. I feel like a giant compared to her. "It's totally thrift store chic."

"Thank you," I say, even though the girl's statement is clearly an insult wrapped inside a compliment. "You're so kind."

Tobin catches the irony in my voice and smiles.

"Well, I think Daphne looks supercute," Iris says. "I love the bohemian look."

"I concur," Tobin says, his smile widening.

The petite blond flips her curly hair over her shoulder and then narrows her eyes as she looks up—way up—at me. "So whom have you trained with? Borelli in LA? Caldwell in San Diego? Iris had to do two years with Rimaldi before they'd give her a scholarship here. It's a good thing he does pro bono work, isn't it, Iris? Oh, by the way, how was the bus ride from Compton?"

Iris purses her lips. A sharp, angular tone comes off her and I can tell she wants to say something rude back, but is biting her tongue.

"I'm from Utah, actually," I say, to draw the attention from Iris.

"Oh, then, Risedale in Salt Lake City?" the blond says, a tiny note of envy coming off her.

"Actually, Jonathan in the back room of Paradise Plants and Floral. Sometimes with an iPod out in the yard, too."

"You haven't had formal training?" she asks, the notes of envy growing stronger. "I had assumed you'd be good, considering Mr. Morgan is allowing you to audition for the vacancy that Cari Wilson's left in the program."

"You play the guitar?" Tobin asks, pointing at Gibby. "That's a sweet Gibson. Where did you—?"

"So what do you sing?" the girl asks, cutting him off.

"I like indie music mostly, but I have a soft spot for more classic—"

"Not what *songs* you like to sing. *What* do you sing?" she says, like I'm a simpleton. "Like, what part?"

"Oh. I don't really know. Contralto, maybe. Or possibly mezzo-soprano." I'd never been able to figure that out in my self-taught lessons. My normal voice isn't high-pitched, like most of the female singers' on the radio. I have a lower, slightly gravelly quality. Like Adele's. But I can also sing higher if I want. Jonathan was always throwing new pieces of music at me, trying to stump me, but nothing ever seemed out of my range.

"You don't know your range and they let you step foot on this campus?"

I shrug, but inside, I start to worry that I am in over my head.

"Well, this is one audition I can't wait to see," she says with a wicked smile. "Come on, Bridgette. I doubt this newbie is Sopranos material. We're wasting our time." She turns on her heel and heads back into the auditorium, with the brunette trailing behind her.

"Okaaay," I say under my breath.

"Don't mind Lexie," Tobin says. "She's not always quite so . . . abrasive. She's up for the lead in the play this year and that's got her on edge. With Cari gone, it's most likely between Lexie and Pear Perkins. She's just worried you'll be new competition."

"She's been a total pain since she took over leadership of the Sopranos," Iris says. "All that power is going to her head."

"The Sopranos?" I ask. "What is she, like, the godfather of the school mafia or something?"

"Pretty much," Tobin says. "But I have it on good authority that they do more shopping than killing these days."

"On the bright side," Iris says, sounding more relaxed now that Lexie is gone, "if you suck at singing, she might actually be friends with you."

"Well, that's a relief," I say, and make a grand gesture of wiping pretend sweat off my forehead.

Tobin laughs. He takes my hand and bows, pretending to plant a kiss on my knuckles. "I think I might be falling in love with you, Daphne Raines."

I laugh.

Iris gives me a not-so-enthused look. "All joking aside. You don't want to cross Lexie. The Sopranos can make your life miserable if they want."

"I'm not really worried about them."

What I am worried about is my audition. I check my watch. It's 3:20. I haven't realized how long I've been talking to Tobin and the others. The next audition should have started by now, and then I am up after that.

The door swings open, and Bridgette, the brunette, pokes her head out. "Have either of you seen Pear? It's her turn, and Mr. Morgan is calling for her."

"Pear Perkins, second call for Pear Perkins," I hear Mr. Morgan yell from inside the auditorium.

"Pear likes to make an entrance," Tobin says.

"I know, but she's really pushing it this time," the brunette says.

"Maybe Lexie offed her," Iris whispers dramatically behind

her hand. "I wouldn't put it past her."

"Be nice," Tobin says.

"I'm just making sure New Girl knows what she's getting herself into. Last year, this freshman was up for the part Lexie wanted, so she put ipecac in the girl's apple juice. The girl puked all over the stage right in the middle of her audition."

"That's just a rumor. She probably had the flu or was nervous or something."

"Well, whatever the cause, Lexie posted a video of it on the school's Facebook page and it got, like, five thousand hits before the admins took it down."

"Nobody ever proved it was Lexie that posted it," Tobin says.

"Yeah, because she posted it under a dummy account. She's not stupid. And proof doesn't matter. Everybody knows it. I'm telling you, Daphne. You don't want to cross her."

"Last call for Pear Perkins," rings out Mr. Morgan's perturbed voice. "Somebody tell that diva she has fifteen seconds to get out here or I'm cancelling her audition."

Bridgette squeaks from the doorway, "Where the heck is she?"

"That's it. I'm calling it," Mr. Morgan says, his voice filled with annoyance. "Next up. Miss Rain. Miss Rain, are you here?"

No answer comes from the auditorium.

"Miss Daphne Rain? Do we have another no-show?"

"Isn't that you?" Tobin asks.

"What?" I'd been distracted by the nervous little melody wafting off Bridgette.

"Daphne Rain, you have sixty seconds to appear on my stage or your audition is also cancelled," shouts Mr. Morgan.

"Oh, that is me," I say, a little dumbfounded. My audition isn't supposed to be for another ten minutes. I haven't had time to finish my relaxation exercises. My throat is still dry. I need more water. I'm not quite ready.

"Fifty seconds!"

I must look panicked, because Tobin takes my arm. "Don't worry," he says, and leads me down the hall several yards to another door. He swings it open. "Backstage," he says. "Just go up those stairs and follow the curtains. Break a leg!" he says, and pushes me through the doorway—which he might have meant literally, because as the door swings shut, I am engulfed in utter darkness.

"Thirty seconds, Miss Rain!"

I stumble forward and hit the stairs. I find the handrail and pull myself up the steps. I grip my guitar tightly in one hand and stick the other out, feeling for the curtains. Something rustles past me, and I hear that low, hissing sound from before. I spin around, looking for what—or who—is with me in the darkness. I can't see anything but blackness all around. My old fear of the dark had started during that hospital stay when I was thirteen. Every time one of the nurses would shut off the lights, it would seem like someone was standing in the shadows. Watching me. It was probably just the painkillers messing with my mind—the sensation had gone away once we went home and I could sleep in my own bed—but it had taken me months before I could sleep without the lights on. For some reason, that old fear comes rolling over me again. I take another step. Something brushes my arm, and I almost scream. Another half step and I realize I'm standing in one of the curtains.

"Fifteen seconds!"

I push at the curtain and see a sliver of light dance between its folds. I trail my hand along the fabric until I come to the opening.

I think I hear someone let out a breath behind me. I look back, sure I'm being watched, and step out into the light of the stage.

"I'm here," I say, holding my hand up to block the sudden brightness of the spotlight that is trained on center stage.

"Nice of you to decide to join us, Miss Rain," the teacher says curtly.

"It's Miss Raines."

"Noted," he says, making a mark in his binder. "You were almost too late."

"Sorry. I was told my audition was at three thirty."

He purses his lips for a moment. "I expect *my* students to be prepared for anything."

"Well, I am," I say.

"Do you have sheet music for the pianist?"

I stifle a smile. CeCe had always thought that was the funniest word. "I thought I'd play my own accompaniment." I place my fingers on the right chords and prepare to start playing, but then, out of the corner of my eye, I notice the curtains at the side of the stage rustling. I stand still for a moment, trying to see if anything is really there. Maybe I hadn't been imagining things when I was backstage. Maybe someone had been there.

Maybe the stranger from the grove had followed me. . . .

My muscles tense. I wonder if I should say something, but my voice is caught in my throat.

"Well, then, what are you waiting for?" Mr. Morgan asks, clearly still annoyed.

I look at him and then to the expectant faces of the students in the crowd. Some of them looked embarrassed or nervous for me, and I can tell by the tone that titters off Lexie and the cluster of friends sitting with her that they're highly amused. I see Lexie pull her iPhone from her pocket and stealthily train it on me.

Do they think I'm going to throw up on the stage like that freshman girl? Or do I look as mentally disturbed as I feel at the moment?

"If you don't want to be in my music program, Miss Rain, then I suggest you get off my stage," Mr. Morgan says.

For half a second, I find myself wondering if I do want to be in *his* music program.

If I want to be *here* at all. I could just walk right off this stage, bike back to Joe's mansion, and demand that he fly me back to Ellis.

But Joe still has that court order. He'd probably never send me back now that I am here. Or he'd get lawyers involved and my mom would end up going bankrupt trying to fight him. If I walk away now, then the sacrifice of leaving my mom so I can follow my dreams would end up being for nothing.

"No. I came here to sing." I force all the fear and nerves out of my body with a deep breath and strum out the beginning of the song. Sometimes, when I play—when I'm really into it—I can feel the notes dancing around me. That's the way I play today. Like my entire world is wrapped up in this song—because this is the moment I've been waiting for. The moment I can actively start making my dreams come true.

When my voice joins in with the guitar, I can feel the energy in the crowd shift. Their surprise vibrates about the room. Along with it are notes of happiness and relief, but I can also pick out the darker tones of jealousy from a certain pocket of girls in the crowd. I take all of it in. Absorbing the vibrations in the room and channeling them into my voice and into my hands. Letting it all come out in my music.

In Ellis, my music obsession made me different.

Here, I can use it to make me stand out.

When I round into my third song, Tobin catches my eye. He gives me a big grin and thumbs-up. The joyful melody that wafts off him has so much energy, it carries me through the rest of the song all on its own.

It isn't until the last line that I notice that someone else is watching from the shadows in the back of the auditorium. Or at least I think I see the flash of fiery eyes in the darkness. I almost falter on the last note, but I pull it off with gusto. I hold my guitar out and take a quick bow when I'm done.

"Well, then," Mr. Morgan says, actually sounding happy this time. "That'll do, for sure."

Tobin and Iris stand up and start clapping. A few others join in. I don't pay them much attention as I jump down from the stage and jog quickly to the back of the auditorium. But I'm standing alone in the shadows—maybe I hadn't seen anything—until someone grabs me by both hands.

"That was utterly fantastic," Tobin says, shaking my hands in excitement. "I've never heard anyone with a range like yours." I expect his touch to hurt the welts on my arm, but as he lets go of my wrist, I notice the red marks are gone.

"No wonder you got a scholarship," Iris says, coming up to us.

"About that . . . ," I start to say.

Mr. Morgan raises his voice above the chatter that fills the room. "Lexie Simmons. You're up."

"I'd hate to be her right now," Iris whispers. "Wouldn't want to follow you. No way."

Lexie approaches the stage. Her inner music pounds out a symphony of dark notes. I don't need to see the not-so-friendly look she throws me as she climbs the stage steps to know that I have definitely crossed onto her bad side.

Tobin catches the exchange. "Looks like you might be needing a little protection from the mob," he says, leaning in conspiratorially. "Perhaps I can offer my services." He pretends to flex his muscles like a strong man in a carnival sideshow. I've got at least four inches on him heightwise, but that doesn't seem to deter him from thinking he can be my personal goon squad.

"What's it going to cost me?" I ask.

"Let me give you the welcome-wagon tour of the town. I'm the mayor's kid, after all. I know all the good places to check out."

I glance into the empty shadows behind us.

"Yeah," I say, and smile. There's one place in particular I want to check out again—and I don't want to go there alone.

chapter fifteen

HADEN

I climb the trellis that leads to the window of my new bedchamber and slip inside. I scan the room. Everything is the same as I had left it. I can hear the soft murmur of voices down the hall, and I am sure my absence has gone undetected. Good thing. I don't want Dax to know how colossally I've screwed up. *What had I been thinking?*

I hadn't been thinking, that's what. Perhaps this girl is a siren. The old stories say they can befuddle men with their music. Such an idea had always been so obtuse to me, but now I understand. My encounter with Daphne had left me more confused than ever.

But sirens were evil creatures of the Oceanrealm, thought to be extinct. Why would the Oracle want me to bring such a dangerous thing back to my world?

No, she isn't a siren.

But, then, what is she?

She certainly isn't a mere Boon. Or at least not like any Boon in the Court's harem. *She doesn't act like one*, I think, rubbing my jaw where she had hit me. And she certainly didn't look like the Boons I'd seen in the Underrealm. Most of the girls who had been brought back by former Champions were waifish and gaunt to begin with, and wasted away quickly. I'd never really seen the appeal of having a Boon before. But this girl is different. My hands tingle with that strange heat, just thinking of her now.

The Oracle had indicated that Daphne is indeed different. Special, somehow. And Dax had suggested that he knew something about it. I shouldn't have acted without all the information—I should have waited here, as Simon had ordered me to. A soldier should always follow commands.

The thought of Simon finding out what I did fills me with dread. He seems to be in communication with the Underrealm somehow, and I can't bear the thought of his reporting my blunder back to the Court. What would they say about me then?

I settle on the bed and open the cloth bag the girl left in the grove. She may not be a siren and she may not be an ordinary Boon, but she is definitely a more formidable opponent than I gave her credit for. I am a warrior, and I decide to attack the problem of Daphne the way I have been trained to do with any other adversary. Which means I need to do some reconnaissance. I dump the contents on the bed. There are mostly papers. I play with a tube of sticky red gel that smells vaguely of pomegranates, and almost jump when a rectangular contraption buzzes in the pile. I pick it up and inspect its smooth surfaces. It buzzes again and lights up. A written message appears on the glass front. It must be some sort of communication device. The message reads:

CeCe: Daph, really need to talk. Call me tonight. May not be at this number after tomorrow.

A knock sounds on my door, making me jump. My fingers slip. I'm not sure what I've done but the message disappears.

"Haden, you up?" Dax calls through the door.

"Uh, yes. Just one moment." I panic at the sight of Daphne's things strewn across the bed. I grab a blanket and throw it over the mess to hide the evidence of my excursion into the world. I dash over to the door and open it halfway, placing my body between the door and the view of the rumpled-looking bed. I stretch and act as though I've just woken up.

Dax looks somewhat surprised to see me.

"Enjoying a nap, I see," Simon says in his overly chipper way. "Very good. Very good. Many Champions ignore the need for proper rest while in the mortal world. This place can be a strain on the body. You were so quiet in here, I was almost afraid you'd run off on some half-baked idea of going to look for this Daphne girl on your own."

I feel heat flushing into my hands and face. "Just being patient. Like I was told." I try to give Dax my most earnest look.

"Very well," Simon says with a huge smile. "All the arrangements for your stay have been made. I'll leave you boys to it." He drops the smile, and a sudden dark look creeps over his usually bright face. "I trust I won't need to clean up any messes while you boys are here. Not like last time?" He turns that dark look on Dax.

"No, Simon. Everything will be fine."

As quickly as it came, the dark look passes from Simon's face. He smiles happily. "Very good, then. Keep those noses clean," he says, tapping his own nose as he leaves.

I brush my nose, wondering if there's something on my face.

Dax waits until Simon is down the hall and we hear his footsteps on the stairs. Dax shivers, then slips inside my room with a couple of large bags made out of a thin, shiny material. He shuts the door quietly and then turns on me.

"Where the Tartarus were you?" he whispers.

I blink at him. "I —"

"Don't even think about lying to me, Haden. I came to check on you an hour ago and you were gone. I had no idea what I was going to say to Simon if you hadn't been here now. What in Hades's name were you thinking?"

"I wasn't . . ."

"Clearly!"

"You were taking forever. How was I supposed to just wait here? I didn't even know what time it was."

"There's a clock right there! You couldn't be patient for a few hours?"

"Well, nobody bothered to tell me how time works here. That's why I went back to the gate. I needed to know if it was still active. So I'd know that I hadn't been waiting for weeks."

"You went back to the gate? Did anyone see you? Did you talk to anyone?"

I shake my head. "No," I lie. I don't want him to know what I did. How Herculeanly I screwed up. "I went right there and came right back. I know I shouldn't have, but I needed the reassurance."

Dax drops the bags on the table in the corner of my room. "It's my fault," he says. "I haven't been the best guide so far. I should have known not to leave you alone. . . ."

His words sting, but I can't deny their truth.

"Are you going to tell Simon?"

"I should, but I think it's best we keep this between the two of us. For both our sakes."

I realize then that my actions have a reflection on Dax. As my guide, he could be punished for my mistakes.

I want nothing more than to ask him again what he knows about the circumstances of my quest, but I cannot bring myself to broach the topic. Any talk of Daphne might cause me to slip. The guilt is eating at me already.

"What's with all the stuff?" I ask him, trying to turn the topic off my ineptitude.

"Oh yes. I come bearing gifts. Every Champion needs his special tools," Dax says, pulling several things out of the bags and placing them on the table. There's more strange clothing, like what I was made to change into before passing through the gate, plus belts and a couple of pairs of shoes.

"New wardrobe makes the man," Dax says. "These clothes are more up-to-date with current fashion than what you're wearing. You'll fit in just right around here. Well, at least in appearance."

I nod. Blending in would be good for recon. I need to study Daphne's movements, just like I did with that hydra I hunted down last year for the Feast of Return. I stalked its movements for days. I knew its favorite places to go. Where it ate and slept. Where it was most vulnerable . . . before I made my move.

Dax reaches down into the depths of the last bag. "Now don't lose these," he says, handing me three small cards made out of a thin, hard material. Two have my picture on them, and the other has a long set of numbers. "Two IDs and a credit card. This ID says you're sixteen; the other one says you're twenty-one. You'll never know when which age will benefit you more. The credit card is how you pay for things. Simon set up the account and will handle the bills—which means he'll know about *everything* you spend money on. Got that?"

I nod.

"Now, this," he says, "is going to be your most important weapon of all." I expect maybe he is going to bestow on me some kind of enchanted sword or maybe even some poison-tipped arrows, but instead he pulls out a thin, black rectangle with a reflective screen. It looks almost identical to the white communication device I'd found in Daphne's bag.

"What is that thing?" I ask, pretending that I have never seen anything like it.

"It's an iPhone," he says. "And it's the most important tool you'll need in the mortal world." He slides his finger across the screen and the thing comes to life. He presses on the different icons, and shows me the functions of the device. "They've improved since the last time I was here. It's so fast. And so thin." He almost sounds as giddy as Simon. "Its primary function is communication. Somewhat like the talismans the Court uses, except it only transports your voice, not an astral projection of yourself."

I nod. I've heard the Heirs speak of their communication talismans but I've never actually seen one. I doubt they look anything like this iPhone object.

Dax hits a few icons and then scrolls through what looks like a list of names. He finds his own name and then a few seconds later, a ringing noise comes from his pocket. He pulls another iPhone out and shows it to me. "See, you need anything and all you've got to do is hit my name and it'll call me. We can talk, no matter how far away, through these.

"However, this next feature is the most important." He clicks on an icon that says YouTube and holds the phone up in front of me. "You know how we are taught to learn? Someone demonstrates and then we repeat his movements?"

"Yes." The Underlords are natural mimics. We learn by repeating what we see or hear, absorbing the ability to do just about anything in a matter of hours. Some of us—including myself—can master any new skill in a matter of minutes. It's how

I've excelled in my lessons. Humans don't have the same accelerated ability, I recall, according to Master Crue's many lectures.

"Well, the same *watch, absorb, repeat* method also applies to recorded videos."

"Videos?"

"I'll show you." Dax taps icons of letters, spelling out the words *how to juggle*. "We'll start with something easy."

I watch as a prepubescent boy with a face full of pus-filled lesions appears on the screen. He holds three round objects in his hands. I listen and absorb as the boy demonstrates how to juggle the objects. When the demonstration ends, Dax hands me three apples from the bowl on the table.

"Try it," he says.

I picture what I have just watched in my mind, and mimic the boy's actions, movement for movement, and juggle the apples perfectly on the first try.

Dax nods in approval.

"Child's play," I say, placing the apples on the table. "How will this help me?"

"Juggling won't help you much. Not unless Daphne has a thing for clowns, but you can pretty much learn how to do anything using this application." He picks up one of the apples and takes a bite. "There are many gaps in your education."

"I've noticed," I say under my breath.

"You aren't as prepared for this world as you might think you are. It's why I didn't want you venturing out on your own yet. Who knows what trouble you could have gotten yourself into?"

Guilt clutches at me, and I wonder if I should tell Dax about what I've done. I don't know how to fix the problem I've created with Daphne. I feel like such a fool. But if I tell him, he would probably have to tell Simon. How can I share my secrets with the one person I trust if he's under orders to report back on me?

"Just don't ask the Internet for dating advice. That's never a good idea, trust me."

"Dating?"

"You'll see."

"What else can that thing do? Can it track someone?" I'm thinking of Daphne and wondering if this *iPhone* can show me where to find her again.

"If you have the right app. Or if you have their address, you can type it into this map function, and it will tell you where and how to find the location." He hands me the phone and then starts putting my new clothes away in a chest of drawers next to the table.

Address. I remember seeing something like that in Daphne's papers. I'd memorized it without even really thinking about it. While Dax isn't looking, I punch the numbers and words into the search bar in the map's feature. After a moment, a small red dot lands on the map, showing me where Daphne lives. I could go there right now if I wanted. I could sneak out again as soon as Dax left.

I shake my head, dismissing the thought. What is it about this girl that makes me act so stupidly? I tell myself it's for recon reasons, but I know there's a part of me that just wants to see her again.

"I have one more thing to show you. Outside," Dax says. "But first, we'd better do something about your hair. Someone might think you're trying to look like a pirate if you go wandering around, looking like that."

"I'm tired, Dax. Can it wait until tomorrow?" Really, I'm itching to study Daphne's things some more. Learn as much about my adversary as I possibly can. I don't want to be caught off guard again.

"Believe me," he says. "You don't want to wait to see this. It's going to change your entire world."

chapter sixteen

DAPHNE

"Wow, this place is perfect, isn't it?" I say to Tobin as we walk on one of the lake paths.

He'd given me a tour of most of the places in town that could be reached on foot. I wheeled my old bike along as he carried Gibby and pointed out different places of interest. My favorite so far is a street of small, boutique-style shops that Tobin said is called Olympus Row. Each of the stores had been designed to look like a shop you would find in a Greek village, with the white stucco walls and blue roofs and doors. It made me feel like I'd been transported to another world. We'd stopped for gelato, and ate it while we watched a group of kids splashing in a fountain before heading for the trails that wind around the lake.

"Don't let it fool you," Tobin says.

"What do you mean?"

"Nothing is ever as perfect as it seems," he mumbles. A strange black note drifts off him. It clashes with his warm vibe.

"What, is this town ripe with conspiracies and secret societies?" I say, trying to lighten his mood.

"Hey, I'm just saying you never know. . . ." Tobin strums a few bars on Gibby. The sound muffles whatever emotive notes he might be putting off at the moment. He sings a couple of lines from a song I don't know and then stops walking. "Hey, speaking of secret societies," he says, his voice much lighter now, "there's this party next week. . . ." He trails off, and I'm not sure I'm following his segue.

"Are you telling me that the Skull and Crossbones are holding a recruitment meeting? Or is it a Masons sort of shindig?"

"Aliens," Tobin says. "It's an alien rave."

"Ohhhh," I say with a laugh. "Hey, what's over there?" I point at the smaller island of the lake, even though I know very well it's the grove. "You haven't shown me that place yet."

"What? Oh, that's the grove. I thought you said you went there earlier today?"

Oh yeah. I had. "I must be all turned around," I say, sheepishly. "Let's go check it out again."

"Uh," Tobin says. "It's just a bunch of old trees. Once you've seen them, that's kind of it. Nobody even goes there. Anyway, about this party . . ."

"The alien one? Come on, let's cross the bridge."

"Yeah, that one. Except without the aliens. I was kind of hoping. . . ." He lets his sentence trail off again, like he isn't sure what to say next.

I'm not sure what to say, either. Crap, had I totally been oblivious again? I'd read Tobin's vibes toward me in nothing but a friend-zone sort of way. But as CeCe had already established, I totally suck at this sort of thing. So much so that I don't date. I'd always been too focused on my music to care whether or not I got asked out, and I never felt like I had the time to spare when I did. Truth is, the idea of dating has always seemed like it's in opposition to my goals. My mom had let herself get sidetracked by a guy, and look where that landed her. I know I'm hesitating too long, so I say what comes to mind first. "I, um, don't really date. . . . It's got nothing to do with you." I cringe, knowing I sound completely lame. "I just feel like I need to stay really focused on the music department. . . ."

"Oh. Yeah, I get that," Tobin says. "Totally focused here, too. The party is *for* the music department. My mom likes to throw a big shindig for them after the first month of school. It's supposed to help everyone bond as a group, you know. She's kind of overly invested in my social life. I just wanted to make sure you knew about it. . . . So you could come. Alone. Of course." He gives me a sheepish grin. A tinge of pink highlights his cheeks. I listen carefully to make sure his friendly tone is still there, and feel relieved when I still hear it under the wavering notes of embarrassment. I would hate it if my social lameness had messed up my first—and possibly only—potential friendship in this place.

"In that case, I'll be there. Assuming I even get into the department, that is."

"Believe me, you're getting in."

"So let's go explore this grove place," I say, eager to change the subject. I grab Tobin's arm and try to pull him down the path toward the grove, but he literally digs in his heels to stop me.

"Seriously, Daph. Nobody goes there. That place gives me the creeps."

So Marta hadn't been making it up that nobody ever went there.

"Why? Do weird things happen there or something? Or are you just chicken?" I ask, trying to sound nonchalant and jokey, but I really do want to know. Maybe I wasn't the first person to have encountered something strange there.

"Call me a chicken all you want. It's starting to get dark. How about we go get cupcakes back at the row. My treat."

"Come on, ya dork. It'll be an adventure." Tobin's resistance is starting to freak me out, but I need to go back to the grove. I'd left Gibby's case behind—which, yeah, I could probably easily talk Joe into replacing for me—but I had also left my tote bag. Along with it, my cell phone, wallet, my school registration forms, and various other bottom-of-my purse junk. Which means Mr. Creepy Eyes could possibly have access to the contact information for all of my friends in Ellis Fields, my Pomegranate Bliss lip gloss . . . *and* my new address. I could only hope he hadn't noticed my tote and had left it there. I need to get it back before he, or anyone else, happens upon it.

"Then I guess I'll have to check it out on my own," I say, and head toward the bridge that leads to the island. Tobin could either follow or let me go alone. I'm pretty sure he'll follow.

"This place has the creepiest vibe ever," he says as we get closer, his reluctant melody echoing on the bridge.

I don't know what he is talking about. The only thing creepy I had found about the grove was the stranger. Its vibe had been what had drawn me to it. I don't know how it can repel anyone else. Then again, they can't hear it singing the way I do. . . .

As we near the grove, I notice that something is different about the grove's song this evening. I stop and listen for a moment. Instead of being a soothing lullaby, it sounds off. Like it's full of broken, discordant notes.

"Something's wrong," I say, leaning my bike against the bridge's railing. "With the grove." I jog toward the ring of poplar trees.

"If something is wrong in the grove," Tobin says, huffing with Gibby in his arms, trying to keep up, "shouldn't we be running away, not toward it?"

"Not in the grove. *With* the grove. I can hear it."

"You're kind of weird, Daphne Raines."

"I know." I pass between two poplar trees into the dark grove of aspens and laurels. I gasp. This place barely resembles the beautiful grove I had sung in this morning. Several of the smaller trees are broken, and mounds of earth have been upturned. One of the aspens looks like it's been struck by lightning: its trunk is scorched, and one of its large branches has been turned to ash.

"What happened here?" I whisper, more to the grove itself than to Tobin.

"This damage looks fresh," he says. "I didn't think anyone came here. Not since . . ."

I jog over to the laurel tree that's shaped like a tuning fork. It's one of the few trees other than the poplars that are undamaged. I find Gibby's case, but my tote bag is gone—along with all of my personal information.

"Not since what?" I ask Tobin, realizing he didn't finish his sentence.

He leans my guitar against the scorched tree. I follow him as he follows the path of destruction, which slopes down the steep side of the island toward the lake.

"My sister," he says. "She used to hang out here. She'd come here to run lines—she was on the theatre track. She's the only one I ever knew who came here."

"Used to? Did she go away to college or something?" But by the way Tobin's tone has changed, I know that whatever made Tobin talk about his sister in the past tense isn't something pleasant.

"She ran away. Six years ago. I haven't seen her since."

"Oh," I say. "I'm sorry." I really am. Here I've dragged him into a place that reminds him of something painful, for my own selfish purposes. I feel like such a jerk. "Hey, we can go back now if you want."

Tobin stops abruptly and takes in a sudden breath. "Is that someone . . . down there . . . ?" He takes off running down the slope. I follow at a slower speed, trying not to trip on a rock or branch and go tumbling into the water head over heels. I come up short when I finally see what he saw. Light from the lamps, which line the jogging paths across the island, reflects off something lying in the water at lake's edge. It looks like the body of a girl, submerged almost up to her chest. Tobin splashes into the water, wing-tip shoes and all, and kneels in the mud next to the girl. He presses his fingers against her throat. I hold my breath while he searches for a pulse.

"She's still alive!" he says, scooping her up. I almost protest his moving her, but it's not like we can just leave her in the water. "It's Pear," he says. "Pear Perkins."

I know that name. "The girl who missed the auditions?"

"I guess we know why," Tobin says, grave notes marring his voice. "I think she's been unconscious for a while."

I climb down the hill and help him lay her down on the sandy bank away from the water. He pulls off his jacket and covers the girl's upper body, but before he does, I see that she has four deep gashes in her arm, just above her elbow. The gashes make my stomach churn, but it's her shoes that make me think I'm going to be sick. Pink and silver platform sandals. Just like the ones the girl I'd hit with my bike had been wearing. I hadn't realized it when it happened, but as I replay the memory in my head, I see that the girl had jogged off in the direction of the grove. I place my hand on Tobin's wet elbow. "I think I know who did this," I say. "And I think it's my fault that it happened."

chapter seventeen

HADEN

"Touch those shears to my head one more time and I swear to Hades, I will blast your face off!"

Dax only laughs, and snips at my hair again. "Just a few more cuts," he says. "I got pretty good at this when I was here before."

Underlords, even Lessers, don't cut their hair. When my father had cut my braid from my head, it was the first time a blade had touched my hair. Cutting a Champion's braid is supposed to symbolize rebirth. The start of a new life. To me, it feels like an insult. With every snip Dax makes, I feel that what little is left of my honor is falling to the floor.

Garrick sulks in the corner. Someone had fetched him new clothes and he's changed out of his grubby robes. His eyes are pink and watery, still irritated from the harsh light of the sun. His hair is shorn almost to the scalp.

"You cut my hair as short as the Lesser's, and I *will* kill you."

"Promises, promises." Dax chuckles again. For a former Underlord, he laughs far too often. Then again, *former* is the word that needs to be emphasized with Dax. "I had to shave Garrick's hair. It was filthy and matted, so I had no other choice. Yours, on the other hand"—he makes one last snip—"is done."

I jump out of the chair I've been forced to sit in through this ordeal and quickly bring my hands to my head. I brush my fingers through what hair remains. It is longer than Garrick's, but I can tell that a slight curl pulls at the edges of my shaggy locks over my ears. "What have you done?" I demand. "You have made my hair curl like a Boon's, or a nursling's!"

Dax shrugs. "Sometimes you don't know you have curls until you cut your hair. Besides, it's not all that bad. The girls will love it." He puts the shears down on the kitchen table and I am sorely tempted to stab him with them. "Now, as promised, you will get your reward. Follow me outside."

Dax is looking giddy again. This concerns me greatly, but I follow him still. Garrick trails behind us out of the house. What I see in the driveway makes my mouth water with anticipation.

"Unbelievable," Garrick whispers. It's the first word I've heard him speak since we passed through the gate.

"Are those automobiles?" I ask.

"Cars," Dax says. "Call them cars. Master Crue's take on English vocabulary is a bit archaic. And these are more than cars. They're Teslas. Very hard to get, but Simon procured them for us this afternoon. There's a Model X and a Model S—but the Roadster is mine." He points out each car respectively.

Garrick, having suddenly found new life, runs to the Roadster. His fingers caress the lines of the car. "Can I . . . Will you teach me to drive?" He looks at Dax with an eagerness in his eyes. He's like a Lesser who's been given an entire hydra leg for supper.

"Lord Haden first," Dax says. "And we'll take the Model S. Neither of you is touching my Roadster until you've mastered driving."

Garrick's shoulders drop and he skulks into the backseat of the car.

"Best thing about these cars," Dax says, placing his hand on the hood of the Roadster. "They're powered by electricity." I see a soft blue pulse radiate out from under his hand into the hood of the car. It is quiet, but the Tesla comes to life under his touch— the headlights gleaming like beacons in the dusk of the evening. "You'll never have to stop for fuel; just give it a zap every few hundred miles. You could drive from here until the ends of the earth and no one could catch you." A wistful look lights in his eyes. I wonder if it's the thought of driving from here until the ends of the earth that seems to enchant him, or the idea of never being caught.

Dax insists on being the one to drive the Model S first so I can watch and absorb how it's done. He takes us up a few side streets until we reach a large, empty, paved area that surrounds a building with a tall spire. He drives us slowly around the lot for a few minutes, explaining the name and function of each part of the car.

"You think you've got it down?" he asks.

I nod, aching to get my hands on the steering wheel.

We trade places. I melt into the leather driver's seat, and the moment my hands touch the steering wheel, I am sure that I know how to drive this thing. I can feel it in every muscle of my body. My foot makes contact with the accelerator. I press it down and it feels as though the car becomes an extension of myself. I press harder and the burst of acceleration sends us rocketing forward. I spin us around the lot several times but it isn't enough. I want to be out on the open road. I want to actually *go* somewhere. The speed makes me feel as if I am one of the screech owls soaring from the roost.

I know exactly where I want to go. Dax would say I am being

foolish. But he doesn't have to be told where we are going or why. I just want to see where she lives. It's recon, I tell myself, picturing the map of her address in my head.

I steer the car out of the empty lot and onto the road. Dax starts to protest that I'm not ready, but I don't listen. I want to fly.

We tear down the street while he shouts commands at me. But he isn't the Champion here. He's the servant. I'm the one who should be in charge. I pick up the speed.

Garrick lets out a cheer from the backseat.

"Now, that was a stop sign!" Dax shouts. "Slow down! You don't know the rules of the road yet."

At the moment, I don't give a harpy's ass about rules. We are only one turn away from her house.

"Flashing lights!" Dax yells. "Flashing lights! Stop now!"

I don't know what he means until I see lights flickering in the distance in front of us.

"Police," he says. "Flashing lights means police!"

A thought surfaces from one of the recesses in my brain. Police are like the royal guard, enforcers of the law. I slam on the brakes. Dax grips the dash as we come to a halt. I hold my breath, waiting for the flashing lights to advance on us. Only after a few moments do I realize that they are stationary. The vehicles with flashing lights are parked along the street. Several people stand out on the lake trail that is adjacent to the street. I think I recognize the shape of one of them.

I lift my foot off the brake and nudge the accelerator. We roll forward slowly toward the flashing lights.

"What are you doing?" Garrick says nervously. I can tell he likes the idea of encountering human police as much as he likes encountering one of Ren's guards. "Let's turn around. Go back."

"I want to see what's going on. Don't you, Dax?"

Dax can't deny it. "Maybe that's not the best idea," he says instead.

I move forward and come to a stop by one of the vehicles with flashing lights. It isn't an official police car, I realize as I read the seal on the driver's side door. OLYMPUS HILLS SECURITY. A man in a blue uniform steps out of the car and I roll down the window. A terrible scent stings my nose, but there are so many new scents in this world that I can't quite place it.

"You'll need to go around," the security guard says. "No rubbernecking."

I don't know what that means, but I give the guard my most earnest look. "What's going on? We live around here. Is there anything we should be worried about?"

"Couple of kids found a girl in the lake. Near the grove." He sighs, realizing he probably shouldn't have said so much. "Now move along." He pats the roof of the Tesla.

As he moves away from the window, I finally get a view of what I came to see. I'd been right when I recognized the curve of her body, even from a distance. Daphne Raines is standing in front of another set of security guards. She's talking with her hands, giving emphasis to her words. I can tell she's upset. There's a boy with her. He's shorter than she is, but he has his arm stretched up around her shoulder. It's a familiar gesture that makes my hands feel hot. A thin stream of blue electricity crackles around the steering wheel.

"Haden, are you all right?" Dax asks.

I'm not sure what causes her to do it, but Daphne looks over toward our car. I hit the accelerator and drive away before she has a chance to see me.

I take us back to the house and pull the Tesla into the garage. Dax waits until Garrick has gone inside the house before he grabs me by the arm at the doorway.

"Did anyone see you when you went to the grove? Can anyone put you near there?"

"No," I lie. "I went there and came straight back," I say as we enter the house.

"Tsk, tsk," someone says from the living room, but it isn't Garrick. "Didn't your mother teach you that lying is bad manners?"

As we round the corner into the living room, Simon stands up from the armchair. He holds a short, fat glass filled with bright red liquid. His voice sounds as cheery as ever, but the look in his eyes says that he's not the least bit happy.

"Simon?" Dax says. "What're you doing here? I thought you were going out for the night."

"So did I." Simon takes a deep swig from his glass and sets it neatly on a coaster on the coffee table. He smiles at me, the red liquid staining his teeth. "I'm here because of what Haden did in the grove."

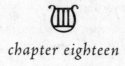

chapter eighteen

DAPHNE

"So let me get this straight," the man in the blue uniform says. "You think Miss Perkins was attacked by a pirate with heat radiating off his skin and green eyes with fire in them? Would you like me to add fangs and wings to that description also? Maybe throw in some sparkles for a little flare?"

The security guard laughs, and his partner pats him on the back like he's oh so funny.

"No, because then you would have a vam-pirate angel and not the person I'd described."

The two laugh harder, and I feel like I'm about to kick someone in the shins. "Vam-pirate angels! You kids read too much, you know that? Your imaginations get the better of you."

"I'm not imagining things," I say. "And I'm not sure why I'm even talking to you right now. Shouldn't the *real* police be here?"

Luckily, Tobin had a cell phone, since mine had gone who knows where with my tote bag. I'd sat next to Pear while he climbed to higher ground to call for help. I'd assumed he'd called 911 until about ten minutes later, when four Olympus Hills security guards came down the island slope to meet us, flashlights in hand. The only ways off the island are the two footbridges that lead to the lake's jogging trails, so the guards had to carry Pear out, rather than bring a car in. Tobin and I had followed with my bike and guitar in tow as one of the guards cradled her body in his arms. She seemed as limp and heavy as the giant bags of topsoil I always had to help my mom heft back to the greenhouse.

We were met out on the road by the flashing lights of the security guards' cars and an Olympus Hills Medical Response vehicle. A small group of bystanders had gathered on the side of the road.

Two of the guards loaded Pear into the medical van, while the other two pulled Tobin and me aside to get our statements about what happened. Tobin told them how we'd found Pear, but when the guards asked why we'd been in the grove in the first place, I confessed what happened in my encounter with the weird boy in the woods earlier today. They'd been following my story until I got to the guy's description. Now they are acting like I am making it all up.

"Listen, miss," the guard says, dropping the jovial tone. "You must be new around here, or otherwise you'd know that the county sheriff's department contracts out our security firm for anything that happens within the gates of Olympus Hills. Which means we are far too busy for stupid teenagers looking for some extra attention . . ."

Tobin had put his arm around me as I told my story, his tone growing darker and stormier as he listened. He drops his arm from my shoulder now. He raises his finger at the guard, along with his voice. "Listen, ya rent-a-cop, my mother is Mayor Winters, which means she signs your paychecks. So how about you finish listening to my friend's statement and take your job seriously, before I call her up and give a report on your performance? One of our classmates was just hurt, badly. Show a little respect."

The two security guards exchange a look. The one taking my statement tells me to go on with my description of what happened. I catch a note coming off him that is pretty much the auditory equivalent of an eye roll when I tell him about how the guy's slight touch had left marks on my arm—marks that are inconveniently gone now—but he doesn't laugh again. When he finishes taking my statement and tells us we are free to go, I get the distinct feeling that everything he's written down is going to end up in the trash.

"I'm not making it up," I tell Tobin when the guards leave us standing by the trail with my bike.

"I believe you," he says. I can tell by the stormy notes coming off him that he isn't just being polite. "I told you, things aren't as perfect as they seem around here. . . ."

I'm just about to ask him what exactly he means when I hear someone shout my name.

I look up and see a man, dressed in nothing but skinny jeans and a canary yellow bathrobe, wandering up the lake path. He's barefoot. And carrying a golf club. He cups his hands to his mouth and shouts, "Daphne? Where are you?"

"Is that . . . Joe Vince?" Tobin asks.

"The one and only." I sigh as I watch Joe poke at a row of bushes with his golf club as if he thought I was hiding in the branches. It's a good thing paparazzi aren't allowed past the security gates or I'm sure this little scene would be on the cover of next week's *OK!* magazine.

"Why would he be looking for you?"

I bite the bullet. "Because he's my father."

Tobin makes a small popping noise with his lips. "You're not a schollie, are you?"

"Goes to show you should never judge a girl by her clothes."

"Daphne?" Joe calls again.

I decide I should probably respond before he brings out half the neighborhood. "Over here, Joe." I wave at him.

Joe drops his golf club and comes jogging toward me. "Oh, Daphne, thank the bloody stars in heaven. You're all right."

"You were worried?"

"I heard there was a girl found unconscious in that grove you were talking about this morning. I tried calling you a dozen times and you didn't answer. Those bloody security guards wouldn't tell me anything. They only gave me a description of the girl they took to the hospital. And I thought . . . I thought . . . I didn't know if . . ."

I realize then that Pear's description would kind of match mine. Tall, tan, and blond. Though she is of the bleached variety and her tan probably comes from an airbrush—while mine is from living in the desert. Really, tall is the only thing we have in common, and I probably still have three inches on her.

"They said she was wearing pink and silver sandals, and I . . ." Joe gives me a stricken look. "And I had no idea what any of your shoes look like." He covers his face with his ring-clad fingers. "I should know that, shouldn't I? Why don't I know that?"

Because you've ignored me most of my life is what I want to say, but when Joe drops his hands from his face, it seems as though he's wiping away tears. Long, low, drawn-out notes come off him, and I realize that he really was worried.

"It's okay," I say to him. "I'm fine. I forgot my phone, that's all." I turn to Tobin. "I should get him home."

"Need help?"

I shake my head. He doesn't need to see any more of Joe in

his grief-stricken state—which was probably spurred on by his vodka-stricken state.

I sling Gibby over my shoulder in her case and take my bike from Tobin. It's a juggling act, but I lead Joe back to the house. I'm hoping I won't have to search for his house keys in the pockets of his robe when Marta meets us at the door. She looks like she arrived a few seconds before us.

"There you are!" she says to Joe. "You let him go out like this?" she says to me with a stern look.

"*Let* had nothing to do with it." I pass Joe off to Marta. "He's your job, not mine."

"Why don't I know what any of Daphne's shoes look like?" Joe asks her.

"Let's get you to bed," she says, ignoring his question as if this sort of thing is an everyday occurrence for her.

"Daphne," he calls down the stairs as Marta leads him up to his bedroom. "I'm glad you're still here. I'm glad you didn't go away."

"Come on, Joe, bed," Marta says, like she's coaxing a dog.

"I'll make it up to you," Joe calls as they disappear down the hall. "On Monday. You'll see. I promise."

I don't know what he means by that, but I have a feeling I'm not going to like whatever it is he has in mind.

chapter nineteen

HADEN

"What are you talking about?" Dax asks Simon as we stand in his living room. "What do you mean, what Haden did in the grove? He's been with us the whole time."

"We both know that's not true," Simon says. "Why don't you ask Haden what he did when he snuck out this afternoon?"

I feel like I've been struck with a mace. "You told him I left?" I ask Dax, like an accusation.

"No," he says. "But what is he talking about? I thought you went straight there and back?"

I don't know how to answer his question. I've lied to him and there are no easy words to explain that.

"Your boy here broke one of the biggest rules of this here Champion gig," Simon says. "And only a few hours into his first day. Apparently, young Haden had a busy afternoon."

"Haden, what is Simon talking about? What did you do?" Dax goes pale. "The girl they found in the lake. When you went to the grove . . . you didn't . . . ?"

I am dumbstruck.

"Girl? What girl in the lake?" Simon says, sounding surprised. "Have you been even busier than I thought?"

"No! I didn't hurt anyone," I say. "Yes, I snuck out, and I may have tried to grab my Boon, but I certainly didn't—"

"Whoa," Dax says. "You tried to grab who? Daphne? When did this happen? What? Why? How?"

"I didn't do anything," I start to say, but I can tell that the guilt is showing in my voice. I let my shoulders sag, resigned to admitting the truth. "I made a mistake, Dax."

His eyes widen. "Did you . . . did you do something to your Boon? The girl they found in the lake?"

"No!" It shakes me to my core that Dax would even ask me such a thing. "I mean, yes, I did something to my Boon but I didn't hurt her. All I did was try to grab her and take her through the gate. And, yes, I know it was a stupid mistake. But that's all I did. I don't know who this other girl is, nor what happened to her."

Dax's face turns red. "That's all? That's all? How did you . . . ? Where did you . . . ? How did you even find her so quickly?"

"When I snuck out earlier, I went to go check on the gate, like I said I did. And she was in the grove, like she'd been placed there just for me. The gate was still active and I thought it was a gift from the Fates. I thought I could be the fastest-returning Champion in the history of the Underrealm."

"That's the damn foolest thing I have ever heard," Simon says. "Don't they train you children anymore?"

"Haden was not one of the Elite," Dax says. He sounds like he's trying to placate Simon, but his words make me feel that he sees me as an inferior Champion as the others do.

"Well, weren't you told this wasn't a snatch-and-grab job?" Simon says. "Do you know what happens if you try to take a mortal through the gate against her own free will? Don't you think there's been some idiot Champion who's tried it before? The gate doesn't work that way. The girl has to *want* to go with you."

"I *tried* to make her say she'd come with me."

"She can't just say it. Every fiber of her being has got to want to go. If not, she dies. And so do you. If you had tried to bring her through that gate, you'd both be a couple of pillars of dust right now. And then where would we be?"

"Ah Hades, Simon, I didn't know you cared so much," I say.

Something flashes in his eyes, and suddenly I regret my snark. In a movement much faster than I thought him capable of, he is in my face. One hand slams the wall next to my head, and the other grabs me by the throat. "Listen, you *koprophage*, we all have things riding on this quest of yours." His breath reeks of something earthy and bitter. "You mess up like that again and you'll be holding your intestines in your hands. Do you understand me?"

I try to nod, but it's impossible with him gripping my throat. I try to raise my hands to push him off me, but Simon stares into my eyes and says, "Drop your arms."

I don't know why, but I follow his order, my arms falling to my sides.

"That's enough," Dax says, approaching.

Simon looks at him. "Be still," he says, and then trains his gaze back on me. "Both of you."

Dax stops moving, and I make my body as still as a tree, and all thoughts of struggling out of his grasp leave my head. I can't move, even though I want to.

"Say it," Simon says. "Beg for it."

At first, I think he means that he wants me to say I understand him, but then I realize that he wants me to invoke *elios*.

I've begged for mercy only once in my life—the day my honor was stripped away—but I have never done it since. Not from

Rowan or the Court. Not from my father. And I have no intention of giving Simon the pleasure.

"Never," I gasp. I try to move again, but my body stays still and uncooperative.

"Good luck with that, boy," Simon says. "Do you know what I'm capable of? I've made men into kings and celebrities, and helped topple governments with only a few sentences. I think I can get a little *kopros* like you to invoke *elios* if I want. Say it."

I feel the word forming in my mouth. I bite my tongue to stop it.

I taste blood.

"*Say. It,*" Simon says, glaring deep into my eyes. His words burrow inside my head and I cannot stop myself any longer from complying with his demand. It is as if he controls my mouth.

"*Elios,*" I croak, before clamping my teeth shut.

Simon lets go, a satisfied smile on his face.

I stay rigid against the wall. Dax remains still also. I see Garrick watching between the rungs in the staircase's banister. I cannot make out the look on his face.

"Now that that's settled," Simon says, straightening his tie, "I have a charity auction to get to. Anyone fancy accompanying me to the ballet next month? I think I'm going to bid on season tickets. No? Well, then, I'm off." He picks up his glass and takes another sip of the thick red liquid. He smacks his lips. "Mmmm. Feel free to help yourselves to the beet juice in the fridge. It's great for the metabolism."

We all watch in frozen disbelief as Simon rinses out his glass in the sink and then grabs his keys. "Good night," he hollers when he leaves through the door to the garage. "Oh, and you can relax now."

With his words, the rigidness leaves my body and I slump down against the wall. I cough, and blood stains my hand. Dax rushes over to help me. I wave him away. I'm not ready to accept his help. Not after he had even entertained the idea that I could have hurt that girl.

But what stings even more than my bleeding tongue and my bruised ego is the look of disappointment in Dax's eyes, knowing that I lied to him.

chapter twenty

DAPHNE

I sit in my private TV room in the east wing of the house, flipping through the channels, looking for some sort of report on what happened to Pear, but apparently the local news comes on much later in California than it does in Utah. I find myself fighting to keep my eyes open. I don't want to fall asleep. Because every time I start to drift off, all I can see are those fiery green eyes staring back at me. . . .

I sit bolt upright when I hear a hissing noise, only to realize that I left the TV on the animal channel. A cobra dances on the screen, hissing at a mongoose. I don't wait to see who wins the fight, and hit the power button.

The clock on the wall says it's just after ten o' clock. Which means it's just after eleven in Ellis. It's been longer than twenty-four hours since I've spoken to anyone back home. I don't have my cell, so I don't know if any of them have tried to text or call me, and at the moment, I feel desperate to hear a familiar voice. I know it's too late in the evening to try my mom, but CeCe and Jonathan are usually up until at least eleven thirty on a Saturday night.

I pick up the handset for the landline and dial CeCe's number. It goes to voice mail after a few rings. I'm not all that surprised, since she never answers numbers that she doesn't recognize. I listen to her voice on the message service, her comforting tone coming through, even on a recording.

"Hey, it's me," I tell the voice mail. "This is my new home number. It might be the best way to reach me for a while. Talk at you later . . . I miss you."

I hang up and try Jonathan. Luckily, he answers.

"Hey, honey," he says, and I can hear him turning off *Saturday Night Live*. "About time you called. Tell me about your day."

And for the first time, the trauma of the day comes crashing in on me, and I burst into tears.

Jonathan coaxes me into telling him what happened, and I relay the story of my nearly disastrous—but thankfully not—audition and how that led me to finding Pear in the grove with Tobin. I tell him about the gashes on her arm, and how the security guards didn't believe me when I said that I thought she'd been attacked. I leave out how I know who the perpetrator probably is—because I know if my mom gets wind of that part of the story, she'll demand that I get on a plane and fly home immediately. She might even come out here and drag me home herself.

Even with everything that happened today, I am not ready to give up and leave.

It's just past midnight when I fall asleep to Jonathan's dulcet, reassuring tones as he tells me that everything is going to be okay.

chapter twenty-one

HADEN

I wake in the middle of the night, knowing there's an intruder in my room. A sudden *thunk*, like something hitting the ground, awakens me, and before I have a chance to sit up, an unexpected weight lands on my chest. Two bright eyes stare into mine. In my confusion, electricity surges into my hands and I am about to strike—until the thing on my chest licks my face.

I blink. "Brimstone?"

The cat meows plaintively in response. She stands with her front paws on my collarbone.

"How did you get here?" I lift her up and get out of bed. I see the bag I'd brought with me from the Underrealm toppled over on the table in the corner. "Have you been hiding in there this whole time?"

She puts her paw on my face.

"Naughty girl," I say.

She hisses.

"Sorry." I stroke her head, trying to soothe her before she gets really angry. "But do you know how much trouble I can get into for bringing a hellcat into the mortal world? Intentional or not?"

She purrs.

"I missed you, too, Brim."

She climbs up my chest, sinking her little claws into my skin as she goes, and then settles on my shoulder.

"You must be hungry."

My thought is to get Brim some food and then figure out how to hide her in my room from the others, but when I enter the kitchen, I find it already occupied.

Dax sits at the kitchen table. A paper sack giving off an unfamiliar smell sits in front of him, and he's holding a tablet of a sort that resembles a larger version of my iPhone. The light coming off the screen illuminates his face in the dark room. A look of worry is etched into his features. I am about to turn around and leave when he looks up from the tablet. He sees me and turns the device off.

"Couldn't sleep?" he asks, his voice sounding strained.

I stand there awkwardly for a few seconds. I am not sure I have forgiven him yet, and I am even less sure if he's forgiven me.

Brim meows.

Dax's eyebrows arch when he realizes Brim is on my shoulder.

"A little stowaway," I say.

"Naughty—"

"Don't make her mad. She's feeling a little touchy on the subject."

"If Simon sees her . . ."

"I know. But I need to get her some breakfast before she decides to eat one of us."

Brim hops off my shoulder onto the counter. She waits expectantly as I inspect the fridge for something to feed her. Either Simon or Dax has stocked the fridge, mostly with foods that I don't recognize. I move aside Simon's bottle of beet juice and find a package of something called cold cuts. I smell it and then hold it out to Brim for her inspection. She sniffs it and bites the corner of the package. I take that as approval and tear it open. She anxiously snatches bits of the meatlike substance from my hand, nipping my fingers in her overexcitement.

Dax pulls something from the paper bag that sits on the table. It looks like meat and cheese wrapped in a really thin, round piece of flatbread. He takes a bite and sighs. "You know I volunteered to be your guide because we're friends, but honestly, I would have done it just for the late-night taco runs. Man, I missed Mexican food."

Dax finishes his so-called taco and then turns his tablet back on. He swipes at the screen a couple of times, and then grunts with displeasure.

"What are you doing?"

"Trying to catch up on things since I was here last." He points at the tablet. "I've been researching local news, that sort of thing. They've already got a write-up on what happened to that girl they found near the grove. It says that doctors concluded that she had a massive heart attack, passed out, tumbled down the slope, and fell into the lake. If she hadn't been found by some fellow students, she probably would have died of hypothermia or drowned. They say she's in a coma."

"Massive heart attack? That means her heart seized up, yes?"

"Yes."

"How old is she?"

"Seventeen."

"Is that normal?"

"No."

"Were there any wounds? Was there blood?"

"It doesn't say."

Brim licks my fingers, greedily searching for more meat. I pull another slice from the package and give it to her whole, distracted by a suspicion that edges into my thoughts.

"What are you thinking?" Dax asks. "You've got that look."

I pick up Brim, who is trying to chew her way into the package of cold cuts. "I noticed a weird smell at the lake. Like death lingering in the air."

"But the girl didn't die."

"Exactly." I look at Dax. My suspicion is going to sound crazy—even to him. "What if Brim wasn't the only stowaway who passed with us through the gate?"

Dax laughs. "You're kidding, right? That's impossible." He looks at me and his laughter dies. "How could it get out?"

"I don't know." I suddenly feel stupid for suggesting it. But if my suspicions are right . . .

"I'll look into it," he says. "Meanwhile, you rest up. You're going to need your strength."

I give him an inquisitive look.

"You're starting school on Monday."

"School?"

"Simon's call. I was hoping you'd get to avoid it, but he thinks it's best if you and Garrick enroll in school. He thinks, with everything that happened today with Daphne and this other girl, it's important that we all act as much like normal humans as possible. He also says the added benefit is that you'll have the chance to interact with your Boon on more common grounds."

I nod. "That doesn't sound like such a bad idea."

Dax makes a scoffing noise. "You might be from Hades and all, but you haven't experienced torment quite like high school before." He swipes at his tablet. "But at least it means no more lurking in the shadows, trying to grab hapless females, and almost getting yourself fried." There's an edge to his voice that tells me I haven't been forgiven completely for my mistake, after all.

Then again, I never actually apologized. It's against my Underlord nature.

"I didn't get very far with her, if that makes you feel better."

"Did she scream or something?"

"No. She hit me."

"She hit you?" Dax suppresses a smile—not very well. "Where?"

"In the face. Hard."

He laughs. "Well, I'll be harpied. I haven't met her and I already like this Boon."

"That's the thing, Dax. This Daphne girl isn't like any Boon I've ever met. . . ."

"Forget those other Boons. There's a difference between the girls who go easily into the Underrealm and the majority of mortal women. You see, most Champions get the chance to choose their Boons—they're usually not preselected for them as with you and me—which means most Champions go after easy prey. Girls who seem like they're already standing halfway in the dark to start with. Maybe that's why they don't last very long. Their spirits were weak from the beginning. But it sounds to me this Daphne girl has got fire."

"True. And a really mean right hook."

Dax chuckles. "She reminds me of someone else I met here . . . ," he says, more to himself than to me.

"Your Boon?"

He doesn't answer my question.

"What happened to her? Why did you come back alone?"

Dax shakes his head. He rarely talks about his time in the mortal world, and he never mentions the girl he was supposed to bring back. All I knew was that he'd returned alone.

"It's not something I can talk about."

"Why?"

"Some things just can't be said." Dax returns his attention to his tablet, his jaw clenched as he swipes at it with a forceful-ness that seems unnecessary. He's grown so quiet that I know no amount of pressing will get him to speak of her now.

But there's a more important question I need answered, so I let the topic of his Boon remain where it stands for now. I sit on the counter next to Brim, and give her another slice of meat so she'll stop trying to eat my fingers, and then bring up the sub-ject I've been wanting to discuss since we were in the owl roost in the Underrealm. It is hard to believe that it has been fewer than twenty-four hours since then.

"When I told you earlier that the Oracle had said my Boon—Daphne, that is—could restore something that had been taken from the Underlords, and I mentioned the word *Cypher*, you acted as though you knew something. You said something about rumors. . . ."

Dax stands up abruptly, leaving his tablet on the table, and exits the kitchen.

I jump off the counter. "You said you would tell me what you know," I call after him.

"Shhhh!" I hear his command to be quiet coming from some-where near the entrance to the garage. I hear a door open and close. The light from Dax's tablet catches my eye. I glance down at the screen and see that he has entered the words *abecie caelum* into a search engine. The second word is Latin for *sky*, the first word is one I don't recognize. I scan the rest of the page and see the words: *0 results found. Did you mean: abecu caelum?*

Whatever Dax had been searching for, he wasn't having much luck.

I hear him coming back and I look away from the tablet.

"Sorry," he says, entering the kitchen. "I needed to be certain that Simon was still out. He has ears like a hawk—I had thought he was well out of range, and yet he still must have overheard us speaking in your room this afternoon. Trust me, Lord Haden. I did not tell him that you had gone to the grove."

"I know," I say. "But he obviously has sources beyond good hearing if he knew about me trying to grab Daphne. I told no one about that."

I remember hearing someone entering the grove just before I left. Perhaps he had someone following me, or he himself had doubled back to the house and had seen me leave and he'd followed. One thing I should have been more careful about was not underestimating Simon, as Dax had instructed.

"What is he?" I ask Dax. "Simon isn't an Underlord, but he's most certainly not human."

"I don't know what Simon is, but he doesn't look a day older than when I first met him six years ago. He could be three hundred years old, for all we know. My best guess is that he's a satyr cloaked in the form of a human. That would explain his heightened senses and slow aging. Not to mention his love for vegetables. But it doesn't account for his certain powers of persuasion, if you know what I mean."

"I do," I say.

No mere mortal—nor mere satyr, for that matter—could bring a lord of the Underrealm to the point of invoking *elios* like that. And the way I couldn't move just because he *told* me I couldn't—it was as if he were controlling my body with his words. If he could do that to me, I imagine most mortals don't stand a chance against his persuasiveness. I look around at Simon's opulent home, and think of the garage full of cars and how easily he had procured new identities for us, and realize just how useful that kind of power would be.

I can't help wondering why he's living in a house with three young Underlords and not off ruling a country somewhere. Then I remember what he had said—that all of us "have things riding" on my quest. Does even he know more about my true purpose than I do? And why hadn't Ren or the Court bothered to fill me, of all the people involved, in on the details?

"What is a Cypher?" I ask Dax. "And why does the Court want it?"

Dax sits at the table, turns off his tablet, and sticks it inside his knapsack, which sits on one of the chairs. He gestures for me to take a seat across from him. Instead, I sit on Simon's polished countertop and let Brim climb back onto my shoulders. She purrs contentedly next to my ear.

"What do you know about the Key of Hades?" Dax asks.

"I know that the Key was more than the instrument that locked and unlocked the main gates of the Underrealm. I know that it was Hades's Kronolithe—the thing that granted him his immortality—and without it, the Sky God was able to kill him. I know that the Key was stolen by the Great Traitor, and because of its loss, we Underlords have been locked inside the Underrealm, godless, for centuries. And this brought an end to the Thousand-Year War between our ancestors and the Skylords."

"All true," Dax says. "Except the war isn't over; it's just at a stalemate, as far as many in the Court are concerned. Why do you think they train us to be warriors? It's because they hope to restart the war someday. Someday soon, if there's any credence to the rumors I've heard."

"But how is that even possible? Only a few of us can pass through Persephone's Gate at a time. And only once every six months. How can the Court wage a war without an army?"

"What if they could open the main gates again?"

"But they would need the Key for that."

"Exactly," Dax says. "And to find the Key, they need the Cypher."

"Daphne? But she's just some mortal girl. How could she help the Court get a Key that has been lost for millennia?"

"That is not a piece of the puzzle I have been privy to."

I can feel my heart racing and energy pulsing through my veins. The Oracle had said that the fate of the Underrealm rests on my shoulders, but part of me had tried to dismiss her words as hyperbole. Had I truly been Chosen for such an important assignment? Could I really have the means to help restore the Key of Hades to the Underrealm? I can only imagine the kind of glory and honor that would accompany such a victory, if Dax's speculations about the Cypher are correct. Had I truly been Chosen by the Fates to accomplish the greatest task that any Champion had ever been entrusted with?

But that is the thing; I hadn't been *entrusted* with anything. The Court hadn't told *me* any of this vital information. As far as I am concerned, I have been sent to the Overrealm blind—thinking I am merely to bring back another Boon for the harem. I had to find out this information from a *servant*. Is that because they have so little *trust* in me that they think I will fail if I have any clue of what an important task is before me?

"How do you even know all this?" I ask Dax.

"There are benefits to being treated with as little regard as furniture," he says. "Many in the Court have a tendency to say too much when servants are around, because they do not care that we exist. What I have told you is what I have pieced together from snippets of conversations and the rumors that circulate among the servants. I can tell you that in the last three years or so, your father has made many journeys to consult the Oracle of Elysium, but it was only now that the Oracle agreed the time is right for obtaining the Cypher."

"What will they do with Daphne? How will they use her to get the Key?"

"I don't know that much. But I heard what the Oracle said in the ceremony—that you are the one who can bring her back to the Court."

Can—that being the word that sticks with me. She didn't say I *will*—there is no guarantee that I will succeed. As it stands at this moment, I am just as likely to fail as I am to succeed.

And with the mistakes I made today, the scales seem tipped too much in failure's favor. . . .

No. That is the way Rowan would want me to think. He would want me to let my fears get in the way. I was the one who was Chosen, not Rowan. I am the one who is here, not him.

The only thing standing in the way of my restoring the full power of the Underrealm is Daphne herself. Part of me worries I'm not prepared for taking on this Cypher, but at the same time, I am glad for the challenge of a worthy opponent. It will make my victory all the more satisfying.

"What is the best way to defeat her?" I ask Dax. "How do I take her down?"

"Take her down?" he repeats, as if I've just said something distasteful.

"You said it yourself. Daphne isn't like other Boons. She's a more formidable opponent than —"

"Whoa," Dax says. "You're looking at this all wrong. First of all, you can't think of her as an opponent. That's you thinking like an Underlord warrior. You're going to have to take a more human approach. You're not here to defeat her; you're here to get her to trust you. You need her to *like* you. Actually, more than that," he says with a weird smile. "You're going to have to get her to fall in love with you."

I stare at Dax, dumbfounded. He might as well have told me I needed to sprout wings and fly into the sun. "How am I supposed to get her to fall in love with me when I don't know the first thing about . . . *it*? Love, I mean."

Dax sighs like he has no idea of how to explain it to me.

And I thought he was supposed to be my guide.

Brim bristles on my shoulder. Her purr turns into a growl. I follow her glare toward the hallway that leads to the garage.

"Simon," Dax says. "She must hear him pulling in."

"Time to hide you," I tell Brim, catching her in my hands before she can go running toward the garage.

"I'll distract Simon with questions about your school arrangements," Dax says as he ushers us toward the stairs. "Hmmm. Maybe he does have the right idea with sending you to school. You need to get to know Daphne on a personal level. Just try to act as *human* as possible. And no more of your little excursions. I mean it, Haden. Especially with Simon on the warpath."

I nod my acceptance and head up the stairs with my cat contraband. I think I hear Garrick's door click shut as I walk down the long hallway, and I wonder how much he overheard.

When I get back to my room, I make a nest of blankets for Brim under my bed and pull out my iPhone. Brim snubs her nest, and instead curls up at my feet. I hit one of the phone's icons and pull up a search engine. I am not sure which question to research first:

"What does it mean to be human?" or "How do I get a girl to like me?"

Because when it comes to both of those queries, I haven't got a clue.

chapter twenty-two

DAPHNE

I'm the first one in the music room on Monday morning. I had to get to school early to pick up my finalized schedule now that I've been accepted into the music program. The official verdict had come via my new Olympus Hills High email account Sunday afternoon. I had celebrated over speakerphone with the crew at Paradise Plants. Jonathan had led the employees in a hip-hip-hurray cheer, and my mother had done a somewhat decent job at hiding her disappointment—in her voice anyway. She hadn't been thrilled about my having found a nearly dead girl in the lake, either. But Jonathan, having been pre-warned, was able to keep her from going into a full-on mother-bear panic. CeCe still didn't know about my getting into the music program—nor about the girl in the lake incident—because she had called in sick, and still hadn't returned my voice mail.

Joe had been gone when I got up this morning—hopefully not out wandering in his bathrobe again—so I'd ridden my bike to school, taking a different path from the one through the grove.

I stand by myself in the music room, drinking in all the sounds of the new room and its state-of-the-art facilities, when I realize that I'm not sure where to sit. I've gone to the same school all my life, sat next to the same friends, and suddenly the idea of not being able to do that today really hits me. I'd known I'd be starting over; I just didn't know what that would feel like until this moment. I finally settle into a seat in the middle row—not too eager, not too aloof—of the semicircle of chairs that face a small stage, and watch students trickle in through the doorway. Some I recognize from auditions, and others are strangers, but there's only one topic of conversation that consumes them all—what happened to Pear Perkins in the grove.

Even the ladies in the main office had been gossiping about it. Which is how I'd heard that the Olympus Hills Medical Center had released a statement saying that Pear had a heart attack brought on by a pre-existing heart condition.

Part of me wants to be filled with relief, knowing it was a medical issue and not something I could have prevented by warning her not to go into the grove, but another part of me can't shake the image of those gashes on her arm from my memory. Could tree branches have really caused those wounds? Or had my theory been correct about the stranger in the grove and nobody had bothered to investigate that angle?

I shake my head, thinking I am being overly paranoid. A doctor had determined that what happened to Pear was caused by a heart attack. Why would the medical center have any reason to put out a false report?

"That's the thing," I hear someone say, coming into the room. I recognize the voice as Lexie's. "If Pear had a heart condition, I would have known about it. We've been friends for, like, ever. And besides, I know all my competitions' weaknesses."

The word *frenemy* comes to mind and I make a snerking sound. Lexie sends a glare in my direction before sitting in the front row with her posse of girls. I imagine they're the infamous Sopranos I've been hearing about.

A few minutes before the bell is supposed to ring, Tobin appears in the doorway. The dark circles under his eyes make me wonder if his nights have been just as restless as mine since the grove. I lift my hand to give a little wave to him, but find myself holding my breath, wondering if he'll respond. I had contemplated looking up his number and calling him to share the good news about my getting into the music department, but I hadn't because I was unsure of where our budding friendship stood after Saturday evening. Finding a nearly dead girl together could serve to either cement our friendship status or crumble it before it even began. And with the crazy story I told the security guards and my omission of the truth—okay, lie—regarding my nonschollie status, I wouldn't blame Tobin if he's decided to have nothing to do with the wacko newbie. But before I can decide whether or not to wave, he sees me and waves first. I respond with a smile.

Tobin slips into the seat next to mine. "I was afraid we'd scared you out of town," he says. "Glad to see you're still here."

"I don't scare away that easily."

"Neither do I." Tobin hooks his backpack over the back of his seat, showing that he's not planning on moving to a new spot before class. Today, he's wearing a periwinkle fedora with a darker blue ribbon above the short brim. "Have you heard what they're saying about Pear having a heart attack?"

I nod. "Kind of impossible not to."

"I know what you mean." Tobin's warm tone drops lower, colder as he leans in close to me. "But do you believe it?" he asks. "I mean, I guess Pear could have had a heart condition and nobody knew it. This place is pretty competitive, so she may have been afraid to show any weakness. I couldn't fathom why Pear would have gone to the grove until I overheard my mother talking on a conference call this morning. Pear's housekeeper said that Pear had forgotten her sheet music for the auditions. They're saying she must have rushed home to get it and cut through the grove as a shortcut. They're saying the stress of it all was too much for her heart and she collapsed. . . . But the thing is, some of those gashes in her arm sure didn't look like they were caused by tree branches."

Relief washes over me, knowing that I am not the only one questioning the weirdness of the situation. It makes me feel a little bit less crazy. "I was thinking the same thing. But why would there be some sort of cover-up going on?"

Tobin looks at me, the strangest notes coming off him.

"What?" I ask.

"I don't think what happened to Pear is the only thing this place is covering up."

This is the third time Tobin has indicated that something less than perfect is going on in this town. What exactly had I gotten myself mixed up in by agreeing to move here? I give Tobin a look, telling him to go on.

"You're going to think I'm nuts—" Tobin stops abruptly. I look up and see that Lexie and Bridgette are standing right next to us, with a couple of Sopranos standing behind them. Bridgette holds a basket of giant muffins.

"I understand you're the one who pulled Pear from the lake," Lexie says to Tobin. She flicks her hand, and Bridgette sets the basket of muffins in his lap. "Consider this our thank-you."

"Um . . . you're welcome," Tobin says. "But it's Daphne you should be thanking. I wouldn't have found Pear if it weren't for her."

"Oh." Lexie blinks at me as if this is the first time she's noticed me sitting there, despite giving me a death glare only minutes before. She picks up one of the giant blueberry muffins from Tobin's basket and offers it to me. "Thanks," she says. "Maybe you're not as useless as I thought. If Pear doesn't recover soon, we will have to consider taking on a new Soprano. We'll be watching you." Lexie drops the muffin in my open hand and returns to the front row with her Sopranos.

"They really are kind of like the mafia, aren't they? 'Consider this our thank-you,'" I say, mimicking the low, raspy Godfather-esque voice.

Tobin laughs. It's nice to hear a tone coming off him that doesn't sound so dark. I want to bring up the topic we were discussing before Lexie interrupted, but at the moment, I want to let him be lighthearted. "'We'll be watching you,'" I say in my God-father voice.

"I wouldn't put it past her to leave a severed My Little Pony head in your bed if you refuse their membership offer," he says, and takes a bite of a muffin.

"Friendship *is* magic," I say.

Tobin laughs harder, accidentally spitting bits of muffin on my shirt. He clamps his hands over his mouth, still laughing. Which makes me lose it, too.

"What's so funny?" Iris says, taking the seat on my right.

Neither Tobin nor I can stop laughing long enough to answer her. She rolls her eyes at us. Tobin squeezes my shoulder. I love the sound of his laugh. It's infectious, just like CeCe's.

"Quiet down," Mr. Morgan calls, entering the classroom from his office. "I have a special announcement!"

"Ooh," Iris says. "I bet he's finally going to give us details about the musical. Maybe he'll even announce the leads." She reaches behind me to smack Tobin on the shoulder in a knowing sort of way. His laughter dies down immediately and he puts his full attention on Mr. Morgan.

"I know many of you were upset that I didn't announce what musical we would be performing this year *before* this week's preliminary auditions," Mr. Morgan says, standing on the small stage before the semicircle of chairs. He sounds far more like a teacher today, rather than the tyrant he was at the auditions. "But that is because some very special circumstances came up just after the beginning of the school year, and I would have been a fool not to have accepted. I am going to end your suspense and tell you all now, as well as introduce our surprise guest...." He stops to straighten his tie, but based on the happy tones of anticipation buzzing in the air, I suspect he's just pausing for the dramatic effect. He smooths down his tie and smiles, practically beaming. "This year, Olympus Hills High will be performing the debut production of a brand-new rock opera. But not just any rock opera—one composed by none other than the 'God of Rock,' Mr. Joe Vince himself!" Mr. Morgan sweeps his hands out dramatically, as if presenting us all with a gift as his office door opens, and Joe—*my Joe*—comes swaggering out to the sudden, uproarious applause and cheers of everyone else in the classroom.

I, however, am completely speechless.

"No way!" Iris practically shouts.

Lexie stands up, clapping, and some of her Sopranos have their hands pressed to their faces like they might just cry. Girls make that gesture a lot when my father is around. At least according to the pictures I've seen in *Us Weekly*.

Joe clasps his hands together and shakes them at the crowd of students. "Thank you, thank you for your warm welcome."

Tobin turns to me. "Why didn't you say something about this yesterday, you big fibber?"

"I had no idea."

"I know holding auditions before announcing the play was unconventional, but we had our reasons," Mr. Morgan says. "As Mr. Vince tells me, the play is a work in progress, and we will be helping him develop the songs over the next few months. In order to do this, he asked me to select the two best singers in our program, and he will then write the songs specific to their vocal range. The rest of the parts will be assigned over the next few weeks to those who impress Mr. Vince with their hard work and abilities."

"I am sure the decision will be very difficult," Joe says, "which is why I left the decision of the lead parts to your instructor. I trust he has chosen the best and the brightest of your group." He looks right at me and gives a little wink.

A redheaded girl in front of me practically swoons, as if the wink were meant for her.

What on earth is going on? Since when did rock stars write high school musicals? Even for high schools their estranged daughters go to? A school she's starting because he just showed up out of the blue and insisted on taking her to for no apparent reason she could discern . . .

And then it hits me. I know *exactly* what Mr. Morgan is going to say next.

And all I want to do is run away.

Mr. Morgan holds out his hands to quiet the class. Everyone is in a tizzy, speculating who will be chosen, or what it will mean to be the star of an original Joe Vince musical production. I can hear the Sopranos fluttering around Lexie, assuring her she's a shoo-in for the lead—especially now that Pear is hospitalized. The class finally falls silent at Mr. Morgan's and Joe's bidding.

"Without further ado," Mr. Morgan says, "I am pleased to announce the leads for the debut production of Joe Vince's rock opera version of the Orpheus and Eurydice myth: *Into the Dark*. . . ."

How quickly could I cross the room and get out the classroom door?

"In the role of Orpheus, we'll have Tobin Oshiro-Winters!"

"Sweet!" Tobin smacks his hands together.

Iris cheers for him, but I'm still too panicked to react.

"And in the role of Eurydice, we have another special treat. . . ."

I feel like my throat is about to close in.

"My very own daughter," Joe says, cutting Mr. Morgan off in his excitement, "will be playing the part." He claps his hands out toward me. "Stand up, Daphne, so the others can meet you!"

All I want to do is hide under my chair, but I'm pretty sure Joe isn't going to stop clapping until I stand up. I do so, pulling Tobin up with me so I won't be the only one in the spotlight. Tobin gives a salute to Joe and Mr. Morgan, and then a Frank Sinatra–esque bow to his fellow students, who call out their congratulations to him. There's not a single congrats thrown my way, but there are plenty of dagger stares coming from Lexie and her Sopranos.

"This is crap," she says, not so quietly, to her friends. "Isn't nepotism illegal?"

Even Iris is staring at me, with her mouth looking like her jaw has come unhinged. "Why did you say you were a schollie?" she finally asks.

This is exactly what I was afraid of all along. I don't even want people to think I'd gotten into the program because I'm Joe Vince's daughter, and now they all believe I'd gotten the lead because my father is writing the play.

Joe gives me a big thumbs-up. So this is what he had meant the other night when he said he was going to make it up to me. If he thinks he is helping me win friends and influence people, he is as delusional as he is a drunk. I can tell from the murmurs and glares being exchanged that my social standing has just gone from New Girl to downright most hated.

Joe and Mr. Morgan go over some of the details of how the next few months are going to work with preparations, but honestly, I tune them out. When the bell rings, a few girls rush the stage. Joe signs autographs for them as he makes his way in my direction. The last thing I want to do is talk to him right now, so I grab my bag, ignore Tobin's offer to help me find my next class, head for the door, and escape out into the hall.

I bump into several people as I try to find my way through the unfamiliar halls of Olympus Hills High, fighting tears of frustration that sting the backs of my eyes. The last seventy-two hours had been anything but ideal. I'd been ignored by my father; accosted in the grove; had found the body of a girl who may or may not have been attacked because of me; was treated like I'm delusional by a couple of rent-a-cops; and now I had earned the ire of almost every student in the music program, and the program was my only reason for being here.

I can't imagine how things could possibly get any worse, I think as I round the corner and find room 108, my humanities class. I push open the door and almost drop my backpack. Because sitting right there in the back row is the boy from the grove.

I can't believe it. There *he* is, looking through a textbook and tapping his pencil against the top of a desk. Just like any other student waiting for class to start. Except he's scanning the pages of his book so quickly, he can't possibly be reading anything.

"What is he doing here?" I say under my breath.

"*You* know Haden Lord?" The question comes from behind me. I glance back and see Bridgette standing there.

"Yes," I say quietly. *But do I know him? Is this even the same boy?* He looks so different under the fluorescent school bulbs—so normal. If the contours of his face hadn't been etched into my thoughts for the last day and a half, I might not have recognized him. His hair is still dark, but more the color of rich coffee than the midnight black it seemed in the grove. It's shorter, too, and waves and curls slightly around his ears, rather than hanging to his shoulders like before. "No. I mean . . . do *you* know him?"

Bridgette shrugs. "I heard they were here."

"They?"

"The Lords are some hoity-toity extended family from the East Coast or something. They send a few of their kids here every few years. These new guys must be younger cousins to the ones who came last time. I guess there was some kind of mix-up, because nobody knew they were coming to school until yesterday. There wouldn't have been room for them if it hadn't been for the big ole donation checks they showed up with."

I raise my eyebrows at this flood of coherent information from Bridgette, who had seemed a little vacant up until this moment.

"What?" she asks. "My dad is on the school board. You didn't think I got into this school because of my smarts, did you? My mom's movies aren't *that* good." She smiles. "Dad was in a tizzy over the Lord boys at breakfast this morning."

"What else do you know about them?"

"There are two of them going to school. One is a freshman, named Garrick, and the other is a junior. Since this is junior humanities, I'm assuming that means this one is Haden. Oh, and they're staying at that really big house on Athena Way."

I nod, even though I don't know which house she's talking about. All of the houses in Olympus Hills seem big enough to hold half of Ellis Fields in their main floors.

Before I can ask any more questions, someone pushes between Bridgette and me, knocking my shoulder into the doorjamb.

"Bridgette," Lexie snaps at her friend.

"Oh yeah. I'm not supposed to talk to you anymore," Bridgette says, and hurries after Lexie. They sit with a group of Sopranos in the first row. Each one deliberately not looking at me.

The bell rings, and the only seat left is in the second row. It's directly behind Lexie. *Great.* But the worst thing about it is that it means I can't see this Haden guy unless I deliberately turn back to look at him. I pause before sitting, to watch him. I wish he'd look up. I want to see his eyes again. I want to know if they're bright and fiery like I remember. I need to know if he's the same person I met in the grove.

"If everyone will sit, we will get started," a tall, thin woman with red, curly hair says. I assume she must be Ms. Leeds, despite the leopard-print miniskirt she's wearing.

I turn my back to Haden and slip into my seat.

"I trust last night's events did not prevent anyone from finishing the reading."

I pull out the iPad Marta had presented me with yesterday afternoon—she said it was preloaded with all of the books I might possibly need at OHH—as a collective groan echoes through the classroom. I would have joined in if I hadn't turned to studying in an attempt to lull myself to sleep at three this morning. I ended up reading a third of the book before my alarm clock went off. It was either that or call Jonathan again, and I didn't think he'd appreciate that.

Ms. Leeds makes a tsking noise. "I was hoping now that Mr. Morgan has announced the subject of the school musical, your interest in our Greek mythology unit would have heightened. Mr. Morgan tells me you will be focusing on the story of Orpheus, the tale of the great musician who traveled to the underworld to bring back his wife, Eurydice, from the dead. It's an interesting story, but I thought we might back things up a bit and study some of the earlier myths of the underworld before revisiting Orpheus. Mr. Morgan will be very pleased if those of you in the music and theatre tracks actually have a clue of what it is you're singing about."

Lexie sits at greater attention as Ms. Leeds opens her notes and sets them on a podium. She's dedicated, I'll give her that.

"Now, who here knows who Persephone is?"

Lexie and I both raise our hands at the same time.

"Ah, we get to hear from one of our new students. Daphne, yes?" Ms. Leeds says to me.

I nod.

"Enlighten us with your knowledge, Daphne."

Lexie lowers her hand.

"Persephone was the goddess of springtime. She lived on earth with her mother, Demeter, until she was kidnapped by Hades and forced to go to the underworld to live with him. Her mother, who happened to be the goddess of the harvest, wanted her back, and caused a big famine until Zeus told his brother Hades that he had to send Persephone home. Hades, being an evil jerk, tricked Persephone into eating six pomegranate seeds, which meant she was now tied to the underworld for six months out of the year. That is supposedly where the seasons of the year come from. Spring and summer are beautiful and lush because Demeter was happy that her daughter was with her, and fall and winter are crappy because that's when Demeter was sad, because Persephone was forced to be in the underworld with Hades during those months."

"Colorful interpretation of the story," Ms. Leeds says. "Though I find it interesting that you refer to Hades as being an 'evil jerk.' Why do you say this?"

"He's the devil, isn't he? Keeper of hell and all that."

"No," Ms. Leeds says. "While most scholars agree that the idea of Hades may have been the precursor to the medieval Christian concept of the devil, they were actually quite different."

"But they both like dead people!" Bridgette says enthusiastically.

I can hear the eye roll coming off Lexie.

"Yes. True . . . somewhat," Ms. Leeds says. "They are both the keepers of the souls of the dead. However, the Christian devil is traditionally known to claim only the souls of sinners, while Hades was believed to oversee all of the dead, whether they were good or bad."

Bridgette nods as if that's what she'd meant to say all along.

"It is also interesting to note that Hades was not only the god of the underworld, but he was also believed to be the god of wealth. As gold, jewels, and other precious metals come from beneath the Earth—which was believed to be the location of Hades's realm. Many people would pray to Hades and make bargains with him in exchange for wealth and power. Some scholars think this may have been where the concept of 'selling your soul to the devil' arose in Christian beliefs. But what about the symbolism of these two figures?" Ms. Leeds asks, looking at Bridgette. "The Christian devil is widely accepted as the embodiment of evil—a fallen angel. But what about Hades? Is he a figure of evil in the Greek mythos?"

Bridgette shrugs.

"Anyone else?" the teacher asks.

Lexie and I raise our hands at the same time again.

"Daphne, since you brought up the subject, I'd like to hear more of your thoughts."

I can hear the frustration wafting off Lexie, but I go ahead and answer. "I think he is supposed to be a symbol for evil. The myth of Persephone clearly shows that. . . ."

"I beg to differ," says someone from the back of the room. I'm certain I've heard his voice before—even if there's no hint of his strange accent now.

"Ah, our other new student," Ms. Leeds says, with a little clap of her hands. "I'm sorry, I should have started class with introductions. Haden Lord, stand up so everyone can see you."

Haden stands. There's one thing about him that isn't different from the grove. He's tall. At least six feet four. I'm not the only one who takes in a quick breath at the sight of him standing there.

"Sweet mother of hotness," Lexie whispers from the desk in front of mine. This must be the first time she's noticed him.

"I don't believe Hades was evil at all," Haden says. "He was purely a man—or god, actually—who was assigned a difficult destiny." He looks at me for the first time since I entered the classroom. His eyebrows arch, but I can't tell if it's a look of recognition or not. His eyes are still jade green but not bright like before, and I can't tell if his pupils are surrounded by amber fire rings from where I sit. "Being the keeper of the underworld doesn't make him evil. Somebody has to do it."

"No. But being a kidnapper and a rapist does." I raise my eyebrows right back at him. "I mean, there Persephone was, minding her own business, picking flowers, when all of a sudden Hades bursts out of the ground in a flaming chariot and grabs her. I mean, you can't just go around grabbing people. That's not okay." I narrow my eyes, challenging him. "What kind of person does that?"

Haden glowers right back at me. "Maybe he didn't see any other options at the moment."

"Hades is a tool. He obviously couldn't find a girl to love him, so he just thought he'd steal himself one. There wouldn't be a story about him being a rapist if people didn't think he was evil."

"Rape didn't have anything to do with it," Haden says in a tone that seems defensive to me. "Her father—Zeus himself—had already agreed to let Hades have her, and according to tradition, taking a woman by chariot from her home to yours is part of the ancient Greek wedding ceremony." He sits down. He wears a long-sleeved, gray shirt with the sleeves pushed up to his elbows. It bothers me that I notice the muscles flexing as he crosses his arms in front of his chest.

I shake my head. "How can you say that? He took the girl by force and made her his bride. The book calls the myth the Rape of Persephone for a reason."

"But there are earlier translations of the story than the one cited in the text." Haden waves his muscular hand. "Maybe Persephone, a virgin"—he winks at me—"went willingly into the underworld in order to explore her own sexual desires." He smirks and leans back in his chair with his arms crossed. I'm sure my face goes white before heat floods my cheeks, but I refuse to turn away from his gaze.

"Well. I'm glad to see at least two of my students have a passion for this subject," Ms. Leeds says. I can see her pretending to fan herself out of the corner of my eye.

My cheeks burn hotter as Lexie and her friends snigger at us.

"Be careful or I'll assign you two to write a term paper together. I am known for my matchmaking skills, after all."

That statement makes me turn away from Haden quickly. I stare down at the text on my iPad. Not because I'm backing down from him, but because the last thing I want is to get stuck working alone with this Haden jerk—for any reason.

Ms. Leeds sits on the edge of the table in front of the class, crossing her long legs. "Haden brings up an interesting point that I hope none of you missed. There are many interpretations and versions of these myths other than the ones featured in our textbook. The so-called Rape of Persephone story actually contradicts many of the other myths in which the figure of Persephone appears. In myths such as Orpheus and Eurydice, and Psyche and Cupid, Persephone is portrayed as quite the formidable queen of the underworld, not as a lilting flower, easily taken and tricked by a man. When I was at Berkley, I wrote a paper on this subject. My research showed that there were very early versions of the Persephone myth that claimed that she was not 'taken' at all. One version suggested that Persephone, tired of being under the constant watch of an overbearing mother, left the mortal world of her own free will in order to fulfill a greater purpose. She recognized the underworld's need for a queen and chose to fulfill it."

"But why would someone change her story?" Lexie asks, not waiting for the teacher to call on her this time.

"As I wrote in my paper: to very patriarchal societies, a tale about a young maiden who takes her own future into her hands, leaves her home and family in search of her own destiny—and possibly a bit of forbidden love—is a very dangerous story indeed. So, therefore, they changed her story to fit their purposes. To make her a victim—a morality tale to warn girls from wandering too far from home, like Little Red Riding Hood. They changed her story to take away her power. That is the true rape of Persephone, if you ask me."

I nod in agreement and notice that Lexie does, too.

For the first time, I feel connected to Persephone's story. Well, Ms. Leeds's version of it anyway. We'd both left our homes in search of a bigger purpose.

Ms. Leeds launches into the rest of her lecture on other underworld myths, and I can tell she's trying to spark another lively debate. But I keep quiet after that, and so does Haden. As Bridgette enlightens the class with her perspective on the plight of beautiful women in Greek mythology, I risk a glance back at Haden. He looks up as if he senses my movement, and for the briefest of moments, his eyes seem to flash a fiery mix of amber and jade green.

I run into Tobin on my way from humanities to geometry.

"Hey, superstar," he says. "You doing okay after your dad's big announcement?"

"Fine," I say, "except for pretty much being nominated for class leper."

I look behind my shoulder, feeling like I am once again being followed. I must look as shaken as I feel when I look back at Tobin, because he puts a hand on my shoulder and asks, "Are you okay? Lexie and her little mafia aren't getting to you already, are they?"

"No," I say. "It's that . . . I saw *him* again. The guy from the grove. At least, I think it was him—he looks different somehow. But still the same."

"What?" Tobin says, dropping his hand from my shoulder. "Did you see him somewhere outside? You didn't go back *there* again, did you?"

"No, he was *here*. He was in my humanities class. He's a student."

The tone coming off Tobin is even darker than it was after we found Pear. "What's his name?" he asks. "Do you know his name?"

"Haden," I say. "I think it was Haden Lord."

Tobin takes in a sharp breath.

I look down at my iPad. "Like I said, I'm not a hundred percent positive it's the same. . . ."

But Tobin storms off before I finish my sentence.

chapter twenty-three

HADEN

"What the Tartarus is that?" Garrick asks, his eyes enlarged with horror as he looks from *it* to me and then back to *it*.

"Harpies if I know," I say under my breath. I'm too busy scanning the room for a certain face to scrutinize the alien mass in front of me.

"Gods, it smells almost as bad as it looks." Garrick picks up his knife and poses as if he is about to prod the glistening mass with the point of the blade. He hesitates and then pulls the knife back. "I mean, do you think it's safe?"

I shrug. I don't want to touch it, either, but it wouldn't bode well for me to show any hesitancy so early in my quest. My eyes move over a group of girls sitting at a far table, and then scan the faces of the people who stand in line at the opposite end of the room. Where is she? Have I lost track of Daphne already?

I'd hung back and watched her leave the classroom after the bell rang, but had lost her trail in the hallway. It is impossible to make out one person's scent in the cacophony of body odors and strange perfumes that permeate this place. I don't know how these humans can stand it. The smell is even worse here in the cafeteria.

As are the sounds and sights that assault my senses. Human

teenagers are just *so* loud. And the brightness that floods in through the long rows of windows above the tables makes my eyes burn. How am I supposed to locate Daphne in all of this chaos? How am I supposed to observe her if I can barely see?

I pull my sunglasses out of my jacket pocket and shove them on my face—despite Dax's warning that wearing sunglasses indoors in public might make me look like a "creeper."

Creep. Daphne had called me that in the grove. Does she still think of me that way? She hadn't looked back at me again before leaving class, and I can't help feeling like a dung spout for the things I'd said to her.

I worry my new strategy is failing. My online research into "how to get a girl to like me" had suggested, time and time again, that to win a human girl over, I had to be mean to her. I'd spent the bulk of class either ignoring her, contradicting her, or acting like a "bad boy," which I gather meant showing off my muscles and leaning back in my chair after saying something sexually suggestive.

So why do I feel like I am in an even worse place with her now than before?

What's more, she'd deserved my derision for the offensive things she'd said—her accusations against the god of the Under-realm had bordered on blasphemy. Hades is everything we Underlords aspire to be, but both she and the text of the book had treated his memory as if he were a villain. How could I not be angered by her words even if I wasn't trying to be rude?

"It's just so vile," Garrick goes on, about the foodlike substance on his tray.

Vile? Harpies, why did saying those things about virginity and exploring sexual desires to Daphne make me feel so vile now?

I mean, it's not as if I know what I'm talking about. Only Champions who ascend to the Court are allowed to mate—and only after they've returned victorious with their Boons.

I can't help wondering if Daphne really is this Cypher, and not just an ordinary Boon. Will she still be *my* mate when I bring her back to the Underrealm? Or will the Court claim her for another purpose? *Gods, I hope not*, I think as I imagine the possibility of she and I together. . . .

"It's wrong. Like . . . like . . . I don't know. What on *earth* could it be?" Garrick's voice trails off in disgusted awe.

That strange heat I'd felt when I first met Daphne in the grove fills my hands. I try to pick up my knife, but little sparks jump off the metal when I touch it. I tuck my hands into the pockets of my hooded sweatshirt, not sure how I could have lost control so easily.

"I believe it's called mashed potatoes and gravy," I say, looking at the sign that hangs over the cash register, where I had paid a woman with the credit card Dax had given me.

Garrick picks up his tray and plops it back down on the table as if to test what would happen. The yellow, congealed *gravy* moves as one mass and slops over the side of the mashed potatoes, laying waste to what I think are kernels of corn.

"Gross," Garrick says almost gleefully.

He had been reluctant when Simon informed him that he would be attending school with me, but this environment has a strange, enlivening effect on him. I don't think I have ever heard a Lesser speak so many sentences in the presence of an Underlord.

A warm breeze rustles through the room, and I look up toward one of the cafeteria doors, which leads to a grassy courtyard where some of the students eat. I expect to finally see Daphne—maybe my strategy is working after all—but instead, the person standing in the doorway is the boy I saw her with on Saturday. The one who'd had his arm around her at the lake. I almost stand to see if Daphne is somewhere behind him, but then he looks in my direction. An expression almost as dark as an Underrealm storm crosses his face. He leaves the doorway and advances toward our table.

"Harpies," I whisper under my breath. I know that look on his face all too well—it'd been perfected by Rowan years ago. My first instinct is to pick up a knife and ready for an attack, but it takes all my willpower to do the opposite. I drop my head and hunch my shoulders, as if making myself smaller will deflect some of the other guy's anger.

"Are you Haden Lord?" the boy asks as he comes to stand at the opposite side of our table.

I don't respond.

"Are. You. Haden. Lord?" he says, more forcefully this time.

I give a slight nod, hoping he'll go away once I've answered his question.

"Then you've got about five seconds to vacate this table."

I can feel Garrick twitching beside me. His gravy-smeared butter knife is in his hand. Do Lessers even know how to fight?

"Don't move. Don't speak. Don't even breathe," I growl at Garrick in a low voice. "Let me handle this." I feel my fingerprints starting to burn into the wood surface as I grip the edge of the green cafeteria table. *Not so hard*, I remind myself, and my fingers relax slightly as the boy comes around the table and stands in front of me. I do not know what I have done to offend him, but if a fight is truly what this boy is looking for, it will not end well for either of us.

"I told you to get lost."

Electric heat courses through my body, but I stay silent, with my shoulders hunched forward. I don't dare respond. Not out of fear of this boy—but out of fear of myself, what I'm capable of doing in this room filled with humans, if I lose control again.

"Do you need me to count to five for you?" he asks.

I try to keep my eyes trained on the yellow gravy congealing on top of my mashed potatoes. I can only hope Garrick will follow my lead and stay still.

"I'm talking to you, creep." The boy leans down and pushes his face right up to mine. He shoves my shoulders. My elbows slide sideways, hitting my lunch tray and sending its contents toppling into both my and Garrick's laps.

Garrick shoots up from his seat. His fists are clenched and red.

"I said not to move!" I seethe at him. I grip the table harder—almost too hard—as electric heat surges into my fingertips. Garrick steps back and loosens his fists, but I need to do something fast to keep him at bay. I remove my sunglasses. Gravy and bits of corn ooze down my pant leg as I slowly stand and face the angry boy. He is not nearly as big as he is acting. I square my shoulders and lift my head, making myself at least eight inches taller than him, and look him in the eye.

But the boy doesn't back down. He sends a fist flying at my face. I see it with enough time to block it, but I don't. If I touch him right now, the electrical current that would leave my hands could kill him. And Simon would surely have my hide for exposing my powers in public. Instead, I duck, and the boy swings wildly at the air above my head. He goes for a lower blow, and I twist out of the way.

The boy's eyes widen, and for a split second, the angry look on his face wavers, and I realize he is not nearly as brave as he's pretending to be. He raises his fists to block his face, thinking I'm going to retaliate.

"If you want our lunch table, then you can have it," I say as calm and coolly as I possibly can, but I can feel my voice crackling with energy. "No harm done."

"No harm?" he says. "This isn't about a lunch table. I couldn't give a crap where you sit. As long as it's nowhere near this town." His voice is shaky, but he stands his ground. "I know you don't belong here," he says. "So I suggest you and your friend go back to where you came from before some actual harm gets done."

His words surprise me, but it's the look in his eyes that makes me take a step back. It's a look of recognition. My shock leaves me unprepared for the blow he lands against my chest with the heel of his hand. I fall backward and my back slams into the edge of the table. I slump onto the bench. The boy pulls his arm back to strike me again while I'm down. I close my eyes, willing myself to take the punch without losing all control.

"Tobin!" A new voice rings out behind us. I know it's *her* without seeing her face. "Stop."

I open my eyes in time to see a flash of long, golden hair as Daphne throws herself between her friend and me.

"What on earth are you doing?" she asks him.

I want to know the answer also, but Tobin doesn't get a chance to respond. I feel a swift movement and burst of heat as Garrick lunges, his fist swinging ferociously in the direction of Tobin and Daphne. I push up from the bench and fling my arm out at Garrick, catching him by the collar of his shirt, and wrench him back just as his red fist is about to slam into Daphne's face.

She stumbles backward and covers her cheek with her hand,

even though I'd stopped Garrick before he struck her.

"Are you all right?" I ask, reaching for her.

She jerks away from my grasp like she had in the grove.

Tobin steps in front of her, angrier than ever. "Don't you touch her." He tries to wrap his arm around her shoulders, but she twists away from him.

"Don't either of you touch me," she says. She looks at me. "And you, stop stalking me!" She stumbles away, still cupping her hand to her cheek.

It's against my nature, but my first instinct is to go after her, and it must have been Tobin's also. We both start in her direction, but a woman steps in front of us. I assume she's a teacher who's been summoned from her lunch, because she's still holding half of something that resembles what Simon had called a sandwich in her hands. "All three of you"—she points to Tobin, Garrick, and me—"principal's office. Now!" she commands as if she were the king of the underworld.

The teacher is a small, middle-aged mortal, and I can hear the arthritis grinding in her knees. It would take me less than a second to disable this feeble mortal and make my escape, but I am in barely enough control to know that probably isn't the wisest course of action. I watch the human boy for cues to the proper reaction. He hangs his head and says, "Yes, Mrs. Canova," and surrenders himself to the teacher. I do the same and give Garrick a stern look until he follows suit, and we allow the teacher to propel us toward the main office. She leaves Garrick and me to sit in two chairs under the watchful eye of a dark-haired woman with glasses that remind me of the shape of Brim's eyes.

The teacher takes Tobin to an office marked VICE PRINCIPAL

JORDAN and knocks on the door. "Your mother just happens to be meeting with the administration. I'm sure she'd like an explanation of your behavior."

Tobin hangs his head lower.

The door opens, and I catch a glimpse of a man who must be the vice principal and a woman in a bright red suit. She looks surprised to see Tobin in the teacher's grasp.

"What's the meaning of this?"

The teacher gives a quick recount of the scene she'd broken up in the cafeteria, and then I hear the woman ask, "What is this all about, Tobin?" before the teacher shuts the door and leaves them to talk it out.

"A guidance counselor will be with you two shortly," she says, and then instructs the dark-haired woman to buzz the "new guy" and tell him, "He's got a couple of fighters waiting out here."

Guidance counselor? I think. Like any of these humans could offer me guidance.

Garrick twitches in his seat next to me. As a Lesser, he's probably even more keen on avoiding authority figures than I am.

"Don't even think about it," I whisper, knowing he's calculating how many seconds it would take him to cross the room and escape. It would take him seven. Three for me. I know because I estimated the distance before I even sat down. "Sit still, keep your head down, and follow my lead. I'll do the talking."

"Why should I listen to you?"

I blink at him. It's an awfully insolent question for a Lesser. "Because I'm giving you an order. We might not be in the Underrealm anymore, but I am still the Champion and you are still my servant. I'm ordering you not to do something now, just like I ordered you not to do something in the cafeteria."

"Follow your orders? You expected me to sit and do nothing after that human dumped food on me? Yeah, right." Garrick surprises me with his bold words, and I have to admit that he is scrappier than I would have ever given him credit for. "You could have easily taken that guy, you know," he says.

"I know," I say.

"But you just let him attack you. You did nothing."

"I know."

"But you could have blasted his face off if you wanted."

"*I* know!" I whisper through gritted teeth. "That's *why* I didn't do anything. Don't you understand that? Now drop it."

"But you could have at least let me—"

"And then where would we be?"

And how badly would Daphne have been hurt if I hadn't stopped Garrick in time? It is harder to control our powers here— I am starting to see that—and humans are far more fragile than the people of the Underrealm. Imagine Ren's wrath if something happened to the Cypher. . . .

"Anywhere but here," Garrick says, bouncing his knee. "I hate this place."

I hate this place as much as he does, but I'm not going to show it. "You should be grateful to be *here*. This place might not be ideal, but I'm betting it's infinitely better than the Pits. You should be clamoring to do what I want. Thanking me. I'm the one who took you away from that miserable life."

"Thanking you?" he says, his voice rising louder than my whisper. "Do you really think I don't *know* why you chose me?"

"What do you mean?" I ask with a lowered voice, but dread his answer. Shame bites at my insides. *What if he really does know why I chose him? What if he knows what I did to him all those years ago—*

"I know you chose me so you could make Rowan look stupid in front of the Court."

His answer rings somewhat true, but it's not what I was dreading he would say. Maybe he has no idea what I did, after all?

"In a way," I say, trying to hide my relief.

Garrick looks away. "But you didn't think about what that would mean for me, did you? You didn't stop to think how Rowan might decide to take that out on me when we return. My life might have seemed *pitiful* to you before, but it's nothing compared to what it will be like when we get back. Rowan will make sure of that."

No, I hadn't stopped to consider that. Just like I hadn't considered the consequences of another decision I'd made concerning him several years ago. Both had been impulsive choices....

I don't know what to say, so I sit and watch the woman with the glasses as she picks up the receiver of a large beige-colored phone.

"You always do what you want for your own benefit," he says, "and don't think about what that would mean for anyone else."

That shameful feeling eats at me again. Maybe he really *does* know.

I don't get a chance to consider asking because the woman with the glasses waves at us. "One of you can go into Mr. Drol's office now." She points to the door we're supposed to enter.

I rise from my chair. Garrick sinks farther into his seat.

"Stay," I say to him, making very certain that he can tell it's an order, not a request.

I open the door, expecting to find another feeble human whom I have to appease, but my jaw pops open when I see who is sitting behind the desk in the counselor's room. "So, honey, how was your first day of school?" he asks.

"What are you doing here?" I ask as I quickly shut the door behind me.

"I thought you'd be happier to see your new guidance counselor," Dax says. He's wearing a light yellow sweater with brown patches on the elbows and sucking on the end of a . . .

"Is that a pipe?"

He nods. "Not lit, of course. No smoking allowed on campus. I thought it made me look older. What do you think?"

"I think you're addled. What are you doing here? What if this Mr. Drol comes back?"

"I am Mr. Drol," he says, raising his eyebrows and biting the end of his pipe. "I am too old to pose as a student like you and Garrick, but I didn't want to dump you here all on your own, so Simon got me a job instead. His powers of persuasion were quite effective on the administration."

I nod.

"But the part I didn't tell him is that this arrangement will give us better opportunities to talk in private. I think I might be recommending twice-weekly counseling sessions for you." He smiles around the stem of his pipe. "You're looking quite emotionally disturbed."

"I feel emotionally disturbed," I say, sinking into the seat across the desk from him. "You were right; this place is torturous."

"So what's this about you picking fights? Do I need to suspend you?"

"Funny," I say. "But I didn't do anything. It was some hot-headed kid. Just came out of nowhere and tried to pick a fight."

"Unprovoked?"

"Yes, but it must have had something to do with Daphne. I saw her with him on Saturday."

"Aha."

"She tried to get in the middle of the fight, you know?"

"Nice!" He taps his pipe on his desk. "I told you I liked this girl."

"She definitely doesn't like me. She accused me of stalking her!"

"But you are stalking her, aren't you?"

"Well, yes, but she's not supposed to *know* that." I throw my hands up. "This girl makes no sense. First, she calls me a perv and a creep, but then she tries to stop her friend from beating me up? And two seconds later, she's calling me a stalker. How does that make any sense? And I don't think being mean to her is working at all."

"Wait, why are you trying to be mean to her?"

"Because I'm trying to get her to like me, as you said I should. This Web site said that girls like guys who are mean to them, so—"

"What? Haden, I thought I told you not to ask the Internet for dating advice!"

"You forget that I don't even know what dating is!"

"Oh no, no, no, no, no," Dax says, rocking back in his chair. "How mean were you?"

"I implied her virginity in front of our entire humanities class," I say sheepishly.

"Oh harpies, we're going to have to do some major damage control now."

"I am all for suggestions."

Dax chews on the end of his pipe for a moment and I can barely resist the urge to rip it away from him.

"That's not helping," I say.

"Oh, hmm. You don't know something she's really interested in, do you? Something you could get involved in to show a common interest?"

"Music. I think she's in the music program," I say, though I have no idea how I am supposed to use music to get close to Daphne when I know even less about it than love.

Dax cringes. "It had to be that," he mumbles under his breath. "I'll see what strings I can pull from my end, and if all else fails, I'll call on Simon—though I'd like to avoid that as much as possible." He moves a stack of papers around and then stands up, with his pipe. "Now, perhaps you should scamper off to class, young Master Lord. No more fighting, you scallywag," he says with a British accent. "I think Mr. Drol should be from Yorkshire, don't you?"

I shrug. "One more thing . . . The guy I got in a fight with . . . He gave me this look that made it seem almost as if he might know *who* I am."

Dax drops his pipe and it plinks across the table. "He what? How? Who was this kid? What did he look like?"

"Short. Part Asian. Japanese, I think. Wears a stupid hat."

"Hmm, doesn't ring a bell," Dax says, but a dark look crosses his face. He walks me to the door. "I've changed my mind. You shouldn't go back to class. I'm suspending you for the rest of the week. Go home and lie low."

"Dax, you can't do that. I'm just getting started!"

"I mean it. Let's let this kid simmer down for a few days while we think about what to do next. It'll probably take me a couple of days to arrange this music program business anyway."

Waiting. More waiting. I think I might go insane.

Dax ushers me out the door just as that Tobin guy and his mother exit the other office with the man I assume is the vice principal. "I trust we won't have any more issues with you after your suspension," the vice principal is in the middle of saying to Tobin. "I would hate to tell Mr. Morgan that he needs to recast your part in the musical."

The mother barely even gives me a glance as they pass us, but Tobin seems to look right through me—as if he's trying to get a better look at Dax, who stands behind my shoulder in the doorway. Tobin comes to a complete stop, his face white as ash. Dax steps back into his office and closes the door.

"Are you okay, Toby?" his mother asks.

Tobin turns away. "Yeah. Whatever. I'm fine." But I can tell from his tone that he's clearly not.

I watch them pass by the glass windows of the office, fighting the urge to follow them. Instead, I turn toward the chairs where I left Garrick, to find that he's already gone. I can only hope he isn't getting himself into more trouble.

That's the last thing any of us needs right now.

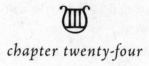

chapter twenty-four

DAPHNE

The landline phone in my room rings. I can hear it from my private bathroom, where I stand in front of the large, oval, Swarovski crystal–encrusted mirror that hangs over the marble-countered vanity. I'm not used to having my own bathroom—there was only one in the bungalow that I shared with my mom and the varied guests or strays we occasionally had staying with us—let alone one so opulent. If I were in a better mood, I might be tempted to pretend I am some sort of diva in my dressing room before a big show. Instead, I am inspecting the faint red mark that stretches across my right cheekbone. It almost looks like I'd merely gone too heavy with my blush, but the pain that pulses under my skin reminds me of a burn. It is almost exactly the same as the marks left on my arm when Haden had tried to grab me in the grove.

The strangest thing is that I didn't think the boy, who I assume is Haden's cousin, based on Bridgette's description, had actually touched me. Haden had stopped him before his fist collided with my face—and yet, I had felt a burning heat slap against my face. I guess it is possible he'd grazed me with his fist after all, but it had happened so quickly, I wasn't sure.

The phone starts ringing for the fifth time since I got home.

I'm in no hurry to answer it. I am home alone, and it is most likely someone for Joe—probably a reporter trying to get a statement about his new musical endeavor with the high school—and I am in no mood to talk about it. I turn on the faucet and splash cold water on my face. When I look up in the mirror again, the mark is gone, but my skin still stings. I prod at my cheek with the tip of my finger, suddenly wondering if I'd imagined the mark there in the first place.

I'd never had to question if I was just imagining things back in Ellis.

Something weird is definitely going on in this place.

Maybe Olympus Hills is dumping hallucinogens into their water supply. Maybe that was the big theory Tobin had wanted to share with me. I laugh at the mirror. *Yeah, right.*

The phone finally stops ringing, and I assume the call has gone to voice mail. *It's probably better to let Marta get Joe's messages anyway,* I think as I wander back into my bedroom and sit on the edge of my plush bed.

The phone starts ringing again. The sound echoes in my large, lonely room. That has to be a reporter. Nobody I know would be that persistent.

I realize it could possibly be CeCe. I'd left her three messages since I'd gotten here, telling her to call me back on this number.

I reach for the phone, and another possibility hits me. Another person might know this number. Someone who might have picked up my bag in the grove and who now has my cell phone—and all my contact listings—in their possession . . .

The phone's shrill ring makes me jump. Despite my better judgment, I pick up the receiver.

"Hello?" I ask tentatively.

"Daphne?" says a male voice on the other end, and my shoulders relax so much at the syncopated, friendly tone that accompanies it that I almost forget I'm mad at him.

"Tobin," I say, trying not to show too much relief in my voice.

"You're a hard bird to get ahold of," he says. "I would have come by your house to see you in person, but I'm kind of grounded. Also, I was worried you might slam the door in my face."

"You deserve both the grounding and the door slamming," I tell him.

"Yeah. I know." He's quiet for a moment. "I just wanted to make sure you're okay."

"I'm fine," I say, brushing my hand over my cheek. "But I might hang up on you if you don't tell me what you thought you were doing in the cafeteria. That Haden guy might be dangerous. Why would you try to take him on like that?"

I would never have confided in him that I think Haden Lord is the guy from the grove if I'd thought that would cause Tobin to go after him. It hadn't crossed my mind that a guy like Tobin would try to pick a fight. I might expect something like that from a stereotypical jock or something, but starting a confrontation seemed so against Tobin's nature. But then again, I'd known him for only a couple of days. I'd assumed he was like CeCe because they share a similar inner song, but maybe I don't know as much about his nature as I thought.

And the fact that this Haden guy hadn't even tried to fight back when Tobin attacked made me question—ever so slightly— if my assumptions about him had been incorrect, too.

"I'm sorry," Tobin says. "I wasn't planning on starting anything with him, but it's like I saw him and something came over me." I hear strange notes coming off him—the same low, cold tone I'd noticed in music class. Right before he was about to confide in me.

"Does this have something to do with what you were going to tell me before?" I ask him.

"Yes. It's just that . . ." Tobin trails off, and I hear someone else's voice in the background. "Yeah, Mom. In a minute," he says away from the receiver. "I've got to go, Daph. I'm not supposed to be on the phone."

"It's just what?" I ask before he can hang up, my curiosity edging into my voice. "You can't say something like that and not finish. *Again.*"

"You're still coming to the party Friday night?" he asks.

For half a second, I don't know what he's talking about, and then I remember that he was in the middle of inviting me to a party for the music department when we discovered Pear Perkins in the lake. "Stop trying to change the subject."

"I'm not. Are you still coming?"

"Your mom is still having the party?" I thought she might cancel, considering what had happened to one of the invitees.

"She's even more determined to throw it after what happened to Pear. She thinks it will be nice for the music department to come together and collectively send their goodwill vibes to Pear. That and she already paid the caterer. Besides, she wants to meet my costar."

"I don't know. . . ." The last thing I feel like doing is celebrating my part in the play, and considering Tobin is the only one in the music department who is willing to talk to me, I'm pretty sure everyone else probably feels the same way. But then again, since Tobin is the only one of them still acknowledging my existence, it might not be the best idea to alienate him by not accepting his invitation.

"Come, okay?" Tobin whispers into the phone. "I'm suspended through Friday, so I won't get a chance to see you until then."

"You're still trying to change the subject."

"The *subject* is the reason I want you to come. I need to show you something."

"Okay. I'll be there. But this had better be worth the wait."

"It is," he says, and hangs up.

chapter twenty-five

HADEN

"A party?" I ask Dax as he pulls a glossy pair of shoes from a box and sets them in front of me. "Are you sure this is the best next step?" It has been four days since I have seen Daphne. Four long, mind-numbing days in which I have been forced to stay inside Simon's house while on suspension, and now Dax wants my second sanctioned excursion into the world to be at a party. "And while wearing *this* around my neck? I'll look like a fool," I say, tugging at the long, striped length of cloth that he has tied so tightly around my collar, it feels like a noose.

Dax swats my hand away and fixes the knot I've loosened. "Everyone will be wearing ties. This is the party of the year."

Simon worked his magic, or pulled some strings, or whatever it is he does, and managed to *procure* me an invitation to the mayor's party—along with a spot in Olympus Hills High's coveted music program. But I don't know which one makes me more anxious at the moment: the thought of pretending to belong in a music class or the idea of going to a human party. I have been trained in the art of combat, not in singing, dancing, and making small talk with teenage girls.

"Someone really needs to make a few adjustments to Master

Crue's lesson plans," I say, slipping my feet into the stiff shoes. "I have no idea what I am doing."

"Just play it cool," Dax says.

He has forced me to don a pair of dark gray slacks and a white button-up shirt. Contrary to his protests, I have pushed the sleeves of the shirt up past my elbows, but I make sure the scars on my arm, which spell out Daphne's name, are covered. I feel overly warm and suffocated in these clothes. "I don't understand. You want me to pretend to be cold?" I fake a shiver. "Like this? What's the point?"

Dax tries to stifle a laugh—not very well—and I realize I've been tripped up by another one of these "figures of speech" that I keep running into. I'm beginning to hate the English language.

"No, I mean, don't go following Daphne around the party. Pretend you barely remember who she is."

"I thought you told me not to be rude to her. Isn't indifference the same?"

"No, what I'm saying is don't act all stalkery. Let her come to you. Let her be the one to engage."

"But what if she doesn't?"

Dax looks me over and adjusts my tie one last time. "Trust me. She will."

"I don't know about all this music business," I say, stalling my departure for the party. "Perhaps joining the music department isn't the right course. I should find a different way to get closer to her."

"No," Dax says. "I think the music angle is your best shot. I've been doing some research into it and found that there's a whole neurochemistry to singing that we can use to our advantage."

I raise my eyebrows.

"There's scientific evidence that when people sing together their brains release oxytocin—that's a neurotransmitter, a chemical, that's associated with social bonding. It causes a sense of well-being and trust toward the person you're singing with."

I nod, liking the sound of that, even though I don't know how to sing.

Another concern eats at me. "But it's forbidden," I say. "Music isn't allowed in the Underrealm."

"We're not in the Underrealm anymore."

"But still . . ." The idea of outright breaking one of the Court's most steadfast rules makes me feel as though my nerves have been left exposed to the open air. "If my father finds out . . ."

"Simon signed off on this plan—granted, reluctantly—so he's not going to tell on you. Not unless you do something impulsively stupid again."

I shake my head, not wanting to rehash what I did in the grove once more.

Dax puts his hand on my shoulder. "I know it goes against everything you've been taught, but sometimes Champions have to make exceptions to the rules. Just be smart about which ones you choose to *bend*." He slaps my shoulder. "Now, go knock 'em dead."

I assume he means that I should make a good impression at the party, and not to follow the literal interpretation of that expression.

chapter twenty-six

DAPHNE

Back in Ellis, throwing a party usually meant a handful of friends, chips, dip, and a movie projected onto the side of my mom's barn. But I get the feeling the mayor's party isn't like anything I've seen in Ellis when I find the garment bag that Marta has spread out on my bed. I'd been planning on wearing one of the maxi-skirts that had come in my boxes of belongings, which arrived earlier in the week, but as I unzip the garment bag, I find the most exquisite blue dress that I have ever seen. It's a cascading silk gown, the color of brilliant blue cornflowers, with a strapless, sweetheart neckline. The boning in the ruched, crossover bodice holds tightly against my chest when I zip up the dress. The gown is lit with shimmering glass beads along the lace-trimmed empire waistline, and ruched blue silk sweeps through the floor-length skirt and trails behind me in a romantic train as I walk.

Marta has left a shoe box along with the dress. Inside, I find a pair of silver satin pumps with a crystal flower accent along the bridge of the open toe.

I pin one side of my hair back behind my ear with a silk flower, and let the rest hang long and loose. I look in my gilded mirror.

The color of my dress makes my eyes pop in my tanned face, and I can't help thinking that the design of the outfit invokes the image of the Grecian goddess of springtime.

For the first time, I feel happy that Marta knows more about what is going on in my life than I do. I would have felt like a real country bumpkin, walking into a party in a maxi-skirt and tee if other people were going to be in gowns like this.

I am about to tear the sales tag from the dress when I see the price. My mother could probably buy two new coolers for the flower shop for how much my outfit costs. Instead of ripping off the tag, I cut it off carefully with a pair of scissors I find in my vanity drawer. Maybe if I can manage to keep the dress looking really nice, I can sell it on eBay after the party. My mom won't take money from Joe, but maybe she'd take it from me.

I am not used to heels, and I am walking very carefully down the stairs, wondering how I am ever going to ride my bike to Tobin's house in this dress, when I see Joe standing in the foyer. He's wearing a slim-fitting suit that no doubt costs even more than my dress, and he's dangling a pair of car keys in his hand. I almost slip on a stair. Joe is going to the music department's party. Of course he is. He's writing the play, after all.

"Ready, love?" he says with that darned cheeky grin of his. "I thought we'd take the Porsche."

"I'm good on my bike. Maybe you should walk. Drunk driving is still a crime, even if you have a wall full of platinum records."

"That stings, Daph. That really does," he says, clutching his chest dramatically. "I haven't had a drink all day." He counts on his fingers. "Three days, actually."

As I get closer to him, I do notice the lack of a liquor smell lingering in the air. He's even splashed on a bit of cologne, removed his longer extensions so his hair now frames his chin, and shaved. He looks better without the stubble.

"Good for you. I can still take my bike."

"Good luck in that dress," he says.

He does have a point. "I'll walk, then."

"Sorry, deary, it'll be dark soon, and if you think I'm letting you out on those paths after what happened to that Perkins girl, you've got another thing coming. I nearly had a heart attack last time."

"She's the one who had the heart attack."

"Sorry. Wrong phrasing, but the gist is, I'm driving you to the party or you're not going at all."

I give Joe a look that shows that I'm not amused. I don't know where he gets off thinking he can pick and choose when to act like a real father. Though I'd be lying if I didn't admit that part of me almost likes it. If his driving me to a party is enough to keep him from yucking it up with his good old buddies Jack and Daniels, it at least says something about him. What that something is, I'm not quite sure.

"Okay, we can go together. If you let *me* drive the Porsche," I say, because a red Porsche is always more preferable to a yellow bike when making an entrance at a party.

"Do you know how to drive a stick shift?" Joe asks wearily.

"No, but I'm a fast learner."

He hesitates for a moment.

"I can always walk. . . ."

"Fine," he says, and hands over the keys. "You look stunning in that dress, by the way. I knew that color would be perfect with your eyes."

"You picked out my dress?"

"Does that surprise you?" he says with a wink and grin.

Part of me wants to go back upstairs and change into my maxi-skirt just to spite him, but the part of me that has never felt so beautiful in my life manages to win out. "Thank you," I say softly.

"Now let's go party, shall we?" he says, offering me his arm.

The mayor's mansion is on the exact opposite side of the lake from Joe's place, so it takes us a while to drive there—mostly because I keep stalling out the Porsche. I am surprised at how well Joe has managed to keep his cool as we grind our way into Tobin's driveway. We stop in a long line of cars waiting for valets at the front door.

"Right here's good enough," Joe says, gritting his teeth. "We'll just let the valet come to us. How's that?"

We idle in silence for a few minutes. There hadn't been much time for talking on the drive over except for Joe's strangled instructions on how to shift gears. "So . . . ," he says awkwardly, and I know an attempt at conversation is coming. Joe gives me a grin that reminds me of the stray dogs my mom is prone to bringing home. Long, reaching notes fill his voice as he asks, "What are your thoughts about the opera? Are you excited to be playing Eurydice? What do your friends think?"

I can't help laughing. Doesn't he realize that because of his "grand gesture," I don't have any friends? Other than Tobin, that is. I'd thought I didn't care about meeting new people when I agreed to come to Olympus Hills, that I'd come just for the music, but after almost a whole week of having nobody to talk to at school, with Tobin out on suspension and the Sopranos' black-balling me, I'd never felt so lonely. In Ellis, I had people to eat lunch with and hang out with on the weekends—here, I spend most of my free time writing new songs so I'll look too busy to care when the Sopranos pass me, talking behind their hands.

And I miss CeCe. I'd never been super-BFF-close with any of my school friends. But CeCe—despite her being almost five years older than me—and I had been supertight ever since she came to Ellis when I was eleven. Except now I've been gone for a week and still haven't been able to get her to call me back. And my calls are all going straight to voice mail. Jonathan says she took the week off with the flu, but I can only think that she's superpissed at me for abandoning her. And it only made things worse that today is her birthday.

But it's more than the friends thing that irks me so much about Joe's big surprise. It's the same reason I wanted to change out of this gown when I'd heard he'd picked it out for me. Anger rises up my spine, and I find myself wishing I had changed.

"I'm not your puppet, Joe. You can't just offer to buy me nice things or dress me up pretty and put me in some play and make me sing the words you've written—and pretend it makes up for every minute of my life that you've ignored me. You should have told me about your plans beforehand. You should have asked me if I wanted to be part of it."

Joe's grin vanishes. "I thought you'd be happy. I'm just trying to help. . . ." As they fall flat, I realize those reaching notes coming off him were the sounds of eagerness.

He really thinks he's helping me, I realize. Mr. Morgan says that Olympus Hills productions usually bring in a huge audience, but with a name like Joe's backing the opera, scouts from all the major music colleges, not to mention Broadway, and probably big recording labels will show up for opening night. This is a billion times bigger than that talent competition I'd wanted to enter back in Utah. Normally, I'd kill for a break as big as this one. I'd work my butt off to take advantage of every second of the opportunity, and a part like this is exactly the reason I'd agreed to come to Olympus Hills. But I wanted to get the part because I'd earned it, because I'd put in the hard work—not because Joe gave it to me.

Maybe Mr. Morgan *had* given me the part because of my audition. Tobin and Iris had said that I'd done an amazing job. But the suspicion (in both my mind and every other student's) would always be there—that I'd gotten the part only because I am Joe Vince's daughter.

I want people to hear my voice when I sing. Not his.

I want them to see me. Not just a shadow of Joe.

"It's fine," I say. "I'm sure the play will be great."

I suddenly feel the urge to put a little distance between the two of us. I pull the car's emergency brake and open the door. "I'll find you when I want to go home," I say, and exit the Porsche.

There are luxury cars galore lining the street in front of the mayor's mansion, and I'm not the only one who's showing up with an escort, based on the number of adults who mill about in suits and fancy gowns. I don't see one maxi-skirt in the group of students who are all dressed more like they are going to the Metropolitan Opera than a school party. Clearly, no one is going to be eating chips and dip.

I walk through the house at the behest of the doorman and follow orchestra music out into the backyard. The mayor's house isn't as large as Joe's, but the yard is at least ten times the size, large enough to accommodate the band *and* space for a dance floor on the stone patio alone. The decor of the party is a modern fusion of ancient Greek and Japanese influences that would make a designer like Jonathan drool. Glowing, cube-shaped lanterns hang from every tree, and lotus blossoms cupping tea-light candles float on the surface of the pool. Partygoers fill the yard, some dancing, others talking in small groups, their happy chatter mixing with the music from the orchestra.

I look for Tobin but I don't see him anywhere in the crowd, so I make my way to the long buffet tables that take up most of the north side of the yard. A spread of every kind of food imaginable sits on elevated tiers on white satin tablecloths. Floral arrangements of orchids, tulips, cherry blossoms, hyacinths, and narcissus cascade from tall Grecian-looking urns on the buffet. I pick up a plate made of thin bone china, from the stack at the end of the table, and make my way through the culinary paradise in front of me. I don't even know the name of some of the foods, but I do recognize the sushi rolls, because Jonathan has a weakness for late-night infomercial shopping and once bought a "create your own sushi" kit. I use silver tongs to pick up pieces from two rolls that look familiar, and then a third one that looks scary. Like it has spider legs sticking out of the ends.

I take two desserts. One is a piece of baklava, and the other is something a waiter informs me is a mini taiyaki—a traditional Japanese fish-shaped treat made from a crispy waffle on the outside with sweet jam on the inside.

Another waiter in a tux offers me a flute of champagne.

"Um, I'm only sixteen," I say, waving the glass away.

I hear tittering notes from behind me. I turn and see Lexie and the Sopranos nearby, each holding a glass of champagne. I look around and notice they're not the only underage drinkers at the party. Considering this is a school-related event, hosted at the *mayor's* house, I am surprised that none of the adults seems to care. That sort of thing would never fly in Utah.

Lexie's eyes seem trained on my every move, like she's judging the way I've arranged the veggies from the sculpture of crudités on my plate. I shove a piece of rainbow roll in my mouth and give her a sarcastic little wave. She drains her glass of champagne, takes a second glass from the waiter, and then says something I can't hear to her friends. I gather the meaning, when two seconds later, she and the Sopranos turn on the heels of their designer shoes in a coordinated move, so all I can see of them are their backs. I swallow my bite of sushi—almost sighing at how amazing it tastes compared to Jonathan's homemade creations—take my plate, and leave the buffet.

I nibble my food and wander the party for a while, looking for Tobin. When my efforts prove to be fruitless, I make my way through the crowd toward the patio and the one somewhat friendly face I've seen all evening.

"I see I'm still being stonewalled by the Sopranos," I say to Iris, and bite off the pointy end of an asparagus spear. "And it seems to be contagious." I use my veggie to point out a line of short freshman girls who have followed Lexie's example and have turned their backs toward me.

"I know. I'd better be careful. I could get totally blacklisted by the Sopranos just for talking to you." Iris smiles, but I can tell from the shaky notes coming off of her that it's something she's actually worried about. She's being polite to me because she's too nice not to be.

I clear my throat. "Have you seen Tobin?" His assertion that he had something to show me is the only reason—besides the food, I'll admit—that I'm still here. I've been waiting almost a week to see what it is, after all.

Iris glances over her shoulder at the Sopranos to see if they're watching. "Haven't seen him yet. Maybe he's in the kitchen with the caterers?"

"Thanks. I'll leave you alone now," I say, and start to turn away.

"Hey," Iris says. "I don't think they're right, you know. I heard you sing at the auditions. You might not have seniority, but you still deserve the part. I . . . I just can't afford to make enemies. Being a schollie and all."

I nod. "Thanks, and I get it." Being a scholarship kid in a world populated by the spawn of the rich and famous is probably anything but easy. I can't blame her too much for being afraid of Lexie and her mafia.

"They'll probably move on to a new target soon," Iris says, trying to sound reassuring. "Like the new guy. Once word gets out that Mr. Morgan let him into the program without an audition, they'll be out for his blood—no matter how hot he is."

"New guy?" I ask.

A weird feeling rushes through me—I can't tell if it's anticipation or dread.

"Over there." She gives a quick nod toward the large magnolia tree that's dripping with shimmering lanterns, near the pool.

I follow her quick gesture. I'm not sure if I expected to see anyone else, or if I knew it would be him all along.

But there is Haden, standing under the tree, nursing a glass that looks like it's filled with Coke, right in Tobin's backyard. There had been one nice thing about the last week: Haden's suspension meant that I hadn't had to think about him—much—in the last few days.

"*He's* in the music department now?" I ask.

But where the heck is Tobin? I have a feeling this party will go south pretty quickly if he sees this unexpected guest.

"That's what Bridgette said."

I don't wait for her to fill in any more details and head toward the tree where Haden stands. He doesn't look at me. Just takes a sip of his Coke and lifts his glass toward a few sophomore girls, who pass him, giggling. The girls are giggling, that is, not Haden. The way his lips are set on his stony face, I wonder if he ever laughs. Or smiles, for that matter.

I stop and watch him for a few minutes, all the time wondering if he's ever going to look up at me, until a girl in a purple satin gown stumbles into him. He catches her before she falls over. She laughs, and I realize it's Lexie. Obviously, no Soprano memo to blackball Haden has gone out yet. She smiles up at him—way up, considering she's way more than a foot shorter than he is, even when she's wearing heels. She tries to wrap an arm around his neck, but he politely pushes her hand away. In her other hand, she holds a champagne flute, and I wonder how many of those she's drained since the two I saw her with.

I'm guessing quite a few, from the way she's swaying in her pumps.

Having a biological father who clearly has a problem with alcohol, I'd always resisted the temptation to sneak a beer behind the Ellis Filler-Up on Friday nights with some of the kids from my old school. And watching Lexie make a fool of herself as Haden walks her over to Bridgette and deposits her nonchalantly with the Sopranos, I still don't see the appeal of getting drunk.

I've watched too many *Where Are They Now?* specials on VH1 at CeCe's apartment to know that talent won't get you very far without a little bit of self-control. It's a miracle Joe hadn't washed up years ago.

Haden returns to his tree, glass of Coke in his hand. He takes another sip and pulls a slight gagging face, like he can't stand the taste. I wonder why he keeps drinking it. And why does he seem to look at everyone here except me?

I scan the party again for Tobin and when I look back at Haden, I catch his eyes on me for a split second before he looks away at the pool.

So he has seen me.

"You're being too obvious," I say, approaching him.

"Pardon?" he asks, his eyebrows raised, breaking up the stoniness of his features.

"You're still stalking me, and you're being quite obvious about it."

"You're being very flattering of yourself," he says.

"Excuse me?"

"What makes you think I'm here to see you?"

"Maybe the fact that you tried to grab me the other night?"

"I haven't the foggiest idea what you are talking about."

"Whatever," I say. "I want my stuff back, by the way."

He raises his eyebrows again, as if he really doesn't have any idea of what I'm referring to. Like he's not the one who took my tote from the grove.

"So we're still playing that game?" I ask.

I don't break eye contact with him until he holds out his hand and asks, "Will you dance with me?"

I am so startled by this proposition, I don't know how to respond. Luckily, the screech of a microphone as the music stops saves me from having to do so. I turn toward the sound.

"May I have your attention?" A woman in a red gown calls into the microphone from the bandstand on the patio. The crowd of students and parents quiet down and turn their attention to her.

Tobin and a very dapper-looking Japanese man, who I assume is Tobin's father, stand by her side. "I am happy to welcome you all to our home today," the woman who must be Mayor Winters says. "You've all worked so hard to get here, and I am as proud of you as I am of my own son. However, I do think Tobin deserves a round of applause for landing the lead in this year's play."

She starts the applause and everyone in the crowd—except Haden, who has retreated behind the magnolia tree, I notice—joins in. Next, the mayor leads the crowd in a rollicking welcome for Joe, who seems to be enjoying the company of several women in short cocktail-length dresses near the bar.

"And where is your costar, Toby?" she asks. "I hear she's quite lovely."

Even from where I stand, I can see the blush in Tobin's cheeks. He finds me in the crowd and points me out to his mother. The mayor attempts to start a round of applause for me, but I am not surprised that it sounds much more feeble than for Tobin.

"I hope you will enjoy the party," Mayor Winters says. "We will be sending the floral arrangements to Pear Perkins's hospital room, so please be sure to sign the get-well card that is circulating the party. We want to do everything we can to take care of our own here in Olympus Hills." She smiles, showing gleaming white teeth behind her ruby red lipstick. "Oh, and do be sure to help yourselves to the spider rolls; they're an Oshiro family specialty."

And with another round of applause, Mayor Winters and her husband head down the patio steps, shaking hands with party guests as they go. The orchestra strikes up again, and couples head out onto the dance floor. I slip past them and head for Tobin, who is accepting the congratulations of a man wearing a pale yellow scarf. Tobin smiles when he sees me approach and excuses himself from the conversation.

"Yowza, Daphne," he says, looking me over. "I take it back. I *was* asking you to be my date tonight."

"Too late," I say with a smile.

He looks even more Frank Sinatra–esque in a black suit, bow tie, and a black fedora sitting on his head at a rakish angle. With my heels on, I tower over him even more than usual, but he doesn't seem to mind.

"Wanna dance?" he says.

"No," I say. "I want to hear about this big secret of yours."

He takes my hand and gestures me toward the house. "Like I said, it's something I need to show you."

chapter twenty-seven

HADEN

To my utter astonishment, Dax's plan to get Daphne to come to me seems to be working. Daphne moves closer and closer as the party progresses. She's standing only a few feet away now.

Between trying to dodge the disgusting-smelling food at the buffet, warding off the attention of some short girl named Lexie, and pretending to be overly fascinated by the tree that grows near the pool, I've done a rather decent impression of being aloof. I don't follow her, and I don't look at her unless I am sure she isn't watching. Which is an experiment in self-control, considering how she looks in that dress.

I had already been fascinated by the curves of her body, but the way that dress hugs and emphasizes them makes me wonder why everyone at this party isn't staring at her. I am astonished that people are actually turning away from her. She reminds me of the paintings of our goddess that adorn the walls of the palace. The blue of her dress brings out the color of her eyes and complements the tanned skin on her exposed shoulders. . . .

I glance away quickly, realizing I've been caught looking.

I take a sip of the dark, bubbling liquid in my glass. It burns my throat as I swallow. When I look up, Daphne is standing right in front of me. She says something snide.

And I ruin everything when I open my big dung spout of a mouth to reply. I'm not even sure what I've said that annoys her so much, but she's staring me down like she'd rather punch me in the face than speak to me again. I can't think of what to do next. The music and smells cloud my judgment. Not to mention *that dress* . . .

Her stare intensifies. I say the first thing that comes to mind. "Will you dance with me?"

I hold out my hand. I don't know how to dance but I hope I will pick it up as quickly as driving. That is, if she'll accept my offer.

I don't get to find out.

The music stops, and the woman I saw in the vice principal's office, the mayor, I realize, calls for everyone's attention. She starts talking and I see her son standing beside her.

Kopros. I am at the home of the boy who tried to attack me in the cafeteria.

I duck behind the tree until after the woman is done talking. I want to try to strike up another conversation with Daphne, but before I have the chance, she heads in Tobin's direction. They speak for a moment, and then she takes his hand and they enter the house. Together.

I'm not going to follow her. That would be against Dax's advice, and the last thing I want is to be accused of stalking her again. I'm not going to go into the house to see what they're doing. But I don't see the harm in watching through the windows. . . .

The lights are on in the house and the shutters open. I walk around the side of the mansion until I am near the gate that leads into the front yard. I see Tobin and Daphne enter an unoccupied room together. Tobin leans down and pulls something from a drawer. I am tempted to climb the trellis next to the window to see what he is showing her.

But I bristle when I hear a familiar, chipper voice speaking to the doorman out front.

"It doesn't matter if the mayor is having a party. She will be delighted to meet with me."

"She'll be delighted to meet with you," the doorman responds mechanically, and invites Simon into the house.

I climb the gate that separates the backyard from the front yard, trying to get a better view into the windows of the foyer. My attention already torn between trying to ascertain what Daphne and Tobin are up to, and trying to figure out why Simon would be meeting with the mayor in the middle of her party, when something else pulls at me. The hairs on the back of my neck bristle, and I suddenly feel as though I am being watched.

I scan the backyard, but it seems as though none of the party-goers has noticed me perched on top of the gate. I look behind me into the front yard, and then beyond to the road. The light from one of the street lamps glints off the visor of the helmet of a man sitting on an idling black motorcycle. His face is completely covered by the helmet, but I can tell by the way his head is angled that he is either watching me or has a strange fascination with cedarwood fences. A catering van pulls up to the curb, blocking him from my view—and me from his.

I tell myself that he is probably just waiting to rendezvous with a party guest and noticed a teenager sitting on the gate in the middle of the mayor's yard, and I turn my attention back to the windows of the room Daphne had entered. Only now she and Tobin are gone, and Simon and the mayor have replaced them in the room, seemingly locked in an intense conversation.

chapter twenty-eight

DAPHNE

Tobin leads me down a long hall toward the front of the mansion. He stops and waits until one of the waiters passes, with a silver tray of tempura shrimp, before we duck through a set of French doors into a room I assume is his mother's office. There are glass cases displaying various vases and artifacts lined up along the edges of the room. Some look Asian in origin, but most of them look like relics from ancient Greece or Rome.

"Is your mom a collector or something?"

Tobin puts a finger to his lips to quiet me. "Yeah," he whispers. "But none of this is what I wanted to show you." He leads me to a large mahogany desk and opens one of the drawers.

"What are you doing?"

From the way he's acting, I almost think he's planning on pulling a heist in his mother's office—and using me as his accomplice—but what he pulls from the drawer is hardly something valuable. In terms of money, that is. It looks like an old family photo.

"Notice anything weird about this picture?"

There are a lot of weird things about this photo. It's at least seven years old, based on how old Tobin looks in the picture, but

I wouldn't have guessed it was his family from appearance. The woman in the photo has long, naturally curly, auburn hair and a daisy tucked behind her ear, and the Japanese man in the photo has hair almost to his shoulders, and wears a beaded necklace and a T-shirt with a windmill design on the front. Besides their faces, they barely resemble the dapper power couple of the mayor and her husband. There's another boy in the photo who looks to be a few years older than Tobin.

"Who's that?"

"My brother, Sage," Tobin says. "He went off to MIT a couple of years ago."

"MIT. I'm guessing he wasn't as into singing as you are?"

"No. He's a mechanical genius, just like my parents."

"Your parents?" Then I recognize the windmill design on his father's T-shirt. "Wait. I've heard your last name before. Oshiro-Winters Wind Energy. Your parents own one of the largest alternative energy companies in the West. They built a wind farm a few miles outside Ellis a few years ago."

"Owned," he corrects me. "They went public and sold out just before we moved to Olympus Hills. They retired at forty, except for my mom going into local politics and all. They were total hippies, and now they're the ultimate yuppies."

"I'll say." I point at the picture. "Your mom looks like she could have been on the cover of a Simon and Garfunkel album."

"But that's not the weirdest thing about this picture. Do you see it?" He points out the way his brother Sage's hand seems to float, as if it were resting on an invisible person's shoulder.

"Is there someone *missing* from this picture?"

"My sister, Abbie."

I think back to the only other time Tobin had mentioned his

sister—in the grove. "Your sister. The one you said liked to go to the grove with her friends. . . . Before she ran away?"

Tobin nods. "It happened six months after my parents got rich and moved to Olympus Hills. They were so upset when she went missing. But not like worried upset, like angry upset."

"Is that why they Photoshopped her out of this picture?"

"Not just this picture. All of our pictures. I can barely remember what she looks like sometimes. They say she dishonored the family. They won't even speak her name these days. But the thing is, Daphne, sometimes, I don't think she ran away. Sometimes, I think . . . that she was taken."

"Taken. Like kidnapped? What do your parents think?"

"They think I'm nuts. She left a note on her computer, and my dad says the PI he hired to check it out couldn't find anything to suggest there was foul play involved. But that note didn't sound like the Abbie I knew. It was more like someone else had written it for her."

"That's insane. I mean, not that I think you're insane. That's just some pretty intense stuff. I mean, you were what, like, ten years old when this happened?"

He nods. "I was the last person to see her, you know. I was out riding my bike around the lake and I saw her crossing that bridge that leads into the grove only a couple of hours before she didn't show up for dinner. She wasn't alone."

I raise my eyebrows, asking the question I can't quite put to words.

"He was a new friend of hers from school—a visiting student from the East Coast. His last name was Lord and he looked an awful lot like this Haden guy."

"What?" I say, completely confused.

"That's why I flipped out at school on Monday. After hearing your description of Haden and hearing his last name . . . Something just came over me and I thought . . ."

"That he was the guy you saw with your sister? But that was what, six years ago? Haden would have been, like, ten or eleven. It couldn't have been him."

"I'm not saying it was him. They just share the same *look*, you know? Maybe he was, like, a brother or a cousin. All I know is that someone from this Lord family was with my sister just before she disappeared." Tobin pulls a small key from his pocket. "But here's where things start to get really weird, Daphne. I think there have been others."

"Other what?"

Tobin crouches next to his mother's desk and starts to unlock a large file drawer. "Other girls who've been taken from this place."

"Tobin!" a stern voice interrupts us. Tobin stops what he's doing and slips the key back into his pocket and shoves the family photo under the desk as Mayor Winters appears in the doorway. "What are you doing in here? I have a meeting."

There's a man with her, but he's obviously not Tobin's father. He's wearing bike shorts and an Under Armour tee, and there's a bike helmet covering most of his head. What kind of meeting was the mayor having with him in the middle of a party?

"Sorry," Tobin says, quickly stepping away from her desk.

"Your father has been looking for you. It is impolite to neglect your other party guests for so long."

The man in the bike shorts grins merrily. "Now, now,

Rosemary. Don't be so hard on the boy. Kids will be kids," he says, with a little bit too much twinkle in his tone.

Tobin clears his throat. "Again, my apologies, Mother," he says with a slight bow, and leaves the room.

I follow after him, wondering if I should bow also. The mayor stops me just before I exit the office. She taps my shoulder with one of her long, manicured, red fingernails. "I hear you're the one who told security you thought the Perkins girl was attacked. You know it's a crime to give a false report, don't you?"

I shake my head. "I didn't lie." I almost add that the guy I suspected of doing Pear harm is currently in her backyard, but I don't like the way she's staring at me. Like she could have me locked up with only a single phone call.

"Tobin is a good boy," she says. "I wouldn't want him to make friends with anyone who might encourage him to behave otherwise." She glances at the desk drawer that Tobin had been about to unlock. Is she insinuating that he was poking around in her stuff under my influence? "Thank you for inviting me to your party," I say, not knowing how else to respond, and leave the room.

By the time I make it back outside, Tobin has been entrapped by his father into greeting their various guests, so I decide it's time for me to make my exit.

I'm already tired of this so-called party.

I don't see Joe anywhere—he's probably off somewhere with that gaggle of women and a bottle of champagne—so I decide to walk home, despite how dark it's gotten. I keep snagging the train of my dress with my heels, so I remove my shoes and leave them on the hood of Joe's Porsche, which is parked along the road.

I set off barefoot on one of the lonely lake paths, only to find myself not quite so alone after all. A very short girl in a very tight purple dress is hunched over a trash bin at a fork in the path— in the process of losing her dinner. She heaves one last time and stumbles in her ridiculously high heels.

"Lexie?"

She steadies herself with the rim of the trash can and looks up at me, wiping the corner of her mouth with the back of her hand. "What are you looking at?"

"Are you okay?" I ask. "Bad sushi?" More like too much drinky, but whatever.

She narrows her eyes at me. "Why do you care?"

I shrug, not sure why, either. "Do you need help getting home?"

"Why would I need help from you? You don't even exist," she says, turning her back on me.

"This stonewalling thing is stupid, you know. You can't pretend I don't exist when I'm the lead of the play." I am so burned out from Joe, the party, trying to process Tobin's revelation, and my encounter with his cranky mother that I'm ready to just lay into Lexie and tell her what I really think of her and her elitist little mafia. Do they really think they're so much better than everyone else?

Lexie reels around, nearly toppling over in her shoes. "You think you're so much better than me, don't you?"

"What?"

"You think you're so great because your dad is some middle-aged rock star." She points a finger at me. "You think you can come waltzing in here with your long neck and your long legs and steal the part that should be mine. I've been working on Mr. Morgan for the last two years to get to be the star, and now it's like he's lost his mind. I mean, you're a contralto or whatever you are. Contraltos never get the lead. And you'd look ridiculous onstage with Tobin. Look at you, you're like a . . . like a . . . giraffe or an albatross or something."

"Ostrich," I say.

"Huh?"

"You called me an albatross, but I think you meant ostrich. An albatross is like a seagull. Ostriches are the birds with long necks. If you're going to insult me, at least get it right."

"What, now you're a freaking brain, too?" She puts her hands on her hips. "But all you really are is a pathetic little brownnoser, or whatever you call someone who uses her daddy to get whatever she wants."

"I barely even know him. I had no idea this play was the reason he wanted to bring me here, so don't blame me, okay?" I reach for her arm. "Let's just get you home."

Lexie pulls away from me. "I don't need your help. I can get myself home." She takes a couple of unsteady steps down the path to the right of the fork that make it clear she does need help.

"Isn't your house the other direction?" I call after her.

She responds with her middle finger. I stand at the fork in the path and watch her disappear around the bend of the tree-lined trail. Most of me wants to just let her go. She deserves to get lost in her drunken state for being such a brat. But then I realize that the path she took leads to the bridge to the grove, and I remember what happened the last time I let someone head in that direction when I should have stopped her.

"Lexie?" I call after her.

She doesn't respond and I can't see her anymore, so I start after her. I've only taken about six steps when I hear a noise that sounds like something falling over, followed by a muffled swearword from

Lexie. I smile, guessing she tripped in her shoes.

But then a horrible noise fills the air. At first, it starts as a low hiss and then grows higher pitched and grating. It reminds me of the screeching squeal of bad car brakes—only higher and much louder. It reverberates around me, making me shiver. When the noise dies away, Lexie's frantic scream replaces it.

Without thinking, I run in the direction of her scream. I think I hear footsteps following me, but it's probably just the pounding of my heart in my ears. I don't dare look back. I round a corner in the path and stumble over something. I fall hard on my knees and see, lying on its side like a lifeless corpse, one of Lexie's gold shoes on the ground in front of me.

At first, I can't find Lexie. The path in front of me seems empty. I look deeper into the woods that line the path, and see her. She's on the ground, backed up against a large tree about ten feet away from me. She holds her hands up defensively and shouts for help. That's when I realize there's someone—or something— else in the trees with her. At least I think I detect movement in the shadows beside her. It's so dark, all I can see is the outline of a large black form standing over her. Or maybe it's just the shifting shadows of tree branches. Then the shadow seems to swoop down toward Lexie.

"Get away from her," I shout, and grab the closest thing that resembles a weapon. Lexie's very pointy shoe. I push myself up from the asphalt path and lob the shoe at the shadowed outline. It passes right through it.

I am sure it's just a shadow now, except it seems to turn in my direction.

That terrible screeching noise fills the air again. It seems to echo off the trees and slice into my ears. I can't tell if it comes from the shadow or from somewhere behind me. I swallow hard and launch myself at Lexie. I wrap my arms around her protectively as the shadow engulfs us. Lexie buries her face against my shoulder, her curly hair blocking my view of the shadow.

I do the only thing that I can think of next. I scream.

My voice echoes around me, almost as loud as the screeching squeal, matching it in pitch. I feel the shudder of the shadow against my skin, but I don't dare look at it. A second later, a burst of lightning explodes just over our heads. I scream again. Lexie flails. The light illuminates the terror on her face before I clamp my eyes shut to protect them from the brightness. My lids are down only for half a second, but when I open my eyes, she and I are alone beside the path. The shadow is gone.

But, no. I am wrong. We're not completely alone. Electricity tingles in the air around me as I push myself up to get a better look at the boy who stands on the opposite side of the path.

chapter twenty-nine

HADEN

Another surge of electricity builds in my chest as I watch her approach. I try to push it down, but I'm fighting the adrenaline rush of what just happened.

"Haden?" she asks. "Is that you?"

So she's seen me. There's no running away now. That would only make matters worse. I don't know where the *thing* went—its scent has evaporated from the air—so there's no point in trying to go after it. She moves even closer. Her eyes lock on mine. She brushes her hands up and down her arms, marveling at the way the fine hairs on her skin stand on end from the electricity that still crackles in the air around us.

She looks up, and I can tell that she's noting that there isn't a cloud in the sky.

"How?" she says. "What . . . what just happened?"

I don't know how to answer that question. I don't know the how or why of it all, either. It should be impossible. The shadow beast—that *thing* that attacked—I think I know what it is, but it shouldn't be possible. How could it be here?

It was the smell that sent me after Daphne. I was still sitting on the gate, intent on trying to read Simon's and Mayor Winters's lips—making a mental note to research how to do that better on YouTube—in order to follow their conversation, when I saw Daphne leaving the party alone. I wasn't going to follow, noting how Dax would approve of my restraint, when I caught the strange smell on the breeze.

It was the metallic tinge of blood in the air, followed by the wafting scent of sulfur.

It was enough to make me forget about Simon and the mayor. I jumped down into the front yard, following the smell. I bypassed the catering van in the driveway, and noticed that the helmeted man and his motorcycle were gone. My footsteps quickened as I realized the sulfuric scent led in the same direction that Daphne had gone. But it was the scream that sent me running.

I wouldn't have believed the scene I came upon if I hadn't seen it with my own eyes. The short girl, Lexie, was cowering against a tree trunk, seemingly under attack by some sort of shadow creature—and Daphne had thrown herself in the middle, using herself as a shield to protect the other girl as the shadow swirled around them. I didn't understand it. Why would Daphne help this girl, who, for all that I could tell, had been cruel to her all night? The thought snapped away from me as the shadowy thing reared back, as if preparing to take a swipe at the girls. Daphne screamed, and the thing seemed to quiver. For the briefest of moments, it seemed to take solid form. I thought maybe I had just imagined it or my eyes were just playing tricks on me, but I caught a glimpse of feathers and claws before it turned back into a misty shadow again.

"No," I whispered out loud. *It can't be.* A pulse of electricity flooded through my body. I directed it into my arms, then hands, then fingertips, and flung it at the creature. The lightning passed right through the misty creature and exploded against a tree only a few feet from the girls. Lexie wailed, clasping her hands over her head. Daphne screamed. The creature became solid once more, long enough for me to see only the look of shock—or perhaps recognition—in its red eyes as it glared at me. It went misty again and then vanished altogether, evaporating into the shadows that surround the path.

Another surge of lightning crackled up my body. I knew I should go after the creature. It's not injured. I'd probably only frightened it away. It could attack again. But how could I stop something that I couldn't strike?

It's the sound of Daphne's gasp that made me hesitate. She'd seen me and was approaching tentatively, leaving Lexie looking as though she had fainted against a tree.

"What just happened?" she asks again.

I don't say anything. I don't even know what I *would* say.

"What was that?"

I shake my head as if to say I don't know. But I do. I recognized it for what it is, just like it recognized me as an Underlord.

But I have no idea how a Keres could have gotten here.

"You saw it, though. Please tell me you saw it?" I can see the pleading in her eyes. She wants me to reassure her that she's not crazy.

"I don't know what you're talking about."

"What? You had to have seen the shadow and the lightning."

"A shadow and lightning?" I ask, edging my voice with incredulity. "That's what you saw?"

"Yes. I mean, no. I mean, it was *more* than that!" She throws her hands up in frustration. Deep red stains paint her palms. Her dress is torn. "Geez, security is going to think I'm even more of a loon."

I swallow hard, but it isn't the thought of security guards that concerns me. "Are you bleeding?" I try to keep my voice even and not betray any sign of panic.

She looks at her hands. "Oh. It's not mine. I think Lexie fell."

We both look at Lexie. She's curled up in a fetal position, her hair splayed out around her head. One of her knees is coated in blood. It smears down her leg.

I know now why the Keres went after her. Master Crue taught us that the Keres are attracted to the smell of blood. It's how they find their victims.

"We need to get her out of here." I scoop the tiny girl up in my arms. She groans a little and blinks at me a couple of times, so I know she's not really unconscious, but it'll be faster if I carry her. "I need you to come with me," I say to Daphne.

She hesitates. I can feel her reluctance to go anywhere with me. I guess I brought that upon myself with what I tried to do in the grove.

"It isn't safe here. We need to get your friend home."

"So you did see something?" she asks. I can hear both the hope and the fear in her voice.

I don't answer.

I set a quick pace for us, hoping to get away from the grove before the Keres decides to return. It seems to be concentrating its hunting activities on this side of the lake, but that isn't a guarantee that it wouldn't stray in order to come after us. I can hear Daphne's breath quicken as she tries to keep up with me. Getting away from the Keres's hunting grounds isn't my only motivation for moving quickly—if I keep Daphne out of breath long enough, she won't be able to ask any more questions.

The short girl regained herself enough to tell me her address and then she nestled her head against my shoulder and seemed to go to sleep. I used my iPhone for directions.

We have just deposited a very dazed-looking Lexie into the arms of an equally confused-looking housekeeper at the girl's home—the air is clear of any hints of sulfur, so I feel safe leaving her in the care of someone else—when Daphne turns to me with a concerned expression on her face.

I know what's coming. . . .

"She isn't my friend."

Or maybe I don't. . . .

"What?" I ask.

"Lexie isn't my friend. I don't hang out with people like her, you know."

"Okay," I say, not sure why she's telling me this.

"She doesn't like me at all. She made that pretty clear, and then she went off toward the grove. I should have tried harder to stop her, but I didn't. Just like that Pear Perkins girl. But I wasn't thinking then. . . ." I can hear the guilt dripping from Daphne's voice, and know why she's telling me all this. She blames herself. "And then I heard her scream. . . ."

"And you went to help her?" I look her in the eyes. "Even though she treated you with such disrespect?"

"Yes," she says. Her cheeks twinge with pink.

I did not expect such bravery from a human. "That was stupid," I say, and look away from her face.

"What?"

"You should have run away."

"I'm not weak," she says, standing at her full height, which is

227

only a few inches shorter than mine. I can tell it irks her to have to look *up* to meet my eyes. "I could have—"

"Fought it?" I ask, unable to hide the amusement in my voice. This girl is unbelievable. "You think you could take on a wild animal or a monster?"

"So you do think some*thing* was out there?"

I look down at her. A soft breeze catches her golden hair, blowing a few stray strands about her face. I feel the sudden urge to reach out and catch one in my fingers. A strange heat tingles through my body at the thought. She startles—as if she can see it in my eyes. I train my face into the stony, emotionless look I have practiced since I was a child. "I think nothing of the sort."

"You're lying."

My stony mask almost cracks.

"I don't think it's a coincidence that you just happened along tonight when something weird was going on in the grove, and I don't think it was a coincidence that I saw you there before that other girl was attacked."

"She had a health scare. She wasn't attacked."

"You're lying again."

I purse my lips. What is she getting at? Does she think I tried to kill that girl? Does she think *I* was the assailant tonight? How on earth am I going to explain my way out of this? How can I ever get her to trust me?

"I think you followed me tonight because you knew something was wrong. And I think you tried to get me to leave the grove the other day because you knew it wasn't safe. You were trying to protect me."

I blink at her, not knowing how to answer. Is she really handing me the explanation I need?

"Maybe," I lie.

"But how did you know?"

I flounder for an answer. "Maybe I . . . just did." I stifle a wince, thinking I probably sound like a complete dolt.

But she nods. "I know what you mean. I felt something like it before Tobin and I found Pear. I just knew something was wrong. Is that what it was like?"

"Maybe," I say, suddenly unable to say anything else. I don't want to tell her more lies that I might need to corroborate later. I clear my throat. "Maybe . . . we should get you home," I say. "I don't know what really happened out there, but I'll go back and take a look around if it makes you feel better."

"And you're not afraid?" she asks. "What if you get hurt?"

"Do you care?"

She bites her lip, turns, and starts down the block. "Maybe," she calls back to me.

Her *maybe* sets that heat tingling under my skin again. I follow her, staying a few feet behind, not wanting to push my luck. After a couple of blocks, she stops in front of a house with a red sports car parked haphazardly in the curved driveway.

"Looks like my father beat us home," she says. "I'm good from here."

"I'll wait until you get inside."

She gives me a look I can't read and then places her hand on top of mine. The tingling under my skin shoots through my body. She pulls her hand back as if I've shocked her without realizing it.

"The strangest thing," she says, looking up at the sky, "is that it was a burst of lightning that scared that thing away, but there isn't a cloud in the sky."

I slip my stony mask back on and step away from her. "Must be some freak of nature."

She squints at me and I wonder if I've used that expression correctly.

"Freak of nature," she mumbles to herself as she heads up the driveway. She glances back at me before slipping into the house and shutting the door behind her.

I may have lied to her about why I'd tried to get her to leave the grove with me before, but I keep my word about going back there now. Lexie had been attacked on the path leading to the island. I don't find much evidence there, but when I cross the bridge and enter the grove, I find that it looks very different from when I was here last. Small saplings have been pulled up by their roots, and holes have been burrowed into the ground. It looks as though someone, or something, has been searching for something.

Is this simply the Keres's chosen hunting grounds, or had it attacked on instinct to protect whatever it had been looking for here?

But Keres are supposed to be mindless creatures—so fearsome they have been locked away in the Pits of the Underrealm for centuries. What would it be looking for?

And the more vital question—how had it escaped the Pits?

"Keres!" I say to Dax when I see him sitting in one of the armchairs, fiddling with his tablet, in the family room. He looks up at me, startled. I pant and claw at my tie, trying to get more air. I'd run all the way here in my dress clothes after inspecting the grove. "They're here. Or at least one of them is."

Dax gives me a cautioning look.

"What's all this?" Simon asks, stepping in from the kitchen,

230

one of his green smoothies in hand. I hadn't realized he was here or I would have called Dax out of the house before saying anything. He's still dressed in the tight-fitting, shiny clothing he wears when he takes his bike out for a ride around the lake each night. Only this time, he'd taken a detour to the mayor's mansion during his ride. "Care to fill me in?" he asks cheerily, his teeth gleaming white as he smiles.

My first instinct is to keep anything I know from Simon, but then I realize that he might be the one person who might be able to help. He's in communication with the Underrealm, so he could possibly get us some instructions on how to send this thing back there.

"A Keres," I say. "I think that's what really happened to that girl who supposedly had a heart attack last week. It tried to attack Daphne and one of her classmates near the lake tonight."

"What?" Dax asks. "Are they okay?"

I nod. "I scared . . . I mean, it got scared away before it did any damage," I say, catching myself before revealing to Simon that I had used my powers in close proximity to a couple of humans.

"Are you sure it was a Keres?" Dax asks. "That shouldn't be possible."

I catch a movement in the corner of my eye and notice Garrick slinking into the kitchen, listening to us as he passes. Lessers have a talent for lurking.

"I saw it. It looked just like the carvings on the walls in the palace."

"Well. That's a relief!" Simon says brightly as he places his smoothie on the table behind the couch, careful to use one of the coasters.

"A relief?" I ask. "We're talking about the most fearsome

monsters of the Underrealm and you think that's a relief?"

"They found an unconscious waitress at that party you went to this evening," Simon says, his voice far too chipper sounding for such a revelation. "I had to do some damage control and convince everyone she'd had a heart attack like I did with that student. But I was beginning to think you had some kinky fetish for stopping pretty girls' hearts, which you and I were going to have to have a little chat about. It's a relief knowing we won't have to have such an awkward conversation. I'd much rather deal with a monster on the loose."

"Then you know how to deal with it?"

Simon smiles, but there's an accusatory narrowing of his eyes. "Any thoughts on how it got here?"

I almost bring up the theory I'd postulated when Dax had told me about that Pear Perkins girl having a heart attack—that perhaps a Keres had somehow stowed away with us through the gate like Brim had. But I stop myself from mentioning it, because the last thing I want is for Simon to try to pin responsibility for this happening on me. It was a highly unlikely theory anyway. A tiny cat hiding in my bag was one thing, but a large, shadowy monster going completely unnoticed by me and the entire crowd surrounding the gate was virtually impossible.

"I think it's more important to focus on how to stop it," I say.

"Leave this to me," Simon says.

"You'll contact the Court, then? You'll ask them how to send this thing back? Or kill it?"

Simon draws one arm across his chest and uses the other to grab his elbow, pulling it tight to stretch his shoulder. "There's no need to bother the Court with this matter."

"But it could go on hurting people."

Simon shrugs. "I don't really care. I just need to clean up after it in order to keep too many people from asking questions."

I realize then that Simon is more concerned with appearances than about the people this Keres could possibly hurt. Or kill, if it gets strong enough.

Which it will, if it goes unchecked.

"Then I'll go after it myself," I say, balling my fists.

"You don't have time for such distractions," Simon says. "Leave this to me. This isn't your concern."

"But that thing almost hurt my Boon," I say. "That does concern me. And I'm sure it's only just started with its attacks. If we don't stop it now . . ."

Simon snaps his gaze in my direction. I don't look away fast enough, and he locks eyes with me. "Drop it," he says. "This conversation is over. Let me handle this."

I find myself unable to speak anymore about the topic—but I know this matter is far from being over.

chapter thirty

DAPHNE

I don't realize that I have been asleep until the sound of a phone ringing wakes me up. In my groggy, disoriented state, I find I am unable to tell if what had happened in the last few hours—the party, Lexie near the grove, strange shadows and lightning, Haden walking me home—had been real, or if I'd merely been having the strangest dream.

I blink several times and my eyes focus on the dirty, torn blue dress that's draped over the back of my vanity chair.

Nope, definitely not a dream.

The clock on my dresser tells me it's early Saturday morning. *Too early for social calls*, I think as I pick up the phone.

It's my mother.

Her voice is bordering on shrill, and the notes of concern ringing through her words are so strong that I panic, thinking she's somehow gotten wind of what happened after the party and is about to demand that I pack my bags and come home. Instead, I realize she's saying something about CeCe.

I sit up in bed with the handset pressed to my ear. "What was that?"

"Have you heard anything from CeCe in the last week?" she asks.

"No, I've left her messages, but she hasn't called back."

"Nothing? No texts or anything?"

"No," I say, not admitting that my cell phone is probably in some guy named Haden Lord's bedroom. Who may happen to be related to a kidnapper, according to my new bestie. "Why?"

"She's gone," my mom says.

"What? What do you mean, gone?" I try to keep the panic from rising in my voice, but Tobin's talk of missing girls is making me as paranoid as he is.

"Demi, you're being overly dramatic and scaring the girl." I hear Jonathan's soothing voice and realize I'm on speakerphone. Probably in the flower shop, the faint buzz of the old cooler in the background. "Hey, honey, how was the fancy party? You took pictures, didn't you?"

"It was . . . nice," I say. "But what's this about CeCe? I thought she had the flu."

"She quit," Jonathan says. "In a note, of all things, and right before we needed to get all the orders in for the Harvest Banquet."

"Why would she quit?"

"I don't know," Mom says.

"When did this happen?"

"I don't know when she left," Mom says. "She called in sick the morning after you went to California and didn't come in for any of her shifts this week. I figured she must have been feeling really poorly, so I went over to her apartment with some of my tummy tea this morning, and, well, she was just gone. Her landlord said she left a check to cover cleaning and a note saying that she quit her job and was leaving town."

"Why?" I ask.

"No idea. She's never seemed interested in leaving Ellis."

"I told you," I hear Indie's staccato voice from somewhere in the background. "She must have taken that new job."

"What's that?" I ask.

"Some woman called the shop a few days ago," Indie says, coming closer to the speakerphone. "She was asking all these employment verification questions. Like how long CeCe had worked here, where she'd worked before, and stuff. I don't get why everyone is worked up about it. So she quit and took a new job in a town that actually has malls and stuff."

Honestly, I can't blame CeCe, considering I'd left Ellis for bigger and better things. It just surprises me that she hadn't called to tell me her plans.

"We were hoping you'd heard more from her," Jonathan says. "I can't get over her not saying good-bye."

"It doesn't make any sense," Mom says. "She always seemed so happy here. Right up until you . . ."

"Right up until I left," I say, finishing the thought for her.

chapter thirty-one

HADEN

"He's not even singing," Tobin whispers to Daphne. They sit on the other side of the half circle of chairs in the music room. It's amusing that he thinks I don't know what he's saying. I can't actually hear their words over the singing, but I have spent the weekend mastering the art of lipreading. What isn't amusing, however, is that Tobin has caught on to the fact that I'm merely moving my own lips along with the rest of the choir. Daphne looks up at me. I stare down at the songbook in my hands. Maybe I should try singing along, but I don't know how to make my voice do what hers does, even if I want to. I feel her gaze leave me and I glance back at her.

"Maybe he's just intimidated," Daphne says. "It's his first day in the program."

My hands grow hot at the idea that she thinks I am afraid. I take a deep breath, tempering myself before I set the songbook on fire.

"Maybe he doesn't know how to sing."

"Then he shouldn't be here at all." The hard-lined look on Tobin's face makes me wonder what exactly his problem is.

"Leave him alone," Daphne whispers to him. "I think I was

mistaken about him. He's not the bad guy I thought he was."

"I think he's exactly who you thought he was."

Mr. Morgan shoots them a cross look for talking while the others are singing. This song is supposed to be for the rock opera that Daphne's father is writing—or so the teacher had explained at the beginning of the class period. It's a chorus piece, which apparently means that Daphne is not part of the song. I find myself wishing she were. I want to know if her voice is as enchanting as I remember.

When the song ends, Mr. Morgan addresses the class. "Very good. Very good. But we still have a lot of work. I want this song ready to present to Mr. Vince for his approval by the end of the week. Now for another matter," he says. "The mayor has asked me to find volunteers to provide entertainment for the Light-up Olympus Festival at the end of November. Does anyone want to sign up to do a musical number as part of a showcase the night of the festival?"

Tobin's hand shoots up. "I will."

"Thank you for your enthusiasm, Tobin. I'll mark you down. Anyone else?"

Tobin's hand goes up again.

"Yes?" Mr. Morgan asks.

"I think we should hear from the new student," he says.

I look up at him. I keep my face expressionless, but I can only hope that the glint of panic doesn't show in my eyes.

"I'd like to hear what he's got. And where better than in front of the whole town? He must be something pretty special to have *earned* a spot in the department without auditioning."

I sit up straighter. My gaze shifts to Mr. Morgan.

Mr. Morgan looks flustered. I wonder what kind of "requests"

Simon made of him to get me in the program. "Well, only if he wants to. It's completely voluntary."

Tobin sets his glare on me. The rest of the class follows his lead. "What say you? Are you up for the challenge?"

If it is possible for someone's expression to say, "You're not fooling me. I know you don't belong here. Try to prove me wrong," all in one narrowed-eyed look, this Tobin guy is pulling it off. It isn't a physical confrontation, but his challenge is just as serious as any one I'd accepted in the Underrealm.

And, oddly, feels just as dangerous.

Like not accepting will prove to him that I'm not who I claim to be.

"Challenge accepted," I say.

As other students volunteer to add their names to the performance list, I catch Daphne's eye for the first time since class started. I want her to see that I am not afraid. Even if, deep down, I really am.

When the bell rings, I pick up my songbook and leave as quickly as I can. I can sense Tobin coming after me, and Daphne only a few steps behind him. I duck around a corner. Leaning against a locker, I listen as Daphne catches up with him.

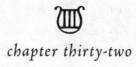

chapter thirty-two

DAPHNE

"Stop, Tobin," I say as I catch up to him in the hallway. "What was all that challenge crap back there? You're not going to try to punch him again, are you? Because you'd probably get kicked out of the play this time if you do."

"I just wanted to see where he goes next."

"To class," I say. "Like everyone else."

"Or so we think."

"I told you, I don't think Haden is a bad guy."

Tobin takes me by the elbow and leads me into a small alcove in the hallway, like he's afraid someone might overhear what he has to say next. "You know there was another attack Friday night?" he says. His voice is low and quiet, but I can hear an edge of accusation in his tone. At first, I think he's referring to what happened to Lexie in the grove and he's mad at me for not telling him about it—frankly, I didn't because I haven't been able to process what happened yet, myself—but then he goes on: "She was a cater waiter at the party. One of the valets found her unconscious near the lake."

"Oh no." I clasp a hand to my face. "What happened?"

"They're saying heart attack again. But I don't believe it. And

I don't think it's any coincidence that Haden was skulking around a party where someone ended up being attacked. I saw him sneaking over my back fence just after we left my mom's office."

I shake my head. "Haden didn't hurt anyone after leaving the party."

"How do you know that?"

"Because he was with me," I say.

"What?" Tobin's face goes ashen. "You left the party with him?"

"Not exactly . . ." I give him a quick overview of what happened to me and Lexie in the grove, even though I know it all sounds insane. But Tobin doesn't balk at my description of the weird screeching noise, the freaky, swooping shadow *thing*, and the stormless lightning. In fact, he doesn't react at all until I get to the part about how Haden showed up just as the weird shadow disappeared. "He *helped* Lexie and me Friday night. That's how I know he wasn't off attacking people."

"Are you sure?" Tobin asks. "I mean, you said you couldn't see who, *or what*, it was that was after Lexie . . . and then Haden just *happened* to show up? How do you know he wasn't the one who was trying to hurt her in the first place?"

I shake my head in frustration. "Because I just do. And I don't think he had anything to do with what happened to Pear, either. I was mistaken about that. He's not evil. He's just *different*."

"What, do you *like* him?" Tobin takes a step back, as if the idea of my liking Haden is repulsive to him. "You have a thing for him even after what I told you about Abbie?"

"No. I definitely don't have a *thing* for Haden. Listen, I agree that there's something weird going on around here. What happened to me and Lexie proves it. But maybe you should stop jumping to all these crazy conclusions about Haden because his last name happens to be Lord. It could be a total coincidence that your sister was friends with someone with that last name before she disappeared. Maybe this guy is related to Haden, but it doesn't mean anything. I'm friends with you, but that doesn't mean if I were to go missing, that you'd be suspect number one." I take Tobin's hands in mine because I know what I have to say next is going to be hard for him to hear. "Are you even sure this guy looked anything like Haden? Was Lord really his last name? You were only ten years old, Tobin. You may have gotten some of the details wrong."

I can hear the anger coming off him before I can see it on his face. I know I've offended him by questioning his theory about his sister's disappearance. But someone needed to.

"You think I'd forget the face of the guy who took my sister?"

"You have no proof that he even did. . . ."

"I do have proof," Tobin says, pulling his iPhone from his pocket.

The bell rings, indicating that our next classes have started, but neither of us moves. I am sick of our conversations getting interrupted and I'm not going anywhere until I've heard everything Tobin has to say. What proof could he possibly have?

"I'm still listening," I say.

"This is what I wanted to show you at the party." Tobin hands me his phone. The camera roll is pulled up on the screen. The small thumbnail photos all seem to be pictures of documents. I click on one of them to enlarge it, and then scroll through the others. They all seem to be dossiers—files containing detailed information about certain people. I look more closely at the information. Not just any people. Each dossier, fifteen total, is about a teenage girl, ranging from the ages fifteen to eighteen, and contains details such as name, date of birth, physical description, last known address, date last seen, and reason for leaving Olympus Hills.

"What is this?" I ask.

"Those are all girls who left Olympus Hills High under mysterious circumstances in the last fifty years. The first one dates back to the early 1960s—when the school was founded. The most recent is my sister, Abbie, six years ago."

"Okay, this is definitely strange, but what does it all mean?"

"It means that in fifty years, fifteen girls have gone missing from this school. That's just enough to be out of the ordinary, but not enough to draw someone's attention. Unless you're someone like me, who's looking."

"What exactly do you mean by 'gone missing'?" I ask, pointing to the file that's pulled up on the phone. "This Kendare Petrovich, it says that she left OHH because she transferred to Juilliard in 2001." I swipe the screen. "And this Adele Berger got pregnant and moved to San Diego in 1982." I swipe through more of the files. "None of these reasons for leaving seem all that mysterious to me. Abbie running away from home is the weirdest. I mean, I left Ellis High before graduating, but you can hardly call that circumstances mysterious." *Well, only a little. The mystery being why Joe even wanted me around.*

"Yeah, but Juilliard has no record of a student named Kendare Petrovich, and there were no Adele Bergers living in San Diego in 1982. I talked to the aunt she supposedly moved in with, and she hasn't seen Adele since she was a kid. Yeah, a lot of people have come and gone from Olympus Hills without graduating, but these fifteen people all have stories that don't check out. Like someone was trying to cover up the reason they went missing."

"Who even made these files? Where did you get these?"

"I made them," Tobin says. "It's something I've been working on for a couple of years."

I look at him, realizing that I don't really know him at all. Underneath his sweetness and friendly tone lies the heart of a full-blown conspiracy theorist.

"I got all these names from my mother's files. I was trying to show you the master list when she walked in last night."

"Have you asked her about this?"

"Yeah, right. And tell my mom I went through her private government files? You have no idea the grounding I would get." Tobin smirks. "My mom is kind of a scary lady."

"Tell me about it," I say, thinking of the icy reception I got from her after we were caught snooping. "I guess it makes sense, though, that, as mayor, she would probably be aware of people who've gone missing in her town. And it makes even more sense that a ritzy place like this would want to keep this sort of thing covered up. Bad PR, you know."

Tobin nods.

"But this still doesn't prove that any of these missing people are connected," I say, putting my hands on my hips. "How does this prove anything about the Lord family?"

"Look at the dates," Tobin says, pointing at the phone. "There's a pattern. One girl has gone missing every three years. There's only one deviation. It's been six years since Abbie disappeared and no others since then."

"Okay, that's definitely eerie." I rub my arms, suddenly feeling cold.

"I thought maybe the pattern had stopped . . . that maybe

whatever was going on had stopped. Until I saw Haden Lord. Which made me remember my sister's friend. Which got me thinking . . . I've only lived here for six and a half years, so I don't really know, but what if there were people from the Lord family in Olympus Hills all those other times people went missing?"

"Bridgette said that the Lord family sends kids here from time to time."

"She did?" Tobin almost sounds giddy at the prospect.

"Yeah, her dad's on the school board. She said they come every few years."

"Like, every three years?"

"I don't know." There's a look in his eye that makes me worry he's drawing way too many conclusions. "Tobin, none of this is proof. This is still just a theory. And it doesn't mean Haden knows anything about it."

"That's why I'm going to get some proof. There has to be a way to figure out if any more Lords were here the same years these girls disappeared."

"What are you going to do, hack the school server?"

Tobin doesn't answer.

"Tobin?"

"I bet records aren't even computerized before the nineties," he mumbles to himself.

"Tobin! You're going to get yourself into trouble."

"I need your help," he says.

"Excuse me?"

"I'm going to look into this records theory for the rest of the day. Which means I need you to follow Haden. Find out where he goes. Who he talks to. What he's doing here."

"Seriously?"

"You've already got an in with him after this Lexie thing. Let's use it to find out as much about him as we can."

I'm about to tell Tobin he's a couple of tubas short of an orchestra, but I notice the swirling, lifting notes in his voice as he asks, "Please, Daphne, help me." It's the sound of hope.

Hope that he'll find his sister.

"Okay," I say. "I'll help."

chapter thirty-three

HADEN

Kopros.

This Tobin boy is getting too close to the truth.

Champions use Persephone's Gate, which always leads to the grove, to enter the mortal realm, but in order not to draw too much attention to any one town, they spread out and alternate quest locations around the world—usually going three years before revisiting a city. Except for Olympus Hills. It has been six years since a Champion had been assigned here.

Dax.

I hear Tobin and Daphne leave the alcove and start up the hall, so I take off before the two round the corner. I head straight for the counselor's office and ask for Mr. Drol.

"He's on his break," the woman with the cat's-eye glasses says. "You're not scheduled to meet with him until tomorrow afternoon."

"This is urgent."

"You can see Mrs. Dunfree instead if you'd like."

"No, thank you," I say, and open the door to Dax's office anyway.

"You can't do that!"

"It's okay," Dax says. "Let him in."

Dax turns off the screen of his computer and swivels in his chair to greet me. He's wearing one of his ridiculous elbow-patched sweaters. "Now, son. What's all this bother?" he says in an exaggerated Yorkshire accent. I shut the door firmly behind me before ripping into him.

"Why did you send me into that party blind?" I say. "You're supposed to be my guide. So why didn't you tell me your Boon was the mayor's daughter, that I'm attending school with her brother? Don't you think these are important things for me to know?"

"Haden," he says, dropping the accent. "I told you. I cannot speak of this to you."

"But this affects me, Dax. It's jeopardizing my quest. This Tobin kid is on to us. He's determined to find out what happened to his sister, and he's not going to stop until he does. How am I supposed to get Daphne to trust me if Tobin is filling her head with vitriol, all because of the mistakes *you* made?"

"I'll take care of it," Dax says.

"How?"

"Keep your voice down."

"*How?*"

He slams his open palm on his desk. "I don't know! I just will."

I take a step back. "Why won't you just tell me what happened?"

Dax stands. "I *cannot.*" His nostrils flare and he takes a deep breath, as if fighting from saying more. His meaning sinks in. He's made an unbreakable oath. When he says he *cannot*, he means it would be physically impossible.

But who could compel him to do such a thing?

"If you value our friendship," he says. "If I mean anything to

248

you, you will stop being selfish for once in your life and listen to me when I ask you not to speak of this again. The consequences for me would be far greater than anything you can imagine."

I nod and pull open the door. I leave the office more confused than ever. But I have to go. Because the one thing I need to ask him I can't:

If Dax had returned alone to the Underrealm six years ago, but this Abbie girl still went missing, then what in the name of Hades had happened to her that he had sworn to never speak of again?

If it hadn't been for the conversation I'd overheard between Daphne and Tobin in the hallway, I might think she is starting to like me, because she keeps glancing back at me during humanities class. Instead, she's probably just trying to figure out whether or not I can be related to a kidnapper. Or worse.

I keep my face blank and pretend to be absorbed in the text of my book. When the bell rings, she stays in her seat instead of hurrying off to her next class. Is she waiting for me to leave? I pick up my book and head out the door. She follows a few seconds later.

I keep my pace slow so she won't lose me in the crowded hallway. When I get to my next class, I duck behind the door. She stands there for a few minutes, satisfied that I'm where I'm supposed to be. I watch her turn and walk back in the opposite direction.

So she's stalking *me* now?

I almost smile at the thought.

"You like her," someone says.

I turn and find Lexie standing behind me, her arms crossed in front of her chest. Two of her friends flank her on each side. They remind me of miniature versions of Rowan and his cronies—but with matching shoes and coordinated skirts.

"Pardon?" I ask.

"You like Daphne. I can tell from the way you look at her."

"I do not."

"You do. I heard the way you two talked the other night. It's obvious you're jonesing for her."

"I am not," I say, not even sure what she means.

"You are. Heaven only knows why. But I'm feeling generous, so I'm going to offer you a little advice."

"Why would you do that?"

"Listen, I don't know what exactly happened Friday night, and I am not too keen on trying to remember, but I'm pretty sure I owe you for helping me home, and I *don't* like being in anyone's debt. So I am going to do you a little favor by offering a little womanly advice. You want Daphne to like you, yes?"

I clear my throat. "Perhaps."

"Then ask her to help you with your performance for the Light-up Olympus Festival. Maybe suggest a duet? All that one-on-one time, working together—it'll work like a charm."

I consider her idea for a moment. It sounds exactly like something Dax would suggest.

"What if she doesn't say yes?"

"She will," Lexie says. "Trust me. I've seen the way she looks back at you."

I'm not so sure about this assertion of hers but I nod and thank her for her advice. "One more thing," I say as she and her lackeys start to head to their desks. "If you really want to be square with me, then you need to do me one more favor."

She narrows her eyes at me. "What's that?"

"Stop shunning Daphne."

"That's a big request. I'm not sure you have the bargaining power for it."

"Suit yourself," I say. "But you should see it more as me doing you another favor. If Daphne's dad is in charge of writing the play and there are still several parts to be doled out, don't you think you should be a little nicer to the one student who might be able to pull some influence on your behalf? I think you'd make an excellent queen of the underworld, don't you?"

Her nostrils flare almost imperceptibly, and I know she sees my point, whether she wants to or not.

"Besides, if you owe anyone anything after Friday night, it's her."

Lexie uncrosses her arms. "I'll take it under advisement."

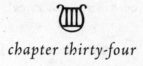

chapter thirty-four

DAPHNE

I can't find Tobin in the cafeteria, so I carry my lunch tray out to the courtyard. I sit under a statue of some Greek poet or whatever. I pull out the stack of homework I'm supposed to finish in order to catch up on the three weeks of classes I missed at the beginning of the year. Between that, rehearsing for the play, my current course load, and now Tobin's "investigation," I am starting to feel a bit underwater.

I try a couple of math problems and then give up. Instead, I pull out a notebook, and decide to make my own dossier of things I know about Haden Lord.

Name: Haden Lord.

Age: 16? 17?

Hair: Dark brown, almost black

Eyes: Jade green (but sometimes look like they have bright amber rings around the pupils?)

Occupation: ~~Part-time pirate~~

I tap my pen on the paper, realizing what I know about Haden isn't very much at all. I take a bite of my chicken salad sandwich, trying to think of something else to add to my list.

"Hello, Daphne," Lexie says as she sits down right in front of me.

"Um, hi," I say. I look around, trying to figure out what she's up to. None of her Sopranos is around, so I'm not sure if this is an ambush waiting to happen.

Lexie tucks her legs under her and opens a prepacked salad, like she's planning on staying for a while. She stabs a cucumber with a plastic fork. Eats it. And then looks at me. "Do you want to know why I hate you?" she asks.

I almost choke on a bite of chicken.

"Not particularly," I say when I've recovered. "But I have a feeling you're going to tell me anyway."

Lexie shakes a little tub of dressing, opens it, and dips the tips of her fork tines into the dressing before taking a bite of salad. She chews it neatly and then repeats the tiny bit o' dressing, lot o' bit of lettuce process before she decides to enlighten me.

"I hate you because you're a natural," she says.

"A natural what?"

I expect the next words that come out of her mouth to be something like *a natural-born loser* but instead she eats another cucumber and says, "A natural at everything I want to be." She scoots an olive off her salad with her fork. "You're a natural blond, naturally fit—hello, all the mayonnaise on that sandwich—and most of all, you're a natural singer. I, on the other hand, have to go to a stylist every six weeks to keep my hair color fabulous, do an hour of Pilates every morning to look this rocking, and I've had six different vocal coaches since I was five years old. Don't get me wrong, I *know* I'm talented, but I've had to *work* to get this voice. You just have it."

"I work hard, too, you know," I say, putting down my sandwich. "And I would have killed for the voice coaches you've had."

"And yet here you are, in one of the best music programs in the country without an ounce of professional training. Don't deny it, Daphne, you *know* you're special. You've just got it, and people can see it. They can hear it."

"So you hate me because you're jealous?"

"No, I hate you because you're an idiot."

"Excuse me?"

"I saw the look on your face when your dad announced that he's writing a freaking opera—just for you. He threw the biggest opportunity in the world at your feet. And you didn't want it. You would have thrown it back at him if you could. Meanwhile, I work my ass off trying to get a big enough part so my parents will even bother to come. Which means you're the biggest idiot I've ever met."

"Why are you telling me this?"

"Because I want to propose a truce. I'll call my Sopranos off if you help me get what I want."

"Let me guess, my part in the play?"

"We both know your daddy wouldn't go for that. No, I'll let you play the damsel in distress. I want to be the queen. Put a bug in your dad's ear that I'd make a good Persephone, and I'll make sure you have a *nicer* time at this school." She packs up her salad and stands. "Sound good?"

"I guess," I say.

"Cool. I like your . . . um"—she scans her finger over my outfit—"barrette, by the way. *Très* chic."

"Thanks," I say, and watch as she walks through the courtyard back into the school.

I pick up my sandwich and take a couple of bites, wondering

how this lunch break could get any weirder than Lexie proposing a truce, when someone very large steps in front of my sun, casting a shadow over my food.

I look up. *Way up.* And see Haden Lord, with a purple paisley tote bag on his arm, standing over me.

chapter thirty-five

HADEN

When I see Daphne sitting in the courtyard during our lunch break, I don't hang back or pretend to be aloof. I walk right up to her with the determination of a warrior and address her as if she were an Underlord of my same rank. "I have agreed to sing during the festivities of lighting up Olympus. I request that you help me prepare. Or perhaps a duet would be prudent."

She blinks at me for a moment, then looks down at the notebook at her side as if contemplating what she's written there. She looks back up at me. "Um . . . okaaaay."

"Very well, then," I say, hiding my surprise that she has actually agreed. "We shall commence rehearsal at your earliest convenience."

"Next week," she says. "I have a ton of homework to catch up on first."

"I bid you a pleasant day, then." I give her a respectful nod and start to take my leave.

"My tote?" she says, pointing at the bag over my arm. I had intended on giving it to her first thing as a peace offering.

"Oh yes." I hand it over to her. "Everything is as it should be, but I took the liberty of charging your phone for you."

I walk away at a fast clip, not giving her time to reconsider our arrangement.

chapter thirty-six

DAPHNE

After Haden is gone, I pick up the list of things I know about him and add *sometimes talks like Thor*.

This day definitely can't get more surreal.

A light flashes in my eyes and I jump, hitting my back on the base of the statue behind me. Tobin lowers his camera and laughs. "That was a good one. I'll give it a 'dazed and confused in the daytime' caption."

"What the crap are you doing?"

Tobin raises his camera to take another picture of me. I push him away. "Go away. You know they don't allow paparazzi past the gate, dork face."

"Come on, it's for the yearbook!" Tobin seems way too happy, considering our earlier conversation.

"Since when were you on yearbook?"

"Since I found out from the librarian that the yearbook staff has commandeered the school collection of yearbooks dating all the way back to the founding year. They're working on a project to scan and digitize all of them and put them online for OHH's fiftieth anniversary. I guess it's supposed to 'nostalgialize' the alumni into sending big, fat donation checks."

"Which means you'll have access to class lists for the last fifty years."

"Exactly. I am going to find every Lord who has ever gone to this school and cross-reference them with the girls who went missing. The investigative avenues will be endless after that."

"That's going to take a while," I say, but it's far preferable to the thought of Tobin getting arrested for hacking government files.

"How's your end going?" he asks.

I show him my meager list about Haden. "But I think the perfect opportunity to study Haden more closely just fell into my lap. He just came over and requested that I help him prepare for singing at the 'festivities of lighting up Olympus.'" I move my arms while I'm speaking, acting like I'm doing an impersonation of a robot.

Tobin laughs. "That's perfect."

I stick out my tongue as he snaps a picture of me.

He puts the camera down and gets real quiet for a few minutes, absentmindedly picking blades of grass.

I fish my phone out of my tote bag and check to see if I have any messages or texts from CeCe, explaining why she quit and left town. I expect to find *at least* a good-bye text, but there's nothing. I try to send her my own text, but it doesn't go through. Like her number has been disconnected. I blink back tears, wondering why CeCe would just cut me out of her life like this.

Tobin brushes my arm, drawing my attention. I give him a small smile, happy to still have a friend like him.

"Just promise me you'll be careful around Haden, okay?" he says. "Don't get *too* close."

I nod, remembering that Haden might be dangerous.

chapter thirty-seven

HADEN

"That was very nice," I say from the doorway of Daphne's bed-room. She jumps and almost drops the guitar she's been playing. I'd caught her right at the end of a song.

She shoots up from the edge of her bed. "What are you doing in here?"

"The door was open . . . and I didn't want to interrupt you."

"What, did you just walk right into the house? An open door isn't an open invitation. Joe always forgets to shut it. And you're not allowed in my room anyway."

"Sorry." I take a long stride backward so I'm now standing in the hallway outside her open door. I jam my hands into the pockets of my jeans because I don't know what else to do with them. "I knocked on your front door. Your servant let me in. She said I could come on up to find you."

"We don't have a servant," she says, like it's an accusation.

"Thin woman? Hair slicked back into a hair . . . ball . . . thing . . . on the top of her head? She seemed too young to be your mother."

"Oh. That's Marta. Joe's assistant." Her tense stance softens a little. "Why are you here?"

"You said you'd help me with the festival song. It's been a week, as you requested. Is this not your earliest convenience?"

"Oh. Yeah. I guess I didn't mean in exactly a week. The festival isn't until the end of November, you know that, right?"

"I don't believe in procrastination."

"Meaning I do?"

It had been a week since I had an excuse to talk to her, and not talking to her was making me feel addled. But I can't tell her that. I point at her guitar. "Will you show me how to play?"

"You don't know already?"

"I've had more important things to do."

"If you were serious about the music program, you'd make time."

"I'm here, aren't I?" I temper myself, remembering that Dax told me to be nice. "I need your help."

Daphne picks up the guitar and brushes past me through the doorway. I follow her to a large living room. She sits on the couch and looks up at me. "You coming?"

I sit on the opposite end of the couch. I set my schoolbag between us.

"How much do you know about playing?" she asks.

"Not a thing."

She sighs. "We'll start with the basics, then. Let's go over finger placement, and then we'll talk about the different chords."

"Actually, will you do that song for me again? The one you were just playing in your room? I want to learn that one."

"You're not ready for that one."

"Please?" I ask. "I want to hear it again."

She locks eyes with me for a moment and then shakes her head in a resigned sort of way. "Okay." She places the guitar in her lap, and I study the way she positions her fingers on the strings, memorizing each tiny movement as she begins to play the song. After a few notes, her voice joins in with the guitar and I almost forget to keep watching her hands. Her voice is soft, tentative at first, as if singing in front of me embarrasses her, but as the song builds, her voice flows out of her with a force that makes me almost quiver. Her words mingle and dance with the sounds her hands make as she plucks and strums the guitar.

I can feel a familiar ache in my own hands as my brain records the movements of Daphne's fingers and imprints them in my muscles. I feel as though I am in a trance. When the song ends, I don't snap back out of it until she says my name.

I hold my hands out for the guitar. "Can I?" I want to give it a try while the memorized movements are still vivid in my mind.

"Knock yourself out." She gives me the guitar. "But don't be upset if you don't get more than the first couple of notes." There's an edge of challenge in her voice.

I place my hands on the guitar, perfectly mimicking her placement when she'd started the song.

She nods. "So far, so good."

I think hard, replaying the song in my mind for a few moments, and then pick out the first few notes.

She raises an eyebrow. A slight smile plays on her lips.

I almost smile myself, liking that surprised look on her face. The stiff strings of the guitar bite my fingers, but it's a welcome sensation as my power of mimicry takes over my hands. I launch into the next few measures of the song, playing with a precision that should make me proud—except even though the movements of my hands are perfect and the notes I play are correct, something about the song doesn't sound right to me. That same warm feeling doesn't fill me the way it did when Daphne played the song and sang. I don't dare join my voice in with the music, but I concentrate harder on the guitar, launching into the more difficult part of the song.

I look up at Daphne, expecting to see a full smile on her face, but instead her lips have twisted into a frown.

"Stop." She snatches the guitar from me, sending my last note screeching. "Get out," she says. Her words are quiet, but they rumble with anger. She points toward the hallway leading to the stairs.

"What? Did I do it wrong?" Why couldn't I make the music sound the same as she had?

"Very funny, jerk. Pretending you don't know how to play. 'I don't know a thing about music. I need your help. Did I do it wrong?'" she says, mimicking my voice in a not-so-flattering way. "Are you just trying to make me feel stupid?"

"No, I swear. I have never played before. I'm just a really fast learner. I'd never even heard music before I heard you sing in the grove the other day—" I swallow hard, realizing I've probably said too much.

She gives me a look that makes me want to wither. "How is that even possible? Music is everywhere. You can't even go to the grocery store without hearing it."

"Maybe I've never been to a grocery store."

"What?

I look down at my shoes.

"What is your deal?"

"My deal?"

"Let me guess: some spoiled rich kid who's never had to lift a finger in his life? Do you have servants who do all your shopping for you?"

263

"My family, they're . . . different. My home is a very controlled environment. Music isn't allowed."

"Seriously?"

"I am serious. There's no music, no television, no movies, no parties, no girls." I glance at her and then train my eyes on the clock over the fireplace. Maybe she'll realize that's why I keep saying all the wrong things.

"Sheesh, and I thought my mom was strict. Your parents sure sent you to a funny school, if they hate the media. Do they know you've joined the music program?"

I shake my head. "My father wouldn't approve."

"Then why did they send you here?"

I hold my breath, trying to come up with a plausible explanation that doesn't involve my telling her that I'm supposed to bring her back to the underworld with me. I flip through the compartments of information stored in my brain until an idea clicks. "Have you ever heard of a *rumspringa?*"

"Isn't that an Amish thing? Where they send their teenage kids out into the world to see everything they've missed out on before deciding for sure if they want be Amish for the rest of their lives . . . Holy crap, you're not Amish, are you?" She throws her hands over her mouth sheepishly, like she's afraid she's offended me.

I almost laugh. The sound gets caught in my throat. "*Definitely* not Amish," I say. "But that is what I'm kind of here for. This is kind of like my *rumspringa*. I'm here to experience the rest of the world before I go back home again."

"So what happens if you choose not to go back?"

"I don't know. Nobody in my family has ever *chosen* not to return." I run my hand through my hair, finding myself still surprised at how short it is. "Choice doesn't have anything to do with it."

I'll return because I must. It's my destiny.

"And where is home?"

I can feel heat rising in my chest. She asks too many questions. She's probably mentally recording my answers to share with Tobin later. "Upstate New York, but my father is Greek," I say, telling her the cover story that Simon made me rehearse before starting school.

"Where is your mother from?"

"The West."

"How did your parents meet?"

"I don't remember." Energy continues to build inside of me. I feel as though I am being interrogated by one of the royal guards.

"Is she as strict as your father?"

"You're curious for a—"

"For what? A girl?"

I was going to say *human* but had caught myself.

"Is that a problem?" she asks, taking my silence for an admission. She stands up. "I'm not allowed to be curious because I'm a girl?"

She's infuriating is what she is. I can feel electric heat rolling under my fingertips. Why is it so much harder to control myself around her?

"Your mother didn't teach you not to be a total misogynist."

I stand up to meet her. "My mother is none of your affair," I say, electricity crackling in my voice.

She stares at me, our faces only inches apart. I know she must feel the heat radiating off me. I wait for her to tell me to get out again, to get lost, but instead she backs away and sits down on the couch, almost crushing the bag I'd placed there. Which is when the bag lets out a hiss. "What the . . . ?" Daphne bounces away from the now-wriggling bag. A second later, a furry little thing pops out of it, launches itself at me, and perches on my shoulder. All the while hissing its displeasure over almost being squashed.

"Well, it's your fault, Brim, for hiding in there!"

Brim growls, baring her tiny fangs.

"Oh my gosh, is that your kitten?" Daphne asks. She sounds strangely amused, and the anger melts from her expression.

"In a way. But she's not a kitten," I say, because I know Brim *hates* being called that. "She's nearly seven years old."

"But she's so tiny! Like, barely bigger than a guinea pig."

I try to pet Brim to calm her, but she swats at me with her claws. "What she is, is angry. That's not a good thing."

"It's adorable." Daphne laughs. "Come here, little girl," she says in a singsong voice, reaching for Brim.

"Not a good idea," I say, and try to pull the cat away from her reach. Brim bites my finger. I snap my hand back, and to my horror, Daphne snatches up the cat. To my utter astonishment, Brim lets her, though she's still growling and hissing.

"I know how to soothe a savage beast," Daphne says, like she's singing. "My mom is always bringing home cranky strays. Grab the guitar. Try the song again."

I scoop up the instrument and sit next to her. I pick out the notes again. After a few seconds, Daphne joins her voice in with my strumming. She sings in a lower, more gravelly tone that carries the same timbre as Brim's small yet ferocious growl. Listening to her feels like the sensation of someone wrapping a warm blanket around my shoulders. But it's been so many years since someone has done this for me; I am surprised I remember what it feels like. . . .

We're halfway through the song when I realize that Brim's growling has been replaced by a steady purr. She's curled herself into a tiny ball in Daphne's hands. Daphne smiles down at her.

I suddenly feel jealous of the cat.

I haven't dared to add my own voice to the music for fear of spoiling it. I don't even know *how* to sing, but as the song rounds into the final lines, the warmth of the music engulfs me to the point that I feel as if something inside of me is pushing its way out to meet it. I cannot help myself. My voice crackles at first and is barely audible, but when Daphne turns her smiling eyes on me, my voice grows stronger, mingling with hers. Our voices ring together, and for a moment, I feel as though I am free. Even freer than I felt in the Tesla. Freer than owls soaring from their roost.

I hold the final note of the song with Daphne, almost afraid to let that feeling of freedom go. Finally, she lets the note fall and I end the song.

I pull my fingers from the guitar strings and find Daphne staring at me. Her head is cocked to the side as if she is listening to something even though the music has stopped.

"What is it?" I ask her.

"Huh. I didn't think you had an inner song, Haden Lord," she says softly. "I guess I was wrong."

I have had five lessons with Daphne in the last two weeks. Each one starts almost the same as the first. She peppers me with questions about my family and my past until she becomes frustrated with how little pertinent information I give her, and eventually she moves on to the music. I bring Brim with me since she seems to have a softening effect on Daphne, who lets her sit on her knee as we play.

My mastery of the guitar is coming along quite nicely, thanks to Daphne's gifted hands. She has even let me play the piano in her father's studio a couple of times. I prefer the guitar, though; it gives me something to hold on to.

It is late in the evening. I am headed back to Simon's mansion after my latest lesson with Daphne. Brim clings happily to my shoulder, enjoying the fresh air, and I carry the loaner guitar that Daphne has sent me home with to practice. It's an ebony black Stratacoustic from her father's collection. "Believe me, he won't even notice it's gone. Besides, he owes me one," she'd said. I think of how her hands had brushed mine when I took it from her.

I am crossing the bridge that leads to the school, taking a shortcut to Simon's, when the smell of sulfur permeates my senses. Brim catches the scent also and jumps from my shoulder. She yowls and runs across the bridge, following the scent.

"Stop!" I shout. But she doesn't listen. *Harpies*. I hitch up the guitar and take off after her, thinking of the consequences of letting a hellcat get loose near a school.

I don't have to go far before I find her. Thankfully, she's just standing on the back end of a parked car, meowing plaintively at something behind the vehicle. That is when I see it.

The body.

She lies on the ground behind a crop of bushes just beyond the parking lot, her hair splayed out around her head like a brown halo. Gashes cover her arms, and her chest has been ripped open. Her heart is missing.

This time, the Keres has done more than cause a heart attack.

It'd ripped it right out of her. I wonder how the town officials will try to explain away this death.

I can't tell what set the Keres off at first, why it had gone after her in the first place, but then I notice a small bandage on the woman's pinky. Probably no more than a nick on her finger from a piece of paper.

My fears were right. The Keres is growing stronger.

Its thirst for blood is making it bolder.

I look more closely at the woman, realizing that I know her. Mrs. Canova, the teacher who had dragged Garrick and me to the counselor's office after the fight.

Garrick.

The realization hits me so hard, I don't know why I didn't see it the moment I first glimpsed the Keres the night it attacked Lexie. There is only one person in the mortal world right now who would know more about Keres than I do. Only one person here who had access to them before we came.

Only one person who could have known how to bring it here . . .

"It's not fair," Garrick says as he and Dax enter the mansion via the garage. "When are you going to let me drive?"

I hear them coming and stand up from the couch, where I have been waiting for them to return.

"Sorry, kid. You've got to be at least sixteen here to get a driver's license." Dax tosses a grease-spotted paper sack onto the coffee table. "Dinner," he says to me.

"Dax picked," Garrick says. "So I hope you like deep-fried fat."

"They're called chimichangas. And they're awesome. Almost as good as tacos."

I wrinkle my nose at the smell. "I'm not hungry."

Garrick flops into an armchair. His leg dangles over one of the arms. I assess him for a moment and notice how he's dropped the small, cowering mannerisms of a Lesser. He has become too comfortable here. "Can't you get me one of those fake ID things you got Haden?" He leans over and digs into the paper bag. He takes out two bundles wrapped in grease-spotted paper. He tosses one to Dax, who catches it without looking up, and then offers the other to me.

"I don't want it." I wave off the foul-smelling food. Garrick doesn't even notice me glaring at him.

"I could get you an ID, but I won't. You're too young. I wouldn't let you near Venus."

"Venus?" he asks mockingly. "Is that what you call your car?"

"She's my little goddess. And I'm not letting you near her again. You tried to eat a chimi in the front seat."

"What's that?" Garrick asks, with a mouth full of meat and cheese, pointing at the guitar Daphne gave me. It's tucked under the coffee table.

"It's nothing."

"It's something." He bounces up and grabs it out from under the table. His greasy fingers leave prints on the black gloss paint. "What the Tartarus is this thing?"

"Put it down," I say, but he doesn't listen.

His filthy fingers are on the strings now.

"Don't touch that." I reach for the guitar just as Garrick slides his fingers over the strings and a discordant jumble of notes fills the air.

"Harpies," he says, almost dropping it. The clatter of notes as it smacks against his leg makes me cringe.

"You dung eater!"

"That thing makes music," Garrick says. I can see the panic in his eyes. Finally, an expression that belongs on a Lesser. "What are you doing with it?"

"Give it back."

"It's forbidden. If King Ren finds out—"

"He's not going to find out."

Garrick squeezes the neck of the guitar hard in his hand. I can feel the pulse of electricity building in his body.

"Don't you dare."

"We should destroy it."

"Give it to me. That's an order, Lesser."

"No."

I can't tell if he refuses because he's concerned about my well-being, or just because he wants to be defiant. Because he thinks he *can be*. He raises his free hand, tiny wisps of blue light crackling in his palm. I've never seen a Lesser use his lightning power before. The electricity is weak, but still strong enough to cause damage to the guitar.

I lunge at him.

Garrick squeals and scrambles up onto the armchair, but he can't get away from me. I wrestle the guitar from him and thrust it at Dax, who tries to stop us from fighting. I grab Garrick by the collar. I raise my other hand. The energy that pulses through me would be enough to knock the teeth from his mouth.

"Why did you do it?" I ask.

"Music is forbid—"

"Not that," I snarl into his face. "Why did you bring *it* here?"

Garrick's eyes go wide. His mouth quivers. "I don't know what you're talking about."

"Yes, you do!"

"Haden, stop," Dax says. "What is this about?"

"The Keres," I say. "Garrick brought it here."

"What?" he says. "That's impossible."

"Think about it. He works in the Pits. He has access to them. He must have brought one with him." I shake Garrick by his collar. "But I want to know why. Did you think it would be amusing? Did you do it to distract me? Why, you little harpy?"

"Stop this," Dax says, trying to pull me off Garrick. "Listen to yourself. Garrick didn't know you were going to choose him to come with us. How could he have planned it? How could he even get a Keres out of the Pits? The barriers of the Pithos prevent it."

Dax's reasoning edges at my rage. I've acted again without thinking it through.

"It was an accident," Garrick says softly. He cowers, holding his hands in front of his face defensively. "It must have attached itself to me. They can do that. Like a second shadow. It was a stowaway, like how you suggested to Dax that first night. I had no idea it was here until I heard you tell Dax and Simon that you saw it. Then I realized what I had done."

"You idiot. Why didn't you tell us?"

"Because I knew you would react like this."

"I don't understand," Dax says. "How is any of this even happening? The Keres can't get out of the Pits. Only Hades himself could summon them through the barrier. I wouldn't believe any of this if Haden hadn't seen it himself."

"The locks on the Pits are starting to fail. The barrier that keeps the Keres out of both the Underrealm and the mortal world is beginning to fall," Garrick says. "Pandora's Pithos is opening."

"But that means more could get out. They could all get out."

One Keres is a dangerous thing on its own. But one can become more when it becomes strong enough to multiply. The Keres are kept weak in the Pits to keep their numbers low. But even a handful of Keres, which hunt in packs, could rip through the Underrealm in a matter of days. If more get into the mortal world, especially depending on the *type* of Keres—disease, fear, violent death, war, pestilence—they can destroy a state, a country. Unchecked, they can multiply and multiply until they destroy this entire realm—and then move on to the others.

We've been lucky with this Keres that is loose on Olympus Hills, I realize. This one is merely a reaper. I've only ever heard of one other Keres escaping into the mortal world since their imprisonment. Humans called it the black plague.

"How can the Heirs stop the Pithos from opening?" I ask.

"They can't," Garrick says. "Not without the Key of Hades."

I finally let go of him. Dax and I exchange a look. We are back to the Key once again. No wonder the Court is so desperate to find it. Bringing the Cypher—bringing Daphne—to them has more importance than just restoring the Underlords' ability to move freely between the realms, even more than restoring their full powers—it is needed to stop the five realms from ceasing to exist.

"That's just a worst-case scenario," Dax says, as though he can read the thoughts that have slammed through my brain. The gravity of it all must be written on my face. "Let's not get ahead of ourselves."

"How do you kill them?" I ask Garrick. "How do we stop this one before it gets strong enough to multiply?"

"You can't," he says. "That's why Hades locked them away."

"You have to know something."

"I don't," Garrick says, and pushes me away from him. "I don't know anything. I'm just a Lesser, remember?"

"You brought this thing here. Accident or no accident, you are responsible for what it does. The lives it takes are on your head. You have to help me stop this thing."

"No," Garrick says. "This is *your* responsibility. *You* brought me here, which means you brought the Keres here. It's not my fault it was attached to me. That's the hazard of living in the Pits. And you and I both know the real reason I was banished to the Pits in the first place. Which means what that monster does is on your head. Not mine."

So he does know his banishment was my fault. . . .

He raises his fist as though he wants to blast me. Tiny threads of blue light encircle his hand. My shame prevents me from trying to stop him.

Dax grabs Garrick's fist. He winces as Garrick's lightning shudders up his arm, but he doesn't let go. "Do not forget your place, Garrick. Haden is our Champion. Your insubordination is a crime, even in this place."

Garrick's face clouds over with the look of a hellcat. Then he drops his head like a scolded kit. "Fine."

Dax lets go of his fist. "Go upstairs."

Garrick grabs the grease-spotted bag and huffs up the stairs.

"Garrick," Dax calls after him. "That's Haden's dinner."

"Let him go. I'm not hungry."

Dax sits in the armchair that Garrick vacated and looks at me. "What did he mean by all that?"

"It's nothing," I say in a tone that makes it clear I don't want to talk about the things Garrick said.

"Haden?"

"I'm respecting your secret. You can respect mine." Dax is the last person in all the realms I want to know what I did to Garrick. Dax is the only one who doesn't look at me with disdain because of what I did when my mother died, but if he knew what I did to Garrick two years later, to get rid of the walking reminder of my shame, he may not be able to look at me at all anymore.

I sit on the couch with the guitar. I want to distract myself, like the way I feel when I sing with Daphne, so I play a few bars.

"That sounds pretty good," Dax says. "I take it things are going well between you and Daphne?"

I shrug. "I don't know. Maybe. Maybe not. I mean, I got her to help me prepare for the festival, and she trusts me enough to loan me a guitar." I wipe at the fingerprints Garrick left on the finish. "But it all seems like such small steps. What if it doesn't add up to enough before the Eve of the Return?" The night I have to tell her the truth and ask her to come with me through the gate.

"Don't let the importance of your quest make you feel like you have to rush—it'll only scare her off. There's a reason we're given six months—other than the confines of the gate—it takes time and patience to win her affection. She'll come around. All the little things will build on each other. Like that song you're playing. It works because you let the tune build as you go. You don't try to play all the notes at once."

I look down at my hands, not realizing I'd started playing an actual song. It's the one Daphne first taught me.

"I can't make it sound like she does, though. I do all the right movements, hit all the right notes, but it still doesn't *feel* right."

"That's because music isn't just about precision and mimicking movements. It's an emotional experience. True music comes from inside. I heard someone say once that the ability to create musical expression from emotional experience is a uniquely human trait."

"Then I probably shouldn't bother," I say, zipping the guitar into its case.

"Don't forget, Haden. All of us Underlords are part human. Your mother—"

"Don't," I say, standing. Why would Dax try to remind me of her? Why would he encourage me to tap into my human side when, all my life, I've been taught to repress it?

I hear the garage door open. Simon has returned from wherever he goes during the day. I don't feel like dealing with him. And I don't want him to try to stop me from dealing with the Keres again.

"Where are you going?" Dax asks as I head out of the room.

"Hunting," I say.

Because Garrick is right. It's my fault the Keres is here.

And now it's my responsibility to figure out how to stop it.

I return to the school parking lot with the idea of inspecting the scene more closely in hopes of finding clues as to where the Keres went next. But I am too late. The humans have already found the body, and the area is cordoned off by Olympus Hills security. I stand in the shadows and watch as they load what remains of Mrs. Canova into the back of the OHMC vehicle—until I notice that someone else is watching me.

I see him at the far end of the parking lot, idling on a motorcycle. He wears the same full-coverage helmet that hides his face, but I am certain he is the rider I saw outside the mayor's party. The same one that seemed to be watching me then, too.

Was he working for Simon or something?

There's only one way to find out. I start making my way

toward him, sticking close to the perimeter of the school, but he must sense me coming, because he revs his engine and peels out of the parking lot before I close in.

I chase after him, running at top speed over the bridge that leads off the school's island, but my legs are nothing compared to his motorcycle. He speeds away and disappears into the night.

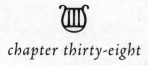

chapter thirty-eight

DAPHNE

I wake to the smell of burning.

A shout from Joe sends me running downstairs in my pajamas to investigate. I find him in the kitchen, muttering swearwords, a smoking frying pan in his oven-mitted hands. The counters are littered with eggshells, spilled flour, and various half-empty containers. Batter oozes out the side of a waffle iron, which sits haphazardly on a stack of *Us* magazines.

"Oi, Daphne," Joe says when he sees me. "Grab a towel, eh?" He indicates the toppled-over milk container that's busy glugging out a waterfall of white liquid from the marble island to the hardwood kitchen floor. "Knocked it over while I was trying to save the eggs à la Vince."

I pull open a drawer and grab Joe's entire collection of dish towels—all three of them. "Where's Marta?" I ask, righting the milk carton. I drop the towels on top of the mess. Much to her displeasure, Marta is usually in charge of breakfast. Which usually consists of cinnamon oatmeal for me and a weird concoction of tomato juice, lemon, and Worcestershire sauce for Joe. Basically, a Bloody Mary sans the alcohol.

The dish towels aren't enough, so I grab an entire roll of paper towels.

"Gave her the day off," he says, spooning a hefty portion of very crunchy-looking scrambled eggs onto a couple of plates. "Thought we could spend the day just the two of us. I've got the whole thing planned out." Joe opens the waffle iron. The tops of the waffles have stuck to the apparently ungreased upper plate of the appliance. He tries to scrape them out with a fork.

"You *planned* something for today?" I can't hide the incredulity in my voice. I'm not sure I want to.

"I thought, after breakfast, we could duck out of Olympus Hills for a few hours. My drummer and his brother are opening up a burger joint that has onion rings to die for, and the planetarium is putting together a light show based on my *Saturn's Ring* album. Which means I was able to pull some strings to get us a private tour." Joe presents me with a plate of food that somewhat resembles breakfast.

"I don't know, Joe. . . ."

He pours a healthy portion of maple syrup over the contents of his plate. "You still like stargazing, right? Because they've got one of the biggest telescopes in the country."

The mention of telescopes and stargazing makes my stomach churn. Or maybe that's from the smell rising up from my plate. I'm pretty sure scrambled eggs aren't supposed to be made with cream cheese and . . . mustard? I push the plate away. "I can't, Joe. I've already got plans."

"But, Daph, I cleared my whole schedule for you."

"Well, maybe you should have thought to make sure *my* schedule was clear before making all these plans. Did you just suppose I'd have nothing better going on? I have a life of my own, you know?"

"Oh," Joe says. "Yeah, I guess you're right. I should have checked with you first." He sounds so dejected, I almost waver.

"I need to get ready," I say, before I can be talked into changing my mind.

I leave Joe at the breakfast table. I look back before heading up the stairs. He stabs a forkful of eggs à la Vince, shoves it in his mouth, and then promptly lets it all fall back out onto his plate.

"Bloody hell," he says, wiping his tongue with the sleeve of his bathrobe.

I stifle a laugh and head for my bedroom. I pick up my phone from my bedside table and dial a number I never thought I'd actually call when he gave it to me.

"Hello?" Haden answers. He sounds surprised.

"Are you busy today? I thought we could fit in another lesson."

"I'm available," he says. There's a touch of eagerness in his voice before he tempers it. "What did you have in mind?"

"A field trip," I say, wanting to get as far away from Joe and Olympus Hills as possible for the day. "I think it's time I give you a more advanced musical education. Pick me up in two hours."

"I don't even know where to start. I mean, there's the classics. Like Tchaikovsky, Beethoven, Rachmaninoff, Shostakovich, Debussy, and then some more modern stuff like the Kinks, the Zombies, the Beatles of course, Bob Dylan, Van Morrison, the Velvet Underground, the Who . . . Ah crap, that's just the 1960s."

"This is starting to sound like it's going to take a year," Haden says.

"I know. This is even more difficult than I thought it would be."

I researched online and found a music store a few towns over from Olympus Hills that still has an old-school listening booth in it. I'd already arranged with the manager—thanks to the generous cash allowance Joe had given me—for us to have use of the booth for the entire afternoon. But that isn't feeling like nearly enough time at the moment.

I take a great big breath and let it out in a puff. "Okay, I'm just going to grab some of my favorites from different decades. This might take a bit." I look up at Haden and see that he's watching my hands as I pluck different albums from the bins.

"What should I do?" he asks.

"Hmmm. Go pick something out. Anything you want."

The strangest look passes over his normally stony face. Hesitancy? Uncertainty? Almost like no one has ever given him the option of picking something out for himself before. It's the first time I'm seeing him with an unguarded expression.

I smile at him reassuringly. "There's no wrong choice. Just surprise me."

He nods and that stony mask of his slips over his face again. I miss the more open look.

I watch him for a moment, his long fingers curling over the edges of the CD cases as he flips through the albums. He glances back at me. I look down at the album in my hands.

After I've got a stack of CDs that's almost as tall as I am, Haden comes back with an album. He holds it up for my inspection. *Shadow of a Star* by Joe Vince. The frown forms on my face before I can stop it. Of all the thousands of albums in this place, he had to choose that one.

Haden pulls the CD back. "I chose wrong, then?" His voice is gray with disappointment. "It's your father's album, yes? I thought it would be good to familiarize myself—"

"Pick something else," I say abruptly. "Anything else."

"Why?" he asks.

The personal question interests me, since he's always trying to deflect mine, but what's more is that I actually find myself wanting to tell him.

"It's a long story."

"I'd like to hear it."

I sigh. "I'd only ever met Joe four times before I came to live with him back in September. The last of those times was when he made a surprise appearance at my tenth birthday party. He made a big deal about giving me his guitar, the first one he'd ever bought with his own money—and he taught me the words to his favorite song. He cried when I sang and he said I had *his* voice, and he told me that *this time* he was going to stay in Ellis.

"I followed him everywhere for the next few days. He taught me to play the guitar, and took me out at night to see the constellations. He told me the stories behind them, and we even wrote a song about the stars together. But five days into what I thought was the best week of my life, he left me standing at my front room window with a telescope, waiting for him until it was almost midnight and I realized he wasn't coming. One of his handlers sent a note the next day, saying Joe had gone back to California. Without even saying good-bye.

"I spent the next year learning every single one of Joe's songs until I could sing them even better than him, thinking somehow if I did this, he'd be impressed enough to come back. But he didn't." I shrug one shoulder. "I'd call him with the hope of singing to him over the phone, but he never answered. He never sent post-cards. Never visited again. And after a while, I moved on from my father's songs and started writing my own. Joe likes to tell people I have his voice. But he's wrong. It's *mine*." I point at the album in Haden's hand. "That song, 'Shadow of a Star'—that's the song I helped Joe write when I was ten years old. It's considered one of his greatest hits—the one that solidified his 'God of Rock' status. But I hate it. I turn it off anytime it comes on the radio."

"I can see why," Haden says.

"You know he had the audacity to invite me to go stargazing again today? He arranged this whole, grand daddy-daughter day and rented out the planetarium's telescope. He didn't even get *why* I didn't want to go. I had to tell him I had plans so he'd drop it."

"So that's why you called me?" Haden asks.

I nod. "Sorry."

He shrugs. "I'm happy to be your other plans." His jade green eyes lock on my mine for a moment. Then he turns away. "I guess I should find something else." He tucks Joe's album into a stack of Top 40 rock and then migrates to the indie section. He comes back a minute later with a new CD. Death Cab for Cutie.

"How's this? I liked the name of the band."

"Perfect," I say, and lead him to the booth. It's a small, glass-enclosed room at the back of the shop. It's such a tight fit for both of us that I can feel the heat radiating off his body as I sidestep around him to get to the stereo. He smells of citrus and soap.

I linger for a second longer than I need to.

"We'll start with a couple of classical numbers," I say. There's an odd tremor in my voice. "And then we'll move on to some more modern stuff."

"Sounds good to me," he says, but I detect a hint of apprehension in his voice. I remember what he said about music having been forbidden to him, and I realize I'm about to take a virtual musical virgin for the ride of his life.

"So what do you think?"

Haden is quiet for a moment. "Can I use the word *beautiful* to describe music?"

"Yes, of course." *What an odd question.*

"I can't think of another word for it."

"That's okay. Music is hard for just about anyone to describe, let alone for someone who hasn't developed a musical vocabulary."

"I'm not used to being at a loss for words."

I believe him. This is the eleventh song I've played for him and he's stayed mostly silent during all of them—verbally anyway. I noticed that by the fifth song, the sphere of silence that normally surrounds Haden had started to wane. It was like when we sang together for the first time, and I had heard a soft, resonating pulse of sound coming off him. And now with each musical number I played for him since then, his inner tone had grown ever so slightly. It is like no other inner song I've ever experienced before.

"It might be easier to describe how it makes you feel."

That hesitant, uncertain expression crosses his face. Has no one ever asked him to talk about his emotions before?

"Sad," he says. "It's a sad song. But optimistic, too."

"Optimistic?"

I'd played him a song called "I Will Follow You into the Dark" from the Death Cab for Cutie album he'd picked out. It is a simple song, just a singer and a single guitar, but it seems to have had a strong impact on Haden. His inner tone beats twice as strong as before. It almost sounds hopeful.

"I don't know if *optimistic* is quite the right word. But it's about two lovers," he says. "Yes?"

I nod.

"They've been together for a long time. They've seen many things and loved deeply. But she's about to die. And he's telling her not to cry or worry. Because she won't be alone. Because he'll follow her into the dark. He's telling her to have hope. Yes, that's the right word for it."

"I guess so. But who would do that? It's kind of a ridiculous notion, don't you think? Can he really promise that he's going to die right after her so she won't be alone?"

"I think it's less about death and more about a willingness to follow someone into the unknown. For love."

"Maybe."

"Would you ever do something like that? If you loved someone enough, would you follow him into the dark?" He looks at me with those jade green eyes and, for the slightest of moments, I think I see dark amber fire rings dancing around his pupils.

My impulse is to look away, but I don't. "No," I say. "I'm not a follower."

"Hand in hand, then?"

I do look away now. "I don't think I'm capable of loving anyone that much." I turn my back on him and move to the stereo.

"Even if it was your destiny?"

I give a short laugh. "Destiny? I don't believe in all that fate mumbo jumbo."

"How can you not believe in fate?" His question sounds like he thinks I'm being blasphemous.

"I believe in goals, and working hard for what you want. And choices. I make my own path; nobody else chooses it for me."

Haden's hopeful tone disappears. That sphere of silence returns, surrounding him and stretching to the corners of the booth. I can't stand it.

I remove the disk from the stereo, and look for a new one to replace it.

"What about to save the person you loved?" he asks.

"Maybe," I say, thinking of my mom. I'd come here to save her—in a way. Well, to save her from losing her shop and her livelihood. But it had been *my* choice, in the end. "Depends on the person, I guess." I find the disk I'm looking for and put the new CD into the player. "Let's try a modern song without lyrics this time. This is by one of my favorite bands, Stars of the Lid. Just concentrate on the music. Open yourself up to the emotion it evokes." I press play and let the music fill the silence in the booth. "It's a beautiful song, one of my favorite pieces of modern music, but it also reminds me of a discordant lullaby. Like something's broken or missing in the music—but in a very deliberate way."

My back is to Haden as the song plays, but I can feel his warm presence only inches away in the tight booth. The air grows heavy, hot, electric, and a new strain of notes fills the booth. But they're not coming from the stereo.

I turn to Haden. His lips are partly open. A red blush paints his pale yet olive cheeks. This new sound is coming off him.

It's the sound that sorrow makes.

"What . . . what is the name of this song?" he asks, with a tremor in his voice.

"'Requiem for Dying Mothers.'"

He purses his lips. His nostrils flare. A wet sheen fills his eyes. "Turn it off. Please. Just turn it off."

"Okay." I turn and hit the stop button. When I look back,

Haden is gone. The glass door to the booth swings shut, and I see him heading out the front of the store.

I find Haden outside. He leans against a wood railing that overlooks the beach, his face buried in his arms.

When we drove to this store, it was the first time I'd glimpsed the ocean in my life. The first time I'd heard the song of the sea. It'd been mesmerizing even through the windows of Haden's car. Hearing it now, so close, mixed with tones of sorrow coming off Haden, it sounds like the ebb and flow of throbbing, raw pain. Like from a wound that can't be closed.

"Haden?"

"Go away. Please," he says. "Don't look at me."

I ignore his request. "Did something happen to your mother?" It's the most intrusive question I've ever asked him, but I have to ask it. The sound of his sorrow is too overwhelming not to. "Did she die?"

"Yes," he says softly. "In my arms. She died in my arms. When I was seven."

"I'm sorry." Tears prick at the backs of my eyes. I can't help imagining myself in his place. "I shouldn't have played that song. . . ."

"You didn't know," he says into his arms, which cover his face. "I try not to allow myself to think about her. But that song . . . it sounded like . . . *felt* like . . . I don't know how to describe it. It reminded me of how I felt when she died." The tone that comes off him changes, warps from sorrow to something else. At first, I think it's helplessness. No, I'd almost say it sounds like shame. He stands up straight now, wiping the tears from his eyes with his shirtsleeve. "You must think I'm disgusting."

"For tearing up? No." I reach toward his face, then stop, not sure what I was going to do. I place my hand on his shoulder instead. "It's a perfectly human reaction."

His face reddens slightly. "That's the problem," he mumbles, and places his hand over mine. His skin is hot, but it's a welcome warmth against the breeze, which carries in the salty cool air from the ocean.

My arm tingles and I feel the hairs on my forearm stand on end as if with static electricity. Haden lets go of my hand. I look up at the darkening, cloudy sky. "I think a storm is coming. Should we go?"

"Yes. I think that would be wise."

I head back to the store to gather my things from the booth, but as I look back at Haden before opening the door, I notice that it sounds like the storm is raging inside of him.

Haden parks behind Joe's red Porsche in my driveway. His car is so silent, I don't notice we've come to a stop until he clears his throat.

"Thanks for the ride," I say, picking up my tote bag.

"Thank you for the education."

"I'll send you some more songs tomorrow. We need to settle on something for the festival."

"We?" he asks. "So you'll do a duet with me?"

"Yes." I open the door. He looks at me.

"Daphne, do you have plans tonight?"

I blink. Is he asking me out? "Um. No . . . ," I say tentatively.

"Then if I were you, I'd take your father up on going to see that telescope."

"I don't think that's—"

"I know I don't really know your father, but it sounds to me like he's *trying* to make a connection with you. Hades knows that my father has never even cared to try with me . . . and my mother . . ." He trails off heavily. His fingers tap on the steering wheel. "What I am attempting to say is that perhaps you should give your father a chance while you still can. There might come a day when the option is no longer available to you."

chapter thirty-nine

HADEN

When Daphne is gone, a hollowness fills me that I cannot explain.

I drive. Out of Olympus Hills. Out onto the open road. Faster and faster. Trying to outrun the storm that chases me from the inside.

I don't know where I am going until I find myself outside the music shop again. I go inside, bells jangling as I let the door slam behind me.

"Can I help you?" the man at the cash register asks, startled.

"I want it all," I say. "I want to buy a copy of every album you've got."

The man raises his eyebrows over his thick-rimmed glasses. "Everything?"

"Yes," I hiss. Is this human an idiot? "That's why I said *every* album."

"Um. Okay. Uh. CD or MP3? I'm assuming MP3, since you can't fit the whole store in your trunk. You probably don't even have a CD player in a car like that, huh?"

I shake my head.

"We've got more selections on digital recording anyway. It'll fill up half a dozen of these MP3 players," he says, pointing at a row of devices, which look similar to my iPhone, in a display case.

"Then give me six of those, too," I say, and set the credit card Dax gave me on top of the glass case.

"Are you sure about this, man? Your parents aren't going to freak when they see the bill or anything, are they? And I'm going to need to see some ID."

"I don't live with my parents." I set the driver's license that says I'm twenty-one next to my credit card. "Don't forget anything. I want every single song you've got."

The man glances from the ID to the card to my luxury car, which sits in the parking lot, and then back to me. "Sweet," he says, a huge grin overtaking his face. "You are in for one wild time, my friend."

Hours later, I sit in my car on the beach. Waves crash outside, and wind from the approaching storm pounds against the roof and windows. One of the MP3 players is wirelessly connected to the stereo. I play song after song, trying to open myself up to each one. To feel the emotion they evoke like I did with Daphne in the booth. Some of the songs make me cringe, but others conjure emotions I have spent most of my life trying to bury: sadness, anger, awe, fear, joy, desire.

Love?

Daphne didn't mock me when I cried in front of her. She didn't think I was disgusting. She didn't tell me to stop before I embarrassed her. She seemed like she genuinely cared.

She cared about *me*.

The hour nears midnight, but I've barely burned through a fraction of the music I bought. The car's control panel warns me that I've let the battery get too low. Just as the music starts to fade,

I jolt the car with a burst of electricity, restoring it to full power. I turn up the volume. Louder. Louder. But no matter how high I turn up the sound, no matter how many emotions I let flood through me, I cannot drown out the thought that has clung to me since Daphne played me that last song in the booth.

I'd known it all along. Pushed way back in my mind so I wouldn't have to think about it. But opening up to her like that—letting her see one of the rawest portions of my soul—and her not rejecting it, I cannot deny reality any longer. The truth is, if Daphne eventually agrees to come with me, if I am victorious in my quest, if I get everything I've ever wanted—whether she's a regular Boon or this Cypher who the Oracle spoke of—she will die.

Just like my mother.

Just like every human who has been brought to the Underrealm—most barely making it through the first two years. Humans cannot survive without the sun.

They *all* die.

And so will she.

chapter forty

DAPHNE

It's nearly midnight, but the restaurant Joe takes me to in LA is packed. Despite the cold wind and the spattering of rain, there's a line wrapping around the side of the building. Joe leads me past the waiting crowd to the front doors. People scream his name and he stops to sign a couple of autographs. Flashbulbs go off, and reporters shoot questions at him.

"Who's your companion?" one of them yells.

Joe wraps his arm around me. "This is my daughter!"

The camera flashes go wild. He grabs me by the hand, and the doorman lets us in without making us wait.

"Sorry about that," Joe says to me. "You'll get used to them. Eventually."

We follow a hostess through the crowded restaurant, passing people I recognize from the gossip magazines. Joe hasn't let go of my hand yet. He waves at his friends, exchanges cheek kisses, and merrily introduces me as his daughter to everyone we see.

Most respond quite diplomatically, but I can hear the tones of utter shock coming off them.

We finally find ourselves at a window booth in the back of

the restaurant. It's quieter here, but the energy of the place still buzzes around us.

The hostess puts two menus in front of us and then offers Joe the wine and beer list. He waves it away. "Chocolate milk shake. With sprinkles." He raises his eyebrows at me.

"Make that two," I say.

A waitress comes and takes the rest of our order. I get a Kobe beef and applewood smoked bacon cheeseburger and onion rings that cost twice as much as the fanciest steak at Ellis Grill. Joe seems to request half the menu. It's his drummer's restaurant, so I am assuming that running up a *huge* tab on opening night is the polite thing to do.

"I'm sorry we didn't get much time with the telescope," he says.

"It's okay. Neither of us can control the elements," I say, watching the rain patter against the window.

"What made you change your mind?" Joe looks a bit sheepish. "About coming tonight. I mean, I'm happy about it. You just surprised me is all."

"Just something a friend said to me." I shrug like it's no big deal. "And I like the stars."

"Me, too," he says. "Do you remember what my favorite constellation is?"

I do. I remember him telling me once when I was a kid. But I don't want to admit that I've held on to that bit of information for this long. I shake my head.

"Lyra. It's supposed to be Orpheus's lyre. His father gave it to him when he was a boy. They say Orpheus was so talented, he *could* control the elements with his music. Animals, trees, rocks, rivers, monsters—even gods were not impervious to it. He used it as a weapon against Hades."

"A weapon?" I ask. Ms. Leeds had said that we would eventually discuss the Orpheus myth, but we've been mired in Homer's *Odyssey* for weeks.

"So to speak. Orpheus had one great love, his wife, Eurydice. She was bitten by a snake and died, but Orpheus was undaunted. Armed only with his lyre, he traveled to the underworld and tried to get her back. He used his music to convince the boatman to take him across the river Styx, and also used it to tame Cerberus, the three-headed dog that blocked his path. But his greatest feat was playing a song so melancholy and beautiful for the god and goddess of the underworld that even Hades himself could not deny Orpheus the opportunity to save his wife."

"So he followed her into the dark?" I ask, thinking of Haden's words from earlier today. "To save her?"

"Well, he tried, at least."

"He failed?"

"Hades gave Eurydice to Orpheus and told him they would be allowed to escape under one condition—that Orpheus was not allowed to look back at his wife until they had exited the underworld. He led her out, using his voice to guide her, but just when they made it to the exit, Orpheus looked back and Eurydice was lost to him forever."

"But why did he look back? They were so close."

"I don't know, really. Some say it's because he thought they'd already reached safety. Others say it's because she cried out because something was wrong. Or perhaps he'd lost faith that she was still there. Most storytellers agree that it was Hades's punishment—that he knew Orpheus would fail."

"Punishment? But he's the one who said they could go."

"To the ancient Greeks, questioning the will of the gods—let alone acting out against it—was the ultimate sin. Orpheus's sheer audacity in thinking he could reverse his fate—get his wife back from the clutches of the god of death—was considered wrong. It's a morality tale. You fight destiny, and it'll come back to bite you in the arse every time." Beyond the noise of the restaurant and the chattering patrons at the tables that surround us, I catch the most melancholy tone wafting up from Joe. "You can't fight your destiny. Believe me, I've tried."

I am about to ask him if he really believes in all this fate stuff or if he's just being melodramatic for the sake of the story, but three servers appear with tray after tray of food. One of the servers asks for a picture of Joe. He poses with her and then digs into a plate of cheese fries like a man who hasn't eaten in days. I bite into my bacon cheeseburger. I'd be lying if I didn't say it is the best thing I've ever tasted—even better than the burgers we'd grill up behind the shop on Sunday afternoons. But I'd never tell my mom or Jonathan that.

"What happened to Orpheus after that?"

"Some say he died of a broken heart; others say he was torn apart by a group of crazed women because he was too sad to pay attention to them. . . ."

I smirk, thinking of some of Joe's more rabid fans I'd seen on TV. It isn't too hard to believe.

"Others say that his father, Apollo, carried him away in his sun chariot. Whatever the story was, the loss of his music was so lamented that Zeus himself threw Orpheus's lyre into the heavens, and it became the Lyra constellation."

I can see why it is Joe's favorite constellation. I wouldn't be surprised if he fancies himself a modern Orpheus. I am pretty sure *he* is the one who first coined his "God of Rock" nickname.

"Is that why you chose Orpheus and Eurydice for the subject of the play?"

"Among other reasons." Joe holds up one of the burgers he ordered. "You have to try this. It's bloody brilliant. It has a fried egg and a slice of beet in it."

I wash down a bite of my cheeseburger with a gulp of milk shake and pull a gagging face at Joe.

"No, really. Try it."

He waves the burger in my face, and I know he's not going to stop until I take a bite. To my surprise, it's even better than my burger.

"That is bloody brilliant," I say, mimicking his accent.

"Eh, watch your mouth, girly," he says with a cheeky smile. He takes a bite of the burger. "Bobby and I first had these in New Zealand. Told him if he ever opened his restaurant, he had to put it on the menu," he says with his mouth full. "Eh, you should come with us sometime. On tour."

I choke on an onion ring.

"You okay there? Put your hands in the air. Maybe try some water?" He smacks me on the back until I stop coughing. "Yes, you should come on tour with us to Australia and New Zealand. You would love it. The stars are so much brighter there, and you can see constellations that you could never see here. We could go tramping up a volcano or something with a telescope. Now, there would be a good trip." He pounds his fist on the table, excited. "Next summer, you're coming with us!" he practically shouts.

"Joe, I don't think—" My desire to see the world and my uncertainty about going on tour with the father I barely know come clashing together. Mostly, it irks me that one evening at the

297

planetarium and a shared burger make him think that we're the best of friends now. That I'd *want* to go with him. That anything has been forgiven . . .

"Joe, my boy!" says an extremely enthusiastic voice.

Joe and I both look up. A man in a trim, expensive-looking, light gray suit stands in front of our table. He holds what looks like a spinach smoothie in his hand. I can't quite place his face, but I feel like I've seen him before.

"Sunny," Joe says. He sits up straighter. "I didn't know you'd be here tonight."

"Why wouldn't I be? Bobby has done a fantastic job, don't you think? Fantastic! Though he could stand to put some healthier items on the menu. Had to have the chef make me something special." He lifts his green glass. He smiles at me. His teeth look as bleached white as teeth could possibly get. "So this is the elusive Daphne. Aren't you going to introduce me to your beautiful daughter?"

"Oh yes," Joe says, wiping his mouth with his napkin. "Daphne, this is Mr. Sunny. My manager."

"Oh." One of the few things I do know about Joe's career is that he's been with the same manager for almost eighteen years. Kind of unheard of in the business, these days. Which is weird, because even though Joe has a polite smile on his face, the tone coming off him makes it clear that he's less than happy to see his manager at the moment.

I take the hand that Mr. Sunny offers. He clasps his fingers around mine as we shake. His skin is as cold as ice. Or I guess as cold as the smoothie he's been holding.

"We were just discussing some plans for the summer," Joe says. "Wouldn't it be nice to take Daphne on tour?"

Mr. Sunny's enthusiastic grin falters at the edges. I'm guessing that traveling with your teenage daughter doesn't do the best thing for your image when you're a rock star trying not to seem middle-aged to the younger generation.

"You haven't forgotten about your obligations this spring, have you?" Mr. Sunny says.

Joe shakes his head.

"Speaking of which, Bobby says you've missed your last two sessions at the recording studio."

Ah, the reason Joe isn't happy to see Mr. Sunny. He's been slacking.

"I've been busy working on the musical for Daphne's school."

"Oh, that explains it," Mr. Sunny says merrily, but the sound coming off him is anything but. "Joe, may I have a word with you in private?"

"Of course." Joe pats my hand as he stands. "I'll only be a minute, Daph."

"You are letting yourself get distracted," Mr. Sunny says to Joe as I watch the two walk away. A mixture of very unhappy sounds is coming off both of them. I imagine Joe is about to get a berating for neglecting his "God of Rock" duties.

"So, you do exist," a man says as he scoots into the booth next to me.

I blink at him until recognition clicks. I've seen him on TV countless times with Joe. Bobby Rox, Joe's drummer.

"I did the last time I checked," I say.

Bobby laughs. He's pink-faced, and I can tell he's on the verge of being drunk.

"Tell you what. We thought the old monk had made you up so we'd stop teasing him about being a eunuch!" he says with a chuckle.

299

"Did you just call my father a eunuch? Because I'm going to need a Brillo pad for my brain to get rid of that mental image."

Bobby laughs so loud that the people at the adjacent tables stare. "We just like to tease the old boy. I'm sure he's got all the right equipment. The guy's as celibate as a monk. In all our years, with all those *groupies* and reporters and *supermodels*, he's never once . . . *you know*."

"Again with the mental images . . ." I point at myself. "Daughter, remember?"

Although a slightly disturbing topic of conversation, this bit of information surprises me about Joe. He's never struck me as the religious type, nor the self-disciplined type, either. My mom had never said whether she and Joe had ever technically gotten divorced. Was it possible he is just that *faithful*?

I shake my head. They'd seen each other only five times in the last seventeen years. That certainly didn't count as a marriage. There had to be another reason for Joe's discretion. . . .

"The old boy probably wouldn't drink so much if he let himself get laid once in a while!" Bobby goes on guffawing, and I'm glad when a familiar face approaches the table.

"Marta, you're here, too?" I ask.

"I was nearby," she says. "Joe sends his apologies. He needs to attend to some business with Mr. Fitzgerald. I've been asked to escort you home."

Normally, I might feel slighted by Joe, but I don't argue with this change in plans. It's nearly one thirty in the morning and I can feel the fatigue pulling at my bones. I've already scheduled a Skype-chat breakfast with my mom, followed by three hours of self-imposed singing practice in the morning, and then I'm supposed to meet with Tobin for lunch so I can tell him everything

I've learned about Haden and the Lord family. It's still not a lot, but I know he'll be revving for an update.

I follow Marta sleepily to her Audi. It's a long drive back to Olympus Hills and I'm not sure I'll stay awake. "Who's Mr. Fitzgerald?" I ask with a yawn as I get into the passenger seat. "I thought Joe was with Mr. Sunny."

"Oh yes. Only Joe calls his manager Mr. Sunny—because of his 'sunny disposition.' He's Mr. Fitzgerald to the rest of us."

chapter forty-one

HADEN

It is nearly dawn by the time I return to the house in Olympus Hills. I have been gone for nearly a day, but I am heady with music and emotion—like an Heir who's imbibed too much nectar at a feast—and I don't care. I bang into the kitchen, singing one of the many songs I have memorized during the night.

Someone is waiting for me, but it isn't Dax, as I expect.

"Care to tell me where you've been?" Simon asks. He sits at the kitchen counter with a mug of his coffee. Based on the dregs left in the pot, he's consumed quite a few cups while waiting for me.

"No." I pick up an apple from the centerpiece on the table.

"Do you know where *I* was?" he asks.

"Nope." I whistle a tune, heading for the stairs.

"I was at a friend's restaurant opening. And the darnedest thing happened. Something that has never happened in all my years. My platinum card had a hold on it."

I stop at the front of the stairs.

"You can imagine my surprise when I called the credit card company to clear things up and found out that somebody in my household put a *fifty-eight-thousand-dollar* expense on my card yesterday afternoon."

I take a bite of the apple. I don't realize how hungry I am until the sweetness touches my tongue. I look at Simon while I chew.

"Not that I'm not good for the money. Not that I don't have the room in my account. They were just *concerned*. As was I. Do you know why I was concerned?"

I shake my head.

"Because someone in my charge didn't come home last night and wasn't answering his phone. I thought maybe this someone had decided to skip town. But you wouldn't do that, would you? Skip town? Abandon your quest? Run away? Like a coward?"

I suddenly find it hard to swallow. "I am not a coward. And I didn't run."

"I know that now," he says. "But you wouldn't be the first to *try*. That's one of the reasons I'm here. I almost came after you. That wouldn't have been pleasant for anyone involved—just ask your friend Dax. However, luckily for you, I took a closer look at the charge on my account. What exactly was so fascinating at Pacific Coast Records that you felt compelled to spend nearly sixty thousand dollars on it?"

"Music."

"Music?" Simon pours soy milk into his coffee and stirs it with a dainty spoon. "Sixty. Thousand. Dollars'. Worth of *music*?" He takes a sip and pulls a face like the milk has gone bad. "You know music is forbidden in the Underrealm?"

"Yes, but I'm only using it to get closer to Daphne. It's part of my quest. Dax said it's okay for Champions to bend the rules occasionally. . . ."

"I know what Dax says. He used the same argument on me when he convinced me to get you a spot in the program. I question whether it was wise."

"It's working. That's where I was yesterday. I was with *her*." *At least part of the day.*

"Do you know why music is forbidden?"

"Because it's too human?"

"Because of the Traitor. Because of what he *did*. He used his music to manipulate the god of the Underrealm. To trick him, deceive him. To distract him so he could steal the Key to the underworld. To trap the Underlords down there. Your god would still be alive today if not for that man's filthy manipulations."

"That has nothing to do with my—"

"That's what music is. It's manipulation. It plays on your emotions. Makes you think and feel things that aren't true. It distracts you."

"I'm not distracted."

"You sure? There's sixty grand and a full day of unaccounted time that tells me differently. You stink of emotion." He pushes his coffee cup away. "I wouldn't be surprised if you were having second thoughts about your assignment." He stares at me, his dark eyes boring into me.

"I'm not," I say softly.

"You sure, boy? I'd hate to tell dear ole Papa Ren that his son is an even bigger disappointment than anyone imagined. Tell him not to keep that seat next to his throne warm for you. Tell him you're just some nursling who can't keep his head on straight around some skirt who can spin a couple of pretty little songs."

"*I'm sure.*"

"Good." Simon takes his cup and plate to the sink. He pulls on a pair of rubber gloves and turns on the water. "Just to make sure, I'm going to be keeping you on a tighter leash," he says, taking a scrub brush the color of limes to his dishes. He cleans them with an intensity that makes me glad I am not a plate. "Under no circumstances are you allowed to leave Olympus Hills again. I have activated the GPS in your phone. I am to know where you are at all times. You will be home no later than midnight every night, and you will give me a full account of your daily doings. If I find that the music program is indeed becoming too distracting, I will terminate that arrangement immediately. You will have to find other avenues for getting close to your Boon. Less emotional ones. Do you understand me?"

Being told that my movements are to be monitored and restricted is irksome enough, but the fact that he's holding the music program out like some carrot he thinks he can snatch away based on my behavior makes me angry.

"You are not my king. I don't have to answer to you in this way."

"I am your father's emissary, which means here, in this place, when you look at me, all you should see *is* your father. I speak for him. I act for him. I report everything back to him. You will treat me as though I *am* him." The cup Simon has just scrubbed clean cracks in his gloved hand. "Is that clear?"

"Yes," I say, leaving my half-eaten apple on the polished mahogany banister, and head up the stairs to my room.

"Good night, then," Simon calls merrily after me. "Oh, and please try to keep your daily spending to at least a ten-thousand-dollar minimum."

I dream fitfully, waking and falling back asleep, for the rest of the morning. I see my mother's face. I hear her voice. I remember that she used to whisper a lullaby in my ear when I was too young to tell anyone. I can't quite hear the little melody, but I can feel it.

I hadn't allowed myself to fully think of her in so long, but once I did yesterday, it's like I can't push away her ghost. She haunts me.

I see her standing in my bedchamber, looking pale and withered. I am sitting at a table, playing chess with Rowan. We are both seven years old. I am bigger than Rowan, but he always beats me when we play strategy games. I prefer to wrestle. I ask our mother for a glass of water and she reaches for the pitcher that sits on the mantel of the fireplace.

She cries out and collapses, falling face-first against the marble fireplace. I hear the crack of her skull against the stone hearth.

"Mother!" I shout, and run to her. It takes most of my strength to turn her limp body over. A gash in her forehead weeps blood. Not knowing what else to do, I clasp my small hands over it, trying to staunch the bleeding, and shout at Rowan to run for help.

"I'm not your servant, Haden," he says, and moves his rook forward to capture the queen I'd left unprotected on the chessboard when I rushed from the table. "We're better off without her. Now come finish our game. I just put you in check."

Blood seeps out from under my fingers, staining Mother's ashy hair red. I can't stop the bleeding. I hear a gasp from the doorway and notice Garrick, small and scrawny, lurking in the corridor, only a few feet away from us, as usual. He blinks at me. The boy is a Lesser. Bred for following orders. "Go!" I shout to him. "Get help! Get my father!"

Garrick, only five years old, half my size and almost as bony as my mother, bounds away. I hear the smack of his sandaled feet against the stone floor as he heads down the corridor toward my father's chambers.

My mother's eyelashes flutter open, but her jade green eyes seem unable to focus.

"I'm here, Mother," I say.

She seems to recognize my voice. She lifts one finger as if she is trying to raise her whole hand but the rest won't cooperate. "Haden, my son," she whispers. "Always remember who you are." Her eyelids slide shut, a low rattle echoes from her throat, and her finger trembles as it lowers to lie as still as her others.

"No, Mother!" I shout at her. "Don't leave me!"

I try shaking her, but she doesn't move. I clasp my hands over her head wound again, determined not to let her go. It takes so long for my father to return with Garrick that my mother's warm blood has grown cold and thick under my hands. "She's dying," I say to him when he finally enters the room with two of his advisors and a couple of servants. My father nods. He snaps his fingers and says, "Clean up this mess," to his attendants. He turns to leave without giving his wife a second look.

"No, no, no," I scream at him. "You have to do something! Save her. Take her to the healing chambers!"

"It's too late," one of the servants says.

The other attendant tries to pull me away from my mother's body. Anger, and another emotion I don't understand, surges through my small body. I scream and kick at the servant's legs. A stinging pain pricks at the backs of my eyes. A terrible wail fills my ears. . . .

I sit bolt upright in my bed. I am cold, but my chest is damp with sweat. My phone wails again from the top of my dresser. I am grateful for the sound—grateful it awakened me before the rest of that memory can play out in my dream. Grateful not to witness what I did next—not to relive the moment of my unforgivable shame.

Brimstone shifts and yawns at my feet. I nudge her off my toes and stumble to get my phone from the dresser. I hurry to answer it when I see Daphne's name.

"Hello?"

"Were you still asleep?"

"Long night."

"Me, too," she says. "But I've been up since seven."

"Did you go with your father, then?"

"Yeah," she says. "And you know, it was better than I thought it would be. Got a little odd toward the end, but it was actually kind of fun."

"I'm happy for you."

"The only problem is, now Joe thinks I'm going to go on tour with him this summer."

"This summer?" A pang of guilt hits me in the chest. Daphne may not ever see a summer again.

"Yeah, can you imagine? I can barely stand sharing a mansion with the guy; can you picture us in a tour bus? And his drummer is kind of a weirdo." She pauses to take a breath. "But, hey, I'm guessing you haven't checked your email yet. Considering you're Sleeping Beauty and all."

"Who?"

"Never mind. Anyway, check your email. I think I've found the perfect song for our duet. I sent you the music."

"Give me a minute." I open my email app. Other than the welcome packet that came from the school at the beginning of the year, her message is the only one in my in-box. I open the file she's sent and peruse it, glad I'd used a YouTube video to learn how to read music since my first lesson with her. "This is good," I say, imagining the sounds of the notes as I read them.

"It's 'Falling Slowly' by Glen Hansard and Markéta Irglová—from one of my favorite movies. It's the first duet I thought of, but after looking at several others, I think it's the best option."

I read over the words. Imagining the lyrics with the notes evokes an uncertain, wanting ache in my chest. "It's perfect."

"It's going to take a lot of practice," she says. "Are you up for spending that much time with me over the next couple of weeks?"

"Yes," I say.

At this moment, there's nothing I want more.

chapter forty-two

DAPHNE

The next couple of weeks are pretty much a blur. Between homework, sitting in on a second round of auditions to help Joe and Mr. Morgan select the other principal roles for the spring musical—I make sure to put in a good word for Lexie for the role for Persephone, not only because of the truce we made, but because she actually deserves the part—and rehearsing with Haden every afternoon and lunch break, I am shocked when I realize that Thanksgiving is already upon us.

Thankfully, Joe decides not to cook Thanksgiving dinner himself, and instead, we join a couple of his bandmates for a private party at Bobby Rox's restaurant. The food is divine, and to my surprise, I enjoy the company. Bobby and his wife, Elle, have the cutest daughter, and Chris Trip, the band's bassist, has everyone in stitches over his impersonations of Mr. Fitzgerald, their overly chipper manager.

When Joe passes up the Thanksgiving champagne and opts for the cranberry juice mixed with Sprite concoction that I order for myself from the kitchen, Bobby slaps Joe on the back and says, "You've been a good influence on our ole boy here, Daphne!"

"Hear, hear!" agrees Chris. "I thought Joe could write his way out of a bottle of Jack Daniel's, but he's even better sober. Those songs he's writing for your school play are amazing."

"They are good, aren't they?" I say. The ones I've practiced with Tobin have blown me away.

Joe smiles down at his plate.

"Yeah," Bobby says. "I haven't seen that level of passion in your work since *Shadow of a Star*."

"The band is thinking of recording an album of all the songs from the musical," Chris says. "Oi, I know, Daphne should record one of the tracks with us!"

"Brilliant!" Joe says.

"What?" I say, almost spilling my fizzy cranberry juice.

"I love it," Bobby says. "Joe showed us a couple of recordings he made during your class rehearsals the other day. You're fantastic."

I blush, pressing my lips together.

"What do you say, Daphne?" Joe asks. "At least one song. You can't say no to an opportunity like that."

"Won't your manager have a cow?" I ask.

"Leave that to us," Chris says, flexing his muscles. "We'll strong-arm him into it."

"Come on, Daph, say yes," Joe implores.

Singing a song on a real live rock album? One that is almost guaranteed to go platinum? The idea both thrills me and terrifies me at the same time. But does Joe really want *me* on his album, or is this just another one of those promises he uses to make himself feel better?

If it were anyone else asking, I'd say yes in a heartbeat.

I think about what Lexie said about my being an idiot for not wanting Joe's help. And then what Haden said about how I should give him another chance at being my father while I still have the opportunity.

"Okay," I say, and the band cheers.

Later that night, as we say good-bye to everyone, Bobby's wife, Elle, takes both Joe and me by the hand. "You're a lucky man, Joe," she says. "I can only hope our little Samara grows up to be like Daphne. She's absolutely perfect."

Joe is quiet the whole way home after that. I hope he hasn't decided that he's made a big mistake.

The day after Thanksgiving is the big Light-up Olympus Festival to celebrate the turning on of holiday lights in Olympus Hills. Which also means it's the day of the big music showcase that Haden and I have been preparing for.

To be honest, I've pretty much back-burnered Tobin's investigation, until I get an urgent SOS. Meet me at the docks in twenty text from him only an hour and a half before the festival is about to begin. I finish fixing my hair and put on the new outfit that Joe let me pick out from Bloomingdale's and head to the lake on my bike to meet him.

I pace the floating dock, the wood creaking under my steps, the whole structure rocking slightly under me. Fifteen minutes go by. Several families and kids from my school pass me on the lake trail, making their way to Olympus Row, where the festival is about to begin.

I wait a few more minutes, and I am about to take my bike and leave, when Tobin finally jogs down the dock, making it rock even more.

"Sorry," he says. "My mom was in a snit over the PA system setup for the showcase. She thinks I should be able to fix any mechanical problem—she forgets I'm not my brother."

"You had me worried," I say, feeling a bit unsteady on the water. "What's going on?"

"I found it," Tobin says, rubbing under his eyes. He looks like he's barely slept in a week. "Ms. Wells finally let me have access to the old yearbooks. I've been poring through them for the last couple of nights. I found what I was looking for." He pulls out his phone and opens the memo app. He holds it up, showing me a list of dates. "These are all the years someone with the last name of Lord attended the school. Do they look familiar?"

I nod.

They're all the same years as the ones those girls disappeared.

"But what does that even mean?" I ask. "Yeah, it's an eerie coincidence. But that's still all it is."

"Coincidence? This is damning evidence. We can use this to find Abbie. I even have the full name and picture of the Lord guy who was friends with her." He shows me a grainy photo of a photo of a guy who bears a vague family resemblance to Haden. "It proves that Haden—"

"What? That Haden comes from a long line of serial killers? That's insane."

"Exactly!"

"I know Haden," I say. "Yeah, he's kind of different and his family sounds a bit off, but he's not some lunatic in training. He's *nice*."

"Ted Bundy was nice."

"Stop it, Tobin. These are serious accusations."

"I know. Which is why you shouldn't see him anymore."

"Anymore? Tobin, I'm going onstage with him"—I check my watch—"in twenty minutes. You're the one who challenged him to this. I'm not going to just cancel on him."

313

"He's up to no good. He's dangerous."

"Dangerous? What's he going to do to me in a large group of people? I've been alone with him several times in the last two months. If he were going to do something to me, he would have done it then. And you know what? Instead of hurting me, he's protected me *twice* now from whatever that thing out there is that's been attacking people."

"You're starting to like him, aren't you?" Tobin asks, like it's an accusation.

"This is ridiculous," I say. "I don't have to answer that."

"You're being ridiculous!" Tobin practically drops his phone in the lake as he gestures at me as if he thinks I'm acting unhinged. "I've got proof your boyfriend is—"

"He's *not* my boyfriend."

"But you like him, don't you?"

"I . . . I don't know."

"You've gotten too close, Daphne. You're letting your feelings for him cloud your judgment."

I throw my hands up. "I don't have time for this." I storm up the dock and grab my bike.

Tobin follows me. "I'm not saying he's a killer. That's the thing—I know Abbie is still alive. I know she's out there somewhere. I can feel it, Daphne. I can feel that Haden can lead me to her."

"I hope we find your sister. I really do. I just think you're looking in the wrong place." I get on my bike.

"Don't go, please."

"I'll see you at the festival, Tobin." I give him a smile so he knows we're still friends. "Good luck with your number."

I set off for the festival, leaving him to follow behind on foot.

I can't quite explain why I'd gotten so defensive of Haden. I just can't believe he's a bad person. Maybe it's because of what he told me about holding his mother when she died. Maybe it's because he's the one who encouraged me to open up to Joe, and I'd actually gotten a positive result out of it. Maybe it's because I enjoy singing with him so much—his voice complements mine so well. Or maybe it's because Tobin might be right.

Despite my better judgment and despite my utter lack of time for a relationship, when it comes to the idea of my starting to like Haden . . . All signs point toward yes.

Crap balls.

chapter forty-three

HADEN

I was born to a race of warriors. My training began when I was six years of age. I have fought and bested Underlords who are twice my size. I have killed a hydra with my bare hands. Placed my head on the altar and left myself to my father's wrath or mercy. I have traveled through Persephone's Gate into a realm unknown to me. But I have never experienced fear quite like the anticipation I feel: knowing that in mere minutes, I am expected to sing with Daphne in front of the entire town.

I'm pressing hard on my knee to stop my leg from shaking, and in turn, the row of chairs beside me, when Daphne sits down next to me. I breathe out a small sigh. I'd almost been afraid that she wasn't coming.

"Want one?" she says, offering me an orangish, discuslike thing. It's speckled with brown spots. "Might help calm your nerves."

"What is it?" I try not to wrinkle my nose at her offering.

"It's a pumpkin chocolate-chip cookie, dork." She makes a teasing face at me. "You eat it."

She drops the said cookie into my hands. It's soft to the touch, yet firm. "You made a pumpkin into *this*?" I sniff it. It smells too sweet to be a squash.

She smirks. "Believe it or not."

I start to take a tentative bite.

"And, no, *I* didn't make it. Lexie and her Sopranos just gave me a whole box of them from Olympus Hills Bakery."

I pull the cookie away from my mouth and cast it onto the table in front of us. "Are you sure they're not poisoned?"

She smirks again, thinking I'm joking. "Good point." She takes a cookie out of the box and takes a bite out of it anyway. I watch, horror-stricken, waiting for any signs of a toxic reaction.

"Mmm," she says, and takes a second bite. "Lexie and I have reached an understanding." She looks up as Lexie, Bridgette, and a couple of the other Sopranos call out their wishes of good luck to us. They're manning something called a Check Your Heart booth as part of the festival. Signs posted around their booth announce free cholesterol tests and blood pressure screening. There's a long line at the booth. I'm not surprised. With there now having been seven "heart attack" victims—three of which were fatal—in the last few weeks, I'm sure the humans are getting anxious about their well-being. The school principal even announced that they're banning something called trans fats from the cafeteria, indefinitely.

If they had any idea of what is really causing the attacks, I doubt they'd be gathering out in the open en masse like this. They'd all be at home with their doors and windows locked tight—not that it would do them much good.

Watching the crowd mill about the festival makes my nerves bristle more. This place could be a feeding frenzy for a Keres. I can only hope it isn't hungry tonight.

Brim and I have gone hunting for the Keres every night for the last two weeks without much luck. Every scent trail has led to either a dead end or another hapless victim. How it manages to keep eluding me, I don't know. If I didn't know that Keres are mindless beasts, I'd almost call this one cunning.

The question that keeps nagging at me is what am I even supposed to do when I find it? How do you attack something that has no form? How do you stop something you cannot touch?

How do you kill a shadow?

I pull out my phone and send a quick text to Dax, telling him that I want him to patrol the perimeter of the festival. I wait for a response but none comes. Dax is supposed to be here somewhere, but I haven't seen him all day. I've barely seen him at all in the last two weeks.

I try Garrick next, sending an order to get his ass to the festival to help with patrols, but that message goes unanswered also. Ever since he admitted knowing the truth about my involvement in his banishment, he's become more and more obstinate to my commands. Like he knows that I know if I push him too far, he'll go squealing to Dax about what I did. He's probably glued to that stupid Xbox device he brought home a couple of days ago.

My "entourage" has been anything but attentive as of late.

"Oh. It's starting," Daphne says, pulling me out of my frustrated reverie. She squeezes my arm with happy excitement.

How can she be so confident?

We watch as the mayor walks out on the temporary stage that has been erected for the night's entertainment in the middle of Olympus Row. Each end of the street has been blocked off to make the festival a pedestrian event. The crowd quiets as Mayor Winters announces the lineup for the entertainment. Tobin will perform first, then Daphne and I, followed by a group number by Lexie and the Sopranos, and then a few more students—but I am too distracted to catch their names. Distracted by the look of disappointment that crosses Daphne's face as she scans the people in the crowd.

I think I know whom she wishes to see.

"He'll come."

"You don't know that." She gives me a weak smile. "Things have been going well between us. We eat breakfast together every morning and we go to school together...."

I nod. Joe had been visiting music class each morning, running through songs and assigning some of the parts. I'd even seen him bring Daphne lunch on a couple of days.

"I just thought he might come tonight." She washes down the last of her cookie with a swig of water from a bottle. "But I guess that's what I get for hoping on Joe," she mumbles to herself.

"It's not our turn yet. There's still time. He'll come." I hope for her sake that I'm right.

"Funny," she says. "Just a couple of weeks ago, I wouldn't have cared if he never heard me sing again."

Tobin takes the stage, to much applause from the audience. Surprisingly, Daphne doesn't light up as she usually does when she sees him. Almost like there's a fresh strain between them. Tobin performs a rocked-out version of one of the older songs in my new music collection. He starts out kind of stiff, like something is agitating him, but once he gets into it, I would be lying if I didn't admit that he's good. The audience seems to agree, clapping enthusiastically when he finishes.

I take the pumpkin cookie—poisoned or not—and shove it in my mouth. (Anything to help stop my urge to run and hide.) Surprisingly, it's the first thing I've eaten in the mortal world that doesn't make me want to gag. Actually, I could eat about ten more. I eye the box sitting next to Daphne.

She looks at me and smiles in the strangest way.

"What?"

"You've got chocolate on your mouth." She reaches out and brushes her fingers over my lips. "There," she says. "That's better," and she absentmindedly sucks the chocolate from the tip of her finger.

If it were possible for an Underlord to spontaneously combust, it could have happened at this moment.

"Come on. We're up," Daphne says, taking my hand.

My mouth runs dry and I regret having eaten the cookie. I down half a water bottle as she leads me to the stage.

Her friend Iris joins us there. Daphne asked her to play the violin in the background, while Daphne is on the piano, and I am the guitarist. Once we'd started rehearsing the song, and I discovered that my voice is supposed to carry the bulk of the lyrics—with Daphne joining in, complementing mine in certain parts—I wasn't sure I could pull this off.

"You can do this," Daphne had said after a few failed attempts during rehearsal. "Your voice is perfect for the song and your playing is technically spot-on. You just need to open yourself up to the emotion of it all. Let the words fall through you—like the song says."

I try to remember that now as I start the intro on the guitar. The first few lines of the song are mine alone, and then Daphne joins in. The timbre of her voice makes me tremble. It sounds like how I imagine her caress might feel. I close my eyes briefly, calming myself. As I play, I concentrate on nothing but the sounds of our voices. Iris's violin in the background fades away, and as far as I am concerned, the audience disappears. All that remains are our voices mixing together—no, more like clasping. Like two lovers who have found each other's hands in the darkness. It's a reaching, yearning sound that makes a wanting ache burn inside my chest.

This time, there's nothing uncertain about it.

When the final note of the song falls, the audience erupts in applause. The sound startles me. I have almost forgotten that Daphne and I are not alone on the edge of her couch, rehearsing. The moment had felt like such an intimate one to me that cheers from the crowd feel intrusive.

Daphne takes my hand and I follow her lead, bowing to the audience.

"Your song," she says, leaning close to me, as if listening to my heartbeat. "It's beautiful."

I tilt my head, studying her face, not sure what she means. Daphne smiles at me, but then her gaze flits to the audience, who stand on their feet, clapping for us. She's still looking for Joe.

I can feel her mounting disappointment until I hear a loud, sharp whistle from the back of the crowd. My gaze follows Daphne's as she finds Joe standing near the kettle corn booth. The smile returns to her face.

"That's my girl!" Joe shouts over the applause. "That's my daughter!" He starts making his way through the crowd. Daphne's smile folds into a frown. Joe's steps are too heavy, lumbering, and he almost pushes over an older man in his haste to get near the stage.

"That's my daughter!" he shouts again. The volume of his voice strikes me as inappropriate, and his voice is tinged with anger. He holds a long-necked, brown bottle in his hand.

"Oh no, Joe," Daphne says under her breath.

"That's my daughter. She's perfect. She's everything a man

could ever want in a child. And I gave her up. I traded her for fame and fortune."

Mayor Winters suddenly appears on the stage. She takes a microphone. "*The* Joe Vince, everybody! How about a round of applause for our local rock star?" She leads the crowd in an awkward spatter of applause. A couple of camera phones flash.

Joe looks around, jerking his head back and forth as if he can't figure out why people are clapping for him.

"Did you all know that Joe Vince is writing the school musical?" the mayor goes on, trying to defuse the situation. "Isn't he fantastic?"

"What? I'm not fantastic. Don't clap for me!" Joe shouts. "I'm nothing but a lying, worthless son of a . . ."

"Sounds like Mr. Vince has been enjoying our little party too much," the mayor says, cutting him off. "How about we find someone to take him home?"

Tobin's dad and another man break away from the crowd. They approach Joe like he's an injured cat.

"Let's go, Joe," Tobin's dad says.

Joe wipes the back of his mouth with his hand. He looks up at the mayor. "You know what I did. You know what I gave up to become the 'God of Rock.' And I'm not the only one here guilty of the same sins." His gaze moves from the mayor and locks on to me. "And now the devil has come to collect."

I take a step back, letting go of Daphne's hand.

Did he really just say what I thought he said? Was he outing me in front of Daphne and the entire town?

But how would he even know who I am? What I've come here for?

Tobin's father makes a move to grab Joe, but Joe takes a swing at him—too slowly—and Tobin's father moves easily out of the way. Joe lurches forward, stumbling. He falls onto the asphalt. I hear the crunch of glass under him as he tries to break his fall with the hand that was holding the beer bottle. More camera flashes go off.

"Joe!" Daphne says, jumping down from the stage. I follow her without even thinking.

He tries to push himself up, but then looks, bewildered, down at his hand. It's covered in blood.

"Bloody, buggering hell," he says, holding his injured hand. "How did that happen?"

"What were you thinking?" Daphne asks. I can't tell if her question is directed at Joe or at Tobin's father for inadvertently causing Joe's fall.

Joe blinks up at her. "Daphne, when did you get here, love?"

"He's drunk out of his mind," I say. "He probably has no idea what he just did. Or even what he's said."

At least I hope that's true. Or at least that Daphne will believe it.

More camera flashes go off as Daphne grabs some napkins from a nearby table. She presses them into Joe's hand. The blood soaks right through.

A Keres would be able to smell that much blood from a mile away.

"There's a first-aid tent at the other end of the street," Tobin's father says.

"No. We need to get him out of here," I say, helping Joe up. I need to get him as far away from this crowd as possible.

"Good thinking," Daphne says. "I wouldn't be surprised if pictures from this little event end up in the newspapers tomorrow."

"I'll take him home," I say to her. Or at least to an area out of sight that will be easy to defend. "Stay here with your friends. Go find Tobin."

"Yeah, right," Daphne says. "I'm not sticking you with Joe. He's my dad."

"You called me *dad*," Joe says. He reaches out and runs his fingers down her face, almost poking her in the eye.

"I already regret it," she says, looping his arm around her shoulder.

"Really, Daphne, I can handle it."

"*I'm* taking him home," she says. "Don't argue with me."

A rotten egg smell wafts by on a breeze. It could be from one of the garbage receptacles placed around the festival or it could be a Keres. . . .

There's no time for arguing.

"We'll both go," I say.

"Stop the car," Joe moans from the backseat. Daphne had ridden her bike to the festival, and Joe was in no condition to walk the lake paths—nor did I want him out in the open—so the three of us had piled into my Tesla.

"We're almost home," Daphne says tersely. I can feel the anger radiating off her. I'm glad it's not directed toward me.

"Stop. The. Bleeding. Car."

I slam on the brakes. Joe is out the door before we even come to a complete stop. He stumbles onto the grass and I hear the sounds of his heaving onto the gravel path that leads to one of the lakefront beaches.

"Nice," Daphne mumbles. She wipes her hand down her face.

"He'll be fine by morning." *If I can keep him alive until then.*

I run through different options in my head. If the Keres has locked on to his scent, then we need to get as far away from town as we can. Maybe take him to a hospital in LA? The cut doesn't look deep enough to warrant stitches but . . . no. I couldn't risk leading a Keres into such a populated area as Los Angeles, and definitely not a hospital. Simon's house, perhaps? Where Dax and Garrick can help . . . But what excuse do I make for taking Daphne and Joe there instead of home . . . ?

I open the door and stand outside my car. I sniff the air to determine if the Keres is on our trail, but the smell of Joe's vomit is too overwhelming.

Joe heaves again. I turn away. It sounds particularly violent.

"What do you think he meant by all that?" Daphne asks loudly, as if trying to cover up the sound of her father's indiscretions with her question. "What he said about trading me for fame and fortune?"

"I don't know." I'd pass it off as alcohol-addled ramblings if his words about the devil coming to collect hadn't hit so close to the mark. "Maybe he really regrets not being there for you as a kid. Like he traded your childhood for his career."

"Do you really think so?" Daphne almost sounds hopeful.

"Daphne. Come here," Joe moans. "I need your help."

She sighs and pushes open her door. "I am not going to hold your weave back as you puke, Joe."

"Dappphhhnnneeee?" he says with a whiny urgency that makes me look at him. He sways in the glow of a street lamp, looking as though he's about to fall over. "Have I always had two shadows?" he asks, pointing at his feet.

"What?" she asks.

I hear her gasp as she sees what I see. Joe does indeed have two shadows. One is shorter, about half his height in length, but the other stretches out to the border of the lamplight.

I suddenly feel as though a cold wind has wrapped around me and pierced into my bones. Two shadows. Two shadows. The Keres has been with us all along. It's attached itself to Joe. He'll be dead in a matter of minutes.

"What the . . . ?" Daphne starts to say as the second, long shadow suddenly curls forward and rises up off the pavement.

I toss my car keys at her. "Drive," I say. "Get out of here!"

Joe moans and clutches at his chest, and starts to convulse as if having a seizure. I know better. The Keres is draining the life out of him.

"No," Daphne says, throwing the keys right back at me. "Joe!" She runs toward her father, but the shadow swirls around him, wrapping him in a transparent black cocoon. "What's happening?!"

A surge of lightning builds in my chest, but I don't know what to do with it. What if I throw it at the Keres, and it merely passes through it and strikes Joe? That would kill him faster than the evil bloodsucker that has him in its clutches. Blue light webs between my fingers, and then engulfs my hand and arm. I can feel it burning the fabric of my shirtsleeve off my arm. It will incinerate my skin next, if I don't throw it soon. I look up at the street lamp above Joe. I pour all my concentration into shaping the crackling wisps of lightning into a blue sphere.

"Get back!" I shout at Daphne.

She looks at me. Her eyes widen as she takes in the ball of lightning I cradle in my hand. I am breaking another one of the steadfast Champion rules by letting her see me this way. *I have no choice but to expose my powers in front of her*, I tell myself. *Either that, or let her watch her father die.*

"Haden, what . . . ?"

"Get out of the way."

She twists out of the way, and I fling the lightning at the street lamp. An explosion of light and glass follows. The Keres sends a screeching, shrieking wail into the night, but it doesn't flee like it did before when Lexie was the victim.

Has it already figured out that it doesn't have to be afraid of my lightning?

The Keres forces Joe to the ground. He wails in pain, calling Daphne's name. Another bolt of lightning works its way through my body. Do I dare take a shot directly at the beast?

Daphne steps in front of me. She plants her feet—staring down at the shadow creature—and screams.

Not out of fear. Not out of anger. But in a determined, deliberate way, focusing her voice right at the black, writhing cocoon. The force of it reminds me of the stories of banshees I heard as a child. The timbre and tone match the horrible, screeching wail that comes from the Keres. The shadow unwinds from Joe, and for a few seconds, the Keres becomes solid, looking like a statue of a monstrous, black, stone angel. Its giant wings bristle, its claws outstretch, its terrible, jagged teeth protrude from its jaws. It flings itself at Daphne, becoming shadow once more.

"Scream again!" I shout at Daphne.

She throws her hands out in front of her defensively and shrieks.

The sound rips the air and the Keres takes solid form again. I can see its terrible claws swipe toward her chest, ready to tear her heart out from behind her ribs.

I fling a bolt of lightning at its abdomen. The electricity catches it midflight and forces it against the lamppost. The Keres explodes into a thousand pieces, raining shards of stone on top of us. Daphne throws her hands over her head. Joe lies as still as death as bits of Keres fall onto his back.

Daphne hasn't looked at me since I killed the Keres. I wish she'd look at me. She's crouched over Joe, kneeling in the debris of broken glass and fragments of stone. She presses her fingers against his neck, and then holds them in front of his mouth.

"He's okay," she says softly. "I think he's just fainted."

I don't say anything in response. I am too afraid to. Not until I see how she sees me now.

Now that she has seen what I can do.

Now that she knows I am not human.

Why doesn't she look at me?

Daphne slowly rises, brushing Keres dust from her arms with her perfect, calloused fingers. Her hair drapes like a golden curtain in front of her face. She can probably see me, but I can't see her.

"You killed it." Her voice shakes, but I can't tell if it's out of fear or relief. "You killed that *thing* . . ." She takes a step closer. ". . . with lightning . . ." Another step. ". . . that came out of your hands." Two more steps. "I saw it." She is only inches from me now. "So don't you dare try to deny it."

"I won't," I say, wishing more than anything I could see her eyes.

"Good," she says, closing three of the six inches that still remain between us. "Then you will know what this is for."

Before I can react, Daphne attacks me. She lunges forward, crossing the last three inches of space between us. Her hands wrap around my neck, and she yanks my head forward against

328

hers. I tense, expecting to be bashed in the face with her fore-head, but instead, her warm lips close over mine. Her fingers slip into my hair, and shooting, tingling pain spreads through my skin wherever she touches me.

Panic overtakes my body. I feel my eyes go wide. I try to raise my hands to thrust her away. Is she trying to steal my breath? My soul?

There are stories of creatures that can do so, I am sure.

But it isn't pain running through my body. It's pleasure. Warm, radiating tendrils of it, curling through me under her touch. Her caress. It feels just as I imagined it would when she sang.

She presses harder with her lips, imploring mine.

I yield.

I melt.

I surrender.

My arms raise now, closing around her, pressing her closer against me. My lips give in to hers, parting, wanting, giving, beck-oning for more in return.

Electric heat swirls inside my chest and shoots through my entire body. I pull away from Daphne just as a blue spark passes from my lips to hers.

She places her fingers on her lips, but I can tell she's smiling.

"What . . . what was that for?" I ask, dragging in a deep breath, trying to calm the fiery nerves in my body.

Daphne tries to laugh, but it sounds like she's out of breath also. She sweeps her hair away from her face. She smiles and her eyes fill with a bright happiness I haven't seen in her before. "For saving my life. And Joe's."

She steps closer again, and I brace myself, hoping to Hades she will press her lips against mine again—wondering how she will respond if I do it to her before she gets the chance.

"For being honest with me," she says. Her hands clasp my arms and she stares into my eyes. I can't help but flex under her fingers. I want her to feel how strong I am. She laughs, and I know she's on to me. Her fingers slide up and down my upper arms. Her touch feels so soothing over the scars in my right arm—my skin left uncovered when my lightning burned my sleeve away. Like I didn't know just how badly the scars pained me until her mere touch made that pain lessen.

Harpies, my scars . . .

I start to pull away from Daphne, but I am too late. Her hand clasps tightly under the scars. "What is that . . . ? What the hell?" Her voice falters, and I know she's seen it.

Her name. Carved and scarred into my skin.

She lets go of me and backs away quickly. "What . . . why? What the hell is that?" Fear strikes into her eyes. "Are you insane?"

"I can explain . . . ," I start to say, but I don't know if I really can. Not without exposing the whole truth. Not without breaking the most steadfast rule the Underrealm has placed on me. Not without losing every chance I have of ever getting her to fall in love with me.

"No. I don't really want to know," she says. "You're sick, Haden. You're sick and you obviously need help."

From the way she looks at me now, I know any chance I had with her is over. She doesn't see her friend standing in front of her. She doesn't see her singing partner. She doesn't see someone she would ever want to embrace again. She looks at me the way I feared she would after I killed the Keres.

She sees the real me.

She sees the monster that has come to take her away.

"Daphne, please . . ."

She lifts her hands defensively in front of her the way she had when the Keres tried to attack. "Don't come near me."

"Daphne, what's going on?" Joe says groggily from behind her. I'd all but forgotten he was here. He rocks up on his knees.

"We're getting out of here." She grabs his arm and pulls him to his feet with one hand, and holds her other hand up to ward me off. "Don't you dare follow us," she says to me. "Or I'll call the police."

I let her go. I let her walk away.

She takes every particle of my hope and happiness with her as she leaves.

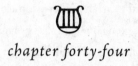

chapter forty-four

DAPHNE

"He's crazy," I mumble to myself as I lead Joe toward the house.

"He's daft," Joe agrees.

"He's insane."

"He's mental," Joe says.

"I don't even think he's human." I know I sound like the crazy one, but there is no human explanation for what I had seen Haden do. What kind of *person* can throw lightning bolts out of his hands?

"Not even human," Joe says. At least I had one person who could corroborate my story.

Tobin is going to flip when I tell him.

If I tell him.

Why wouldn't I tell him?

I unlock the front door, take Joe into the house, and then lock the door again behind us.

"And I can't believe I kissed him!"

"I can't believe you kissed him. . . . Wait, who are we talking about?" Joe stumbles, trying to put one foot in the front of the other as I lead him up the stairs. I realize we haven't been having a conversation; he's just been drunkenly parroting me.

"Never mind," I say, and propel him down the hall toward his bedroom. He falls into the nest of satin sheets on his bed, and settles his hands under his cheek against his pillow. He reminds me of a child.

I pull off one of his boots, and realize that my hands are still shaking. The only time they had stopped trembling since that *thing* attacked us was when I'd kissed Haden. Now the thought of that, and my name freaking carved into Haden's arm, make my hands shake even more. I tug on Joe's second boot. He smacks his lips and wiggles his foot, trying to help me.

"Who did you kiss?" he asks with a yawn.

"Haden," I say, figuring that Joe won't even remember in the morning.

"Oh," he says. "Don't kiss him. Haden is the devil."

"What?" His boot pops off his foot, and I stumble backward, almost tripping over one of the various empty beer bottles on the floor. I drop the boot on the ground. "What do you mean?"

Joe snores in response. I shake his shoulder. "Joe? What did you just say? Joe, can you hear me?"

But it's no use. He's out cold, and I doubt he'll wake up until morning. And by then he'll have no idea what he said to me.

I gather up the empty beer bottles on his floor and take them down to the recycling bin in the kitchen. He had been sober for almost two months now. I wonder what set him off on this binge. There's a half-empty case of beer bottles on the counter. I pull out a bottle opener and start popping their tops off, and then pouring their contents down the drain, finding myself angry that I even have to do this.

Joe seems to live a charmed life—so why does he keep trying to drown himself in this stuff? What is so terrible that he is trying to numb himself from thinking about?

I pick up a new bottle, but before I pop the top off, wind rattles the window over the sink. I jump, almost dropping the bottle. I check the window lock, not knowing if it would do any good against someone who can throw lightning.

What the hell is that all about?

And why is my name cut into his arm?

That is a whole level of psycho I wasn't prepared to deal with.

I look at the beer bottle in my hand. If there is one thing I'd want to numb myself from remembering, it would be the moment I found those scars on his arms. The moment I went from wanting him to realizing he's a sick freak. A sick freak who I *kissed*!

Now that's a memory I'd like to erase.

I should have listened to Tobin's warning to stay away from Haden. He probably really is from a long line of wack jobs. Even Joe seems to think he is a bad person . . . if he is even a person at all . . .

He'd even called Haden the devil. . . .

I shake my head at the possibility of even entertaining Joe's drunken ramblings. I've never been a religious person, and the idea that a living, breathing incarnation of the devil is walking around Olympus Hills and practicing duets with me is about as crazy as believing in fairy tales, or even Greek mythology, for that matter!

I dump the last of the beer down the drain, wash the scent of it off my fingers, and go to my room. I don't need to escape reality; I need to figure out what the hell is going on.

I flop down on my bed, ready to call Tobin—hoping his phone isn't still turned off for the musical showcase—and admit that he's probably right, when I see my iPad sitting on my nightstand, where I'd left it after studying last night. I turn it on and the text from my mythology book appears on my screen. I remember how defensive Haden had been that first day in humanities class when I tried to compare the Greek mythological character of Hades to that of the Christian devil. It was almost as if he had been offended.

Isn't it supposed to be gods who can strike people down with lightning?

Haden, a *god*? That is even more preposterous!

I do a search in the mythology book for all the references of Hades. More in an attempt to put my mind at ease than to prove this line of thinking correct.

Haden already has two strikes against him as far as this Hades theory goes. First, he'd already admitted to being part Greek. And second, there is the name thing. *Haden* is only one letter off from *Hades*. But that feels a little *too* on the nose.

I scan the first page that references Hades, but it is merely a genealogy chart of all the gods. I go to the second reference and find a physical description of the god.

Hades, god of the underworld and brother to Zeus, is usually depicted as being extremely tall, standing at least seven feet in height . . .

Haden is tall. At least six feet four. But being tall doesn't make someone a supernatural being. I mean, look at me.

. . . with a muscular build.

Another check mark for Haden. It had been a little hard to ignore his muscular build when being held in his arms. . . .

Hades is most often depicted as having a dark beard, and pale skin from spending most of his time in the underworld.

Haden doesn't have a beard, but his hair is definitely dark and his skin is pretty pale for someone with an olive complexion—almost like he doesn't get out in the sun much.

Physical objects attributed to Hades are a chariot pulled by four fearsome black stallions . . .

Haden has a black car, but that is hardly the same as having a chariot and horses.

. . . a bident, the Key of Hades, and a three-headed dog named Cerberus.

Ha. There. Haden doesn't have any of those things. And he has the world's smallest cat, not the giant, snarling, three-headed dog that is pictured in my book.

Hades's most impressive possession is the Helm of Hades, a special helmet or cap that can turn the wearer invisible. . . .

This one strikes a strange chord inside me. I've never seen Haden with a hat, but I remember the way he seemed to materialize out of the shadows the first time I met him in the grove. And then there's what happened when I was backstage at the auditions. I'd been completely alone, and yet it had felt like someone had been back there with me . . . some *invisible* presence.

I scan the rest of the pages with references to Hades. I reread the story of Hades's abduction of Persephone and can't help ruminating on Tobin's theory about those girls—his own sister included—who have gone missing whenever Lord family members happened to be in town.

But there's nothing in the book that says anything about Hades having the ability to produce and throw lightning. The only Greek god with that power is supposed to be Zeus.

I laugh derisively at myself. This is insane! Maybe there really was some sort of poison—or psychotropic drug—in those cookies Lexie gave me. My laugh takes on a harder edge, almost a sob, and I know that I am on the verge of a full-scale freak-out.

Tobin is right. I'd allowed my judgment to get clouded, just like he'd said. I'd let Haden in. I'd *kissed* him.

I'd almost fallen for him.

I may not know what Haden is, but something is definitely wrong in Olympus Hills, and I have no doubt now that Haden and his family are at the center of it all.

Which means that now I am, too.

chapter forty-five

HADEN

I enter the house through the garage. Simon's car is gone, but Dax's Roadster is here. I slam the door so hard, the windows shake. Dax is sitting in front of the TV in the family room. He sits up when he sees me come in. Concern mars his face. Laughter echoes from the television. I grab the remote and fling it against the wall. The screen of the TV goes black.

He shoots up from the couch. "Haden?"

"Where the Tartarus were you tonight?"

"Out."

"Out? That's all. That's *all* you're going to give me?"

"What's wrong? Did something happen?"

"Yes, something happened," I hiss at him. "And it's your fault. If you'd been here to patrol the festival for the Keres like I'd asked, then none of this would have happened!" I try to push him. Hard. But he grabs my shoulders. Dax has always been stronger than me.

"*What* happened?" he asks.

"It's all ruined. All of it. It's over. She's never going to trust me again. She's probably never even going to look at me again."

Dax lets go of my shoulders. He has the audacity to look upset.

Joe wouldn't have been attacked if Dax had been there. I wouldn't have had to expose my powers in front of Daphne.

I take a swing at him. It's an impulsive move, and I think I've caught him off guard for once, but he grabs my fist midair. He uses it to force me into one of the armchairs. "Sit down. Shut up. And tell me what exactly the Tartarus happened!"

Dax doesn't raise his voice often, but when he does, it has the same effect as a punch to the jaw. Reason returns to me, and I realize there's no one to blame for what happened tonight. Not Dax, not Daphne, not Joe, and not even myself.

I had made the prideful mistake of thinking I had any control over any of this. What had happened had happened. No matter how I disliked it, it was what fate had wanted.

"What I don't get is why would fate choose me for this quest, and then rip away my chances for success right when everything was starting to come together?"

"Maybe you're supposed to go down a different path," Dax says. "Maybe because you're supposed to make your own fate."

I glare at him. "That's blasphemy."

"Maybe. Maybe not. Does anyone really know?"

"You're addled."

"You still haven't told me what happened."

I'm quiet for a moment. "She kissed me."

"Nice," Dax says. "How is that a bad thing?"

"It's what happened afterward. . . ." I launch into the story of Joe being attacked by the Keres and how I killed it.

"You killed it?" he asks, interrupting me. "You killed a Keres? Are you sure?"

"It exploded into a thousand little pieces. I'm pretty sure it's dead."

"How?"

"I don't really know. It's like it had a reaction to Daphne's voice or something. It became solid just long enough for me to blast it."

"That's intense."

"Tell me about it. I don't even know what I would have done otherwise."

"You still haven't gotten to the part where Daphne kisses you," Dax says. "Get to the goods."

As amazing as Daphne's kiss had been, I can barely muster the words to tell Dax the rest of the story. He lets out a low whistle when I get to the part when Daphne saw my scars and ran away.

"I can see how that would complicate things. She probably thinks you're a total nut job."

"A what?" I shake my head, getting it. "Never mind."

"So what are you going to do now?"

"What can I do?" Fate had brought this down on my head. Perhaps as punishment for my acts of disobedience? My hubris? "She's never going to talk to me again."

Dax starts to say something, but a dinging chime rings through the house. I stand up, searching for the origin of the noise.

"It's the doorbell," he says.

"Ignore it," I say.

"I bet Garrick forgot his keys."

"Let him sit in the cold for a bit." I don't want Garrick to be a part of this conversation. He'll probably go squealing it all to Simon.

Dax sighs and heads for the front door. I sit back in the armchair and bury my head in my hands. I'd been a fool for ever thinking I could pull this off.

"Seems I was wrong," Dax says, coming back into the family room. "And so were you. You have a visitor, Haden."

I tug at my hair and look up at Dax . . . and find Daphne standing right next to him.

She crosses her long, tanned arms in front of her chest. "I want answers," she says. "And I'm not leaving until I get the truth."

Daphne has planted herself beside one of the armchairs and shows no signs of leaving anytime soon. I pull Dax aside.

"What am I supposed to tell her?"

"Try the truth."

"I'm not supposed to do that until the Eve of the Return."

"I'd say your ox is in the mire."

"I have no idea what that means."

"It means that based on the dire circumstances, an exception is in order."

"As in, I'm harpied if I do, and harpied if I don't?"

"Exactly. Always best to go for the truth in these situations."

I drag my hand through my hair and turn toward Daphne. She looks at me expectantly—but not in a good way.

I huff out a big sigh. "So . . . this is going to sound a bit addled. . . . But . . . you see . . ." I look at Dax, hoping he can help me find the right words. He just shrugs. *Damned useful guide he turned out to be.* "Here's the thing. I'm not from around here, and I'm not from the East Coast, either. I'm from somewhere much farther away than that. I'm from—"

"The underworld," Daphne says, finishing my admission for me.

"Ummm . . . what? How did you know?"

"It was kind of a stab in the dark, but thanks for confirming it." She taps her fingers on her arms. "Still not sure I believe it, though."

Dax makes a gurgling noise like he's either choking or laughing. "I told you I liked this girl."

Daphne looks at him, her eyes narrowed. "Do I know you?"

"This is Dax. He's my cousin, sort of," I say. "But you've probably seen him around school. He's a guidance counselor. Mr. Drool."

"Hey," he says. "That's Mr. *Drol*. Though I do see my mistake in name choice now."

"No," Daphne says, shaking her head. "I haven't seen you at school. Have we met elsewhere?"

He shrugs.

"He's supposed to be my guide. But you're not helping all that much at the moment," I add pointedly to him.

"Guide? As in, you've been here before?"

"Yes," Dax says.

"Six years ago?" Her voice has an accusatory edge to it, and I realize the direction she's headed with this line of questioning. Tobin's sister. That isn't a road Dax and I want to go down at the moment. Not if I want a chance at salvaging this situation.

I clear my throat, stopping Dax from responding. "We were talking about the underworld. . . ."

"Oh yes," Daphne says. "So are you a god or something?"

I almost laugh. "No."

"You're not Hades, then?"

"No."

"Who is Hades, then?" Her eyes flick to Dax. He shakes his head. "Does he exist?"

"He did."

"Did?"

"He's dead."

"Gods can die?"

"If you take away their totem, yes. But we're getting off topic."

"Who are you, then?"

"I am Lord Haden, son of King Ren—the current ruler of the underworld. Champion chosen to fulfill a sacred quest."

Daphne steeples her fingers. "And let me guess. That quest is to bring me back to the underworld so I can be your queen or something?"

Her expression is cool and calm, and I wonder if she's really as unfazed about all these reality-rocking revelations as she seems. For the first time since she walked away from me this evening, I wonder if I still have a chance of pulling this quest off. Of convincing her to come with me. Maybe this is the way the Fates wanted it to be. I am not to be a failure, after all.

Hope rises in my chest. I can practically taste the nectar I will be served upon my victorious return. I can see the expression on my father's face when he will be obliged to offer me the seat at his right hand instead of Rowan. All I have to do is make Daphne understand.

"Yes, in a way. I was chosen by the Oracle. I've been sent here to convince you to return with me. You are my Boon."

Daphne scowls. "Your Boon? Like your prize?" A shakiness creaks into her voice, and I realize too late that she's not as cool with all of this as she's been pretending to be. "That's disgusting. That's beyond wrong."

"You're not just a prize," I say, lifting my hands. "You're not just any Boon. You're the Cypher."

"What the hell is that supposed to mean?"

"I don't exactly know. We have a theory." I glance at Dax, but he doesn't jump in to help me. "I'm supposed to take you to the

Underrealm so you can help the Court of Heirs find the Key of Hades. It's kind of vitally important."

"Take me?" Her voice wars between sounding angry and afraid. Anger wins out. "You think you can cut my name into your arm and act like I belong to you? You think you can just take me?"

"No," I say, trying to step closer to her. She moves away, putting the armchair between us. "I made that mistake once—when I tried to grab you in the grove—but I won't make it again. Coming with me has to be your decision. I need your consent. You have to say yes."

Daphne stands up straighter, pulling herself to her full height. I wonder if anyone has ever told her she looks like an Amazon warrior when she's angry.

"Then, no," she says.

"Pardon?"

"You're some fancy-pants prince. Go tell your king daddy or this Oracle or whoever that I say *no*. Tell them to choose somebody else."

"I can't, Daphne. I can't just choose somebody else. Number one, because nobody would listen to me. I'm not exactly the Court's favorite person. And secondly, because you were chosen by the Oracle. You were chosen by fate. You're *the* Cypher. This whole thing is a whole lot bigger than you and me." I can feel it in my soul how important this all is. "You can't just say no. This is your destiny."

"It has to be my choice but I can't say no? That's some pretty messed-up logic, you know."

"This has nothing at all to do with logic. It's about destiny. Our destiny."

"Shove your destiny. I don't believe in destiny or gods or oracles—even if they *are* real. What I believe in is myself. In my choices and my plans. I've got my plan for how my life is going to turn out, and it certainly doesn't involve being dragged down to some mythological world of the dead. So my answer still stands. *No.*"

"What if the fate of your world depended on it?" Because if Garrick is right and the walls of the Pithos are falling, and bringing Daphne to the Underrealm is the only way to stop it, the Fates of both her world and mine are hanging in the balance.

She grips the edge of the armchair so hard, it looks like she might pierce through the fabric with her fingers. "Then I'd say, find another way."

"There is no other way. This is what the Oracle decreed, so it's what must be done."

"Actually," Dax says from the couch. The expression on his face makes it seem as though he's been enjoying a really good show. "There might be another way."

"What?" Daphne and I say in unison.

"Well, not another way, per se. But perhaps a way to find out some more information on all of this. See if there is another option even available."

"What is it?" Daphne asks.

"What if you could talk to an Oracle again?" Dax says to me.

"She resides in Elysium. That would be impossible."

"There's more than one Oracle, Haden. You know that. Even one or two in this realm."

"*If* we could find one, what difference would that make? The Oracle of Elysium has spoken. Her words have been sealed."

"Not all Oracles speak from the same source," Dax says. "Another one might be able to give you more information. Look at things from a different angle. Let you know what other options might be available to you. If any."

"What are you doing?" I whisper.

"Helping."

"How is this helping? You can't make her think there are other options when there aren't."

"You don't know that unless you find out for yourself."

"It isn't my place to find out for myself."

"Yes, it is, Haden. You've been conditioned all your life to obey without questioning. To treat your father like he's the new Hades. Like he's a god. They tell you your impulsiveness is your weakness, but it's not. And I never should have encouraged you to restrain it. Your impulsiveness is your greatest strength—because it's the only time you think for yourself."

I shake my head at Dax. "Thinking for myself is what got me into this mess. My most impulsive act was what caused my father to disown me in the first place. I can't do this—"

"Yes, you can. But you need to stop thinking like an outcast. Stop thinking like an Underlord. Or even a want-to-be prince. You're half human, Haden. Start thinking like one. Humans question. Humans think for themselves."

I glare at Dax. "This is what you wanted all along, isn't it? This is why you've encouraged me to open up to my emotions—to my humanness. I thought you were my friend. I thought you were on my side. But all you've wanted is for me to fail. From the very beginning."

"What I want is for you to make your own path. To find love. To *live*. Just like me."

"Like you?" How could Dax call anything about his life since he returned from his time as Champion *living*?

"Excuse me?" I hear Daphne say. "Still here, remember?"

Both Dax and I snap our attention back to her.

"Yeah. Hi. I know you think you all are whispering, but you

might as well be shouting from the rooftops. I gather Mr. Drool here knows where to find one of these 'other Oracles.'" She steps out from around the armchair, no longer barricading herself behind it. "I want to go see her."

"I can get you a name and city," Dax says. "Assuming she hasn't moved to a new town in the last six years."

"That'll do." Daphne looks at me. "You're coming with me."

"I thought you didn't believe in all this 'fate mumbo jumbo,'" I say, quoting the way she put it when we were in the music shop.

"I don't, but I believe *you* believe it. And if I can convince this Oracle lady to tell you that you've got the wrong girl, then you'll believe her."

"You can't change an Oracle's mind. It doesn't work that way."

"We'll see," she says, sounding far too confident.

"So what's it going to be?" Dax says. "Are you going with her?"

"Before I agree," I say to him, "I want you to tell Daphne what happened to your Boon."

Dax's face goes ashen, confirming what I've suspected for some time now. Ever since I found out that Tobin's sister went missing. Ever since Simon insinuated that Dax tried to run away while he was here last—and how unpleasant it would be if he had to send someone after me.

"You know I can't say anything about that," he says.

"Then I'll say it for you. She died, didn't she? You fell in love with her. You didn't want to take her back to the Underrealm, so you consulted this other Oracle for help. But you didn't like what she said, so you tried to run away with your Boon. . . . But something went wrong. And she died."

"That's the basic gist of the story," Dax says, his voice barely audible.

"Was her name Abbie?" Daphne asks.

He nods.

A small sound escapes her lips. It almost sounds like a sob.

"You still want to go find this other Oracle?" I ask her.

"Yes," she says, sounding more determined than before.

"Then we can leave in the morning."

"No," she says.

"No? I thought you—"

"We don't know how long it's going to take to find this Oracle chick, and reviews for finals start on Monday," she says. "And I have rehearsals with Joe's band, and stuff for the music department. I can't just push pause on my life right now and go."

"Then when?"

"The semester ends on December eighteenth. I wasn't going to head back to Ellis Fields until the twenty-first, but I'll tell Joe that I decided that I want to fly home early. That'll give me two days that I don't have to be accountable to anyone. We'll go then."

I nod, trying to appease her in some way, but I wish I could get this over with right now. The sooner she realizes her destiny is to go with me, the better.

I insist on driving Daphne back to her house. She may not like it, but I plan on sticking close to her for the next three weeks because now that we've made our plan, I don't like the idea of letting her out of my sight. It feels like tempting fate. Or at least tempting Simon. If he were to get wind of how many rules I've broken or find out that I am planning on leaving town with my Boon, taking an unprecedented detour on my quest . . . I don't like to think about the endless possibilities of what he might do.

chapter forty-six

DAPHNE

The next three weeks pass too quickly and yet at the same time feel like they couldn't go any slower. I find myself avoiding Tobin and Joe as much as possible, and pour myself into studying for finals, as if my life depended on how well I do on those tests. It's too hard to be around people I have to pretend to be normal with. To pretend like everything is okay. But I don't talk to Haden, either, even though he always seems to be close by. Like he's afraid to take his eyes off me.

He probably thinks I am going to run.

If I were smart, I probably would.

My seventeenth birthday passes with little fanfare. Joe offers to throw me a "birthday party to end all birthday parties," but I can't muster the energy for such a thing, so instead I opt for eating a bowl of ice cream and a cupcake in front my MacBook while on a Skype call with my mom and Jonathan. I open the packages they sent while they watch. Mom's gift is a painting of the view of Ellis from the front windows of Paradise Plants that she'd done with oils on Masonite board.

"Hang it over your bed so you'll dream of home," she says.

I smile even though Ellis has never been what I want my dreams to be made of.

Jonathan's gift is a collection of romance novels. "You're lacking a mysterious man in your life," he says. "I was hoping we'd get a lot more juicy stories after shipping you off to that fancy-schmancy school. You haven't dated any celebrities or kissed any princes and neglected to tell us, have you?"

It takes all of my control not to tell them right then and there what is going on with *Prince* Haden, and our plans to sneak out of town to consult this Oracle lady. But I can't. Because *when* I get all this Cypher crap straightened out, and send Haden packing to the underworld on his own, I'm going to go back to my life in Olympus Hills and follow my plan to become a music star. But if my mom gets one whiff of any of this underworld business before I can squash it, any chance of my having a life outside Ellis will be over. She'd probably lock me up in our house until I'm old and gray. And I am not going to let that happen.

"No interesting encounters to report," I lie through my teeth.

"Well, get on it, girly," Jonathan says. "Some of us have to live vicariously through you."

I laugh uneasily, but my mom punches him playfully on the arm. "Don't encourage her," she says. "We want Daphne to come back, remember?"

I smile, tears pricking at my eyes, and I wish there was a way to hug them both through the computer.

The night after my last final, I pack my bag as if I am headed for Ellis Fields instead of some undisclosed location with a supernatural boy I barely know. I'm worrying about how I am going to convince Joe when I come down for breakfast that I don't need a ride to the airport—I'll pretend to take a cab—and get to Haden's house instead, but it turns out I don't have to.

There's a note in Marta's handwriting explaining that she and Joe have gone to LA so Joe can lay down some more tracks for a new album. It says not to expect them back before I have to leave, and that a car service will take me to the airport. Even though it makes sneaking away easier, I admit that I am hurt that Joe didn't bother to see me off. It feels like I've barely seen him since the festival, what with all my studying and all the trips into LA he's been taking to work with his band. Maybe I *should* have let him throw me that party.

I call the number for the car service on my itinerary and cancel the driver.

With that obstacle down, I make a piece of toast and shove a couple of water bottles into my bag. I don't know where we are going yet, but Dax had alluded to the fact that the trip might take more than a full day. I've got enough packed, but the idea of staying overnight in some strange town with Haden makes me shiver.

My phone rings. It's Tobin once again. He's been so busy researching the names of the different Lords who have lived in Olympus Hills—to little avail—that he hasn't really noticed that I've been avoiding him. As much as I want to answer and tell him everything I've learned since the night of the festival, I don't. Number one, because then it would make all of this seem real and not just like a crazy fever dream I'll wake up from. And number two, because it means I have to tell him what I've learned about Abbie, and I'm just not ready to do that yet. I can't, because then that will be real, too.

I let the call go to voice mail, but he doesn't give up. While I'm finishing getting ready to leave, he calls two more times, and then sends a text.

Tobin: 911! I must show you something. Call me!

I wonder if he's found another bit of information that I can't tell him will lead to another dead end, but I decide to respond or he's probably not going to stop all day.

Me: Can't talk now.

Tobin: Then I'm sending it to you.

A few seconds later, my phone buzzes again. He's texted me a picture. It's of a list of names.

Me: ?

Tobin: That's the list of names of girls who've gone missing from town. The one in my mom's files. I went to double-check it last night to make sure I didn't miss anything . . . and I saw that a new name has been added. Look at the bottom of the list. . . .

I enlarge the picture and scan through the typewritten names—and then land on the name *Daphne Raines* written in crisp, clean handwriting at the bottom.

Tobin: Your name is on a list with a bunch of missing girls! What does that mean?

I know exactly what it means. The mayor—Tobin's mother—isn't only aware of the girls going missing in her town; she is complicit beforehand in letting it happen.

But I can't tell Tobin this right now. I can't tell him via text—or phone call, even—that his sister is dead and his parent is somehow involved in what happened. I can't think of a worse betrayal than that.

A new text comes in, but this time it's not from Tobin.

Haden: Are you ready to go? I can be there in fifteen minutes.

Talking to Tobin will have to wait until I get back. I send him a text.

Me: I really can't talk about this now. Call you later.

And then I send a text to Haden, telling him I'm on my way over to his place. I know I could wait for him to come pick me up, but I can't stand the thought. I don't want to sit around waiting one more minute. I need to be moving. Maybe I'm crazy for going anywhere with an underworld prince who's full-on admitted that he wants to steal me away. Maybe I'm crazy for thinking I can change his mind. But I have to do everything in my power to try.

Haden is loading a duffel bag into a Tesla Model X in his garage. It's a strange car, with three rows of seats and doors that raise up like falcon wings instead of opening outward. Haden nods when he sees me, and an expression of relief crosses his face—as if he'd convinced himself I wasn't really coming.

He takes my suitcase and places it in the trunk next to his.

"Where's your Model S?" I ask, referring to the car he usually drives. It had kind of become synonymous with him in my mind. His electric black chariot . . .

"Dax took it out this morning," he says. I can tell by his tone that things are still strained between the two of them. "I almost stole his Roadster but figured this car would be more comfortable for a longer journey."

"So Dax isn't coming with us?" I wasn't sure if he would, but I had kind of liked the idea of having a buffer in the car.

"He said something like, 'This is *your* journey to take, Haden.'"

"How very Gandalfy of him."

Haden raises his eyebrows like he has no idea what I've just said. "Are you ready?"

"As I'll ever be." I look around the garage. "Did he give you the information?"

"Yes." He hands me a slip of paper.

I open it up. "Seriously?" I laugh, but it sounds more like a groan.

"What?"

"Sarah Smith. Las Vegas, Nevada. That's all he told you?"

"Yes. Is that a problem?"

"Only because there are probably, like, a hundred or more Sarah Smiths in Las Vegas!" When Dax told me he could give me a name and a town, I had pictured something more like Ellis. You can walk into any shop on Main Street and give any shopkeeper the name of any resident and you can get step-by-step directions to their house. "Vegas is huge, and Sarah Smith has to be one of the most generic names in the world. You sure Dax isn't yanking your chain?"

"He wasn't yanking anything," Haden says.

This time I raise my eyebrows.

"Oh. I mean, he was quite earnest when he gave it to me."

"Okay, sparky. We better get on it, then. I'll start making phone calls to every S. Smith in the Las Vegas phone directory while you drive."

"Just one last thing," Haden says. He opens his duffel bag and riffles around in the contents, then zips it back up without taking anything out.

"What was that for?"

"Just making sure we didn't have a stowaway. Brim wasn't too happy when I told her she couldn't come."

"That's too bad." Even taking a cat along would feel a little less awkward than the two of us on the road together. Alone. To Las Vegas.

"Believe me, sharing close quarters, like a car, with a hellcat is not a good idea. I should know; I've had to keep her hidden from Simon in my room for the last three months."

"Poor baby," I say, meaning the cat, not him.

"I just hope she doesn't get out of my room. She might follow us all the way to Vegas."

"She could do that?"

"She and I are bonded in a way. She can find me anywhere."

"Who's Simon?" I ask. "The person you're hiding her from?"

"My guardian, I guess you could say, and my father's emissary. As in, the person I'm going to be in deep *kopros* with if he gets wind of this trip before we get out of here."

"Let's get this over with, then," I say, gathering that *kopros* is the Underlord slang for stuff that starts with an *sh* and ends with an *it*.

I'm in the process of buckling my seat belt, and Haden is pulling out of the garage, when he suddenly slams on the brakes. I look up and see that Haden's younger cousin—Garrick, I think— is standing in the driveway, blocking our exit.

Haden honks the horn and waves at him to get out of the way. Garrick doesn't move.

Haden puts the car in park and gets out. "What are you doing, Lesser? Get out of my way."

"I can't let you do this," Garrick says.

"And how do you intend to stop me?"

"I'll tell Simon. I'll call him right now. You're not allowed to leave town. I heard Simon tell you so."

"Simon doesn't need to know. He's gone to LA on business. He won't even be back until Monday."

"So what, you're just going to run away the first chance you get? What about the rest of us? What about me? What happens when Simon finds out you're gone? What happens when I go back through the gate without you?"

"I'm not running away, Lesser. You think I'm a coward?"

"I don't believe you. I'm going inside to call Simon! I'm telling him you're going to this Vegas place."

Haden grabs his cousin. Garrick tries to pull away. I get out of the car, thinking I can intervene. Talk some sense into Garrick. But I don't get the chance. Haden places his thumbs behind the boy's ears and his index fingers on his temples and presses until Garrick's eyes roll into the back of his head and he crumples like a rag doll. Haden catches him up in his arms before he hits the ground. I cover my mouth, holding in a shriek.

"Open the door," Haden says, dragging his cousin's limp body toward the car.

"What did you do?"

"I put him in a black sleep. It's an old Underlord negotiation technique."

"Negotiation?"

"If a man refuses to negotiate, you render him unconscious."

"That's crazy."

"He would have told Simon. There was no other way to stop him without resorting to violence. Now open the door."

I pull open the back door, and Haden shoves Garrick into the backseat. The boy lies motionless on his side.

"Will he be okay?"

"He'll have a raging headache when he wakes up in a couple of hours, but by then we'll be halfway there." Haden slams the door. He pulls his phone out of his pocket and tosses it into a bucket of rags in the garage. "Simon *is* eventually going to figure out I'm gone, especially if I'm not back by Monday, but I want to make sure he can't track us. Give me yours." He gestures for me to give him my phone.

"Mine, too?"

"I wouldn't put it past him."

"How would he . . . ?"

"Trust me. He has his ways."

I surrender my phone and watch Haden drop it into the bucket. He gets back in the car. "You coming?"

I sit in the passenger seat again.

As we sail out of the driveway, I glance back at his unconscious cousin in the third row, and I wonder if I've made a grave mistake.

chapter forty-seven

HADEN

Daphne is silent the whole first hour of our trip. She keeps glancing at Garrick, who still lies unconscious in the back row. Sometimes, I catch her gaze darting to me. Her eyes linger on my upper arm. The sleeve of my T-shirt covers my scars, but I know that's what she's thinking about. No wonder so much tension fills the space between us.

"I didn't do that," I say, breaking the silence.

She startles at the sound of my voice.

"I didn't cut those scars into my arm. My father did. So I wouldn't forget my quest. It was the most painful thing I've ever had to endure. And I've endured a lot. . . ."

"Oh," she says. The tension in her relaxes ever so slightly.

Another half hour passes.

"So what did you do?" she asks. "To piss your dad off so much? I got the gist a few weeks ago that you're kind of on the outs with him."

"That's putting it lightly. My father disowned me." I'm not sure I want to talk about it, but Daphne shifts in her seat, turning her body toward me. Maybe talking is the best thing for getting her to open up to me again. "I cried," I say. "When my mother died, I cried."

"What? Your father disowned you over that?"

"No. It's what I did after he punished me for crying. . . ." I realize I need to back up the story more for her to understand. "I have a twin brother. His name is Rowan. But you have to understand that twins are very rare in my world. The first two sons of the Underrealm were created by our god, Hades. They were the first twins—the eldest of whom became the father of our race, while the younger twin became the progenitor of our greatest enemies, the Skylords.

"Because of this, firstborn sons are treated with great respect—made Lords and trained as warriors and Champions—while younger sons are deemed Lesser, and treated with suspicion and disdain."

"Like your cousin Garrick?" Daphne asks. "You called him Lesser."

I nod, but don't tell her that Garrick is actually my half brother and not my cousin. "When my mother learned from the healers that she was carrying twins, she was overcome with dismay that one of her sons would be forced to live as a Lesser. So when Rowan and I were born, she allowed no one to be present with her. That way, no one other than she would know which one of her children was the eldest. Before she would allow my father to see us, she made him swear an unbreakable oath that neither of her children would ever be cast out of the ranks of the Underlords."

"Smart," Daphne says.

I sigh. "Some say that my mother granted us the greatest favor of our lifetimes—but unfortunately, her actions caused Rowan and me to become rivals from the moment we drew our first breaths. Everyone speculated as to which one of us was the true Lord, and which one of us was undeserving of our status.

Everything we did was considered to be a competition. In the beginning, I was my father's favorite. I was bigger and stronger than Rowan and resembled my father with my dark hair and olive skin, while Rowan was slighter and fairer like our mother.

"But as we grew older, it became apparent that Rowan had inherited more of my father's cunning and cold temperament, while I was called nursling well past my second year because—as I am told—I clung to my mother's skirts and screamed when my father tried to pit me in fights with the other boys my age. That is when the Court started to whisper that perhaps I was too human for my own good—that I had inherited too many of my mother's human traits. My father's favor had already started to shift toward Rowan before my mother's death."

I pause, changing lanes so I can pass a slow van and pick up speed. "Rowan is the one the Court wanted to send here, not me." I shiver at the idea of that sociopath sitting here with Daphne instead of me. What tactics would he have used to coerce her into agreeing to be his Boon? The thought of her saying yes to him . . . "Be happy he isn't here."

"Noted," she says, like she's realizing there could be worse things than being stuck in this car with me.

"It wasn't until my mother's death that I fully realized my father's disdain for me. For her . . . When she collapsed, I sent a serving boy—Garrick—to fetch my father. My father took so long to come, and when he finally arrived with a couple of members of the Court . . . it was like he didn't care at all.

"I begged him to help her. I yelled at him to do something. To save her. We have these places called healing chambers, and I thought if he brought her there, she would get better. But he wouldn't listen to me.

"One of his servants grabbed me and pulled me away from my mother's body. I screamed and kicked, trying to escape. And then I started to cry. . . ."

I stop speaking when I remember the stinging sensation that pricked behind my eyes and the warm liquid that welled up in them and then escaped from the corners. At the time, I didn't have a word for the water that made tracks down my face and tasted salty as it ran over my lips and down my chin. *Tears*, I found out later, when I heard the Heirs hiss the word to each other whenever I neared, like I'd done the vilest of things.

"Crying is forbidden past the age of two, and once an Underlord reaches the age of six, he is supposed to be a man. At seven years of age, crying like that is considered disgusting. My father told me to shut up and be still, but instead, I wailed terribly at him, the tears coming faster and harder. The servant who held me was shocked by my tantrum; he let me go; and I fell to my knees.

"I remember looking up at my father just in time to see the back of his ringed hand come sailing at the side of my face. He hit me so hard, I thought my teeth were going to shatter. 'No son of Hades cries,' he said to me.

"That was when I retaliated. I told my father that he wasn't *Hades*, that he wasn't *my* king, and that I didn't want to be his son anymore. I was so angry, I could feel a burst of lightning forming in my chest. I'd only been in training for a few months and I didn't know how to use it properly yet. But I stood in front of my father and demanded that he help my mother. I told him that if he didn't, I would blast him.

"Speaking to the king like that, even if you are his child, is considered to be a sin akin to heresy. I had questioned his authority in front of the Court. Threatened to harm him. I expected him to hit me again—part of me wanted him to. But instead he laughed at me. Laughed at my tears. And that's when I lost control. I attacked him. With a great, raging scream, I lunged at him and threw a lightning bolt at my father, the king of the Underrealm."

"Whoa," Daphne says under her breath.

"He deflected it easily, and sent his own bolt at my feet. It ripped the ground right out from under me and I went flying. I hit the floor and crumpled into a ball. When the ringing in my ears ceased, I realized that the room had fallen completely silent. The servants and the members of the Court who were there looked at me like I had just committed the most unforgivable act in our realm. And that's when I realized I *had*. I'd dishonored my father, blasphemed against his title—the name of Hades—physically attacked the king, and brought shame upon myself.

"I tried wiping the tears from my face and begged for his forgiveness. I groveled and laid myself down in front of him in supplication, hoping he would show me mercy.

"But it was too late. I saw it in his eyes. His disdainful glare made me feel hollow all the way down to my bones. He said, 'You are no son of mine.'

"And that was it. My life as I knew it was over. I was removed from the royal living quarters, dropped to the bottom of my rank, stripped of my honor, and forced to carry this shame for the rest of my life. The only reason I wasn't thrown out of the Underlords and made a Lesser is because of the oath my father made to my mother when I was born. Rowan gladly stepped into the role of favorite son, and I've been trying to win it back—along with my honor—ever since. I didn't think I'd really get the chance until the Oracle of Elysium chose me for this quest."

"I'm sorry," Daphne says after a few long, quiet minutes.

"Sounds like you've got even worse daddy issues than I do."

I can tell she's trying to lighten the mood, but mine grows darker. I am the one who had encouraged her to open herself up to her father—only to be the one who is supposed to take her away from him again.

"They call me the boy who cried," I say. "They equate my showing that kind of emotion to the ultimate sign of my weakness. They act like it's the crying that was my undoing—but that is only because it would be dishonorable for them to speak of someone physically attacking the king."

"Sounds like a great place to live. Can't wait to get there!" Daphne says sarcastically.

"Well, when you put it that way . . ." I try to grin sheepishly, but it comes out more like a grimace. I am quiet for a few minutes, staring down the long stretch of highway in front of us. "I think I'd do things differently, if I were king. I'd bring music back to the Underrealm, for one thing. And I wouldn't treat you like a prize. You'd be my queen. My real queen, not just a figurehead like my mother and the others who fill the role. I think that's one way the Underlords have gone wrong—what's missing from my world. I've heard that things were different when Persephone and Hades reigned together. Things changed after she left. . . ."

"She left? Like, for good? I thought she was bound to the Underworld."

"She was bound to Hades. After he died, she left. She stayed for a while, but then she was so overcome with grief that she went through her gate to the mortal world one spring, and never came back. Or at least that's how the old stories go."

"How did Hades die?"

"The Sky God killed him."

"You mean Zeus?"

"That's what humans call him."

"But weren't they brothers?"

"They were. But they had been at war for nearly a thousand years."

"Why?"

"Because of us. The Underlords." I check the map on the car's GPS and see that we're halfway to our destination. Then I glance in the rearview mirror. We've passed through thicker patches of traffic, but now we're alone on the road, except for a green BMW a few hundred yards behind us.

"I don't know which version of the Persephone story is the correct one," I say. "Whether she was stolen into the Underrealm by Hades or if she chose to go with him to be his queen, but I do know that he was devoted to her, and we Underlords are the proof. Persephone's mother, the Terra Lady, or Demeter, as your book calls her, wasn't too happy about Persephone and Hades's union. As goddess of the Overrealm, the mortal world, she was the one who gifted the harvest to the fields and fertility to the womb. She cursed her own daughter, so Hades and Persephone would never be able to have children. Hades couldn't stand the sadness that overtook his wife, and so he decided to create children for her. His first attempt went horribly wrong. You've seen the results of that."

Her mouth pops open. "You mean that thing that attacked Joe? That was supposed to be a child?"

I nod. "It's called a Keres. They're an experiment gone very wrong, and certainly not the bouncing little baby Persephone had wanted."

"I'm sure that came as quite the surprise."

"Have you ever heard the story of Pandora's Box?"

"Yeah. A woman was given a box and told not to open it. But her curiosity got the better of her, and she opened the box only to accidentally release horrible evils on the world."

"Close," I say. "But in the real version, the box is actually a prison, and the things inside are the Keres. We call it the Pits. Short for *Pithos*."

"So Hades imprisoned his first creations?"

"He had no choice. They were monsters. There are different kinds of Keres. Some of them are reapers—like the one we destroyed—and he used to use them to help collect the souls of the dead on the battlefield. But even those proved to be too bloodthirsty—instead of going after only the dead, they started to attack the wounded also. There's one thing everyone who was attacked in Olympus Hills had in common. They were bleeding. Wounded, I guess you could say. Even if it was only a paper cut. Eventually, the reapers were locked up, too. You can probably imagine why."

She nods. "So then Hades, having botched it the first time, still decided to try again?"

"He was more careful this time. He created the Underlords after his own image, out of mud from the river Styx, fire from the heart of the Underrealm, and shadows from the shades of the dead. Persephone herself breathed life into the first two. Twin sons named Life and Death. They were gifted with the Helm of Hades—the ability to be nearly invisible in the dark—and the fire that burns in their eyes. The twins were the light of their lives."

Daphne shakes her shoulders like something has made her feel cold. "It's that nearly invisible in the dark thing that really creeps me out. You shouldn't have followed me backstage at my audition like that. You freaked me out so much, I almost couldn't sing."

"What are you talking about?" I ask her. "What auditions? I never followed you backstage anywhere."

"After we met in the grove, didn't you follow me to the school? There was some sort of invisible presence with me backstage. Wasn't that you?"

I shake my head. "I didn't follow you to the school."

Her eyes widen as she looks at me to make sure I'm not lying. "I did hear a weird hissing sound, like before the Keres attacked. Maybe that's what followed me—but wouldn't it have been attacking Pear at that time?" Her shoulders convulse again. "And I could have sworn I saw your eyes flashing in the shadows of the auditorium. Someone was watching me."

"I swear to you, Daphne, I went straight back to Simon's place after the grove. If someone was watching you, it wasn't me."

But the question that haunts me is: who was it?

As far as I knew, Dax had been with Simon at that time, and Garrick had been sick and locked in his room at Simon's mansion.

Could there be another Underlord in Olympus Hills that I don't know about?

"Where does the lightning come from?" Daphne asks like she's eager to get off the disturbing topic of invisible people following her. "I thought that was a Zeus thing?"

"It is. The Underlords were gifted with the ability to throw lightning bolts from the Sky God himself. But that's where the story takes a darker turn. You see, Hades was already in trouble with Zeus for creating the Keres by accident, and the Sky God fancied himself the only god who was allowed to create new life out of the elements. So he stole the twins and claimed them as his own creations—his own children—and even gave them his lightning bolts as supposed proof of his paternity."

"I can imagine Hades and Persephone were not too happy about that."

"To say the least. Hades opened the gates to the underworld and unleashed a couple of the reaper Keres to bring back his children from the Skyrealm. They kidnapped Death and brought him home, but Life wasn't so lucky. He'd fallen and scraped his knee earlier in the day, and the Keres, unable to restrain themselves, tore the poor child apart."

"That's terrible."

"Not as terrible as the war that followed. It went on for hundreds of years, trashing everything in between the Skyrealm and the Underrealm—namely, the mortal world. Hades caused volcanoes to erupt, sending ash and fire into the sky, and then Zeus would retaliate. Did you know that almost every culture in your world has a legend of a great flood that almost destroyed the earth? That's what happened when the Sky God opened the heavens in an effort to drown out the Underrealm. He failed, luckily, because Hades was smart enough to lock the gates. Nothing living can get through them when they're locked."

"Rain is living? Well, it has a song, so I guess that would probably mean it's alive."

"A song?" It's my turn to sound surprised.

"Everything has an inner song. Everything living, that is. I can hear it. You probably think that sounds crazy. Most people do."

"I'd say it sounds far less addled than 'hello, I'm an underworld prince and I'm here to take you to live with me in the land of the dead' and all."

A smile on my behalf cracks her lips for the first time since she learned the truth about me. It's fleeting and small, but I see it out of the corner of my eye before it goes away.

"How did the war end?" she asks. "I mean, the world is still here, so I imagine it stopped."

"It's more of a stalemate, really. The war has been at a stand-still since Hades was murdered."

"How did that happen?" Daphne asks. Her voice sounds almost void of the hostility she's shown me all day—it's been edged away by curiosity. "You said a god has to lose his . . . totem?"

"That's the closest word in your language for it. We call it a Kronolithe. It's his symbol, object of power. It's what gives him his immortality. It means 'Kronos's stone.'"

"Kronos? That name sounds familiar. Wasn't he one of the first gods, in Greek mythology?"

"Yes, he was the father of Zeus and Hades and many others. He was a greedy, prideful ruler and he feared that his children would overthrow him someday—so he ate them as soon as they were born. All except for Zeus. His mother wrapped a rock in a blanket and fed that to Kronos instead. Zeus then killed his father and cut his siblings free from his father's stomach. Once Kronos was overthrown, they decided to draw lots and divvy up control over the five realms. Each new ruler was given a piece of the stone Kronos had eaten. I am not sure how it works, but those pieces of Kronos's stone are what make them gods. Zeus became the Sky God, and he fashioned his Kronolithe into an iron thunderbolt. Poseidon, who was chosen as the god of the Oceanrealm, made his into a trident. Hades drew the lot of overseeing the realm of the dead, and he made his Kronolithe into a golden bident—kind of like a two-pronged staff. That's where Christians get their stories about their devil carrying a pitchfork. But it was also a Key."

"The Key of Hades? I read something in my mythology book about that. It was what he used to lock and unlock the gates to the underworld. So the Key and the bident were one and the same? But how did he lose it? The book said he never let the Key out of his sight."

I smile at Daphne. Her enthusiasm for the subject surprises me for someone who claims to want nothing to do with my world.

She gives me a look that I can't read.

"What?"

"You look different when you smile," she says. "You should do it more often."

"I'll try," I say, but my expression defaults to my practiced mask. Why does smiling in front of her make me feel so . . . vulnerable? "As for the answer to your question, I don't really know. There are lots of versions of the story, and I have no idea what's myth and what's real, but according to the version Master Crue taught us—"

"In what, like, Underlord primary school?" It would be impossible not to catch the sarcasm in her voice.

"Something like that, I guess. According to that version, it was a traitor who stole it. A man who begged for one thing but took something else instead."

"Who was he?"

"Orpheus." There's a bite to my voice when I say his name. We've been taught from the age we were nurslings to despise him.

"The musician?"

I nod. "He used his music to confound Hades—manipulate his emotions. He begged for his wife to be returned to him, and the goddess and god of the Underrealm were so moved by his songs that they agreed to let him take her back to the mortal world. It wasn't until he was almost gone that they realized that Orpheus had taken something else while they were distracted. The Key.

Hades sent an army of Keres to stop him. They grabbed Eurydice, but Orpheus escaped. Hades went after him in his chariot, but he never returned. He was ambushed without his Kronolithe, and the Sky God struck him down. Some say Orpheus was working for the Sky God; others say it was Orpheus's father, Apollo, who orchestrated the theft, and that Hades's death was unintentional. Others say Orpheus knew nothing of what he was doing and acted purely out of fear—he'd stolen the bident so he could lock the main gates, thinking nobody would be able to take his wife from him again. Whatever the case, the treacherous deed was done. Hades was slain and the gates of the underworld have been locked tight ever since, and the war has been at a virtual standstill."

"This may seem like an obvious question, but if Hades was the ruler of the land of the dead, and he, you know, *is* dead, then why isn't he still in charge? And what about your mother? Why wouldn't she still be with you there?"

"It doesn't work that way. There are many different lands within the Underrealm, and three different places souls go when they die. Tartarus is the land where people go if they have outright wronged the Gods. It's a place of eternal torment, like what Christians and other religions believe to be their version of Hell. People who die with glory and honor—like victorious Champions, war heroes, and the like—go to the land of Elysium. It is what you would think of as heaven. But everyone else becomes a nameless, faceless shade in the Wastelands. They're kind of what you would think of as zombies. Hungry, insatiable, mindless souls.

"Normally, someone like Hades would have gone to Elysium, but as the stories go, fearing reprisal, the Sky God refused to give his brother a proper burial, and dishonored him by scattering his body throughout the Overrealm. As a result, Hades became just another shade, forced to wander the Wastelands. Most people believe Tartarus is the worst possible fate that could befall a soul, but I think it's the Wastelands. Because even though you're in torment, you're still yourself."

"I agree," she says. "So do you ever get to visit your mother in Elysium?"

"My mother wasn't a Champion or a hero. Only the honored go to Elysium. She is just another shade now."

"But there is more than one way to be honorable," she says. "Doesn't being a good person count for anything?"

I don't know how to respond to that. I've never thought of honor in any other way than I have been taught to consider it. I've never imagined my mother being anywhere other than lost to me forever in the Wastelands. "I don't know," I finally say.

"So what happened to the Key?" she asks.

"Nobody knows. But Dax has a theory that we need the Cypher to find it."

"And that's supposed to be me?"

"Yes."

"We'll see about that," she says. "Hey, wait a second. So how did you get here? If the gate is locked and all?"

"Through Persephone's Gate. It's kind of like a back door to the underworld. Demeter built it to ensure that Persephone would always be able to return to the mortal world without Hades's consent. I guess she was afraid he might try to stop her, depending on his mood. But I know what you're thinking. Why don't we just use that door to come and go from the Underrealm as we please? Use it to launch another attack on the Skyrealm? It's because the gate only opens once every six months and it was originally built to transport only a single person. We can maybe get a handful of Underlords through it at once. It's reserved now for the transport of Champions and their Boons."

"And what's up with that? Why do you need Boons? Are they your mates?" A pink blush brightens her cheeks. "Erm . . . I mean, are Underlord girls just really ugly or something?"

"There are no Underlord women. I don't know if it's a remnant of Demeter's curse or just the will of the Fates, but no female child has ever been born in the Underrealm."

"Oh," she says. "So that's what's with all the girl snatching."

"Nobody is snatched. The Boons must give their consent to come."

"But do they really know what they're getting themselves into? Consent isn't really consent if she doesn't know what she's saying yes to."

I am silent for a long while. I can't deny that there is truth to Daphne's words. I never knew why my own mother had agreed to follow Ren into the Underrealm—what he promised her to get her to come—but I doubt she knew that it would lead to her eventual death. A pang of guilt hits me. Daphne doesn't know that saying yes means that she very well could be agreeing to a much shorter life span. *But that is if she is only a Boon,* I try to tell myself. *If she is the Cypher, could that mean she would survive longer than an ordinary girl? Perhaps finding the Key to the Underrealm will grant her immortality, too, when it is restored to the Underlords.*

But how exactly will the Court use her to find the Key? What will be the cost?

"The Boons live very comfortable lives of luxury," I say at last. "I imagine that appeals to many girls."

"Some," she says. "But I don't fancy giving up my free will for comfort."

"That doesn't surprise me."

"And I don't fancy finding this Key for you people, either. You think I want you restarting this war and trampling my world again in the process?"

"It's not just for opening the gates. The Key is also needed to stop the locks on Pandora's Pithos from failing. Imagine what would happen to your world if more of the Keres got out. They would multiply and do far more damage than any fight between the Lords."

"Oh," she says, quietly. "Could that really happen?"

"I don't know for sure. There are rumors. . . ."

"So you don't know anything, really."

I start to say something, but she stops me.

"I don't want to hear any more. I'm not going to be your Cypher, so stop trying to use scare tactics on me."

We are both wordless for a long time after that. Daphne fiddles with the touch screen, trying to find a radio station, but we're too remote to get anything clear. There's only one car in front of us and one car behind.

"All my music was on my phone," she says, turning off my radio.

"I have half a dozen MP3 players. . . . But I left them all in my other car."

Daphne starts to hum to herself. It's a song that sounds vaguely familiar to me, but I can't say that it's one of the ones I downloaded from the music store. I listen to her, melting into the melody, until a sudden pain pricks behind my eyes. I rub at them and realize I've got tears welling in the corners. I wipe them away quickly, but not fast enough for Daphne not to notice.

"What is it?"

"That song. I think I've heard it before. I think my mom used to whisper it to me when no one was around. It made me feel . . . safe. Protected. Maybe even happy."

"She loved you," she says. "And you loved her."

I shrug, but the tears build faster in my eyes. Almost to the point that I can't see the road. "I don't even know what that feels like."

"You just described it," she says. "I think you're feeling it right now."

I wipe the wetness from my eyes. "That's just blubbering. What else would you expect from 'the boy who cried?'" I say sarcastically.

"It hurts and it makes you feel vulnerable, but there's nothing wrong with crying like that. My mom always says that tears are the price we pay for having love and compassion in our lives."

"Sometimes it feels like too high a price."

She shakes her head. "You know, I don't think it was losing control of yourself that made your father disown you. It had nothing to do with that. I think it's because he was afraid of you."

I blink at her, the tears drying up. "Afraid of *me?*"

"At seven years old, you stood up to the king of the underworld. You challenged him. You were just a little boy who loved his dying mother and that gave you strength. A strength he couldn't even fathom. I bet that scared the crap out of him. Like that Kronos guy, who was afraid his children would become more powerful than he was—but you know, instead of eating you physically, he ate at you emotionally. Your father needed to knock you down as far as he could. Because if you could challenge his authority as a boy, then what would you be capable of as a man?"

chapter forty-eight

DAPHNE

"You mind if we make a pit stop?" I ask Haden. I'd been waiting for him to have to pull into a gas station or a charging station at some point, but his car never seems to run out of juice.

"We're only an hour and a half outside of Vegas."

"That's nice," I say. "You might be made out of fire and shadow and all that jazz, but I'm human, which means I need to eat. And honestly: *I have got to pee.*"

Haden lets out a short laugh. It strikes me again how different he looks when he smiles. It happens so rarely, it feels like getting a glimpse at a Christmas present through the edges of the stiff wrapping paper.

"There's an exit up ahead with a diner," I say, checking the map on the touch screen.

There's a moan from the backseat. In the mirror, I watch Garrick push himself up to a sitting position. He presses his hand to the sides of his head like he's trying to keep his brain from throbbing.

"Good," I say. "Looks like our prisoner has woken up. I bet he could use a Coke or something."

✄

"I'll place our order," Haden says, rubbing his hands on his pant legs to get rid of the stickiness from the menus. "Take Garrick with you and find a place to sit."

He says that like this place is crowded, but we're the only ones here. Other than the trucker at the counter, nursing a milk shake.

"And watch him," he says, nodding at Garrick.

"Okay," I say, and lead Garrick to a booth in the back of the diner, but I'm not quite sure what I'd do if Garrick tried to bolt. Sit on him, maybe? I've got at least twenty pounds on the scrawny kid. But from the way he collapses into the booth and rests his head in his arms, moaning like Joe with a hangover, I'm guessing he's not going to try to make a break for it anytime soon.

Haden heads to the counter, and Garrick looks up at me over his elbow. "He didn't tell you the whole story, you know. About what happened when his mother died."

"You were awake when he told me about that?" I had a feeling Haden wouldn't have shared his story with me if he'd known Garrick had been listening. Then again, Garrick already knew how it went. He'd been there, after all.

"I was in and out, but I heard enough to know Haden left out the part when he gave me this scar," he says and runs his finger over the thin white line that mars his pale cheek. "He threw a broken crystal chess piece at my face. All because I tried to help him clean up after his father left and the servants carried out his mother's body."

"That's terrible," I say. "But I mean, his mom just died and he was only seven."

"I was only five," Garrick says.

"And you were a servant already?"

"I'm a Lesser. I was born to serve." He sniffs and rubs his nose in his sleeve. "Working in the palace was a lot better than working in the Pits, though. I've been there since I was seven."

"You work in the Pits. With those awful Keres?"

"Thanks to Haden."

"Haden?"

"I bet he didn't tell you that part of the story, either. . . ."

"What story?" Haden asks, sliding into the booth across from me. "What are you two talking about?"

"I was just about to tell Daphne what you did to me two years after your mother died," Garrick says. He has no inner song, no tune coming from him, but I can tell he's trying to upset Haden from the very loaded glare he throws his way.

It works. Haden goes ashen and a nervous little melody, like the tapping of anxious fingers against a table, comes off him. "We don't need to talk about that," he says.

"But she should know," Garrick says. "If you're going to give her your woe-is-me, disgraced-prince sob story, you really should tell the whole thing."

"This is not the time or place," Haden says, almost as if it were an order.

"But she wants to know," he says. "Don't you?" He turns that pointed glare on me. I can't deny that I am dying with curiosity now.

"Tell her how you couldn't stand having me around after I witnessed what you did when your mother died. Tell her how you lied just so you could get rid of the walking, talking reminder of your shame. Tell her how you had me banished to the Pits. Tell her how two little words could have saved me from seven years of living a nightmare, being clawed at by every terrible thing that lives in the blackest part of the Underrealm, fighting for scraps, and praying to the gods that I'll make it one more day. Or when things are really bad, that I *won't*."

My breath catches when he says this. I look at Haden for his reaction.

From the dark tones coming off him, I expect him to lash out at Garrick, to order him to be quiet, but instead, he lowers his head, as if resigned to letting the truth come out.

"Tell her," Garrick says. "Or do you want me to?"

Haden sucks in a deep breath and lets it out. "When Garrick was seven, two years after my mother's death, he was found with one of my mother's pendants in his possession. It was made of rubies and shaped like a pomegranate. It was her favorite. He was banished to the Pits for stealing it from the palace."

"But I didn't steal it," Garrick says. "She gave it to me. You knew that. You knew she gave it to me, but you told them that I took it."

"Haden?" I ask. "Is that true?"

"In a way. He would have taken it if she hadn't given it to him."

"But she did give it to me—"

"Because she caught you trying to steal it." Haden looks at me like he wants me to understand. "My mother and I walked in on him going through her stuff. He was supposed to be cleaning, but he pocketed the pendant right as we walked into the room. She saw him do it. We both knew she did, but instead of demanding it back or calling for the guards, she told him he could have it. I asked her why, and she said that Garrick was only different from me and Rowan because his mother wasn't able to protect him the way she had protected us. She said that if letting him have the pendant would help his life be a little better, then the least she could do was let him have it. She said that we should show compassion and mercy for everyone."

"A lesson you forgot as soon as she was gone. As soon as it was convenient for you."

Haden lowers his head again. "I made a mistake and I've felt shame for it every day of my life."

"You turned him in for stealing it?" I ask him.

"After my mother died, my father chose a new Boon from the harem to become his queen. He wanted to give her the pomegranate pendant, but when it came up missing from my mother's possessions, the Court originally concluded that I was the one who stole it. When my father demanded to know what had happened to it, I told him that Garrick had taken it—and when they found it on him, they didn't believe that she had given it to him. . . . I didn't corroborate his story."

"How could you do that to your own cousin?" I ask.

"We're not cousins," Garrick says. "We're brothers."

"Half brothers," Haden says quickly. "And I did it because I hated Garrick at the time. He was right; he was a walking reminder of my dishonor. A walking reminder of what my life would have been like if my mother hadn't protected me with that oath. It hurt me every time I looked at him, and so I wanted to hurt him back." He sits up and looks Garrick in the eye. "I didn't know how bad it would be. I didn't know they'd banish you to the Pits. I thought maybe a few lashings . . . I didn't know." He pauses for a moment and then says, like it's the most painful thing he's ever had to say, "I'm sorry."

I hear the shift in Haden's tone, and I know he's being sincere—I can hear the remorse coursing off him—but Garrick treats him like he's just spat in his face.

"Take your apologies and shove them up your ass," he says.

"Garrick, please," Haden says.

Garrick looks at me. "Be careful, Daphne. Haden's selfishness and his obedience are a dangerous combination. He'll do anything to try to win his honor back. If he's willing to let a little kid be thrown into a Pit full of monsters because he didn't like seeing him around, what do you think he's going to do when he doesn't get what he wants from you?"

His words strike a dissonant chord inside me. His view of Haden doesn't match the remorse that I hear in Haden now. They just *feel* wrong to me.

But then again, I barely know Haden at all.

What *would* he do if I couldn't convince the Oracle to change his mind? What would he do when I continued to say no? Because I'm sure as hell . . . or Hades . . . never going to say yes to helping him.

"Watch your back, Boon," Garrick says. "Because nobody else is going to do it for you."

"I'm not a Boon," I say through gritted teeth.

A very round woman appears at our table with a loaded tray. "Well, howdy, folks," she says. "I've got chicken noodle soup, sodas, a salad, cheese fries, and cheeseburger! Whose poison is whose?" She looks down at us, and her grin fades. "Oh no, oh, dears, you're not all headed to a funeral, are you?"

After the waitress leaves, Garrick grabs his bowl of soup and Pepsi and moves to the next table over like he can't stand sitting close to Haden anymore. But instead of eating, he lays his head on the table and moans, as if his exchange with Haden has zapped up all of his strength. I keep a close eye on him in case he decides to make a run for it anyway.

"You know," I say tentatively, "if you stopped treating Garrick like a Lesser and more like your brother, he might start to forgive you."

He nods as if he might actually consider the idea.

Haden and I sit across from each other in awkward silence for a few moments, but the smell wafting up from my cheese fries and bacon cheeseburger reminds me of how insanely hungry I am. I pick up a fry, and a long string of gooey, melty cheese trails behind it. I catch the slight curl of Haden's lip while he watches it.

He pulls his own plate closer to him and starts picking the croutons out of his salad.

"You seriously got a salad?" I ask him, trying to lighten the mood.

"Yes?" he says, and then pushes the glorious pile of grated cheddar cheese off the lump of iceberg lettuce on his plate. "Is that a problem?"

"We're at a greasy spoon. You should at least have the decency to get something greasy. That's their specialty. This," I say, pulling his plate away, "doesn't even fall into the proper definition of *salad*. This is just lettuce."

"I like lettuce," he says, but the grimace on his face betrays how he really feels.

"How do you maintain all that muscle if you eat like a rabbit?"

"We eat *different* things in the Underrealm."

"He doesn't like anything," Garrick says from the adjacent table. "He's the pickiest eater this side of Tartarus."

"You mean you don't like bacon cheeseburgers?"

"I've never tried a bacon cheeseburger."

"You've never . . . ?" I place my hand over my heart like this news wounds my soul. "We are changing that right now."

I take a knife and cut my burger in half. I shove a rebellious piece of bacon back under the sesame bun and present it to him like it's precious cargo. Which it is. I don't take sharing my bacon cheeseburgers lightly.

"I can't," Haden says, trying to nudge my hands away.

"I will be morally offended if you don't at least take a bite."

"Just eat it so she'll shut up!" Garrick says. "I've got a headache."

Haden takes the half burger from my hands and holds it gingerly. "If I'm going to eat this *thing*, you have to do something for me first."

"What?" I ask reluctantly.

"Tell me how you did what you did to that Keres. How did you know how to make it go solid enough for me to kill it?"

Garrick nearly knocks his Pepsi off his table. "You killed a Keres?" he says. "That's impossible!"

"Not with Daphne's help, apparently."

"What did you do?" Garrick asks. He almost sounds angry.

"I . . . screamed at it," I say with a shrug.

"What?"

"But how did you know to scream at it like that?" Haden says. "Plenty of people have probably screamed at a Keres before, but I've never heard of one becoming solid as a result."

"I don't really know," I say. "I was just scared and tried the first thing I could think of; I didn't really know what would happen." I take a sip of root beer. "It was like how I calmed your cat that one time. You know how I told you that I hear the songs that living things put off? People or animals or even plants? Well, when I was a kid, I figured out that if I imitate the tone an animal puts off, they're more likely to listen to me. I use it all the time on the strays my mom brings home. Some of them can be pretty wild until I give them a good talking to."

"So you were trying to charm the Keres?" Haden asks. The grease from the burger is starting to run down his fingers but he doesn't seem to notice.

"I mostly thought I'd imitate the screeching noise it was making and see what happened. It actually seemed to make it angrier. I'm just glad you were able to kill it before it attacked me." I point at the burger. "Now, are you going to take a bite of that before it gets cold?"

"Do I have to?"

"I answered your question, so yes."

Haden bites off a small corner and starts to chew.

"So?"

"It's . . . actually, it's . . ." His eyes widen and he drops the burger on top of his salad and stands up. His gaze goes out the window and then darts to the trucker at the bar. He scans the whole restaurant quickly, as if looking for someone.

"What's wrong?" I ask.

"That green car out there," he says, pointing to a BMW at the far end of the parking lot. There are only two other vehicles in the lot. A big rig and Haden's Tesla. "It was behind us most of the way here."

"So? They probably just made a pit stop, too."

"Then where are they? There's nobody else in here."

"Maybe they went across the street to that . . . *abandoned* gas station?" I start to see Haden's point. "You think they're following us?"

"There's one way to find out." He tosses a wad of cash on the table. "Grab your food to go. Come on, Garrick."

"Harpies," Garrick mumbles.

I take two big bites of my burger and a swig of root beer and then follow Haden as he leads Garrick by the elbow out to the Tesla. We're all trying to look as nonchalant as possible as we buckle in. Haden pulls out of the parking lot and around to the road behind the diner, then pulls over to the side.

"What are you doing?"

"Just give it a minute."

About forty-five seconds later, the green BMW pulls out of the parking lot and starts in the direction we went. This still seems like a coincidence to me, but it's enough to set Haden off. He slams his foot down on the accelerator and whips his car around so we're blocking the BMW. The other car comes to a screeching halt. Haden bursts out of the driver's-side door.

"What are you doing?" I call after him.

Wisps of blue light crackle between the fingers of the hand he holds behind his back. Someone gets out of the green car, but I can't see who it is until Haden has him by the throat. His camel brown fedora falls to the dusty ground.

"Tobin?" I jump out of the car.

"Why are you following us?" Haden shouts. A sphere of blue light swirls in his hand above Tobin's nose. "Who sent you?"

"No . . . no . . . nobody," Tobin stammers.

"Let him go!" I shout. "It's just Tobin. And . . . Lexie?" I see her now, cringing in the passenger seat of the BMW.

Haden lets go of Tobin, but he still holds the bolt of lightning in his hand. "Why are you here?"

"You kidnapped one of my best friends," Tobin says. "Why wouldn't I be here? And what the hell is that?" He points at the crackling blue light in Haden's hand.

Haden extinguishes the bolt of lightning and shoves his hands behind his back like it was nothing.

"Kidnapped?" I ask Tobin. "Why did you think I was kidnapped?"

"You disregarded my texts about the list so quickly, I thought something must be wrong. I thought I'd walk past Haden's place to see what he was up to . . . and I saw you leaving with him."

"And of course your brain immediately went to kidnapping."

"Only because I saw him shove a body into the car first and then take your cell phone away. I was too far away to do anything, and then when you guys went flying out of the garage, I kind of freaked."

"And how does Lexie come into all this?" Haden asks.

"She happened to be driving down the street. I didn't have a car, so I kind of commandeered hers."

"You mean *you* kidnapped *her* so you could stop me from kidnapping Daphne?" Haden asks. "Talk about irony."

"Hey, I offered to pay for gas," Tobin says.

"If you thought I'd been kidnapped, why didn't you call the police?"

"Because the call would have been rerouted to Olympus Hills security, . . . and you know how reliable they *aren't*, and . . ." He shoves his hands in his pockets. "I thought if I followed him to wherever he was taking you, I might be able to find Abbie."

"Oh." Suddenly any humor I'd found in the situation is gone. Tobin was still desperately searching for his sister, who could never be found.

"But you're telling me you aren't kidnapped. You're heading heaven knows where with this guy on purpose?" he asks.

"Vegas," I say. "We're headed to Las Vegas."

Tobin's jaw drops ever so slightly. "Why?" he asks like he doesn't quite want to know the answer.

I look from Tobin to Haden. Haden shakes his head once. I ignore him. "We're headed to Las Vegas to find an Oracle," I say.

It's time to start telling the truth.

"You people are insane!" Lexie says from the backseat of the Tesla. "Insane! Oracles? Monsters? Underworld princes or whatever? You've all flown over the cuckoo's nest and you're trying to drag me with you!"

Overall, I'd say they've taken the truth—or partial truth— rather well. Especially Tobin. He sits stoically in the middle row of the Model X, his hands clasped in his lap.

Haden was the one who insisted that both he and Lexie come with us now. Tobin had come willingly, saying that he wasn't going to let me go off to Vegas with Haden alone. Lexie had been another story. I thought we should let her drive herself back home, but Haden had made the valid point that we couldn't trust her to not tell somebody where we went. Which means between her and Garrick, we have two captives in the car.

"This Oracle," Tobin asks. "Do you think she can tell me how to get my sister back?"

"Possibly," Haden says as he changes lanes. We're about twenty minutes outside of Vegas and the traffic has gotten heavy.

Both he and I have evaded most of Tobin's questions about Abbie. I plan on telling him the whole truth, but not here. Not now. That is a private conversation that doesn't need Lexie shouting about our sanity in the background.

"There's no such thing as Oracles!" she says.

"Can somebody make her shut up?" Garrick responds, holding his head.

Maybe I should have let Haden knock Lexie out in order to get her in the car. Instead, I'd held her Hermès purse hostage until she agreed to get in.

Haden changes lanes again. He glances in the rearview mirror. "Harpies," he mumbles.

"What is it?"

"I think we've got another tail. Don't look back. Use your mirror. But I think that motorcycle is following us. He's been in my rearview mirror for the last hour. He changes lanes every time I do."

I pull down the sun visor and angle the vanity mirror until I can see who he's talking about. There's a rider dressed in all black leather on a black bullet bike behind us. He's wearing a full-screened helmet that makes it impossible to see his face.

"Who do you think it is?"

"I don't know, but I certainly don't think it's another one of your friends. Simon said he'd send someone after me if I ever left town again. He also said it wouldn't be a pleasant experience." A strange tone comes off his body and he white-knuckle grips the steering wheel. It makes me wonder if he's thinking about what happened to Dax and Abbie when they tried to run away. "I think I've seen this same guy around Olympus Hills a couple of times. He's probably been following us since we left, but I was too distracted by Tobin to notice."

"Do you think we can lose him?" Tobin asks.

"Maybe." Haden glances at me and then points at the touch screen in the center console of the car. "This thing has a Web browser. Use it to get on to YouTube. I want you to do a search for evasive driving techniques in heavy traffic."

"Seriously?" Tobin asks.

"I am being completely earnest."

"Awesome," Tobin practically squeals.

"Or maybe 'how to lose a tail in a car chase' or something like that."

I type in a few options until Haden tells me to stop. I click on the video and we watch as we idle in traffic. I guess I shouldn't be surprised that YouTube has an instructional video on evasive driving techniques, but still, I'm not sure how this is going to help. I can barely understand anything the drivers in the video are saying, let alone remember any of it.

"Okay, that's good," Haden says. "Everyone buckled in?"

When traffic breaks up a bit, he changes lanes, then changes again until we're speeding down the HOV lane.

"This is so not legal!" Lexie shouts from the backseat.

Haden swerves the car back into the left lane and then the middle lane. I can't handle it. I grip the oh-crap bar above my door and close my eyes as hard as I can. I get a little carsick from the jerking motions of the car as Haden weaves through traffic. At one point, we're sailing forward at another, we're flying in reverse!

Lexie screams.

Tobin cheers like he's on a roller coaster.

And Garrick groans like he's about to throw up.

I suddenly question whether I ever want to get my license if there are drivers like Haden on the road.

The car stops reversing and whips to the right. I can tell we're getting off the freeway. Three more sharp turns follow, but I don't open my eyes until we come to a stop. We're sitting in an alley somewhere in Las Vegas proper.

"I think we lost him," Haden says, breathing hard.

Garrick opens the door, stumbles out into the alley, and pukes. I cringe at the sound.

"We need to find a place to hide. We've got to get off the streets before we're spotted again. Find someplace to stay overnight if we have to."

"We're in Vegas," Lexie says. "Pick a hotel, duh."

I raise my eyebrows, surprised to get a suggestion from the "captive" portion of our audience. A hotel is the obvious answer.

"I can't use my credit card," Haden says. "Simon tracks all of my spending; he'd find us in minutes. I've only got about sixty dollars in cash after the diner."

"I don't have much cash, either." Between getting a new outfit for the festival and buying Christmas presents to bring back to Ellis, I am pretty much tapped out in the cash department.

"I could charge it on my mom's card," Tobin suggests.

"No," I say, dismissing the idea without explanation. I don't want Tobin's mom getting wind of our location, either. "I guess we could try to get a cheap motel room off the strip."

"Um, no," Lexie says. "No way! If I'm going to be held hostage in Vegas, it is not going to happen in some bedbug-ridden, pay-by-the hour motel. We're going to the Crossroads Casino and Hotel. My dad is one of the owners. I can get us a room."

The Crossroads? I have never stayed in a hotel, let alone in Vegas, but the name strikes a familiar chord. "And how do we know you're not going to just rat us out and try to make a break for it?" I ask her.

"Because we're in Vegas. And you know what they say: what

happens in Vegas stays in Vegas. You guys can go search for this 'Oracle' all you want. I'll go run up a spa bill on my daddy's tab and hitch a ride home with you guys when you all come back to your senses."

"Won't your parents mind?"

"They've gone to Belize for the holidays—without me. They've been gone for three weeks already, so they won't even know." She crosses her arms around her orange purse. "Frankly, this little ride on the crazy-town express is the most fun I've had in months. So, no, I'm not going to rat you out and make a break for it. I'm going to get a chemical peel, a mani-pedi, and run up a room service bill like you've never seen."

Considering I've never seen a room service bill, I don't doubt it. I also don't doubt that she's telling the truth. It seems very *Lexie* to turn a kidnapping into a luxury weekend getaway.

"Now head up this street and turn left," she orders.

"You heard the woman," I say to Haden.

chapter forty-nine

HADEN

We decide to ditch the Tesla in a parking garage several blocks from the hotel and head out onto what Lexie calls the strip. At first, I am worried that we will be easily spotted out in the open, but this street is so cram packed with people, it's a struggle just to stay together as a group. A cluster of people, dressed in red pointy hats with white balls on the ends, sing as they walk in front of us, but they don't sound nearly as good as Daphne. The hotels are lit up like beacons, and large evergreen trees strung with lights are every-where. I don't know how much of this is normal Vegas fare and how much of it is for of the humans' upcoming Christmas celebration. People bump into me as we walk, making me feel off balance, and a strange smoke chokes my lungs. I see that it's coming from a group of men who line the road, smoking what I recall are cigarettes. One of the men sees me looking at him and he shoves a flyer into my hand. "Good times, good times," he mumbles as I pass.

I look down at the paper and see a mostly naked woman, wearing only two thin strips of red material lined with white fur, standing in a very . . . provocative position.

"You planning on making a visit to 'Sexy Mrs. Claus'?" Daphne asks.

Heat rushes into my face and hands. I drop the paper, feeling strangely ashamed that she saw me looking at it.

"Don't take anything from anyone," Tobin advises me. "And avoid making eye contact."

I nod and pick up my pace, hoping not to get lost in the chaos of the strip. I am glad when we enter the hotel, but I can still feel the grime from the street clinging to me. The lobby is so bright, it hurts my eyes. A sea of potted red flowers fills most of the space, encircling another tall evergreen tree strung with shimmering lights, stretching up to the vaulted ceiling. Garish, glittering globes of green and red hang from almost everything. Loud, grating, overly cheerful music fills the lobby from an unknown source, and an additional barrage of noise and flashing lights come from an area called the casino. It's all so overwhelming, I almost want to retreat back outside.

I don't understand why humans would want to come here to relax.

Garrick collapses into a plush chair in the lobby, looking as though he might vomit again. If I find this place overwhelming, I'm sure his throbbing head can barely handle it.

"Hey," Tobin says to Daphne, pointing at the entrance to the Crossroads Blues Club on the other side of the casino floor. "Isn't that the club where your dad got his big break?"

"Yeah," she says, after thinking for a moment. "I thought this place sounded familiar. Some big talent scout saw him play here . . . which means this is also the place where my parents met. Weird."

"I'm going to go talk to the front desk," Lexie says, and makes her way through the crowd in the lobby. I can't get over the amount of people here. Daphne is right; finding this Sarah Smith in a city this overrun feels improbable, if not impossible.

"So how do we find this Oracle?" Tobin asks. "The sooner I can get a lead on Abbie, the better."

Daphne and I exchange a look.

"I think you need to tell him," I say. I feel gutted at the idea that, because of me and my family, she has to share such horrible news with her best friend. I'd do it myself, but I know he'll take it better from her than from me.

"Tobin, can I talk to you for a minute?" Daphne asks him. "In private."

"Yeah, of course."

I watch her lead him to an empty bench near a fountain in the lobby. The spray of the water drowns out their voices, and I am too far away to read their lips, but I can tell from their body language that Daphne is filling Tobin in on what Dax told us—or didn't tell us—about what happened to his sister. She places her hand over his. His bright face darkens, and he crumples forward against her shoulder. I turn away, no longer able to watch.

It's a good ten minutes later when Lexie returns from the front desk. "There's some big teen talent contest or some garbage being hosted by the club tonight, so the place is pretty booked up. I couldn't get the penthouse, but I did manage to swing us a two-bedroom suite. A room with a king and the other has two queens. I don't know how you all want to deal with your sleeping arrangements, but I finagled the room, so I call dibs on the king."

"I don't care," Tobin says, approaching with Daphne. "As long as I'm not sharing a bed with *him*." He gives me a pointed look that says that even though I wasn't here six years ago, he's holding me responsible for what happened to his sister.

"Tobin, I—"

"Save it," he says. "I'm not giving up on Abbie until that Oracle looks me in the face and tells me there's no way to get her back."

"I don't think . . ." I let my sentence trail off, not seeing the point of trying to dissuade him. Some people won't see the truth, no matter how hard you point it out to them.

"Now can we go to our room?" Tobin says.

"Yeeessss," Garrick answers, sounding like he's about to black out again.

"Suit yourself," Lexie says, handing us each a key card. "I'm headed to the spa."

Daphne hangs back. "I think I'm going to stay down here for a while," she says.

She doesn't quite sound like herself.

chapter fifty

DAPHNE

I realize as I sit with Tobin near the fountain, that the lobby of a Vegas hotel isn't the best place to tell him the worst news of his life—but it's too late. I've already made up my mind to do it, and if I stop now, I don't know how I'll find the courage to do it later.

"I know what happened to Abbie," I say before my words fail me. "She's gone, Tobin."

"Yeah, she was taken by one of these Underlords, right? That's why I need to go see this Oracle. She'll tell me how to get her back."

"It's not that simple." My voice catches, and I clear my throat.

"What is it, Daphne?" he says, like he can see the trepidation on my face. "What's wrong?"

"I am afraid . . . I'm afraid she's dead."

He pulls his hand out from under mine. "How do you know that? You *can't* know that!"

"I met the Lord who was *supposed to* bring her back to the Underrealm with him. . . ."

"What do you mean, 'supposed to'? Like he didn't . . . ?"

"Your sister really did run away, Tobin. Or at least she tried to. The Lord who was supposed to take her, Dax is his name. . . .

They fell in love and tried to run away instead of going back to the underworld. But something went wrong. Somebody came after them. And she died."

"What went wrong?" Tears flood his eyes. "What happened?"

"I don't know." I bite my lip, trying to hold it together. "I don't know any more than that."

Tobin covers his eyes with his hands. He crumples forward and I catch him, leaning his head against my shoulder. He quakes as I hold him, giving off notes so strained with sorrow that it drowns out the Christmas music and hotel noises. They wrap around me and I feel as though I am engulfed in a cocoon of his grief.

"There's more, Tobin." I don't want to say it, but I have to. I can't keep the truth from him any longer. I would want to know if it were me. "That list you showed me. The one of all those missing girls. Those have to be all the girls who have been taken to the underworld; these Boons as they call them. . . . And if my name is on your mother's list now, before . . . before I was even taken . . . that means . . ."

Tobin's sorrowful melody shifts suddenly into harsh, broken notes. He lets go of me and I can see the anger flashing in his eyes, not just hear it coursing off him. "It means my mother knew," he says, finishing for me. "She knew that my sister was one of their targets. But why wouldn't she try to stop them?"

"Tobin, I—"

He looks at me, anger hardening his face. Or maybe it's determination. "I'm going to get her back," he says. "I'm getting Abbie back."

"But she's dead. . . ."

"That Orpheus guy did it. That's what your dad's play is about, isn't it? He went down there and got his wife back."

And failed. "I don't think it works that way. . . ."

"I'm going to get her back."

I feel Tobin clinging to this idea like it's the only thing keeping him from falling into a dark hole of despair. I can't bring myself to tell him that even the son of a god had failed at trying to bring his loved one back from the world of the dead. Instead, I just nod and let him keep holding on. In the meantime, I can feel myself slipping off the edge.

When the others retire to our hotel room, I can't bring myself to follow. Talking to Tobin had done exactly what I feared it would— it had made all of this real. Far too real. The soft, filmy coat of denial I'd been looking at everything through had been eaten away by cold, harsh reality. Tobin's hope only makes it worse. It makes him seem naive and delusional, and made me realize that I could no longer deny what is happening. That the world, as I have known it for seventeen years, is a lie, that it hides terrible secrets like monsters and vengeful gods, Cyphers and Keys, and a selfish underworld prince who isn't going to stop until he gets what he wants: me.

Is there even anything this Oracle can do to help me stop it? Is there anywhere I can hide where they wouldn't just hunt me down? And if I do escape, would the consequences of losing the Cypher be as catastrophic as Haden had tried to make me believe?

Do I really have a choice in any of this?

I wander the hotel, looking for a distraction. Anything that can bring back that easy film of denial. Anything that can help me forget. I try going into the casino, where people sit at machines, looking like dull zombies, but someone barks at me when I try to step off the carpet walkway that leads through the area. No kids allowed. I keep walking until I find myself at the Crossroads Blues Club—the place where my parents met all those years ago. The place that led to a drive-thru wedding and a three-day honeymoon before Joe got a call from that talent scout and he ran off to become a rock star. I expect someone else to yell at me when I walk into the club, but instead, the man in the entry takes one look at me, slams a green stamp on my hand, and tells me that the right half of the room is reserved for "contestants and their families."

The club is dim and smells thick of booze—which seems fitting since it reminds me of Joe. This is the place where it had all started. I probably wouldn't have ever been born if my parents hadn't both ended up here that fateful night.

I laugh to myself at that word. *Fateful*. Fate. That thing Haden clings to and I desperately want to escape.

I want to forget.

A waitress stops at a booth with a tray of shot glasses. She sets it on an empty table and starts flirting with a group of frat boys who've called her over.

I've always despised Joe for his drinking. I've never understood his need to drown out the world. But at that moment, I get it. Because all I want is to forget—if only for one night. I want to stop feeling. I want to be numb.

I want to make it all go away.

While the waitress is distracted, I snag four shot glasses—two in each hand—and retreat to a secluded booth in the back of the club. Where I can drown in the dark.

chapter fifty-one

HADEN

"How many of those have you had?" I ask Daphne when I find her in the Crossroads Blues Club. There's some sort of talent competition going on, and the place is packed. A teenage boy is onstage, playing a wicked solo on the bass guitar. Daphne sits in a booth near the back of the club. In front of her sit a few small glasses filled with an amber liquid that gives off a sharp, woody smell. She looks a bit green in the face.

"Two," she says, holding up two fingers. "Two sips, that is. I keep trying to down a shot whole, but the taste makes me gag."

I had begun to worry when it started to get late and Daphne hadn't come back to the room. Garrick was passed out on the couch in the suite and Tobin was raiding the mini-refrigerator and giving me sidelong death glances, so I decided to go looking for her. Somehow, I knew she'd be in the club. And from the looks of her, I'd been right to be worried.

"I think two shots will get me buzzed," she says. "I think a third shot will get me properly drunk. It may take four or five before I black out. I don't know. I've never had alcohol before."

"How did you even get those?" I'd used the ID that said I was twenty-one at the entrance of the club, but because of the talent competition, the place is overrun by underage kids and their families. Daphne has a bright fluorescent green stamp on her hand to indicate she isn't legal.

"Stole 'em off a tray."

"That takes some guts."

"Don't worry, I'll leave some money on the table."

"That's not what I'm worried about."

"I haven't decided if I'm going to keep trying to drink this one yet," she says, running her finger around the rim of the glass. "I don't drink. I swore I never would because of Joe. My mom is always giving me lectures about how kids of alcoholics have to be real careful—how underage drinking increases their risks of losing control. I don't like not being in control. It doesn't fit into my plan. Everything I've done my whole life has been part of my master plan. Teaching myself music, rehearsing day and night, practicing self-discipline. It was all leading toward the same goal. I knew exactly where I was going and how I wanted to get there. And then you had to come along. . . ."

"Can I sit?"

She shrugs. "It's not like I could stop you."

"You could if you wanted to."

She looks up at me. "Could I?"

I purse my lips.

The guy with the bass guitar finishes his solo, and the crowd goes wild with applause. A table of who I assume are judges hold up white cards with numbers on them. The audience gets even more excited.

She slides over in the booth. "Knock yourself out." She pats the seat next to her, and I figure she's inviting me to sit next to her, not punch myself in the head. So I sit.

She scoots the shot glass closer to her. "I've been in denial since the night of the festival," she says. "Thinking I have some sort of say in all of this. It's just . . . telling Tobin about his sister made all of this suddenly feel very real. Too real." The tip of her finger curls over the lip of the glass into the amber liquid. "And I haven't got the slightest idea what to do."

I want to tell her to give in. I want to tell her to stop fighting her destiny. I want to tell her to agree to come with me. Instead, I say, "I don't think you're going to find the answers in the bottom of that glass."

"Yeah, but maybe I'll find some distraction. I want to forget for a while," she says, holding the glass. She sighs and looks up at the girl on the stage. "That was supposed to be me, you know?"

"How so?"

"It's funny," she says, "that I'm here. This weekend. In Las Vegas. Trying to save myself. Because that was part of my original plan."

A girl onstage goes to the microphone and starts singing. She's good, but not half as good as Daphne.

"My plan was to be here for this very competition." She points up at the sign over the stage. "All-American Teen Talent Competition. I was headed to the preliminary auditions for this competition the day Joe showed up in Ellis and told me I was coming to live with him. Before I met you. This was the plan. I was going to kill it at the auditions and make it past the preliminary round and end up here." She laughs a little to herself. "I told Jonathan that I'd settle for second place, but that wasn't true. I knew I'd end up here. Some big talent scout or college recruiter was going to see me sing and give me my big break. My big ticket out of Ellis Fields. Away from that small-town, nobody life." She gives a short little laugh.

"I didn't know that the final competition was going to be at the Crossroads, though. That's just kind of . . . weird."

I nod.

"I guess it wouldn't have mattered. They would have just sent you to Ellis Fields instead of Olympus Hills. I'd still be in this mess, and the plan would still have gone to hell." She smirks like she finds it all pretty funny. From the way she's talking so openly, I'd think she's already had more to drink than a couple of sips.

"You know?" she says, seeming to speak to the shot glass instead of me. "Why the hell not? Let's get good and drunk. My life is probably over anyway." She picks up the glass, like she's going to down it in one gulp. "Bottoms up!" she says, pinching her nose.

"No," I say, putting my hand over the top of the glass, stopping her. "I've got a better idea for a distraction." I set the glass on the tray of a passing server. "Come on." I pull her from the booth.

"What are we doing?" she asks, but she doesn't protest being propelled from the club out into the casino.

"You'll see. First, we need some leverage."

I tell her to wait outside the club entrance and I make my way nonchalantly to an unoccupied slot machine. I watch how a woman in a giant, tentlike dress uses the machine next to mine. Then I pull a quarter from my pocket and put it into the slot machine. I pull the lever and place my hand on top of the machine and send an electrical pulse into it from my fingertips. The woman next to me goes nuts as the entire row of slot machines comes to life, blinking and beeping and announcing a winner. "Jackpot!" she shouts. "Jackpot!" All eyes are on her as I pull a slip of paper from my own blinking machine.

Five thousand dollars. Not bad for my first attempt at the slots.

"What was that?" Daphne asks as I lead her back inside the club.

"I told you. Leverage."

I walk right up to the table where the MC for the competition waits while the contestants perform on the stage. She's a middle-aged woman who is sporting more cleavage than shirt.

"What are you doing, Haden?" Daphne whispers.

I lean in close to the MC, and she looks up at me, a bit more than startled. I set the slip of paper on the table in front of her. "How about a late entry?"

"I'm sorry, sonny. I can't do that."

"You've got to. You see my friend over there?" I gesture to Daphne, who stands very tentatively a few feet behind me. She probably thinks I've gone insane. "It was her dream to be part of this competition, but something came up that threw off her plan, something that was kind of my fault, and now I'm trying to make it up to her. And I need you to help me." I smile at her in a way that, hopefully, doesn't make her think of me as a "sonny" and slide the paper closer to her so she can see the amount of money she can redeem it for. "Just let her sing, please?"

"All right, honey," she whispers. "Can't say no to a boy with a smile like that. And this ain't too bad, too." She picks up the slip of paper and tucks it into the front of her shirt. "I'd think about telling you my room number, sugar, but it's obvious you've got a thing for your friend over there."

I whisper a few more things to her, and then when the latest contestant finishes and the crowd applauds, the MC heads up to the stage.

"What did you just do?" Daphne asks, quite accusingly.

I smile at her.

"What. Did. You. Do?"

"Seems we've got one more number for you all," the MC says. "Daphne Raines, come on up here, hon!"

"What?" She balks at me. "I can't. I don't . . . I don't even have a guitar!"

"Then ask that guy," I say, pointing at one of the contestants. "Smile at him and he'll give it to you."

"I don't know what to sing."

"It'll come to you."

"There are hundreds of people here."

"So?"

"This is crazy," she says.

"This was *your* plan."

She groans, but I know she wants to sing.

"Go," I say. "Before the judges put a stop to it."

Daphne hugs me. She pulls away too quickly and heads for the stage, stopping only to beg a guitar off a guy who all too willingly hands it over.

She stands on the stage, adjusting the guitar over her shoulder. I can't help thinking she looks as bright and intangible as a ray of sunshine, standing in the spotlight. She leans into the microphone. "This is a song that I wrote with my dad. You may have heard it before." She looks in the direction of where she left me standing. "For you, Haden."

She strums the first few notes on the guitar and then starts singing. "Shadow of a star . . ."

Her voice echoes out from the speakers, filling the club. The entire room comes to a standstill. All other sounds, voices, movements stop. Or maybe that's just me. Maybe I'm the one who stops, everything else disappearing. Nothing else exists. I can't

404

even breathe, for fear of missing a single note of her song. Watching her is like staring into the sun, but I can't look away.

When she finishes, the room remains frozen for a full three seconds, then explodes into cheers and applause. The judges hold up their cards. I can't see what they say from here, but they make Daphne happy. She throws her hands up in the air and curtseys at the same time. I've never seen anyone look so alive.

And that's when it strikes me. How can I take Daphne away from this world? How can I take sunshine and life into a place of shadow and death?

For the first time, I hope more than anything that the Oracle will tell me I am wrong. If my god were still alive, if I could pray, I'd send down a prayer. I'd beg him to tell the Oracle another way. I'd cry to him for another choice.

Because Hades help me, I'm falling for this girl.

Daphne runs toward me from the stage, the biggest smile on her face. I want nothing more than for her to throw her arms around me. If she doesn't do it, then I will.

"Are you Joe Vince's daughter?" a large man asks, stepping between us.

Daphne stops short. "Yes."

"Ah. I thought so. Do you mind if I get a picture of you for our 'before they were stars' wall? We've got a picture of your dad up there," he says, pointing to a wall of framed photographs. "You're going places, kiddo. I'll be kicking myself if I don't get a picture now."

"Um, yes," she says, but her gaze flits to me.

She smiles at the man as he takes a picture with his camera. "Someday, we'll hang this right next to the picture of Joe!"

When the man leaves, Daphne goes to the wall of photos. I

follow her. There, right in the center of the wall, in a big black frame, is a picture of a much younger-looking Joe Vince. He poses for the photo with his arm around a girl who looks very much like Daphne.

"Is that . . . ?"

"My mom," she says. "Wow. This must have been taken the night they met. They were only together for a few days, you know."

"I didn't know. . . . Who's that with your mom?" I point to a second woman in the photo, standing off to the side a bit. She and Daphne's mom wear matching silver bracelets that look oddly familiar to me. Like the one Brim wears as her collar.

"Oh," Daphne says. "That must have been Kayla."

That name strikes me so hard, I feel like the wind has been knocked out of my chest.

"She and my mom were best friends until Kayla took off. I think that's one of the reasons my mother never let me leave Ellis. Her one trip outside town—spring break, her senior year—didn't exactly go as she'd planned. She ended up with a one-week marriage, a surprise pregnancy, and Kayla ended up running off with some guy to New York or something."

I stare into the eyes of the woman in the photograph. Jade green eyes just like mine. Kayla hadn't gone off to New York with *some guy*; she'd gone to the Underrealm. And I know exactly who she went with.

I search the faces in the background of the photograph and find the one I'm looking for: Ren. My father. He looks smaller than I remember in the picture, less regal, wearing blue jeans and a flannel shirt. This is almost eighteen years ago. Back when he was a Champion. Perhaps only hours or days before he returned to the Underrealm. It's obvious he's watching the three main people in the photograph, but his eyes aren't locked on my mother like I'd expect. The person he's intently staring at is Daphne's mom.

"Come on," Daphne says. "Let's go."

"Don't you want to stick around to see if you won?"

She shakes her head. "Singing was prize enough. Besides, it wouldn't be fair if I took home the trophy, since you bought my way into the competition."

chapter fifty-two

DAPHNE

"Tonight was fun. Thank you," I say with a yawn as Haden slides the key card through the door lock. We'd stopped at an ice-cream parlor in the hotel and I'd forced him to try a scoop of mint chocolate chip. Despite his protests at first, he'd gone back for a second helping. "I think you've got a sweet tooth."

He gives me a small smile and pushes open the door.

Garrick is out cold on the couch, Lexie is tucked away in the king room, with the door shut and the TV on a low murmur, and Tobin is asleep, sprawled in the middle of one of the queen-sized beds, with a few empty bottles from the minibar scattered around him. He looks like such a mess that I am happy Haden stopped me from taking that shot at the club. If I'd been able to stomach it, I know I wouldn't have stopped until I was completely hammered.

Haden pulls the latch on the lock and stands behind me. My arms prickle with static energy as I become aware of the electric current that surrounds him. I also become very aware of the fact that there is only one bed left, and two of us.

I had wanted a distraction when I was in the club, and Haden had given me one—but not in the way he'd expected.

He was the distraction.

He'd known what I wanted—no, *needed*—before I even knew that I needed it. He'd been in tune with me in the same way I could discern the emotions of others.

A lesser guy would have let me get drunk, maybe even tried to hook up.

But Haden had stopped me from making a mistake, and helped me in the best way possible. What he'd done is unselfish and so surprising that it makes me see him in a new way—and not at all like the person Garrick had tried to convince me he is.

I am *aware* of Haden in a whole new way.

"Um, wanna flip for the bed?" I cringe, hoping that it didn't sound as awkward to him as it did to me. "I mean, with a quarter. Not like gymnastics or anything."

"Thanks for the clarification," he says from behind me. He's standing so close, I can feel his breath brushing against my hair. "But I'm all right taking the floor."

Again with the being selfless.

I don't argue with him and get my pajamas from my suitcase and change quickly in the bathroom. The awareness that he's just on the other side of the thin door makes goose bumps prickle up on my skin.

When I return to the bedroom, I find that Haden has made a nest out of the blankets from the closet for himself between the two queen beds. He wears a pair of light cotton pajama pants . . . and no shirt. I am not sure I have seen someone with such defined abdominal muscles before. He lies on his right side so I can't see his scars. His eyes are closed, but I know he's not asleep as I crawl into the empty queen bed. I lie on the side closest to him. I am motionless for a long time, watching him breathe. He's so still, except for his chest lifting and lowering ever so slightly, that he reminds me of a shadow. As sleep starts to creep into my mind, I relax on my side and let my arm drape over the edge of the bed. My hand dangles a few inches above his mouth. His warm breath sends tingles up my arm. After a moment, I feel his fingers close tentatively around mine.

I don't pull my hand away.

A cool breeze awakens me the next morning. For a moment, I don't know where I am until I realize that the cold wind is actually the air-conditioning kicking on. I open my eyes and find that I am lying on my back in the hotel bed.

And Haden is gone.

The blankets he'd used are folded neatly and stacked at the end of my bed. I sit up and look around the room. His duffel is gone, too.

Sunrise peeks in between the curtains. Garrick is lying on the floor next to the couch like he'd rolled off it in the middle of the night, and the door to Lexie's room is still closed. Tobin moans and rolls over onto his back on the adjacent bed. He holds his hand over his eyes.

"Tobin?" I whisper. "Do you know where Haden went?"

"No," he moans. "But I heard him leave a couple of hours ago."

"Oh."

Where did he go? *Why* did he go?

Is he having second thoughts about finding this new Oracle?

Has he changed his mind about me?

I thought maybe after last night he might . . .

Then again, maybe I'd imagined what had happened between us. That new awareness of each other—a connection. Maybe falling asleep with our hands clasped had only been part of a dream?

Or maybe he's just as freaked out about all of it as I am.

The hotel room door opens and Haden slips back inside, with his duffel bag slung over his shoulder. He acts like he's trying to be quiet at first, like he's slinking back in, but then comes to a halt when he sees me sitting up in bed.

"Oh good, you're up," he says, but I can't tell if he's happy to see me. That strange sphere of silence surrounds him and his face is devoid of emotion. He holds up a sheet of hotel stationery. "I found her," he says. "I found the Oracle."

"What? How?" I ask, practically jumping off the bed.

"I only require four hours of sleep, so I thought I would get started on the day. I used a courtesy phone in the lobby and started calling every S. Smith in the Las Vegas directory like you suggested. . . ."

"This early in the morning?"

"Yes. Is that a problem?"

"If you're a normal human being, yes."

"Oh. That explains why so many people hung up on me."

"What did you even say? How do you know you've found the right Sarah?"

"I said my name was Dax Lord and I was looking for a Sarah Smith who had helped me out with a problem a few years ago. I had no luck until the thirty-second S. Smith. An elderly man answered. He seemed quite happy to have someone to talk to and after he gave me a quite lengthy lecture on his political views concerning fluoridated water, I told him I was looking for a Sarah Smith, and he told me he had a granddaughter by that name, but that she'd been committed to Sunny Ridge Mental Hospital a few years ago. Because she kept claiming to have visions of the future.

And then he gave me a health update on each one of his relatives, but I think Sarah sounds like the woman we are looking for. Don't you think?"

"Uh, yes, definitely worth checking out. But how are we getting into a mental institution?"

"I called Sunny Ridge. I've got the address right here." He waves the paper. "Visiting hours are from eleven a.m. to six p.m. We can go as soon as you want."

"Do you still want to do this?" I ask. I know he agreed to take me to the Oracle only because he thinks she'll convince me that there are no other options than to surrender to my so-called destiny. I thought after last night, he might change his mind. . . .

Haden stares at me for a few seconds, amber rings of fire dancing around his pupils. I wish I could read their meaning.

"Yes," he finally says, sounding more determined than even I had been when Dax first told us of this option.

I want to ask him what he'll do if the Oracle doesn't give him the answer he's looking for.

"Freaks!" Lexie says, pulling open the door to her room. She's clad in a hotel robe and has a sleep mask advertising the hotel spa pushed up on her forehead. "Do you realize it's seven a.m.? On a Sunday morning? Stop yammering right outside my door!"

Haden drops my gaze. "We'll go as soon as you're ready."

I nod, not knowing how long it will take me to *ever* be ready for this.

"You people realize you're going to visit a person who is clinically insane in order to find out your future, right?" Lexie says. "I mean, who's crazier, the person who's been put in a mental institution or the person who asks that person for advice?"

"The rest of you can always stay in the car," I reply, ringing the admittance bell at the main entrance to Sunny Ridge. It's a small, shabby building at the end of a quiet street. Not the place where I would expect to find an Oracle living.

"No way." Lexie slings her purse over her shoulder. "I so want to see the look on your faces when this so-called 'Oracle' starts drooling on your shoes and you all finally realize how gonzo you've been acting. I wouldn't miss that for the world."

"I'm not missing this, either," Tobin says. "This Oracle lady had better have some answers about my sister." He reaches out and rings the bell a second time.

"I wouldn't mind staying in the car," Garrick says.

"Not you." Haden snags him by the back of his collar. "I'm not letting you out of my sight again." He had caught him trying to use the hotel room's phone while the rest of us were getting ready to leave. "You might be here unwillingly, but I have a feeling Simon isn't going to care about that if he finds us," he had said to Garrick, and ripped the phone out of the wall. Which meant we'd had to go to the hotel buffet for lunch instead of ordering room service. "He's going to be in an 'order you to walk off a bridge, ask questions later' kind of mood, don't you think?"

"What are you even going to say to get in to see this lady?" Lexie asks. "I doubt they're going to let a bunch of teenagers stroll into this place."

"Maybe we can pretend to be a traveling choir or something?" Tobin says. "We sing to the sick."

Lexie snorts.

There's a rustle behind the door and it opens. A short,

gray-haired woman dressed in scrubs is there.

I fumble to find something to say and almost go with the traveling choir idea, but the woman claps her hands together excitedly. "Oh, you must be Haden and Daphne and the others!" she says. "Sarah has been waiting for you."

chapter fifty-three

HADEN

"Did you tell them we were coming?" Daphne whispers as we follow the woman through the building. The floor is made out of a hard substance I believe is called linoleum, which tries to stick to my shoes with every step.

"No. I didn't tell them anything."

"Here we go," the woman says, ushering us into what must be some kind of common room. It is a warm room, even though it has several barred windows along the walls. It is filled with plush chairs, small tables, and a large green table in the center, with a small net stretched across the middle. Two men are using paddles to smack a small white ball back and forth across it. An older woman with stringy white hair sits in the corner, glaring at the wall. It sounds like she's having an argument with it. Others seem to be wandering almost aimlessly about the room. "Sarah will be so pleased you're here. She's been talking about you all week." She points us in the direction of a young woman who appears to be painting . . . with her fingers . . . at an easel at the far end of the room.

I take a step back. "That can't be her."

My memory jogs to my encounter with the Oracle of Elysium.

Her skin was blue and glittery, and her veils swirled about her as if blown by an invisible wind. She emitted the power and majesty of the divine. But this young woman, this supposed Oracle in front of me, looks all too . . . human. Her skin is pale and peachy, and her hair is unkempt and matted in places. She licks the paint from one of her fingers and then looks up from her artwork as if she can feel my gaze on her.

"Haden!" She smiles and waves with a familiarity that makes it seem as though we are old friends. But I don't know how she sees me—her eyes are milky and clouded over with blindness. "You came!"

She wipes her hands on her robe and bounds over to us. She clasps my hands before I can pull them away and then grabs Daphne in an embrace. "And you brought her! I knew you would."

"Is this some big joke?" Lexie asks. "Are you guys pranking me?"

Sarah takes Daphne and me by the hands and pulls us toward a table near her easel. Lexie, Tobin, and Garrick follow tentatively behind. I notice then how quiet the room has become, and glance around. The gray-haired woman who brought us here and all the other patients have disappeared without my noticing. "You have many questions, I know, but we don't have much time. Come sit. Please."

I am hesitant to take the seat she offers.

"You are flummoxed by my appearance, Haden. I know. You also wonder what I am doing in this mortal vessel, allowing myself to be kept in an asylum. This is not my true appearance." She taps her finger against her nose. "I am in hiding. Witness protection, you might say."

"What did you witness?" Daphne asks.

"Everything," Sarah says with a coy smile. "I see all the paths. All the possibilities. Not just the ones the gods want me to see."

"So there is another way?" Daphne asks, leaning closer to this Oracle. "I have other options? I don't have to be a Boon or a Cypher or whatever?"

"You were never meant to be a Boon."

Daphne gives me a satisfied look. "You hear that?"

"But you are the Cypher. Your role in this is much greater than you can imagine, Daphne, Daughter of the Music." Sarah reaches her bony hand across the table and places it over Daphne's. "Being the Cypher is your destiny, no matter what path you take."

"Ha," Lexie says. "Your destiny is to be a zero. That's hilarious."

That satisfied expression slips right off Daphne's face.

"I do not mean *cipher* as in the absence of value. Quite the contrary. You are *the* Cypher. You are the key to all of this."

"What do you mean?" I ask, confused. "Do you mean that Daphne *is* the Key of Hades?"

"No. Daphne is the Cypher. She is the key to *finding* the Key."

I nod, realizing that Dax's theory had been correct all along. "But how? And why *her*?"

The Oracle cocks her head and seems to stare at me with her unseeing eyes. She plays with the mats in her hair. "Oh, I see now. My sister from Elysium told you very little of your and Daphne's destinies."

"Excuse me," Daphne says, pushing up from her chair. "Can you please stop talking about me in the third person? I am right here. And I don't like being referred to as an object. I am not a key or a Cypher. I am just a normal human girl."

"*No, you're not. And you never were*," Tobin says from behind her—but his voice echoes out of him and I know it's Sarah, the Oracle, speaking through him. Her milky eyes have rolled up into the back of her head. Lexie gives a little shriek and backs away from Tobin. "*You have many names, Daphne Raines. You are the Cypher. The Anoichtiri. The Daughter of the Music. The Descendant of the Great Musician. The Vessel of His Voice. You are the Keeper of Orpheus's Heart and Soul.*"

"Whoa, what?" Daphne asks.

"She's a descendant of the Traitor?" I ask. "How can that even be possible?"

"*Orpheus brought back more than the Key from the Underrealm. When Eurydice died, a casualty in the Thousand-Year War between the Underrealm and the Skyrealm, not only did Orpheus lose his new bride, but he also lost the child she carried in her womb. Distraught with grief, he prayed to his father, Apollo, for help in getting them back. Apollo had also heard the prayers of many mortals, whose homes and lives had been destroyed in the cross fire of the war, and he was determined to put a stop to it. In exchange for instructions on how to traverse the dangers of the Underrealm and bring back his wife, Orpheus agreed to steal the Key from Hades. It was intended to be a bargaining chip for Apollo to use to negotiate a cease-fire between the gods.*

"*While Orpheus failed to save Eurydice, he carried with him the child and the Key, the Kronolithe of the original Lord Hades.*"

"You guys," Lexie says, hugging her purse to her chest. "I don't know how you orchestrated all this, but the joke isn't funny anymore. Can we go?"

"No," the Oracle says through Tobin. "*Our time is growing very short, and you all must listen and be quiet. Many have anticipated the arrival of the Cypher for thousands of years. Nearly eighteen* years ago, it was predicted that she would finally arrive in the form of Demi Raines's daughter. They tried to get you then, but they failed. The time was not right. The Champion was not right. You have remained protected in the Fields of Ellis, a safe haven for the servants of Apollo. But now that you have left, now that you have come to me, the wheels have been set into motion. The others will know soon whatever I tell you. The Oracles are connected that way. Whatever I say out loud will be known by all."

"Then why aren't you showing me?" I take her hand and press it against my forehead. I realize now that this is why the other Oracle showed me the instructions for my quest, rather than spoke it out loud.

"I cannot," she says, drawing her hand away and speaking for herself once more and not through Tobin's voice. She sounds exhausted, like that trick had drained her of most of her energy. "I do not retain all of my abilities in this human vessel."

"Then tell us the rest," Daphne says. "I need to know where I come from before I can decide where I'm going."

"Are you sure?" I ask her. "If we set this into motion, there will be no turning back."

Daphne nods.

"The irony of all of this is not lost on me," Sarah says. "You came here, Daphne, to try to escape your fate, but coming here was always meant to be one of your first steps on your path to your destiny.

"When Orpheus stole the Kronolithe, it locked the Underlords in the Underrealm, rendering Hades mostly powerless, stripping him of his immortality. Hades sent Keres through Persephone's Gate to go after Orpheus to retrieve the Key and destroy him for his betrayal. Knowing he could not hold such a prize for long while being pursued, Orpheus hid the Kronolithe where it could not be retrieved. He placed on it a lock that only his heart and soul can unbind. The Keres soon caught up with him and tore him apart, leaving his child for dead. But Apollo found the child, and took him to the Amazons to be raised by one of their own. The child grew, married one of the Amazonian daughters, and had a child of his own. The Amazons were eventually slaughtered by the Sky God for refusing to hand him over, and the family fled to a new safe haven—where their posterity has remained protected, and oblivious to their heritage, until you chose to leave. You must see this, Daphne: you are the last descendant of that child. But not just any descendant. You are the one who has inherited the heart and soul of Orpheus. The one who can retrieve the Kronolithe. But before you can retrieve it, you must find it."

Sarah pulls a golden chain from around her neck. Dangling from the end of it is a large golden pendant with a circle of symbols in the middle. One of them is the raised outline of Lyra—Orpheus's lyre. "You will need this. It is the Compass, and it holds the Instrument of Orpheus. They say the Instrument was cast into the stars, but that is not so. It has been with me all this time—I have fashioned it into a compass of sorts—but I have merely been waiting for you. Waiting to hand you your destiny."

Sarah tries to press the pendant into Daphne's hand, but Daphne pulls away. She jumps up out of her chair. "I don't want that."

"You must take it." Sarah stands, meeting her. "There isn't much time, Daughter of the Music. You must take your destiny."

"You can't just try to hand me my destiny. I don't want it. I don't want any of this. You said there were other options. Other paths that you can see."

"There are many paths. And we choose our paths with the decisions we make. But escaping your destiny is not as easy as it seems. The moment you chose to leave the haven of Ellis, your and Haden's destinies became irrevocably intertwined."

Sarah turns to face me. The temperature of the room drops drastically, and I'm forced to suppress a shiver. A pulse of energy fills the air, and her words echo inside my mind. *You have two paths before you now, young Haden. Both paths are fraught with peril. Both will bring you pain. However, one will lead to the honor you have craved since you were a child, while the other will lead to the end of Lord Haden, prince of the Underrealm.*

Two paths? Two destinies? How can that be? "Which path is which?"

You decide that by the choices you make. The first choice will be upon you soon.

"What does that even mean?"

Sarah stiffens, bolt upright. Her eyelids open and close rapidly over her blind eyes. "My time is up. You must take this, Daphne, so I can fulfill my purpose." The Oracle presses the Compass into Daphne's hand. Daphne seems too stunned to protest this time. Sarah whirls toward the doorway of the common room. "They're here," she whispers. "Sooner than I thought."

"Who's here?" Tobin asks, regaining his own voice. "I need to ask you about . . ." He stops speaking as the door to the common room edges open.

"My time is up," Sarah whispers over and over again, while rocking on her heels. "My time is up."

The door opens wider. All of us stare at the opening, anticipating who . . . or what . . . might enter that has the Oracle in such a state. The door creaks open another inch. . . .

And in prances a tiny, gray feline barely bigger than my two fists combined.

"Brimstone?"

She meows a greeting—or more likely a scolding—and bounds right at me. I stoop down to greet her, and she jumps onto my shoulder, sinking her tiny claws into my skin to anchor herself.

"What are you doing here? How . . . ?"

I look back at the doorway. If Brim has found me, then Dax probably isn't too far behind. . . .

"I'm sorry, Haden," Dax says, filling the doorway. His voice is thick with warning.

And Dax would come here only if something was very wrong. . . .

He lurches forward into the room, and Simon follows right behind him, holding Joe Vince by the elbow. Both Dax and Joe hold their hands stiffly at their sides, as if they are unable to raise them.

"Joe?" Daphne says. "What are you doing here? And with Mr. Fitzgerald?"

Joe shakes his head, his mouth clamped shut, as if he's unable to speak.

"Simon," I say. "You brought him here?" I ask Dax.

"I'm sorry, Haden. I had no choice. He forced me to tell him that I sent you to Vegas, and then he used Brim to track you. He knew she was here this whole time."

"Now, isn't this just the super-duperest of reunions?" Simon says in the jolliest of voices. "I wish I had my camera to capture the moment, because this must be my lucky day." He smiles, his white teeth gleaming. "I came looking for a runaway prince, and in addition, I find the Cypher . . . and the Compass!"

"You heard all that?" I ask.

"I have good ears," Simon says. "But the Oracle only confirmed what I'd already suspected of Daphne. Management was treating this particular quest in a peculiar way." His smile widens, reminding me of a nursling who has just been offered a fistful of sweets. "Now, Haden, hand over the girl and the Compass, and I might let at least one of you survive."

"No," I say, resisting the urge to do what Simon wants. I can feel his words nudging at my subconscious. "You're going to have to be more persuasive than that if you think I'm going to let you walk out of here with her."

Simon shrugs and turns a toothy grin on Tobin. "How about you, then, young man? Bring Daphne to me. Pretty please? And Garrick, why don't you help?"

Dazed expressions cross Tobin's and Garrick's faces. Before I can stop him, Tobin grabs Daphne by the right arm, and Garrick takes her by the left from behind. Holding her by her elbows and shoulders, they propel her toward Simon.

"Tobin, what are you doing?" Daphne says, struggling to get out of their grasp.

Energy swirls inside my chest, and I channel it into my hand. Electricity crackles between my fingers. "Let her go!" I demand, threatening Tobin with the bolt of lightning.

"I . . . I can't help it," Tobin says through gritted teeth as he and Garrick push Daphne closer to Simon.

"Don't hurt him!" Daphne shouts at me. "Tobin, Garrick, let go of me!"

"They're being controlled," Dax says to Daphne.

"Very astute," Simon says. "All it takes is a *please* most times.

You know what they say: you can catch more flies with honey than vinegar."

"Why would I want to catch flies?" I ask.

Simon raises his eyebrows. "Seriously? That's the part of all this you question?"

I change my focus from Tobin to Simon, hefting a pulsing sphere of lightning in my hand.

"Tell them to let her go or you're the one I'm going to blast."

"How can you hit me without frying Dax?" Simon says, moving so Dax, still frozen, is in front of him—using my only friend as a shield.

I extinguish the bolt, but stay in a ready stance.

"Now, boys, that's close enough," he says to Garrick and Tobin. "But make sure she can't get away."

They stop moving, but they keep their hands clamped on Daphne's shoulders. She struggles and stomps hard on Garrick's foot, but he doesn't let her go.

"What's the point of this, Simon? You can't take her to my father without her consent, remember? You can't just compel her to go through the gate."

"Why on earth would I take her to King Ren when she's worth so much more to the Skylords? I imagine access to the Kronolithe of Hades would be very appealing to them. And once the Underlords are finally exterminated, I'll be free to do as I please, instead of having to constantly babysit snot-nosed children with delusions of grandeur."

"You're going to sell her?" I ask. "I thought you were King Ren's emissary."

"More like his slave. I made a deal with the Court years ago. I wanted to be rich. I wanted to be the best salesman this world has ever seen. I got my wish. Hell, I've literally sold the Brooklyn Bridge to three different billionaires in the last decade alone. I made a star out of Joe Vince when nobody would give that poor sap the time of day. But I've been bound to the Court ever since. They own me. But if they're all dead . . ."

He moves ever so slightly away from Dax. I take advantage of his mistake and rush at him, a bolt of lightning building inside my chest. I raise my arm to fling it at him, but he swings around, looking me in the eye, and commands, "Be still!"

My body goes stiff, my arm still raised. I am frozen like a petrified tree. I cringe, fighting to break loose from Simon's mental hold.

"You think I like being at the beck and call of you little dung eaters? I'm a broker. A dealer. And you've got one of the finest artifacts I've ever encountered. This girl is my ticket to the life I should have had when I made that deal with the Court. In fact, my buyer is on his way here now.

"Daphne, be a dear and give me the Compass," Simon says, turning his full power of persuasion on her.

She starts to lift the Compass in her hand, but I can see her struggling against Simon's will. To my surprise, she clutches the Compass to her chest instead of handing it to him. "No," she says. "And I'll never go anywhere with you."

"Well, isn't that a neat trick," Simon says. "Our little Cypher seems to be impervious to my charms. Must be because you've got a few drops of god blood running through your veins. Never mind. That's why I brought a little leverage. Joe?" He snaps his fingers. "You can move now."

Joe lurches forward, as if falling out of a trance. He makes a move to grab Daphne out of the boys' grasp, but Simon commands him to stop. He freezes once more.

"Now, I could just get one of these boys to tear that Compass out of your hands and give it to me. But I think a little game of Simon-says might be more fun. You know the rules, don't you, boys and girls? You do as Simon says"—he reaches behind him and pulls a dark, glossy weapon from his belt—"or you're *out*."

"Gun!" Lexie shrieks. She tries to flee to the corner of the room, where Sarah stands motionless, staring at her easel. It's as if the Oracle isn't even conscious that we are still here.

"Not so fast," Simon says, stopping Lexie. "I think we have our first player. What's your name, dear?"

"What?" she says, sounding even smaller than she looks.

"Your name!"

"L-Lexie."

"Simon says, come here, Lexie." He beckons her with the gun. "It's okay. I only bite if you don't listen to me." Unlike Daphne, Lexie is unable to resists his persuasive orders and goes to him. "Simon says, hold out your hands. That's good. Now take this." He places the gun into her shaking hands, wraps them around the handle, and gently places her finger on the trigger, positioning her arms so she's pointing it at Joe.

chapter fifty-four

DAPHNE

"Simon says, get ready to shoot."

Lexie nods, tears streaming down her face.

"No," I say to Mr. Fitzgerald—or Simon, rather. "Don't do this."

"Now, now, Daphne. Give me the Compass and come with me to rendezvous with the Skylords, and we can avoid this mess." I don't know if the others can hear it, but a strange resonance rattles through his voice when he gives his *requests*. It permeates everything around him, engulfing me. It takes all of my mental strength not to give in.

"Don't do it, Daphne," Haden says. I can see him struggling to break free from the hold Simon has over him. I can hear pain aching from his body.

I shake my head. I don't know what it all means to be a Cypher, and I don't know what this Compass thing is supposed to do, and I had sure been reluctant to take it from the Oracle—but the moment Sarah had pressed it into my hand, it felt like it belonged there. Like it belongs to me. No, more like it is a piece of me. Giving it away would be as impossible as tearing off my own arm.

"Then we'll get to play our little game after all," Simon says.

"Guns are such barbaric things. I much prefer to use my words. . . . That is why I am going to give you until the count of ten to decide to listen to me. But if you let me get to number one, your friend here is going to shoot your father."

I clutch the Compass closer to my chest, looking from Simon to Joe. I know I can't give it to him, but I can't let him hurt my father. Tobin and Garrick still hold me tightly. I can't break free from both of them. Deep, low notes of fear and panic fill the room, from five people unable to move.

"Ten," Simon says. "Nine."

Lexie sobs, her arms shaking along with her hands now.

"Don't do this, Lexie, please," I beg her. "Don't listen to him."

"I can't lower my arms," she says between her tears.

"Eight," Simon says. A gleeful tone dances around him. He really does think this is fun. "Any last words, Joe? Speak now or forever hold your peace."

"Daphne," Joe says, able to speak again. "Don't give yourself over to him. Not for me. I'm not worth it."

"Seven."

I lower the Compass, holding it out in my hands.

"No, Daphne," Haden says.

"Six."

I shake my head. It will feel like ripping out my own heart, but I need to give in. "I have to, Dad."

"No, you don't, Daph. I don't deserve it. I don't deserve you. Not after what I did."

"Oh," Simon says. "We're having a last-minute confessional. This should be good."

I look at Joe as he hangs his head. I recognize the tone coming off him as remorse. "What are you talking about?" I ask him, but part of me fears that I already know the answer. It had been scratching at me since I realized Tobin's mother is somehow in on what is going on in Olympus Hills—and is covering up for the Underlords. That town isn't just any town—it is a staging ground for the Underrealm. A place for them to find their Boons and take them away and let the local government cover up their messes. I'd seen Simon once before he was introduced to me as Joe's manager at Bobby's restaurant. He'd been at the mayor's party—the man in the bicycle helmet she'd been meeting with. That was probably the night my name had been added to her list. Which meant that I'd been brought to Olympus Hills for the Underrealm's convenience, rather than Haden's being sent to Utah. And the person who brought me there was Joe. . . .

"I traded you, Daphne," Joe says, confirming my worst fear. "I traded you for fame and fortune."

My hands fall to my sides. I can barely keep my grasp on the Compass. My heart drops and feels like it's being crushed underneath the weight of his words. Suddenly, all the sound stops. There is no music. No notes. No vibrations. The rush of silence makes my head swim and I feel my legs wanting to give way. "How could you?" I ask, but my words are barely audible, and a low, rumbling song of sorrow begins to grow deep inside of me.

"I didn't know, Daphne. I didn't know you even existed at the time. It happened after I'd only been with your mother for three days. This man came to me. He claimed to be a talent scout at first. He said he'd heard me play at the Crossroads and he offered me a deal. He said I could be famous; I could be the 'God of Rock'; he could grant me every dream I had ever had; and all I had to do was stick my hand in a bowl of glittering water and swear that someday I would give him my child in return. I didn't know your

429

mother was pregnant with you; I swear it. I thought I could cheat the system. I agreed to the deal, thinking I would just never have any children. That's why I left your mum. That's why I haven't touched another woman since. . . . I didn't even know you existed until you were three years old. . . . That's why I stayed away from you. The guilt was too much to bear, and I knew if I got attached, it would only be harder. And I tried, Daphne . . . I've tried to take it back. I've tried to stop this from happening."

"Then why did you bring me to Olympus Hills?"

Joe's face crumples. "They couldn't get to you in Ellis. Simon said I had to bring you to them instead. . . . I had to have you in place by the time they sent someone for you. . . . I am so sorry, Daphne."

"But why?" I ask. I am too stunned to cry. Too stunned to be angry. "Why did you still go through with it?"

He shakes his head. "I can't explain it."

"The water," Haden says. "He made an unbreakable vow."

"I couldn't stop it. I couldn't resist. And Simon compelled me not to tell you. But that's why I was writing the play for you. I wanted you to know how Orpheus survived the underworld, how he escaped, so maybe it could help you. . . ."

"We're done now," Simon says, his weird, resonant tone permeating the room again. "We've still got a game to finish. I believe we're at number six."

Lexie whimpers.

The silence that buffered me before is completely gone now. I hum to myself, trying to drown out Joe's song of remorse mixed with the frightened notes coming off of everyone. I can't concentrate, otherwise.

"You're not getting tired of holding that heavy gun now, are you, Lexie?" Simon says. "Raise those hands a little higher."

I shift the tone of my hum so it matches the resonate vibration coming off Simon's persuasive voice. I don't know if sending his tone back at him will have any effect on him as it had on the Keres. I've never used it on a person before, but I have to at least try it.

Lexie complies with Simon's order, but she raises her hands only about an inch. The gun is aimed just below Joe's heart. Tobin's grip on my arm loosens ever so slightly. I look at Simon. Sweat beads on his forehead. I can see the veins bulging at his neck. It must be taking all his strength to keep this many people under his control. Is he starting to lose his grip? I hum louder, directing the tone at him.

"Five." He wipes at his nose. "Stop that," he says about my humming. "It's annoying."

I increase the volume.

"Four," he says to spite me.

"Daphne," Tobin whispers, squeezing my arm twice.

"Please, Daph, don't trade yourself for me," Joe sobs. "You can still run. You can still—"

"Three! Two!" Simon screeches through gritted teeth. Blood drips from one of his nostrils. "What's it going to be, Daphne?"

"Don't," Haden says, with an almost imperceptible shake of his head.

Simon's mouth starts to form the word *one*, and I can see Lexie cringing, her finger on the trigger.

"Stop," I say. "Take it. Take the Compass. Take me." I hold the Compass out to him in my left hand, as far as I can, with Garrick gripping my shoulder. "Just take it, okay?"

Simon steps away from Dax and reaches for the Compass. I swing my right arm as Tobin's grip on me falls away, and I slam my fist right into Simon's already bleeding nose. He stumbles backward, clasping his face. "Why, you little bi—"

At that moment, a burst of lightning combusts from Haden's petrified arm. He twists his hand just enough to send the bolt into the fluorescent light above Simon's head. Glass and shattered plastic rain down on us.

chapter fifty-five

HADEN

Lightning swirls and builds in my chest—threatening to explode through my rib cage if it doesn't find a place to go. When Daphne hits Simon, his hold on me weakens enough for me to channel the energy into my frozen arm. Brim, still clinging to my shoulder, yowls in protest, but I twist my hand enough to aim the bolt above Simon's head.

The force of the bolt's recoil throws me backward as the light fixture above us explodes. Tobin grabs Daphne, pulling her out of harm's way as shards rain from the ceiling. Simon covers his head and shrieks, "One!" just as Lexie drops the gun.

It clatters to the floor.

His hold on us is broken.

A large hunk of plaster from the ceiling hits Joe, and he sinks to the ground. Garrick runs for the door.

Simon scrambles for the gun, crawling over plastic shards to get to it. Dax goes after him, but Simon sends his elbow back, slamming it into Dax's neck. Dax rolls over onto his side. "Stop breathing," Simon says, glaring into Dax's eyes.

Brimstone yowls from her perch on my shoulder, her claws sunk deep into my skin, but it's enough to get me moving again.

I push myself up from the floor in response to her protests, in time to watch Dax clutch desperately at his own breathless throat and Simon reach for the gun. I go after him. But I'm too late. His hand closes over the handle as I lunge at him. He thrusts the gun against my chest.

"No!" Daphne screams.

Simon shrieks with pain and yanks his hand back, dropping the gun—a small gray cat is attached to his wrist by her teeth. Brim, who had leapt from my shoulder when I went for Simon, has sunk her tiny fangs into his arm.

He shakes his arm violently and sends Brim flying. She hits the top of the table—hard—and rolls a couple of times across the surface, then lands on her four little feet next to Sarah's finger paints. She hisses and spits, turning in a circle and baring her minuscule teeth in anger.

"Are you an idiot?!" I rasp. "You've made her angry."

"I'm not afraid of your kitten," Simon says, sucking the blood from the small puncture marks in his wrist.

Brim shakes and growls. The noise grows deep and fierce.

"She's a full-grown hellcat, you harpy mouth. Do you have any idea what happens when you get a hellcat really mad?"

Simon's eyes widen. He goes for the gun, but I kick it under one of the couches. A crack echoes through the room as the table Brim stands on collapses under her weight. Lexie shrieks and cowers in the far corner of the room—with good reason. A giant paw, bigger than my own head, swipes at Simon's back, sending him crashing into Sarah's easel. A great, hulking, three-headed panther—almost as large as my car—glares down at me. She huffs huge breaths simultaneously from her three mouths, making my hair float up for a second before settling back down around my ears. A swift movement catches the corner of my eye.

"Watch out," I shout to the beast as Simon takes a swing at her with a piece of wood from the broken easel. The wood cracks and splinters against the panther's back.

The beast's three heads roar in pain. Simon has only made her angrier. Turning her attention away from me, she pounces on him.

I try to rouse Dax, who lies in a faint in the middle of the floor as Simon's screams fill the room. Daphne runs for Joe and tries to pull him up. She still clutches the Compass tightly in her hand. The beast has Simon by the throat now. She shakes him violently back and forth. His limbs flail in the air like he's made of nothing but bloody rags. The panther releases him, and lets him try to crawl away before she pounces on him again, flips him over, and tears at his stomach.

Hellcats always play with their prey before killing it.

Simon's screams turn to whimpers. The beast turns away from what remains of his body. His blood saturates the fur on her muzzles. Her giant paws are soaked in it. Anger and frenzy cloud her eyes and she bares her teeth at me while crouching, preparing to attack. Her tail twitches wildly behind her, taking out what remains of the table.

Tobin grabs Sarah, pulling her out of her stupor, and they run along the side of the wall, trying to get out of the way. But one of the beast's heads catches the movement, and she swats hard in their direction. Her claws tear into Sarah's side, flinging her across the room. She bounces off the window, as if she were only a pebble, and lands in a crumpled heap.

"No!" Daphne shouts.

"Blast that thing!" Tobin says, pointing at the beast.

"It'll only make her angrier." I push myself up to my knees.

"The only way to stop a hellcat is to stab it through the top of its spine." I pick up a broken metal table leg from the ground. "Tobin, get Lexie and Daphne out of here. I need to stop Brim."

"No," Daphne says. "I'm not leaving."

"Go." I rise slowly, cautiously. The beast's eyes lock on the metal bar in my hand.

"I've calmed Brim before" Daphne says. "I can do it again."

"This isn't the same. She's not herself. She'll tear us apart and then the rest of the people in this hospital." I can't bear the thought of slaying Brim—*my* Brim, my family—but I will have to try, for all our sakes. She and I are bonded. She always finds me. The beast will pursue me if I run, ripping through anything or anyone who gets in the way. In a city this big, that could mean hundreds of casualties.

"Let me try."

Brim growls, the sound echoing off the stark walls.

"Get out of here!" I shout at the others. I brandish the bar in front of me and send a pulse of electricity crackling around it.

Tobin and Lexie make a break for the door. The panther looks as though she is about to spring after them. Daphne waves her arms, grabbing the cat's attention away from them.

"Brim," Daphne says, in a gravelly voice that sounds like the growl coming from the beast. She holds her hands out in front of her and slowly approaches the three-headed panther.

"Don't," I caution.

One of the beast's heads snaps at her.

Daphne is undaunted. "It's me, Daphne. You like me, remember? Haden and I sang to you."

Brim snorts through all three of her noses.

Tobin and Lexie try to escape through the doorway, but a sharp squawk from Lexie snatches my attention. I turn slightly away from Brim and Daphne to see the man from the motorcycle chase—or at least I assume it is the same man, as his face is still obscured by the helmet—standing in the doorway, blocking their escape. He has Garrick by the back of his collar. Lexie tries to push him out of her way, but he responds by shoving Garrick at her. The two stumble to the ground. Tobin takes a swing at the masked man's stomach. The man blocks the blow and then slams his gloved fist across his jaw, sending him sprawling. Tobin shouts as he hits the back of one of the couches.

The noise distracts Daphne momentarily and her gaze breaks from Brim's eyes. The beast sends a paw out and swipes Daphne's feet right out from under her. She hits the ground, her elbow slamming against the linoleum first, and the Compass flies out of her grasp. It sails up into the air and then slides across the floor until it comes to a stop only a few feet from the doorway. My attention is torn in two directions as the panther crouches over Daphne, growling, and the man in the motorcycle helmet stoops down and grabs the Compass.

"No," I shout, forcing a bolt of lightning through my chest and into my hand. I don't know which direction to throw it. Brim roars. I run for Daphne, but throw the bolt over my shoulder to try to stop the man as he runs to the door. The lightning hits the doorjamb as the man jumps through it. I try to take aim with a second bolt, but I am too late. The man escapes.

I whirl back around toward Daphne and the beast, with the long bar in my grasp. Daphne lies on the ground; the beast is on top of her. The panther rears back her three heads.

Daphne opens her mouth. I expect her to scream, but instead she starts to sing. It's a faint, strangled sound at first.

"Oh, star of mine . . . ," she sings. The panther stops midstrike and stares at her, two of her three heads cocked with curiosity. "High in the sky. Were I a bird, to thee I'd fly."

I recognize the words. It's the lullaby that my mother used to whisper to me. The one that made me want to be able to soar like owls from their roost.

Daphne sings another line of the song.

The beast seems mesmerized by her voice. I come up behind her, the electrified metal bar in hand, and take aim at the top of her spine. I want Brim's death to be as quick as possible.

Unwavering, Daphne keeps singing.

The beast sighs, and I raise the electrified bar, ready to strike.

Daphne catches my attention by shaking her head. "Don't!" her eyes say to me. "Sleep, my little starling." She whispers the last line of the song.

Brim's three mouths yawn and then her body convulses with a great shudder as it curls in on itself. Seconds later, she is a little ball of fur again, curled up and snoring on top of Daphne's chest.

"I . . . I can't believe that worked," I say, taking in the odd scene. It would have been a pleasant picture, if not for all the blood. I've never felt gratitude so strongly before as I do in this moment. I know Daphne did this not only to save herself and Brim—she'd done it for me. So I wouldn't have to lose the one thing I had left that had always loved me.

Daphne sits up, cradling tiny, sleeping Brim in her arms. "So that's what happens when you get a hellcat mad."

"I told you she wasn't good company in tight quarters."

"Well done, Daphne," Dax groans, struggling to get up from the floor where he lies.

438

"Nice of you to finally join us again," I say.

He gives me a pointed look that quickly softens as he pats his chest, as if trying to force more air into his lungs. He winces and closes his eyes, needing rest before trying to stand.

Daphne checks on Joe. "What happened?" he moans, starting to regain himself.

"Sarah," she says, suddenly remembering the Oracle. She sets Brim on the ground and rushes toward the woman, who looks like nothing more than a crumpled pile of bloody bathrobe and matted hair. Daphne turns her over, brushing the hair from her face. A raspy, croaking noise slithers out from between Sarah's lips. It sounds like she's trying to say the word *Compass*.

"He got away," Daphne says frantically. "That man stole the Compass. What am I supposed to do?"

"You will get the Compass back. You will use it to seek the Key. Only you can open the lock that guards it. You are the Anoich . . ." Sarah winces and takes a panting, shallow breath as if she's just run up several flights of stairs. "Anoichtiri. Your heart and soul will open the lock. . . ." Her next breath is faint, more of a wheezing. She trembles. "My time has come. . . . Daughter of the Music." Her eyes roll back into her head and a faint smile crosses her lips. Her back arches against the hard floor. A glittering blue light emanates from her body and a gale-force wind whips around us. When it fades away, Sarah lies limp and lifeless on the linoleum.

The sky outside grows dark, as if a large cloud is blotting out the sun. In the dimness, I notice a different light. It's a strange, pulsing glow that reflects off the walls and windows. The origin of it comes from somewhere near Simon's body—or rather the amulet that lies on the ground beside him. It blinks with a green light, almost like a beacon.

"What is that?" Daphne asks, leaving Sarah. "Where did it come from?"

"I don't know." I am unsure if it belongs to Simon, or if the Motorcycle Man dropped it when he made his escape.

I kneel next to Simon's body and reach for the amulet—but he grabs my wrist. He's still alive—despite his body having been torn open, his intestines spilling out of his gut. "*Elios,*" he whispers, blood trickling from his mouth. Tears of pain stream from his eyes. "*Elios,* please."

"What is he saying?" Daphne asks.

"He's begging for mercy." But I don't know why. There's nothing I can do to save him now.

"We can't leave him like this," Daphne says, baffling me once again with her concern for those who've wronged her.

"You're right," I say, placing my hand over Simon's chest. She turns away as if she knows what I am about to do. I send a shock of lightning into his rib cage until his grasp on my wrist falls away.

After a moment, Daphne turns back to me. "Are you okay?" she asks, extending her hand toward me to help me stand.

"I will be." I pick up the amulet. It's slick with blood and almost slips through my fingers. I catch it up, curling my fingers around it, and reach out to take her extended hand.

But her hand is no longer there. I look up to see why she's pulled it away—but she's gone, too. Daphne has disappeared.

Darkness and firelight have filled the common room. *No, not the common room. I'm somewhere else.* The oily smell of torches burns my lungs. I blink several times and my vision focuses on a black, looming throne in front of me. A man wearing a golden breastplate sits upon it.

I fall back to my knees. I know where I am.

I am in my father's throne room once again—in the confines of the Underrealm. . . .

chapter fifty-six

DAPHNE

Sarah is dead and the Compass is gone—and it feels like a piece of my soul has gone with them. A deep emptiness pulls at me. Sarah said I'd get the Compass back, but she didn't say how.

Joe winces as he tries to sit up. Haden crouches over Simon.

Blood pools out of the man's mangled body. How he's still alive is a mystery to me—perhaps it has something to do with his strange powers. I can only imagine the agony he must be in. The broken tones and notes that surround him sound like the embodiment of misery. "We can't leave him like this." I don't know if I mean we should call for an ambulance . . . or something else . . . but I know there's nothing any paramedic could do for him.

"You're right," Haden says. The tone that comes off him is a mixture of reluctance and determination. Strength and yet tenderness. Relief and yet . . . grief. It's the sound of mercy.

I turn away, knowing what Haden must do.

The notes that surround Simon fade away into silence, and I know the deed is done. I turn back to Haden and offer him my hand—hoping to fill it with something that might make this empty sensation go away.

Haden picks up the pulsing amulet, almost dropping it,

and reaches for my extended hand. Just before his fingers touch mine, a bright burst of light pulses out of the amulet in his other hand.

All the life seems to drain out of his eyes, and he collapses at my feet—his hand still outstretched as if trying to reach me.

"Haden?" I gasp. "Haden, what's wrong?"

I grab his shoulders and shake him, but I get no response. His eyes are open and he's breathing—but it's like nobody is home.

"What happened?" Dax says, trying to stand. "I blacked out again. What . . . ?"

"I don't know. He grabbed this amulet thingy off the ground, and then there was this flash, and he just collapsed."

"Amulet?" Dax stumbles toward us. He kneels next to me. "That's no amulet. That's a communication talisman." He tries to pry it from Haden's rigid grasp, but he pulls his hand back sharply as though the talisman burned him. "It has some sort of invisible shield around it."

"What's going on?"

"We have to snap him out of there," Dax says, slapping his hand against Haden's jaw. "We have to get him back here!"

"What do you mean? Where did he go?"

"This thing, it's a communication talisman. It's like a between-realms cell phone. Only instead of transporting merely your voice to the person who's calling you, it transports your soul so you can converse face-to-face—like astral projection. Someone must have been trying to communicate with the owner of this amulet, but Haden answered the call." Dax slaps him again with an urgency that makes me shake.

"Who? I mean, where is he, then?"

"This is Underlord craftsmanship. So my guess—his father.

443

Haden's in the Underrealm, and he probably has no idea what's going on."

"Can he get hurt there?" I ask. Haden's father is the one person Haden seems truly afraid of. What would he do if he thought Haden had gone off the rails with his quest?

"Yes," Dax says. "If something bad were to happen to him there . . . the connection between his soul and body could be severed permanently."

He grabs Haden's shoulders and shakes him with what strength he can muster. "Snap out of it!"

I could run right now, I realize. I could take off this very second. Haden isn't here to stop me, and Dax is in no condition to follow. I could escape all this destiny nonsense. I wouldn't have to be this Cypher or vessel or Anoich—something or whatever—if they couldn't find me. I could choose to go.

I could be done with all of this if I just run right now.

I reach for the keys to the Tesla that dangle from Haden's pocket. His body convulses in my grasp. His mouth forms what looks like a scream, but no sound comes out. Tears well in the corners of his wide-open eyes.

I drop the car keys and cup my hands under his chin. "Haden!" I say into his ear. "Haden, come back! I need you here."

chapter fifty-seven

HADEN

"What's your report?" my father demands. He rises from his ebony throne.

Report?

What's going on?

How am I even here?

Where is Daphne? And Dax and the others?

A few short months ago, all I wanted to do was return to my home in the Underrealm—to leave the chaos and discomfort of the mortal world behind. I dreamed of my return. Longed for it. Now I am desperate to figure out why I am here—and how to get back to where I was only seconds ago.

"Have you found Haden yet?" my father says. He must think he's speaking to someone else. My head is lowered, so he must not recognize me—or perhaps it's because he never looks directly at a subordinate if it isn't necessary.

How did I get here? And how do I get back?

I look at the amulet in my hand and the answer dawns on me. A communications talisman. I've heard the Heirs speak of them and how they work, but I have never actually seen one before. I try to cast it away, but it seems to be seared into my hand. I can't let it go.

"The Court grows restless over the boy's insolence. Lord Lex has proposed a vote of no confidence in my rule. They're going to depose me if I can't reassure them that Haden is still following the plan. Tell me you've got good news." I hear him move closer, the sword at his hip slapping against his thigh as he walks. He must think I am Simon. "Answer me or I'll blast you!"

I raise my head. "It won't do you much good, seeing as how Simon is already dead."

My father startles at the sound of my voice. "What is the meaning of this?" he says, drawing his sword. "Where is my emissary? How did you get this talisman?" He must be flustered to spare so many words for me.

"Simon's dead," I say, rising to my feet. "I killed him." Brim had done the deed, but technically I had finished it.

"You?" He narrows his eyes at me. "I don't believe it. Simon was one of my best, and you're nothing but a weak, simpering nursling."

"And yet I still scare you enough to cause you to draw your sword."

Ren glances at the blade he brandishes in his hand. He lowers it ever so slightly. I glance around the throne room and see that we are completely alone. It's unlike Ren to be without his royal guard, attendants, and advisors. He must be sorely agitated or in dire need of privacy. Is the Court truly turning against him?

"Besides, Simon may have been a fierce opponent, but he was hardly *your* best. He'd betrayed you," I say, hitting on what I suppose to be a sore spot for Ren. "He'd turned on you. Your *loyal* servant was planning on selling the Cypher—the Key along with it—to the highest bidder. The Skylords."

"You know about the Key?"

"Yes."

"Where is the Cypher? What have you done with her?"

"Why should I tell you?"

"Are you planning on betraying me, too, then?" Ren shoves the tip of his sword so it's only inches from my face.

"Can you even hurt me with that here?" I say, referring to my astral state. I am outside of my body, so how can he cut me?

"No," my father says. "But your soul is made of energy, which means I can still hurt you with this." Streaks of blue lightning crackle up his sword, swirling around the blade. I can feel the heat and the rhythm of electricity and I know he's not bluffing. "Do you know what happens if I cut you off from your body while you are here?" Ren says loudly enough that I can hear him over the pulse in my ears. "You'll never find your way back to it. You'll become just another one of those nameless, faceless nothings that roam the Wastelands. Banished to being a hungry, desperate shade for the rest of eternity."

"You won't do it. You need me."

Ren responds by slashing his electrified sword in the air, sending the swirl of lightning sailing at my chest. I grit my teeth, absorbing the blow and letting it flow back out of me the best I can. I've taken worse hits in training, but the pain is still enough to force me to my knees.

"That was just a warning blow, boy," Ren says. "Just to show you that I can touch you here. The next one won't be so pleasant." He walks back to his throne and picks up a small vessel made of pottery, from under the ebony seat. I take a few deep breaths while his back is turned, to regain my strength.

He returns with the vessel and holds it out in front of me. "This is water from the river Styx, the River of Unbreakable

447

Vows. On the Oracle's behest, I made a vow with this water during the Choosing Ceremony, in which I covenanted that whoever brought the Cypher to me would become my heir. My successor. That is what you want, isn't it, boy? You want to belong. You want to sit at my right hand. You want your honor restored. I am prepared to give you all of that, but you must do one thing for me." He dumps the water from the vessel onto the ground in front of where I kneel. It splashes and pools around my knees. "You make an unbreakable vow that you will bring the Cypher to me. The words will be written in the water, and I can use that to show the Court that you haven't forgotten your quest, that you haven't gone off the path. To prove to them that you are worthy of being called *my son*."

I look up at my father, meeting his eyes for the first time since my return. I wonder if I will see that same disdain he usually looks at me with. But instead, I see something very different. A look of fear crosses my father's eyes. It mars the near-perfect mask of nonexpression on his face that I have always tried to emulate—and I realize why he hadn't filled me in from the very beginning about Daphne's true importance. I know why his Oracle had kept the details from me. Because now that I know what he needs Daphne for—to find the Kronolithe of Hades—I know just how much power I have in my hands. I have Daphne. I have everything he wants: the missing link to finding the Key to the underworld, to finding the object that can turn my father into everything he pretends to be—a god.

I have the power here. The leverage.

Daphne isn't only the key to finding the Kronolithe; she is also the key to getting me everything I had ever wanted, and more.

"That is what you want, isn't it, my son? One little vow is a small price to pay to have all the honor and the glory of the Under-realm bestowed on your head."

Vows made on the river Styx are nothing to be taken lightly. An unbreakable vow is just that—unbreakable. I'd already seen how such oaths control Dax and Joe. What little free will I have in the matter would be gone. I would not be able to stop myself from bringing Daphne to him when the time came.

"I should have made you vow *before* sending you as Champion. That addled Oracle tried to convince me it would backfire, but I see now she was playing games with me. I'm not leaving it up to your impulses anymore. You will bring her to me, no matter what."

"What will you do with her?" I ask.

"Whatever it takes."

"The Oracle says you need her heart and soul. Will you sac-rifice her?"

"Yes. If needed."

"Then my answer is no. You can't have her."

Because I realize now the price for what Ren is offering is too high. I will not give Daphne to him. I will not let her die. I cannot trade her for what I have always wanted—because she is what I *need.*

My father tears into me with another bolt of lightning. This one comes so fast and strong that I cannot brace myself. The light-ning grips me like a great taloned bird sinking its clutches into my rib cage, and slams me against the altar. I sink to the ground. My body writhes against the marble floor as the bolt ravages through me. I scream. Tears flood my eyes. The pain is too much to stop myself.

The lightning dissipates, and I hear the echo of my father's laughter. He mocks my agony. Or perhaps it is my tears that set him off. I had never wanted to let him see me cry again, not since the day Mother died. I have tried to suppress and fight my emotions, to keep the human side of me at bay. I have let him push me down. I think about what Daphne said about my father being afraid of me when I stood up to him as a child.

What I might be capable of now if I had not cowered to his will earlier in my life . . .

Beyond my father's derisive laughter, I think I hear another sound.

Like Daphne calling my name.

"You would put concern for some human girl over your duty to me?" Ren asks. "To your entire realm?"

Haden, come back! I think I hear Daphne call. *I need you here.*

I try once again to cast away the talisman, but it is still branded to my hand. I roll onto my side—it takes all my strength to do so—and look at my father. "I love her."

That's barely something I want to admit to myself, let alone to him, but at the moment, it feels like the most powerful thing I still have inside of me.

"Love? You would put such a silly notion over having your honor restored?" His derisive laughter starts to sound more desperate and hungry to me. The sounds of a man with few options left.

"You can't restore my honor. It was never yours to take in the first place." If it hadn't been for Daphne and my time in her world, I would have never realized that. There is also one more thing I would not realize, either. The clues finally click together in my head. . . . "What do you know about honor anyway? You failed your quest, didn't you? You shouldn't be king now. That's why they're trying to take it away from you."

"What do you know about anything?"

"Eighteen years ago, the Oracle predicted that the child of Demi Raines would be the Cypher. You were sent to the mortal world as Champion in order to bring her back. The idea was to make her your Boon, your mate, and the Cypher would be the child you created together. But you failed. Someone else got to her first. A musician named Joe Vince swept her off her feet, and before you had any say in the matter, she was pregnant. There was no way you were going to convince her to come with you now. So you struck a deal with Joe. He didn't know what he was really agreeing to when he traded the soul of his firstborn child for fame and fortune. But you had the proof you needed to *claim* that you had still secured the child of Demi Raines for the Underrealm. I imagine you carried back the words of Joe's vow in a vessel of water like that one." I point at the vase he'd used to pour the water in front of me. "You also brought back a Boon—my mother, Kayla, for good measure. But she wasn't the prize you needed, and that's why you scorned her. That's why you hate me. Because I am more like her than Rowan is. It's why you treat me like I'm a failure—because I am the reminder of your own."

"I didn't fail. I am king here. You best remember that."

"But you won't be for long, will you?" I try to grab the side of the altar to use it to push myself up. I am too drained of strength and fall back to my knees. "You succeeded your father and became king because you had *technically* fulfilled your quest. But there are those in the Court who question your eligibility. And then there's the matter of your deal with Joe not being enough. That's where I came into play. Your deal with Joe will give you Daphne's soul. Is it supposed to come to you immediately when she dies—bypassing

Elysium or the Wastelands, where it would get lost forever? But the problem is, you need her heart, too. Which means you need her alive—and no living person can cross through Persephone's Gate unless she does it willingly. Which meant you needed a Champion to finish this for you. You needed her to be brought back as a Boon. Rowan was your first choice—he's always been your favorite—but you got nervous. You decided to consult the Oracle and got the shock of your life when she chose me."

"You're proving right now you weren't up to the task, as I thought."

"I'm proving I'm not your little puppet. You think I care if you remain king? Call in the Court right now. I'll tell them to their faces that you should be overthrown."

"You think you know some things, but you don't know the half of it, nursling. I'm the one holding this realm together. I'm the only one who has any reason around here. Yes, there are Heirs who want me ousted, and, yes, your fulfilling your quest is the only thing stopping them from taking over. But my remaining as king is the only thing that is stopping your precious human realm and all those humans you *love* from being destroyed!"

"What do you mean?"

"As you should know, the Pits fill the space between our realm and the Overrealm. But what you aren't privy to is the knowledge that the locks on Pandora's Pithos are starting to fail, and my authority is the only thing keeping some of the Heirs from ripping through the walls of the Pits in order to use it as a bridge out of the Underrealm—setting all the Keres loose on both our realm and the mortal world in the process. There are Heirs who will stop at nothing to get their hands on the Kronolithe in order to reignite the war with the Skylords. They're sick of being locked away. They think the Underlords should rule everything. I'm the one who believes in the order of the realms. I'm the one who wants to keep the stalemate in place—and if I need to sacrifice one little Cypher to find the Kronolithe in order to remain in control, then so be it!"

"You're lying," I say.

Garrick had told me the locks on the Pit are failing. I know it is a possibility the Keres can get out on their own—but the possibility that the Court would let them out *on purpose* is something I can't believe.

Haden. Daphne's voice echoes in my mind, giving me the strength to keep talking back to Ren. "You want the Kronolithe so you can become a god. You want to *be* Hades, not just use his title." The idea of my father as an all-powerful, immortal deity makes me quake where I kneel.

"It's an added perk, yes. But believe me, I as your *god* is a much better option than the alternative." Ren forms a new bolt of lightning in his hand. It rumbles and cracks as it surges with power. "What is that human saying? 'Third time's a charm'? Or, no, maybe I'm looking for 'Three strikes, you're out.' I am guessing your soul can't take a third blast without breaking the link to your body. So this is it, boy. You make the vow to bring her to me and I will make you my son once more, my eldest son—my heir—or refuse and it's good night, sweet prince, for you."

Sarah's words about my destiny come to me then. *You have two paths before you now, young Haden. . . . One will lead to the honor you have craved since you were a child, while the other will lead to the end of Lord Haden, prince of the Underrealm.*

453

I don't know why destiny chose me for this. I don't know why I would be given more than one path. But the Oracle had said that *I* would decide which path is which by the choices I make—and that the first choice would be upon me soon.

"What is it going to be?" Ren asks, a great sphere of lightning encircling his hand—aimed at me.

I can feel my soul wavering. It can't survive that kind of blast.

"You realize that if the Heirs get their way," Ren says, "she'll die, along with all your precious friends. You give her to me, and maybe I'll let you have whatever is left of her after I get the Key."

Haden! I hear my name again. This time, it sounds like Daphne and Dax together.

Thoughts of Daphne fill my mind. The sound of her voice when she sings. The touch of her skin as I held her hand as she slept. The way she didn't mock me when I cried. The way she makes me feel human. That mean right hook of hers . . .

"I'll make the vow," I say.

"Wise decision." Ren snuffs out the bolt in his hand and walks closer to me, his feet making tracks in the puddle of water from the River of Unbreakable Vows. He stands over me, towering so high that it reminds me of what it felt like to be a child trapped under his shadow. "Do it now."

I place my hand that has the talisman branded to it in the puddle. The water edges over my fingertips. It feels cool and calming compared to the pain that I have endured today. I look up at Ren as he glowers down at me, and can't help wondering how that expression will change when I make the vow. How will he look at me then? "I vow, on the water of the river Styx, the River of Unbreakable Vows, that I will . . . *never* bring Daphne to you."

Before Ren can react, I send a surge of lightning into my hand.

It hits the water and explodes, electrifying the wet ground all around us. The blast sends Ren flying through the air toward his throne, and me sailing backward.

I hit the altar with a soul-shattering crack, and darkness surrounds me.

chapter fifty-eight

DAPHNE

Haden's body convulses in my arms, like he's having a seizure. He twists and writhes in silent agony. And then he goes limp and still. So still and breathless that I think the worst.

No. No, he can't be dead.

"Haden, come back!" I say, smacking his face.

Nothing.

I try a softer approach and press my lips to his forehead. "Please, Haden," I say, brushing my hands through his hair and then pressing my fingers against his neck. No pulse. No nothing.

"Daphne," Dax says. "I think he's gone. . . ."

Haden lets out a great, gasping groan and sits bolt upright, like he's waking from a horrific nightmare.

"Haden!" I throw my arms around him, holding him to me. "I thought you were dead."

Haden's vision seems to focus and he takes in the surroundings of the Sunny Ridge common room. The carnage of the events with Brim and Simon surrounds us. I can hear his heart pounding out a frantic melody.

"For a moment, I thought I was, too," he says, his voice sounding more like a croak.

He flexes his fingers and a charred object that vaguely resembles the talisman falls from his hand, leaving a raised, blistering welt of its size and shape in his palm. "That actually worked," he says, like he'd caused that kind of damage on purpose. "Scrambled the connection to the Underrealm . . . Sent me back here." He pinches his leg like he's making sure he's truly back inside his body. "Half expected to wake up a shade in the Wastelands instead."

"What happened?" I ask, searching his jade green eyes.

"He tried to force me to make an unbreakable vow that I would bring you to him. He said the only reason he hadn't done it before making me Champion was because the Oracle tried to tell him it would backfire. . . . So I thought of the way you tricked Simon, and I . . . made it backfire. Quite literally."

"How?" I ask.

"I vowed I would never let him have you, and electrified the water—scrambling the connection in the talisman. Almost killed myself in the process, though." He raises his singed hand like he wants to brush his fingers against my cheek—but doesn't quite have the strength to do it.

"Harpies. Talk about burning bridges. I knew you had it in you!" Dax slaps Haden on the shoulder.

Haden cringes. "'Scuse me?" he asks, his speech starting to sound slurred.

"Sarah and I have met before, remember? She told me *things*. . . ."

"You didn't care to share?" I ask.

"I wasn't at liberty to discuss it. The decision needed to be Haden's alone. I'll tell you more later," Dax says. "We've got another problem on our hands."

"Seriously?" Haden says, dropping his hand. "We almost all

457

died in the worst children's game I have ever heard of; I almost had to kill my man-eating pet; I stood up to my lunatic father—who has a major god complex, by the way—and had my soul electrocuted *three times*; and now you're telling me there's another problem?"

"Ha!" I laugh.

"What?" he says.

"That is the most human I have ever heard you sound!"

A clap of thunder rolls outside the darkened windows.

"Save the flirting for later," Dax says. He points up. "Skylords are coming. Simon made a call before he came in here. I have a feeling his *buyers* are just about to show up. They'll be wanting to take delivery of the goods, if you know what I mean."

"Harpies." Haden looks around. "Where did everyone else go?"

"I sent them to pull up the car," Dax says. "Daphne and I were getting ready to carry your body out. I just hope they didn't take off without us."

Rain starts pelting the windows. There's a clash of white lightning that makes me jump, followed by a roll of thunder so loud, it shakes the building. "That's some storm."

"Not a storm," Dax says, helping Haden to his feet. "We've got to run for it."

He and I lead Haden out of the empty hospital. Brim follows at my heels. Haden leans so heavily against me, like he can barely put one foot in front of the other, that it makes me dread finding out what else had happened to him in the Underrealm.

"Where are the patients?" I ask.

Dax explains that Simon had requested that the staff take all the patients on a walk—which is why no one had come into the common room during the commotion. Thank goodness.

The rain is so thick, my clothes are soaked through almost immediately after we exit through the back doors of Sunny Ridge. Lightning rakes the sky above the hospital. To my relief, Tobin, Lexie, Garrick, and Joe are waiting inside the car at the curb. Joe holds his wadded-up jacket against the top of his head, as if staunching a wound that must have been caused by the falling debris that had knocked him out. I am glad he is relatively okay, but at the same time, I can't bring myself to say anything to him. I don't have the time or energy right now for the anger that might unleash.

Dax insists on driving. I imagine Haden lets him only because, at this point, he can barely keep his eyes open. I sit with him in the third row. We fly out of the parking lot as a strike of lightning explodes against a power pole. The downed lines flail out at us like electrified tentacles. Dax whips us out of their way and out onto the open road. If I'd thought Haden was a crazy driver, that was nothing compared to the way Dax maneuvers around lightning strikes and traffic to get us to the freeway.

"Who are these psychos?" Lexie shouts. "Are these more lightning freaks from your family?"

"Worse," Dax says. "Skylords have lightning *and* thunder. But they are family, in a way. They're kind of like our second cousins a few times removed."

"What?"

"They're the sons of Life," Haden mumbles beside me.

"How?" I remember the story he told me about the twin sons Hades created and the Sky God stole. "I thought Life was torn apart by the Keres when he was just a kid."

Haden nods.

"The Sky God pieced him back together," Dax says, swerving around a slow-moving semi. The windshield wipers can barely keep up with the barrage of rain on the windows.

Tobin screeches as lightning strikes the tail end of the semi truck. He holds his hand to his face like he is merely stifling a sneeze. Brim jumps into my lap. I stroke her bristled back reassuringly.

"He can do that sort of thing, among others," Dax says.

"So the sons of Life are the Skylords and the sons of Death are the Underlords?" I ask, remembering that Haden had said something about that earlier. "The descendants of two twins locked in epic battle."

"Sounds about right. Except the Skylords have daughters, too."

"They do?" Garrick asks, sounding surprised.

"Yes," Dax says, like he knows this for sure. "Oh yeah, they can run through the clouds," he says, pointing at the churning, gray sky above us. I can't see any Skylords, but they must be up there in the clouds. "They're like the new and improved model."

"This was my worst trip to Vegas ever," Lexie says as we sail past a billboard that says, NOT EVERYTHING THAT HAPPENS IN VEGAS STAYS IN VEGAS. GET TESTED!

"Where are we going?" Haden asks. His head is leaning on my shoulder now.

"Ellis Fields," I say. "Sarah made it sound like Ellis was some sort of safe haven. Like we could hide there without being found. I hope she's right."

"Good plan," Haden says, sounding almost completely out of it. "You should stay there. Be safe. Forever."

The idea of being trapped in Ellis is one that had haunted me my whole life. I'd kicked against it as hard as I could while still trying to respect my mother, but at this moment—and I can't believe I'm admitting this—the idea of going back, of *staying there forever*, sounds more appealing than touring the world as a music star ever did.

The tempest chases us as we head for my hometown. The traffic is thin; probably most people are staying off the roads in this storm. Normally, it's supposed to be a two-and-a-half-hour drive between Ellis and Vegas, but the way Dax is driving, we'll be there in half the time.

Haden's head lolls on my shoulder, and I worry he may be in worse shape than I'd thought. And what is to come of him and Dax and Garrick? Would they stay in Ellis with me? Or would they make a new plan and move on? Now that Haden had quite literally—from the sounds of it—burned the connection between him and his father, he has to be in more trouble than I can ever imagine. I can't help thinking about the Oracle's predicting that he may cease to exist. Would the path he chose today lead to his eventual death? Had he traded his life to spare mine?

And *why* would he do that?

I am lost in thought for so long that I almost forget that we are running for our lives—until a blast of lightning takes out the speed limit sign we've just careened past.

"Take the next exit," I call to Dax from the backseat.

"What exit?"

"The one coming right up."

"I don't see it."

Is the rain blocking his view that badly?

"Quarter of a mile," Tobin says. "Right up there."

"There's nothing."

"Trust me, there is." Tobin leans forward and grabs the

steering wheel. He yanks it to the right and we swerve onto the exit ramp just before missing it.

"Where did that come from?" Dax asks.

"Turn left . . . right now," I shout.

He follows my instructions even though they seem to bewilder him. "Oh, there's the road," he says, as if he can see it only now that we're on it. "What now?"

"Keep following this road. It will take us through the canyon for a few miles before we get to town."

We fly up Apollo Canton Road, dodging lightning. At one point, a strike hits the canyon wall beside us, and a tumble of red rocks starts to fall. We barely make it through before it crashes into the road. Lexie isn't the only one of us who screams.

"Daphne, I don't know about this!" Dax says. "Where do I go now?"

"Straight ahead," I say as Ellis starts to come into view. "We're almost to town."

"What town?" Garrick says.

Joe groans like all of this is too much for his head.

"The one right in front of us," I say. I can see buildings and homes through the rain, nestled in the heart of the canyon. Lit up like little lighthouse beacons beyond the storm. My mom's shop is there. Home is there. The walls of red rock surrounding the town that had once made it feel like a prison, now make it look like a fortress of safety. "You can't see that?"

"Daphne, we're heading straight for a giant mountain!" Dax says.

From what I can tell, it isn't raining over the town. That and the fact that Dax and Garrick can't see it reassure me that Sarah was right. Safety is only half a mile away.

Lightning crashes right in front of us. Dax yanks on the wheel hard, and we swerve in a circle, spinning donuts in the red mud that covers the road to Ellis Fields.

"Just keep going!" I shout. "We're almost there."

The car speeds up. Thunder shakes the car, and a lightning bolt rips a hole in the road right where we would have been if we hadn't surged forward. Dax clutches the wheel hard and clamps his eyes shut. He's bracing himself for impact as we pass the WELCOME TO ELLIS FIELDS city limits sign. A second later, he relaxes and looks around, stunned.

"Well, I'll be harpied." He whistles under his breath.

"Where the Tartarus did this all come from?" Garrick asks, staring out the windows as we roll into Main Street, Ellis Fields.

I direct Dax to stop the car in front of Paradise Plants. The road here is dusty and dry as always. I get out of the car, followed by Dax and Tobin, and stare in disbelief at the storm we've left behind. It's like a great fence of rain and clouds circles the whole town, but above us the near-evening sky is dusky but clear. Out on the sidewalk, a couple walking their dog stops and stares, pointing at the strange phenomenon. The door to Paradise Plants starts to open. I brace myself, expecting to see my mom or Jonathan for the first time since I left. I don't know what I am going to tell them.

Can I possibly tell them the truth?

I hear the bells over the door and out walks Indie. She snaps a photo of the wall of rain with her phone. Then she sees me.

"Daphne?" She waves. "What're you doing here so early? Did you see that crazy storm?"

"Yeah, just drove through it. I decided to come early for winter break," I say. "Thought I'd bring some friends home for a couple of days to meet my mom."

"Oh," Indie says. "Didn't you know? Your mom isn't here. She and Jonathan went to Salt Lake City this morning."

"What?" I ask, taken aback. "What could get my mom to leave Ellis? She wouldn't even come to see me off to Olympus Hills."

"I don't really know. They took off in a big hurry. It has something to do with CeCe; I know that much."

Dread pulls at my stomach. I listen to the thunder rolling in the sky beyond the outskirts of town. My family is out there somewhere. "What about CeCe?"

"I don't know exactly. Jonathan called here this morning all in a panic. He said something about how he thought CeCe hadn't left here on her own. It was like he thought she'd been taken or something. . . ."

"Taken?" There was that word again. It had haunted me in Olympus Hills and now followed me here. I want to sit down in the dust right here and now. On top of the day I've had, this last bit of information is more than I can bear. People aren't supposed to disappear from Ellis. Bad things don't happen here. This is supposed to be the safe place. My haven.

"Jonathan said he found a receipt for a bus ticket from Saint George to Salt Lake City in the stuff CeCe left in her apartment. Only the station said the ticket had never been redeemed. Jonathan said he remembered that CeCe had some friends in Salt Lake, and they just took off and left me here. Your mom said she was going to call you."

Yeah, but my phone is in a bucket of rags back in Olympus Hills. She could have left a thousand messages without my knowing it.

"I think they're totally overreacting, if you ask me," Indie says. "So what if she didn't take the bus after all? I still think she jumped at a chance for a new job to get out of this hellhole."

"Daphne," Lexie calls out from the car. "I don't think Haden's doing so well."

Dax and I exchange a worried look.

"Um . . . carsick," I say to Indie.

"Yuck. I'm out, then. I'm supposed to finish watering plants before I can lock up."

She goes back in the shop, and Dax and Tobin help me get Haden into the house. He's grown very cold; his fingers and lips look blue. We settle him on the couch and I pile blankets from the linen closet on top of him. Each one smells like a piece of home to me.

Brim curls up in a ball on top of Haden's chest and starts purring. My mom always claimed that the frequency of a cat's purr has restorative properties that can help a person heal more quickly. At the moment, I hope she's right.

"This place is . . . quaint," Lexie says, coming through the door, followed by Garrick and Joe. Garrick plants himself at the kitchen table, looking as forlorn as possible. Joe lingers in the doorway, like he's not sure he's welcome here. "You guys have running water, right?" Lexie asks.

"Yes," I say. "But if you're looking for a bathroom, you'll have to trudge to the outhouse in the backyard."

Lexie looks like she's about to faint in horror.

"I'm kidding. The bathroom is upstairs, second door on the left."

"Oh good," she says, but from the bewildered sound of her voice, I'm sure she thinks that a house with only one bathroom is almost as archaic as one with an outhouse.

She makes her way up the stairs, with Tobin trailing behind

465

her. Garrick lays his head on the kitchen table. Joe clears his throat from the doorway.

"You can come in, Joe," I say, but I don't look him in the eye as he enters the house.

He starts to approach me as if my invitation to join us had meant more than that. "Daphne, I . . . ," he starts to say, but I hold my hand up to stop him.

"Don't, Joe," I say, barely able to keep my anger in check. "I don't want to hear any more of your apologies right now. I don't have the energy. I don't know if I ever will."

"Daph, please." He holds his hands out in front of him.

"I forgive you, Joe, for what you did. But that doesn't mean I can *forget*." I know that Joe hadn't intended on trading *me personally* to the Underrealm when he made that deal, but knowing that he would give up the *idea of me* for fame and fortune still stung like hell. It sucks knowing your father would have chosen to make it so you never existed in order for him to become a rock star. "Now respect me when I say I don't want to talk about it."

Joe nods and slinks to the kitchen table, where he sits across from Garrick. Both of them bury their heads in their arms.

Dax opens the fridge and asks if he can make a taco for a snack with the meat and tortillas he finds in a couple of Tupperware tubs.

I nod my approval and I find myself wondering just how long I'll be stuck in this house with all of them. It's not like they can all stay in hiding forever.

But where do we even go from here?

How do you combat a race of beings that can control the weather?

Guilt eats at me. This is all my fault. My very existence,

apparently, is putting everyone in this house in danger. My instinct is to figure out a way to protect them, but I don't even know where to start.

The things Sarah said about my origins and my destiny come back to me. She'd called me many things other than just the Cypher. She said I was the Keeper of Orpheus's Heart and Soul. The Vessel of His Voice. I remember Joe telling me about how Orpheus was such a great musician that he could control the elements with his voice—animals, trees, rocks, and such. Even monsters and gods were not impervious to it. I think about how I was able to calm Brim when she'd gone all beast cat, and how my voice had caused the Keres to go solid enough for Haden to kill it. I'd even been able to use Simon's persuasive tone against him to weaken his hold on my friends.

Did inheriting Orpheus's voice mean that I had inherited his supernatural abilities with music, too? Maybe my musical OCD isn't an impairment at all—maybe it truly is a gift, like I had always thought. Maybe Orpheus had been able to hear the tones and sounds that the world and people around him gave off—and tapping into that was how he used music to control the elements.

Maybe this is why I've always felt my voice was meant for bigger things than what Ellis had to offer.

There's a small potted bonsai tree on the coffee table in front of me. Its serene tone reminds me of Asian meditation music. I'd always thought it had a calming effect. I listen to it for a minute, soaking in its song. Then concentrating all my energy at the little tree, I hum the same tone back. *Move,* I tell the tree with my thoughts as I hum. *Come to me.*

Just when I start to think that this whole idea is as cracked as possible, the little bonsai tree—pot and all—lurches forward a good two inches. As if it is actually trying to come to me.

I jump and glance around the room. Nobody else seems to have noticed what I've done. *What I can do.* I decide that, for the moment, it might be best to keep this new development to myself. Until I know how I want to use it.

I start nodding off to the sound of Haden's rhythmic breathing. It reminds me of sleeping beside him in the hotel. I am about to give in to the slumber that pulls at my mind when Tobin shakes me awake.

"Daphne?" He sticks a framed photo in front of me. It's one that normally hangs on the wall between the bathroom and my bedroom upstairs. "When was this taken?"

I blink a couple of times and focus on the picture. "Last winter. The town has a Christmas party every year. Jonathan made us all matching elf costumes."

"Last winter? As in, a year ago?"

The urgent notes coming off him make me sit up—the usual syncopated beat that had attracted me to him has increased in rhythm tenfold.

"What's going on?"

"This girl," he says, tapping the glass. "Who is she?"

I look at the photo and see who he's pointing at. Her untamed red hair curls out wildly from under her elf hat, and she looks so pale compared to the rest of us desert folk in the photo. She could never spend much time in the sun because of her fair complexion. "That's CeCe Caelum."

Dax makes a noise from the kitchen.

"The girl who's missing?" Tobin asks.

I nod.

He sinks into Jonathan's easy chair with the photo on top of his knees.

"What is it?"

"That's my sister," Tobin says, holding his fingers splayed over his mouth. "That's Abecie."

"What?" Dax says, dropping the taco onto his plate.

"Are you sure?" I ask. "I mean, you're Japanese and CeCe . . . um, isn't."

"Half sister," Tobin says. "But I never thought of her that way. My mom had her before she married my dad."

I nod. The reason Tobin reminds me so much of CeCe in both tone and personality finally makes sense. Almost all that time she'd been missing from his life, she's been in mine.

"She's alive," he says.

Dax grabs the photo from Tobin. "Abbie," he says. "I've been looking everywhere. . . . And she was here. That's why I couldn't find her."

"You said she was dead," Tobin says, standing. "Daphne said that you told her that she died!"

"Not exactly," Dax says. "I just didn't deny the idea."

"Why would you do that?"

"It was better for people to think she was dead—for her protection—and I had vowed not to speak of her. Or of what happened. I . . . I don't know why I *can* speak about her now. . . . The Oracle must have released me from my oath when she died. . . ."

"Then you'd better start explaining." Tobin looks like he wants to punch Dax in the face.

"What do you know about Abbie's biological father?"

"Not much," he says. "I know my mom hates his guts. She

469

never treated Abbie the same as me and Sage. It was like Abbie was some burden she had to bear."

"Abbie's father was a Skylord."

"Whoa, you mean Abbie is like those people who were chasing us? She's part Skylord?"

Dax nods. "Though her powers were mostly dormant when I met her. Your sister wasn't just any Boon I was sent to fetch. The Court was desperate to have her, so they made a deal . . ."

"With my mother," Tobin says, and I can hear a string of discordant notes rattle through him. "I started putting the pieces together after Joe admitted to the deal he made—why my mom was covering up those attacks in Olympus Hills. My mom was always all about her work when I was little. She was obsessed with this new wind turbine that she and my dad engineered. She said it had the power to change the world, but they couldn't get the backers they needed to finish it. That is until some mysterious benefactor came along. He made my parents' company take off the way it did. . . . And then they sold the company to him and brought us to Olympus, and she took over as mayor. That benefactor must have been Simon. My mother is working for the Underrealm, isn't she? And she didn't just know that Abbie had been chosen to be taken—she traded my sister and her allegiance for the money she needed to finish her life's work, didn't she?"

"Yes," Dax says.

Tobin nods, anger ringing off of him, as he accepts the terrible truth. His mother had not only traded Abbie like Joe had traded me—but she had done it *knowingly.*

"If Abbie chose to run away rather than fulfill my mother's end of the bargain," he says, "I can see why my parents act like she's *dishonored* our family. My mom must be in pretty deep with the Underrealm because of it. But what I don't get is how she even got involved in all of this in the first place. I mean, this is all just so insane. I've been searching for the psychopaths responsible for what's been going on in Olympus Hills, and it turns out I've been living with one of them all along? How does that even happen? How did she get hooked up with Simon in the first place?"

"You see," Dax says, "centuries ago, all humans worshipped the gods of the five realms. But as those selfish gods kept warring against each other and decimating the earth in the process, humans started to turn away from them in favor of softer, friendlier versions of deities. Instead of a vengeful Sky God, they wanted more of a divine father figure. Most humans lost faith in the realm gods, but there are still select groups who worship and serve them. Secret societies who keep their dealings very private. They're rewarded with fame, fortune, power, or whatever they desire in return. Your mother was sought out by Simon, the leader of one of these groups—of Hades, the god of wealth, worshippers, because she had something the Underrealm wanted. Your sister."

"You mean there are more people who've made deals like Joe and Mayor Winters?" I ask.

"Yes," Dax says. "Olympus Hills is home to many of their members."

"Wait!" Lexie calls from where she stands on the stairs. I didn't realize she'd been listening in on this conversation. "You mean, like more of my neighbors could be involved in this sort of stuff . . . maybe even *my* parents . . . ?"

"You're Lexie Simmons?" Joe asks from the table. "Your father is one of the owners of the Crossroads Hotel, right?"

She nods.

"There are all sorts of stories about people making deals with the devil down by the crossroads," he says. "That's why I played at the Crossroads Club all those years ago. I had some silly notion something might happen, but never thought it really would. Only it wasn't the devil who came knocking. . . ."

Lexie sits heavily on one of the steps, as if the weight of realizing she may not be immune to all of this is too much for her at the moment.

"So the Court wanted Abbie," Tobin says, bringing the topic back to his sister.

"Abbie was chosen by the Court because they thought they could use her to reinvigorate the bloodlines of the Underlords," Dax says. "They wanted to use her for prime breeding stock for the Court."

"That's disgusting." Tobin balls his fists like he wants to take his rage out on Dax.

"I agree," Dax says. "I fell in love with your sister, and she fell in love with me, and the thought of her being used by the Court in that way . . . I knew I couldn't bring her back there. We found the Oracle and she gave us instructions. Sarah told Abbie to find a place to hide until I could come back for her. . . ."

"But why did you leave her in the first place?" Tobin asks.

"Because that was part of the bargain I made with the Oracle. I had a role to fulfill before Abbie and I could be together. I've been trying to find her since I returned—doing research, and sneaking off to check out our old haunts, and searching some of the hiding places we'd discussed. I thought I had a line on her about three weeks ago, the night of the festival, but it turned out to be a dead end. I was beginning to think I might never find her. No wonder. She'd found the best hiding place in the world. It seems as far as the Skylords and the Underlords are concerned, Ellis Fields doesn't even exist."

I can't help wondering if CeCe—I mean, Abbie—had been bound by a similar oath not to talk about all this stuff. Otherwise, she would have told me. I considered her as much my real sister as Tobin did. A pang of guilt hits me. Over the last couple of months, I'd been so hurt by the thought that she was trying to cut me out of her life, I hadn't stopped to consider that she might really be in trouble.

"But it sounds like someone *did* find her," I say. "She's missing again."

"Marta," Joe says. "It could have been her. She might have recognized Abbie when we were here."

"Marta is in on this, too?" I ask.

He nods. "She's one of Simon's lackeys who's supposed to keep an eye on me."

"But it could have been the Skylords, too," Dax says. "If Marta spooked her and she ran from town, they could have gotten to her. They've wanted her back ever since they found out the Underlords were after her."

"I can't believe it," Tobin says. "I got this close, and now she's gone again. She could be anywhere."

"We'll find her," Dax says. "The Oracle told me we'd be reunited again if I helped Haden find his true path."

chapter fifty-nine

HADEN

I wake several hours later. Daphne's house is empty. For a moment, I wonder if I have been abandoned. I wouldn't blame them. Daphne should have left me back at Sunny Ridge. I am surprised she didn't run the first chance she got.

I hear voices—laughter—from outside the house. I wander out the back door and find the others gathered around a table on the deck. They pass food to each other—chimichangas, most likely Dax's suggestion—and talk like they're merely in the cafeteria back at school.

"You should have seen the look on his face!" Dax says.

The others laugh.

"Whose face?" I ask.

The group falls silent and they all look at me expectantly. Like they've been waiting for me to tell them what we're going to do next. I walk to the edge of the deck and lean against the railing. I look up at the sky. There are more stars above us than I have ever seen during my time in the mortal world. This place is beautiful in a whole different way from Olympus Hills. I wonder if Daphne will be happy staying here.

A streak of lightning rips across the sky, blotting out the stars, and thunder rolls in the distance. The air feels arid around here, but I can smell rain on the horizon. The Skylords are still out there. Waiting.

What else is out there waiting for us? Who is the Motorcycle Man who took the Compass and what does he plan on doing with it? Who is he working for? What will Ren do to retaliate?

Another thought creeps into my mind—the same thought that haunted me while I slept off the effects of the day. . . .

Dax approaches with a plate of food.

"Are you hungry?"

I shake my head. I'm starving, but I can't bring myself to eat. Not with the sick, heavy feeling that sits in my gut.

He places the plate on the railing between us. "So what exactly happened down there?" he asks softly.

"Like I said, my father tried to force me to make an unbreakable vow that I would bring Daphne to him, but instead I vowed that I never will."

"That was brave," he says.

"What if I made a mistake?"

"You didn't."

"How do you know that?" I search his face, looking for the truth.

"Because I believe in you. That's why."

"I'm not sure you're putting your belief in the right place. My father said some things when I was down there. He tried to convince me that he was about to be overthrown by the Court, and if they succeed, some pretty terrible things are going to happen."

"Like what?" It's Tobin who asks the question.

I can see the others are listening now. I turn to face them. All their eyes are on me—except Daphne's. She stares intently at the food on her plate.

"He said that if he is unable to convince the Court that I will bring Daphne back, then they will revolt. That they'll tear through what remains of the locks on Pandora's Pithos to get out into the mortal world. That they'll come after the Kronolithe themselves and reignite the war with the Skylords." I can see that the full meaning of this has not reached everyone. "Between the Keres that would be let loose on the earth when the Pits open, the hungry shades and the tormented souls of Tartarus that will eventually wander out the gaping hole between the realms, and the Underlords surfacing so they can reignite the war between the gods—basically, all hell is *literally* going to be set loose on the world. We're talking end-of-the-world, apocalypse-level violence and destruction."

"Do you think he was telling the truth?" Dax asks, his eyes as wide as I've ever seen them.

"I don't know. I thought, at the time, he was making it all up so I would give him Daphne—but I can't shake the feeling now that he might have been telling the truth. He seemed too desperate. I've never seen him like that before."

"If you'd believed him," Daphne says from the table, looking up at me, "would you have made the vow to give me to him?"

I think about it for a moment—the thought of Daphne in my father's control. The thought of his sacrificing her so he can become a god, no matter how altruistic his motives supposedly are. The idea of losing her . . .

"No," I say. "There has to be another way to stop this." Two days ago, I would have never believed that I would say something like that.

I kick at a warped floorboard on the deck. "Guess I can kiss that wreath of glory good-bye, huh? Nobody is going to be showering me with honor anytime soon." I had meant that statement to be a lighthearted comment. To ease the tension everyone is feeling, but it came out more sullen and forlorn than I'd expected.

"You are honorable to me, Prince Haden." Dax puts his hand on my shoulder and stares into my eyes with a fierce determination. He looks like a warrior about to take up the charge. "I will follow you wherever you lead."

I am surprised at the sting of tears at the backs of my eyes.

"So what *do* we do now?" Garrick asks. "You kind of screwed us all over."

"I think . . . I think the only thing is to go after the Kronolithe myself. *If* I can find it before the Underlords break out, then maybe I can stop all this before it even starts. Make some sort of bargain that doesn't involve Daphne giving up her heart and soul."

"Where do we start looking?" Dax asks.

"There is no *we* in all of this. This is my responsibility. You all will stay here, where it is safe, while *I* search for the Kronolithe."

"Like hell there isn't a *we* in this!" Daphne interjects before I can say anything else. She stands and moves until she's just a few feet from me. She has the same determination in her eyes as Dax. "There's at least a *you and me*. This is my fight, too."

"Saving the Underrealm isn't your fight."

"Honestly, I don't really give a crap about the Underrealm.

But I do care about stopping the mortal realm from getting destroyed by the spillover. I'd kind of like a world to actually tour when I grow up. Not to mention, keeping my friends and family safe."

"I can't let you be a part of this, Daphne. It means going back out into that." I gesture at the barrage of lightning on the horizon. "It means facing whatever other dangers that are coming for us. My choices put us on this path, not yours. You should stay here, where you'll be safe."

"You seriously think you can stop me from coming?" Her hands are on her hips and her hair blows about her face in the evening breeze. She looks as powerful and unrelenting as the lightning storm. "Two hours ago, hell, even ten minutes ago, I was determined to stay here and hide from my destiny, but now you're telling me there's a freaking apocalypse on our hands because of me, and you think I'm going to sit back and let you try to stop it on your own? You heard the Oracle as well as I did. Our destinies are irrevocably intertwined. Even if you find it, you can't *get* the Kronolithe without me, so suck it up."

"I thought you didn't believe in all this destiny crap."

"I thought you didn't believe in having a choice in any of this." She stares back at me, her jaw set. My heart aches at the sight. She has just witnessed the brutal deaths of Simon and Sarah, had been nearly killed herself by a three-headed beast, had lightning hurled at her for close to one hundred sixty miles, and has been told she's public enemy number one for the gods, and yet she's willing to run into battle with me.

"And I think I might have an idea of where it is anyway," she says.

"You do?" Dax asks.

"Where?" I say, unable to hide my skepticism—and hope.

"Back where we came from. We need to go back to Olympus Hills."

"Seriously?" says Lexie. "You think some ancient god's Key is just lying around in some random, master-planned community in California?"

"First of all, I don't think anyone here still believes Olympus Hills is some *random*, master-planned community anymore. Secondly, Orpheus supposedly used Persephone's Gate to escape the underworld, which means he came out in the grove, doesn't it? Before Olympus Hills even existed. The gate has always opened there, right? He couldn't have gotten far with the Keres on his tail. Not while carrying his baby and the Kronolithe. I'd bet anything that he hid it somewhere in or near where Olympus Hills stands now."

"That actually makes a lot of sense," Dax says. "The Oracle implied that no one but Daphne would be able to retrieve it. Maybe it's hidden somewhere only she can see."

I consider Dax and Daphne's hypothesis. It seems unlikely that the Kronolithe has been under our noses this whole time, but then again, one of the things I had learned in my training is that the best hiding place is often in plain sight. Either way, it is the best lead we have. "Fine. Daphne and I will return to Olympus Hills to seek the Kronolithe. Dax, you watch over everyone here until we return."

"That could take months!" Lexie says.

"Like Tartarus I'm going to let you two go off alone," Dax snarls. "We are in this together. I told you I will follow you anywhere, and I meant it."

"I'm coming, too," Tobin says, standing. "My sister is still out there, and she and my mom are involved in all of this. If I'm going to find Abbie, my best chance is to stick with you guys." He looks at me and shrugs. "Besides, I kind of think you're not such an ass hat after all. I mean, after what you did for Daphne, you might make a halfway decent *human being* someday. Count me in."

"Me, too," Lexie says. We all turn and stare at her in surprise. "What?" she says, like she has no idea why we're so incredulous. "If something is going down in Olympus Hills, you'd better believe I'm going to be a part of it. And there's no way I'm waiting here."

"I want to help, too," Joe says. "I got Daphne into this situation, and I want to help get her out of it." He looks at her for her approval.

She nods ever so slightly.

Garrick clears his throat. Everyone looks to him, waiting to see what he has to say. "I think you are all a bunch of lunatics," he says. "But I also don't like the idea of sitting around in the middle of the desert, letting you guys have all the fun. . . . Count me in—as long as somebody lets me *drive* on the way home."

I laugh uneasily. The sound ripples through the group.

"We should leave under the cover of night," I say. "Midnight. Skylords don't see as well at night, and the roads will be emptier."

They all nod like they're taking an order from their captain.

"It's settled, then," Daphne says. "We'll follow you into the dark."

After a few minutes, the others scatter. Garrick takes the rest of his dinner out into the yard, and Dax and Tobin wash the dishes so Daphne's mother won't find our mess when she gets home. Joe fills a couple of water bottles while Daphne and Lexie gather road-trip snacks from the cupboards. Brim picks at the dinner I've left abandoned on the railing.

I stand on the deck, watching the storm that awaits us. Hoping for a break that doesn't come.

I don't hear Daphne approach. I don't know she's there until she slips her hand into mine. I wrap my fingers around hers.

I don't know what the future holds. I don't know how or if we'll get through this. But for the first time in my life, my destiny is in my own hands.

ACKNOWLEDGMENTS

First off I must express my extreme and undying gratitude to my editor, Greg Ferguson, for guiding me through the journeys of writing my first four books, and to Andrea Cascardi for picking up the reins to help me finish this one.

Many, many additional thanks go to everyone who works tirelessly on my behalf: Margaret Coffee, Michelle Bayuk, Bonnie Cutler, Erin Molta, and Torborg Davern from Egmont USA. My agent, Ted Malawer, who championed this story from the very first time I told him about the inklings of the idea over five years ago. Michael Stearns and my foreign agents, who spread my stories across the world, and the designers who wrap them in such beautiful packages.

To my true friends and steadfast family who celebrate with me when there are blue skies, but most importantly stand by my side when the storm clouds gather and the lightning threatens to strike—and for whom I am always ready do the same. Extra special shout-outs go to my music experts and amazing friends, Michelle and Brent Sallay; my mom and dad; my siblings, Kim Webb Reid, Rachel Headrick, and Shani Despain, for always lending their enthusiasm, support, and listening ears.

Lastly, but most importantly, to my dear husband and our two amazing boys: I would follow you into the dark. No question about it. I.L.U.R.U.T.T.M.A.B.A.

Turn the page for a sneak peak at the
second book in the INTO THE DARK trilogy

THE ETERNITY KEY

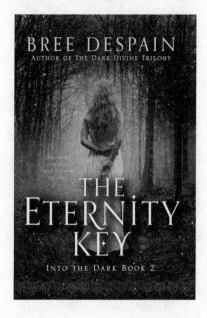

Available in Hardcover and eBook in May 2015

chapter one

HADEN

Lord Haden, *prince of the Underrealm*, has ceased to exist.

I have ceased to exist.

Since I was a nursling, I'd been taught that life is nothing but a thin golden string. It's spun and entwined in a grand tapestry of the gods' design, then pulled and severed at a predetermined length. Nothing can be done to change this, nothing can be said, and no bargain can be made. Once your thread has been measured—that's it. No choice. It's the will of the Fates.

I'd believed this myth every second of my existence, and yet, as I'd learned all too recently, if you clawed at the design hard enough, the tapestry would unravel just enough that you could grab on to another string. Follow another path.

Since that realization, I have burned the connection between myself and my realm, ruined what little standing I had reclaimed as a Champion chosen by the Oracle of Elysium, and destroyed all hope of becoming my father's heir. I brought this upon myself with a single decision.

And I would do it all over again.

Because this is a fate of *my* own choosing.

I am rewriting my destiny.

Something I didn't even know was an option until I met *her*.

Daphne Raines—the girl who was supposed to grant me the chance to win back my honor. I had been Chosen for a quest to the mortal realm to convince her to come back with me to the underworld. It quickly became clear that there was something special about her. She wasn't a mere Boon to fill the harem of the Court.

Daphne is the fated Cypher—the only one who can find and retrieve the lost Kronolithe of my long-dead god: the Key of Hades.

I knew it was up to me to ensure that the Kronolithe was found, and use it to stop the Court of the Underrealm from breaking through the walls of the Pits and freeing the Keres. There would be terrible consequences if they were to take this action: all hell would break loose on the mortal world, spilling out from the schism created between the realms, and war with the Skylords would inevitably follow, not to mention the death toll and havoc the Keres would leave in their wake.

With the fate of the five realms hanging in the balance, I'd chosen to leave the safe haven we'd found in Ellis Fields in order to return to Olympus Hills to search for the Key.

Much to my surprise—and admittedly distress—Daphne and the others had chosen to go with me. "Even if you find it," she'd said, "you can't *get* the Kronolithe without me, so suck it." I'd known she was right, even though I had wanted her to be wrong. Because of our choices, our new destinies were now irrevocably entwined. If the realms can be saved, salvation will happen only if we do it united.

And so we'd escaped into the dark, together. . . .

Rain pounds on the hood of my car now as I sit outside Daphne's home in Olympus Hills. I realize I am gripping my steering wheel tight, as if I were once again silently maneuvering the Tesla Model X down an unlit canyon road in a torrential rainstorm without headlights. It had been a slow, tense, and quiet escape during the darkness of midnight. No one said a word for almost an hour, as if even a whisper might alert the Skylords of our presence or break my concentration on the wet, black road in front of us.

In our favor, Underlords see far better in the dark than Skylords do, and the Tesla, with its silent electric motor, had provided us the stealth we needed to make our exit. The Skylords, who can control rain as well as lightning and thunder, had intended the storm to prevent us from escaping, but instead it had provided the cover we needed to pass through the unlit canyon unseen. However, the mere memory of that storm is enough to raise the hairs on the back of my neck. I had never been so terrified in all my life—not even when facing the imminent destruction of my soul at my father's hands. Because, this time, the lives of Daphne, Joe, Tobin, Lexie, Garrick, and Dax—the only people left in all the realms who still believed in me—were in *my* hands as we crept along the cliffside road.

It may have been two weeks since that harrowing experience, but sitting in the rain now not only served as an unwelcome reminder of that long drive, but it also felt like a warning as to what is still to come.

I will one of my hands to release its death grip on the steering wheel and use it to take a swig from the coffee cup that's been my only company tonight. I gag, almost choking on the cold swill. I don't know how Simon could have loved this stuff. I take another sip, not because I want to taste it again, but because I need to stay awake. I've barely slept a scant few hours in the days since our

3

return from Ellis. I may require less sleep than a human, but even I have my limits.

As if Dax can read my thoughts—which I am not entirely sure he *can't* sometimes—my phone lights up with a text from him.

Dax: You're there again, aren't you? Come home.

I stare at the screen, not sure I am going to reply, when another message comes through.

Dax: You've barely slept in weeks. You can't keep up this pace of looking for the Key all day and guarding Daphne's house all night.

I pry my other hand from the steering wheel to answer.

Me: I'm not at Daphne's. I am merely getting a bite to eat.

Typing it feels easier than saying it to his face. I've never been good at lying to Dax. I drop my phone in an empty compartment in the dash, hoping that will be the last of the conversation, and pinch my nose between my eyes. Sleep pulls at me, but I won't let my eyelids shut.

I grip my coffee cup with both hands, sending a small pulse of electric heat from my palms into it, hoping to warm it up enough to make it palatable again. An abrupt knock sounds against the passenger-side window. I jump in my seat, and a surge of electricity escapes my hands, nearly incinerating the cardboard cup before I drop it in my lap. I hold my hand out, blue light crackling between my fingers, toward the car door as it swings open.

A tiny gray cat jumps through the dark opening, landing on the passenger seat. She yowls at me.

"Hello to you, too, Brim," I say, knowing I've been caught.

I extinguish the lightning in my hand and pick up the cup from my coffee-stained lap, wishing I hadn't warmed the contents quite so much. Brim jumps over the center console onto my shoulder as Dax follows her into the car. He settles himself into the passenger seat and pulls the door shut. His hair is damp, and rain has soaked the shoulders of his jacket.

"Liar," he says, not looking at me as he digs into a paper sack that he's brought with him.

"You used Brim to track me?" I ask, not realizing that is still a sore spot until I say it. Brim and I share a special bond, and because of it, she can find me anywhere. Simon exploited that fact to follow Daphne and me to the Oracle in Las Vegas, and that unfortunate choice had resulted in both Simon's and the Oracle's deaths. Brim might look like a harmless puff of fur, but Simon had made the mistake of ignoring one of the most steadfast rules of the Underrealm: never get a hellcat angry.

I scratch Brim under her chin to let her know there are no hard feelings about her being used to find me once again. Brim purrs next to my ear.

"I used my common sense to find you," Dax says. "Brim came along for the ride. We brought you something." He fishes in the paper sack.

"If that's another taco, Hades help me . . ." Since Simon is gone, Dax has taken over most of our meals, which means I've had more Mexican takeout in the last two weeks than I'd ever care to have in a lifetime.

"It's chamomile tea," he says, handing me a capped cup, and pulls out a second for himself. It smells sweeter than the coffee I've been nursing all evening, like flowers and honey. I'm about to take a tentative sip when he says, "It'll help you sleep."

I put the tea in a cup holder. "I don't need help sleeping."

"Those dark circles under your eyes tell a different story."

"What I mean is that I'm not going to sleep. Not when it's raining."

"You need sleep. *Go home.*"

Brim meows as if agreeing with Dax. *Furry little traitor.*

"Maybe you didn't hear me: *it's raining. I can't leave.*"

"Yeah, Haden, I can see that," he says, gesturing out the windshield. "And it's just rain. There's no lightning. No thunder. Rain doesn't always mean Skylords are about to swoop down on us. Relax. We're safe."

"You can't know that."

"It's been two weeks."

I don't like being reminded how much time has passed since we returned to Olympus Hills. I don't know why I really expected anything different, but part of me had thought we would have found the Key by now. Despite all our searching, we haven't made any progress. It's like I can feel every second that ticks by without the Key now.

It's not just the rain that keeps me up at night. It's the nightmares. The visions of Keres ripping through the realms, devouring everything—and everyone . . .

I know if I tell Dax about my dreams, he will say that they were just that, *dreams,* but part of me worries they're a premonition of what is to come if we don't find the Key. Just like the rain feels like an omen now.

As if something else were coming . . .

"If the Skylords were coming for us, they would have come by now," Dax says, and I know my thoughts are painted on my face. All my life, I've practiced hiding myself behind an expressionless mask—a necessary skill for someone from a place where emotion and affection are considered weaknesses—but I seem to have lost my knack for it of late. Ever since I let Daphne see the real me . . .

"Deal with it, fearless leader; we got away," Dax says, and lifts his tea as if proposing a toast in my honor.

A sick feeling washes over me, and I know it's not from my steady diet of fast-food tacos and coffee. I hit the lever for the windshield wipers, wiping away a thick coat of rainwater. In the distance, I watch one of the lights go out in Daphne's house. It isn't her window that goes dark, but I wonder if she was the one who turned out the light. *Can she see me out here now?*

Her bedroom is in the back of Joe's mansion. I'd contemplated climbing the fence and camping out under her window, but I'd barely gotten past the point in which Daphne was referring to me as a creep and a stalker, so I didn't want to push my luck. Instead, I sit in my car like a sentinel. Making sure there's no sign of trouble.

Making sure she's safe.

"You should tell her." Dax's voice is so quiet when he says it, I almost wonder if he said anything at all. "No, wait, scratch that," he says, bolder now. "You *need* to tell her."

I raise an eyebrow with a noncommittal "Huh?"

"That you're in love with her, you idiot."

Panic rises up my throat, burning like vomit. Admitting to myself that I am in love with Daphne had been hard enough—and it had taken the imminent threat of my death to get me to do it.

"I can't," I say.

Affection is weakness, I hear my father's voice echoing in my head. My jaw aches as I remember his ringed hand slamming into my face when I was a small child. I'd been punished, disowned, stripped of my honor because I'd shown affection for my mother when she died. My love for her had caused me to take a stand against my father, and I'd lost just about everything because of it.

Dax shifts in his seat. "Despite what your father and Master

Crue and all the other Heirs may have taught you, loving someone isn't a sin. It isn't a crime, either."

Love gave you strength. That's what Daphne had told me when I related the story of my mother's death to her. Deep down, I'd known she was right. And I know that my love for Daphne was what gave me the strength to stand up to Ren once more—to try to weave my own destiny. But the idea of *telling her* terrifies me more than the threat of the Skylords and the wrath of the Court combined—because I turned my back on the Underrealm, my father, my chance to be his heir, gave up being a prince, and possibly endangered all the realms, because of my love for Daphne.

That love is all I have left.

It's the only thing that gives me hope.

And if I confess to her and learn that she does not reciprocate my feelings—then I will have truly lost *everything*.

My fingers shake as I reach for what remains of my coffee cup instead of the chamomile tea. "I can't," I say again. Even if I *wanted* to tell Daphne, I wouldn't be able to find the words.

Against my will, my thoughts flit to Rowan—my twin brother, the one my father and the Court would have chosen as the Champion to collect Daphne if the Oracle of Elysium had not intervened. *Rowan* was the one who had a gift for words. He was the smart one. The cunning one.

A small smile plays on my lips because I like to think that even Rowan, with all his manipulative skills, wouldn't have been able to trick Daphne into falling in love with him enough to return with him to the Underrealm. She'd have seen right through his lies. As far as I know, my brother is incapable of loving anyone other than himself. All he cares about are power and pride.

Then again, only four months ago, before I was sent to the

mortal world, before I met Daphne, before I refused to hand her over to my father, all anyone would have said I cared about was getting my honor back.

But I proved I wouldn't sacrifice her to do it. Rowan would have handed Daphne over without blinking, if he were in my place. He would have done anything necessary to succeed where I had failed.

Dax clears his throat, pulling my thoughts away from Rowan.

"So are you hoping that, by sitting outside her house every night, she'll figure it out on her own?"

"I don't sit out here every night. Only when it's raining."

"It's January in California. It's rained every night."

"It didn't rain yesterday."

"And yet you still found a reason to stay here half the night."

"There was rain in the forecast. I needed to know she was safe."

"Harpies, Haden. Sometimes rain is just rain. Come home. Unless you know something I don't know?"

I hesitate for a moment. There was something—something I saw when we stopped for breakfast at that diner outside Vegas. The same one where Daphne, Garrick, and I had stopped for lunch on our way to find Sarah, the Oracle, and ended up meeting up with Tobin and Lexie. Thinking we were in the clear after we escaped the rain, we'd stopped for sustenance and to retrieve Lexie's car. I hadn't thought anything of the trucker who had been in the diner when we stopped there the first time—just a man in a hat with a scruffy beard who seemed to like pink, creamy looking drinks—but when I saw him there again, at four in the morning no less, I'd started to worry.

I watched him down two of those pink drinks while the others ate piles of what Daphne had referred to as "buttermilk pancakes," then he threw a few bills on the counter and left without giving us a second glance. I'd let myself relax then, even grunted in response when Daphne dared me to try bacon dipped in maple syrup, thinking I'd been a complete lunatic for being anxious about the man—but then I could have sworn that, through the diner's dirty windows, I saw the man's truck rumble to life before he even got inside it. As if he'd started it with the brush of his hand over the hood. Like the way I could start my Tesla with my lightning powers.

Much to the others' protests, I'd insisted we leave as soon as the trucker pulled out of the parking lot. I didn't mention what I saw because I didn't see the man or his truck on the road. He wasn't following us, and he wasn't up ahead. I'd convinced myself that having my soul fried less than twenty-four hours before, followed by the tense drive out of the canyon, was making my mind play tricks on me. (For all I knew, there had been someone else in the truck to begin with.) And I didn't feel like contradicting my passengers, who were treating me like I was some kind of Hercules for successfully executing our daring escape from Ellis.

My pride had gotten the better of me then, but the more days that passed and the more rain that fell, I had started to wonder if we had really escaped at all.

"No . . . It's just a feeling," I say, my pride getting to me once again. "You know. As if I'm still being followed."

"They didn't follow us."

"You're the one who is always telling me to trust my instincts."

"Right . . . But, you know, if someone were watching us, you sitting outside her house every night is pretty much the same as erecting a huge, Vegas-style THE CYPHER LIVES HERE neon sign, right?"

I hadn't thought of that.

"And if you kill yourself via sleep deprivation, then you'll truly be no use to anyone." Dax places his hand on my shoulder, next to a now-sleeping Brim. "How about you let me take up the watch tonight so you can go home and sleep? There is that school thing tomorrow and all."

I try to take a sip of my coffee but all I find are the scalded dregs in my charred cup. Brim's purring snores next to my ear seem particularly hypnotic. My eyelids feel heavy as I look up at Daphne's house. All the lights are out now. I'm not going to be much use at school if I fall asleep in class. With Simon gone and Daphne knowing the truth, I normally wouldn't see the point in continuing with the school charade—except I don't like the idea of leaving Daphne unprotected all day long. Besides, I welcome the excuse to actually be close to her, instead of sitting outside her house at night.

I look out over the lake across the street from Daphne's quiet home and notice that the rain is finally starting to let up. I contemplate going home to sleep so I'll be prepared for tomorrow. My fingers are on the ignition button, ready to start the car, when a bolt of lightning rips the sky above the lake. Rolling thunder explodes with it, causing me to flinch at the nearness. But in the half second before my eyes clamp shut, I think I see someone standing on the lakeshore. Staring at me. When my eyes open another half second later, no one is there.

I jump out of my car and run toward the lake. The wet sand on the shore grips at my shoes, slowing my pace. Dax follows, calling, "What are you doing, Haden?" as if he hadn't seen anything. Brim yowls in protest over having been awoken so abruptly, sinking her claws into my shoulder.

I cast about in the rain, but I don't see anyone. I start to think I'd imagined seeing someone—perhaps I'd drifted momentarily asleep—but I make out what looks like a pair of boot prints in the sand before the lapping water of the lake washes them away.

"There," I say, pointing to the now-gone prints. "Didn't you see him?"

"*Him?*" Dax shakes his head. "I saw lightning, but nothing else."

I stand on the beach, frantically searching the shoreline with my eyes, that creeping feeling that I am being watched plaguing me. The rain, lighter than before but still a steady downpour, soaks through my thin shirt. Brim jumps from my shoulder and bounds back to the car, seeking shelter from the rain.

"Come on," Dax says. "It was just lightning. You don't want to be standing in the water if it strikes again."

I cross my arms for warmth and turn back toward Daphne's house, watching for any signs of trouble. Any thoughts of leaving, and any sleepiness, have vanished. I don't care if I have to stand in the rain all night; I'll do whatever it takes to keep Daphne safe.